THE DUBLIN GIRLS

Dublin, 1950s: Nineteen-year-old Nell Flynn is training to be a nurse and planning to marry her boyfriend, Liam Connor, when her mother dies, leaving her younger sisters destitute. To save them from the workhouse, Nell returns to the family home — a mere two rooms at the top of a condemned tenement. She finds work at a biscuit factory, and at first they scrape through each week. But then eight-year-old Róisín, delicate from birth, is admitted to hospital with rheumatic fever, and fifteen-year-old Kate, rebellious, headstrong and resentful of Nell taking her mother's place, runs away. When Liam finds work in London, Nell stays to struggle on alone. She's determined that one day the Dublin girls will be reunited — and only then will she be free to follow her heart.

CATHY MANSELL

THE DUBLIN GIRLS

Complete and Unabridged

MAGNA
Leicester

First published in Great Britain in 2020 by
Headline Review
an imprint of Headline Publishing Group
London

First Ulverscroft Edition
published 2020
by arrangement with
Headline Publishing Group
London

A catalogue record for this book is available
from the British Library.

ISBN 978–0–7505–4837–3

Published by
Ulverscroft Limited
Anstey, Leicestershire

Set by Words & Graphics Ltd.
Anstey, Leicestershire
Printed and bound in Great Britain by
TJ Books Limited, Padstow, Cornwall

I dedicate *The Dublin Girls* to my three sisters, Eilis, Jane and Marie.

All Dublin girls with no resemblance to the three sisters in my story.

1

Dublin City, 1950

Water dripped on to her head and shoulders, running down the thick rubber apron over her feet as Nell stretched to hang the heavy biscuit tins on the hook above her. Her arms ached and her fingers were red and sore from rubbing. It was beyond her how people could send the tins back in such a filthy state. By now, she was flagging and had lost count of how many she had washed, guessing it was near one hundred. As she dropped another sticky tin into the large vat of water, the sound of the siren that heralded the end of the eight-hour shift almost brought tears of relief. She had yet to receive her first week's wages, having already worked a week in hand, and wondered what she and her sisters would eat tonight.

Outside on the Dublin streets, cold wind blew in her face, making her shiver as the traffic gathered momentum, belching gassy fumes into the air. She was still coming to terms with the buses that now replaced the electric trams. She glanced across to where twenty-two-year-old Liam was waiting, a shopping bag hanging from the handlebars of his bicycle. She broke away from the stream of workers flocking through the factory gates, and walked towards him. In spite of how he made her heart race, she must stay strong.

'What are you doing here? I . . . we'd agreed.'

'No, Nell. I didn't agree.'

She glanced down. 'I have to go. You know how it is.'

'Only too well. Don't tell me you like it in there? You're sacrificing your career, everything you've worked for.'

'I can't think about that now. I thought you understood.'

'You're nineteen. You can't replace your mother. Won't you reconsider, or at least let me help?'

'No, Liam. They're my family. My responsibility.' She walked on.

At first, he didn't follow, but then he was riding alongside her. 'My mother asked me to give you this. Go on, take it. You'll offend her if you don't. I'm not giving up on us, Nell.' He handed her the bag and cycled away.

Dear Liam. If only things were different. But they were what they were, and she had to get on with it, even if it meant letting go of what she loved the most. Tears gathered when she thought about Ma. Her death — so sudden, only weeks ago — had changed the course of their lives. A heart attack, the doctor said. With Kate and Róisín still at school, finding work had been Nell's priority if she was to keep a roof over their heads.

She inched the bag on to her shoulder and walked along Peter's Row until she came to Wood Street. Standing on the factory floor all day aggravated her already painful chilblains, making her feet throb as she cut through and

2

crossed over the Halfpenny Bridge that linked one side of the city to the other. It was early November and the evenings were already drawing in. Tired and hungry, she reached Dominick Street. She glanced along the row of shabby, neglected Victorian houses, once occupied by wealthy English lords and their families before Ireland gained its independence. Now home to Dublin's poor.

For as long as Nell could remember, they'd lived on the top floor alongside a host of decent families whom her mother had called the salt of the earth. The women no longer stood gossiping in the doorway in the late afternoon. The majority had been rehoused by the Dublin Corporation, moving to new estates in Inchicore, Cabra and Raheny. Now, only a few families remained in rooms on the floors beneath them. Tonight, the dingy hallway was dark and smelly, but light from the street lamp filtered through the broken fan-light. Bulbs were no longer replaced. As she passed through the hall, Joan Kinch — the oldest of eight children, whose mother had been a good friend to Ma — bounded down the stairs.

'Are ye coming for a stroll down O'Connell Street later? We can take a look in Clery's window. Sure, me mam will keep an eye on Róisín.'

'I'm sorry, Joan. I can't.'

Exhausted, she climbed the eight flights of stairs. The squabbles and noisy rows that penetrated the walls appeared to echo through the house tonight as she reached the top two rooms, which she shared with her siblings. When their father was alive, they considered themselves lucky to live at the top of the house, with large sash windows overlooking the street below. The other advantage was they were further away from the noise and brawls that took place at night. Her parents worked hard to give them a decent life compared to some. Her mother had kept their little home spotless, with a nourishing meal waiting. Now each time she came through the door a lump formed in her throat, and after three weeks she still found it difficult to come to terms with how their lives had changed overnight.

Róisín rushed to greet her, wrapping her thin arms around her sister's waist.

'Hello, pet. It's freezing in here. Why's the fire out?' Nell asked.

Kate, her long auburn hair over one shoulder and her nose buried in a library book, glanced up. 'I tried my best, but it kept going out. I can never light that thing.'

Nell bit back her frustration. 'It won't light without fuel. Now, put that book away and go down to the yard and bring up a bucket of coal.'

'Ah, I hate going down there in the dark.'

Nell glared at her. 'You should have thought about that earlier, shouldn't you?'

Kate, used to having everything done for her by their mother, was in for a rude awakening.

'You'd better pull your weight around here, Kate, or things will get a lot worse.'

Kate scowled at her sister and snatched up the coal scuttle.

4

'I'm hungry.' Róisín held her tummy. The eight-year-old had never been strong, and although she went to school most days, their mother's death had hit her the hardest. She looked up, and a curly lock of fair hair fell across her face.

Nell smiled. 'I know, honey. You peel the spuds while I get the fire going.' She raked the ashes and placed small pieces of wood on top.

'Mrs Kinch called up with some of them pig's trotters she cooked earlier.' Róisín wrinkled her nose. 'I hate them. They make me sick.'

'Well, I hope you said thanks. Did she ask you questions?'

'She wanted to know how we were managing.' Róisín burst into tears. 'I miss me ma. I want her to come back.'

Nell stood up. 'It's all right, honey. But we have to make the best of things. Otherwise those nosey parkers from the St Vincent de Paul will come round, and we don't want that, do we?'

The two rooms comprised a parlour, with a fireplace and two comfortable armchairs their father had picked up at the auction, a double bed where their parents had slept, and a table and four chairs. Above the mantel was a statue of Mary, two brass candlesticks with candles and matches in case of a power cut, and a framed family photograph portraying happier times. The adjoining room, where Nell slept, had a small scullery in the corner — sectioned off by a curtain — with cupboards, a heavy black gas cooker and a large earthenware sink. Their father had died before he got round to plumbing it in, so their mother had had to go down to the yard and wash the clothes in the wooden tub with a washing board and a cold water tap. The walls in both rooms showed signs of damp, and her mother had put in for a Corporation house. They were all excited about the prospect, despite the reports in the *Evening Press* that most of the close-knit community who had already moved were unsettled.

Kate struggled in with the coal, and soon flames were shooting up the chimney. She put the potatoes on the gas ring to boil.

'What else have us to eat? What's this?' She opened the shopping bag on the table where Nell had placed it as she came in. 'Have you got shopping, then?'

Nell nodded. If she mentioned where it came from, Kate would assume she was seeing Liam again and think about the nice treats he used to bring them. The bag held a pound of sausages, a loaf of bread and some lard.

'Set the table, Kate, and I'll cook these,' she said.

Nell placed the links of sausage and the lard on a plate and took it to the scullery, where she pricked the skins before dropping them into the hot fat. To lift her mood, she switched on the radio, and her hips swayed as she worked to the beat of Rosemary Clooney singing 'This Ole House'.

'I love the smell of Donnelly's sausages,' Kate said as they sat round the table. 'Ma always fried onions with them.'

'Well, we have none.' Nell tucked into her

6

dinner and then glanced across at Róisín, whose small trusting face looked up at her big sister. 'Come on, pet, eat something, it'll make you feel better.'

Róisín picked up her fork and played with her food. 'Lucy Flanagan said . . . she said if we didn't have a mam or dad, I'd get took away. I won't, will I, Nell?'

'No! Definitely not. Take no notice.' She patted the young girl's hand.

'But we might have to move,' Kate chirped in. 'There's hardly anyone left in the tenements. Where do you think they'll send us?'

'I don't know, Kate, and right now I'm struggling to pay for this place. The rent's due on Friday.'

'Ma managed.'

Nell swallowed. 'Ma struggled, and if you weren't so wrapped up in yourself, you'd have noticed. The money Da left her didn't last, and what she earned as the priest's housekeeper kept us going.'

'She never said.'

'You need to grow up and consider yourself lucky to have stayed on at school when girls your age are working in the biscuit factory. We both might have to do the same if we are to stay together.'

'No. No, I won't.' Kate glared at her. 'Miss Leach says I have great potential . . . and besides, I'm not working in any old factory.'

Róisín whimpered, and Nell patted her hand to comfort her.

'That's enough, Kate. This isn't helping.'

Filled with despair, anger spread through Nell like a fire and she gripped the table. If their mother was here, she'd have slapped Kate.

The door knocked and Mrs Kinch, who lived on the floor below them, walked in. 'It's only me. I want to make sure youse are all right.'

Nell smiled. 'We're okay, thanks, Mrs Kinch. Please, sit down. Would you like tea?'

'No, sure I'm grand. And call me Amy. I'm going to be keeping an eye on youse for a while, so I am.'

'Thanks, Amy.'

Kate glared at Nell, then got up and took Róisín away and sat her by the fire.

'How're ye gettin' on at the biscuit factory?' asked the older woman.

'Well, okay, I suppose.' Nell leant her arms on the table. 'Have you any idea when you might be rehoused?'

'No, but it won't be long, love. Ten of us. And with the kids growing, we're cramped.'

Nell nodded. 'By the way, thanks for the crubeens.'

'I'd be able to do more for youse if the aul' fella didn't drink.' Amy gave a little laugh. 'Ah, sure that's the way of it.' She glanced over at Róisín lying on the rug in front of the fire. 'Sure, that child's dead on her feet. I'll be off and let you settle down for the night. You know where I am if you need ought. And, Nell, you'd better let the housing people know about your mam.'

Nell had put off writing the letter, knowing how much a new house would have meant to her ma. Amy went on, 'The Corporation won't give youse a house now. Sure, if push comes to shove, you can always move in with us.'

As kind as Amy Kinch was, the thought of that happening filled Nell with despair.

2

Nell got out of bed and tiptoed across the room.
She could hardly see the rooftops outside the
grimy window. The sky was grey and overcast,
and seagulls swooped overhead. A sign of rough
weather at sea, Ma used to say.

She glanced into the room, at the double bed
where her sisters slept. Kate's long hair spread
across the pillow. At fifteen, her figure was
creeping into the contours of womanhood.
Róisín, her curly honey-blonde head the colour
of Nell's own short bob, was just visible above
the blanket.

The smell of last night's dinner hung in the
room and she opened the top half of the window.
Dressed in her warmest clothes, she sat on her
bed. The noise of a door banging below them
was a familiar sound, but this morning it echoed
through the house. Mr Kinch worked on the
docks; she set her clock by him. A quiet, polite
man, until drink turned him into a foolhardy and
boisterous drunk who remembered none of the
nasty things he'd said to his wife and his
neighbours, the following day.

She boiled herself an egg, leaving the
cornflakes and milk for her sisters. She placed a
slice of bread under the grill and, as she waited,
her mind drifted to her brother, Danny. At the
age of twenty he had seen no future in Ireland
and felt he could best help the family by

10

emigrating along with many others. Their parents had given him their blessing, but her mother had cried buckets after he'd left.

Their father died shortly after that, devastating the family. Danny returned for the funeral and decided to stay, but within months he contracted consumption and died. It wasn't uncommon, and Nell had known many men and children who had died of the disease. Nell was sure that losing her son and then her husband, so close together, had contributed to her mother's death.

Now the responsibility of the family rested on her shoulders and filled her waking hours. She scraped a small amount of butter on to her toast and dipped it into the egg. The yellow dripped down the eggcup on to the plate and she mopped it up, wondering how her money would stretch this week. When their father was alive, they were always sure of a decent meal and good clothes on their backs, even if they were from the second-hand market.

As she put on her boots, Nell noticed the soles were wearing thin. She missed her father, not least for his talent to repair their footwear, but also his ability to keep calm in a crisis. What would he do in this situation? He was a Protestant, her mother a Catholic. It made no difference, Ma always said, as they were praying to the same God. But Father John had refused to marry them in front of the main altar because of it; their vows were taken at the side altar.

Nell and her sisters were brought up in their mother's faith, but it was well known that Protestants got the best jobs. However, as things stood, she had welcomed the job she was offered. She was sure her father's dedicated service, over many years, had swayed the application in her favour.

She shrugged her coat on and wound a blue scarf around her neck. Before leaving, she glanced again at the sleeping girls. Kate was always a puzzle to her. Even in their present plight, she seemed to think it was her right to carry on her education, despite knowing that Nell had given up her chance of a nursing career.

With no choice but to trust Kate to get Róisín ready and drop her at the school gate, she hurried downstairs. Families were stirring, quarrels erupting and babies crying — all part of normal life, living in a tenement. As she walked towards the factory, fifteen minutes from home — ten, if she ran — Nell's worries about paying the rent multiplied. The small allowance she had received as a trainee nurse wouldn't pay the rent. The biscuit factory paid more, but she hated the work. Yet what else could she do?

* * *

Jacob's biscuit factory had dominated the skyline for as long as she could remember. Until his death, her father had worked there as a cooper, making wooden containers for shipping biscuits abroad.

This morning, as she turned into Wood Street with ten minutes to spare, her mind flitted back to her first day at the factory, two weeks ago. She would never forget the sweet smell of the fancy biscuits; the almonds and sugar icing filled her senses as she walked into the factory. The supervisor had kept her waiting, and Nell had stood in the middle of the floor, her face flushed from the heat of the enormous ovens, waiting to be shown what to do.

She'd watched the dough swirling around in the big mixers before falling into a trough, then noisy machines rolling the dough on to sheets that men fed into the hot ovens. Women worked in rows, decorating biscuits by hand. Embarrassed, standing in view of everyone, she had picked her nails until the supervisor walked towards her.

'Come along, then — and stop gawping,' the woman had snapped.

Nell followed the woman with buck teeth, through to where golden biscuits were being packed. The aroma intensified, and the whiff of chocolate was so strong it made her mouth water. She continued through to a room that was light and airy, with large windows, and she hoped this was where she would be working. But they had gone up some stairs to where women were packing biscuits into tins decorated with colourful labels, which then moved along a conveyor belt where they were sealed around the edges.

Her heart quickened when she was taken to another part of the factory where the temperature dropped and a draught swept around her ankles. Girls and women were scrubbing tins next to a stack piled high, ready for lowering into the large vats for washing.

'I'll leave you in the capable hands of your chargehand,' the supervisor announced. 'You'll have a ten-minute tea break, and you know the rules.' With that, she walked away.

Disappointed, Nell stepped into a vacant space between two women, the tantalising aromas of the lovely biscuits replaced by caustic soap and swishing water.

Now into her third week, she still dreaded the day ahead. She walked past the hot ovens, where the steel floor felt warm beneath her feet, towards the cold wet room where she worked, and her spirits dropped to an all-time low. She was tying the heavy apron around her waist when the chargehand — a pleasant woman in her forties — approached her.

'Nell, I want a word in the break.' That was all she said, leaving Nell to wonder what she'd done wrong and in fear of losing her job.

The morning dragged. At eleven, everyone stopped working and rushed upstairs to the canteen, but Nell lingered behind. Was this the end of the line for her at the biscuit factory? If so, she dreaded to think what fate awaited her and her sisters.

'I won't keep you long,' the chargehand said. 'I'm sure you are ready for your break.'

Her words gave Nell hope and, straightening her shoulders, she removed her wet apron.

'You've done well in the short time you've been with us,' the woman continued. 'In fact, you've overreached your daily quota.'

'Is . . . is that good?' Nell asked, tentatively.

The woman smiled. 'There's an opening in the

labelling section, and I will put your name forward.'

'Oh, thank you.'

'Now, you'd better hurry if you want that cup of tea.'

Most of the women took their breaks in groups, laughing and joking, but Nell hadn't yet made any friends and didn't like to push her way into their conversations. Instead, she usually went home for lunch, despite having little time to make herself a sandwich.

When she reached the canteen, it was buzzing with noise and the clatter of crockery. She fetched her tea and glanced around for somewhere to sit.

'You can sit over there,' one woman told her.

Nell sat down and smiled at the woman next to her, who just burst into tears and rushed from the room.

'Take no notice of her,' another said. 'She won't last long. Not got the stamina.'

Suddenly, the siren pierced the air, making Nell jump. Everyone scrambled to their feet and made their way back towards the stairs.

Heartened by what the chargehand had said to her earlier, for the rest of her shift Nell washed the tins with renewed vigour. Her spirits uplifted, she smiled as she listened to the women singing 'Roll Out the Barrel' and joined in with them.

3

Instead of the usual tiredness on returning from her day at the factory, tonight Nell felt optimistic and took the stairs two at a time. She wasn't surprised to find Róisín alone and Kate down the street with one of her friends.

'I'm cold. And Kate said she'd be back to light the fire before you got home.' Róisín was sitting in her coat and scarf, looking pale and tired.

'Don't worry, pet, I'll soon have the place warm.' She pulled the young girl towards her, wrapping her arms around her. There were only a few pieces of coal in the scuttle, and they were down to their last sack; she would have to think of a cheaper way of heating the room.

Once the fire was lit, she removed Róisín's coat and sat her in front of the flames, placing a blanket across her knees. Róisín had always been delicate, and their mother had worried about her poor appetite.

'I've good news to give you,' Nell told her, 'but first I must get fresh water for the spuds.'

As she struggled back upstairs with the heavy bucket, a figure in dark clothing was ahead of her. 'Ah, Nell. Just the woman I want to see.' It was Father John from St Saviour's Church. He was the last person she wanted to talk to right now, and he didn't even offer to carry the water.

She followed behind, spilling some of the water in her efforts to keep up with him, until

16

they reached the top landing, where he stood back to let her go through into the room.

'What can I do for you, Father?' She placed the bucket in the corner of the room, reminding herself not to fill it so full next time.

The priest removed his heavy black coat and sat down. 'It's more what I can do for you. I won't beat about the bush. Since your mother died, you seem to have forgotten your religious duties.'

'Sorry, Father. I don't like to leave Róisín. She's not always well.'

'The church is only feet away, girl. It's not an excuse.' He raised his eyebrows as Nell busied herself filling the kettle and putting a light underneath the saucepan. 'I hear you're working. That must be a help, but you can't be managing on that? Have you been to the St Vincent de Paul?' She wasn't sure which question to answer first. 'And what about your other sister, Kate?'

'What about her, Father?' Nell placed a cup and saucer on the table in front of him.

'Well, now. In the circumstances, she can't continue at school.'

What he said was true, but she couldn't help the growing resentment she felt towards this middle-aged priest who offered no comfort other than to preach.

The door opened, and Kate burst in. 'Hello, Father John. To what do we owe the honour?'

'Concern for the welfare of your souls, young lady,' he replied quickly. 'So much so, I've dragged myself up these dark stairs to do my duty.'

17

'You shouldn't have troubled yourself.' Kate, as self-absorbed as ever, ignored Nell's warning look as she poured tea for the priest and placed the last of the biscuits on a plate.

Throughout the conversation, Róisín slept in the chair by the fire. Kate pulled over a chair to join her.

The priest sipped his tea and crunched a biscuit. 'Are you keeping up with the rent?' he probed.

'I'm doing my best, Father. I hope you'll excuse me if I cook the dinner, we're all hungry.' She moved towards the scullery.

'Aye! I'll be away, then.' He crunched another biscuit and drained his cup. Standing up, he slipped his coat on, then looked across at Kate. 'And as for you, young lady. I don't see why you can't take over where your poor mother, God rest her soul, left off. Call at the house after school tomorrow.'

Kate's mouth opened and closed. 'I don't want to be a cleaner, thank you, Father.'

He glared at her. 'You must help your sister to keep this family together. I'll be expecting you. If not, I'll just have to tramp up these stairs again.'

Nell, despite stifling a giggle, knew pride came before a fall.

★ ★ ★

Kate was deep in thought as she walked home from school with Róisín. No one would dictate to her — and certainly not Father John. Her plans were above cleaning or factory work. Ma

18

had become housekeeper for the priest after their da died, because she was a mother with children to feed and rent to pay. But that wasn't Kate's life; she had ideas of her own. And she'd only agreed to go along with it to please Nell and to get her to stop whining on about money.

Besides, Nell was up for promotion, she'd told them last night. So that should solve things. As the oldest, she was duty-bound to take their mother's place.

Kate missed her ma, but wished she hadn't died before they had been rehoused. They could have had a brand-new house, with their own bathroom and an indoor toilet. Now, they would probably be stuck in the slums for ever.

Back at the dreary room, she changed out of her school uniform and put on her best dress and beige woollen duffel coat, bunched her hair into a ponytail, then took Róisín to Mrs Kinch because she didn't want to stay on her own.

'Ah, sure, that will suit you fine, so it will,' Amy Kinch said when Kate told her where she was going. 'It'll take the weight off your sister's shoulders.'

Outside, Kate cringed. Suit her fine, my eye. If her life turned out like Mrs Kinch's, she'd die of shame. She had no intention of going to see Father John. But as she walked past the church on her way towards Dorset Street to browse the shop windows, a young man was placing his bicycle against the railings and turned towards her.

'You don't have the time, do you?' he asked. 'Only my watch has stopped, and Father John will lecture me if I'm late.'

She had never seen him before and was immediately struck by his good looks and dark hair; the way he smiled at her made her heart race. 'It's . . . it's just past four o'clock,' Kate replied. 'Have you come about the job?' She couldn't bring herself to say cleaning.

'Well, yes, I guess so, but as I'm late, it won't go down well.'

He unzipped the top of his black bomber jacket to reveal a grey jumper, and he wore smart blue trousers. As he removed his bicycle clips, Kate noticed his slender fingers and clean nails, and wondered what he worked at.

'What job is that, then?' She didn't think she was at all cheeky in asking.

'I'm here about the clerk's job. What about you?'

Her face coloured. 'Oh, I . . . I just want a word with Father John.'

'Well,' he half smiled. 'I'd better get it over with.'

She walked with him to the presbytery. 'If we go in together, he'll be more lenient with you.' She felt the heat blooming on her cheeks, and her heart thumped as she stood next to him.

'It's worth a try.' He straightened his shoulders and Kate pressed the bell.

Minutes later, the door opened, and the priest frowned at them both.

'Well, now. You're late, Michael. Not a good start.'

'I'm sorry, Father. I've come straight from work and the traffic is heavy this evening.'

20

'No excuse,' the priest replied. 'Well, you'd better come in.' As the flustered young man stepped over the threshold, Father John turned his attention to Kate. 'Come back in half an hour, Kate,' he said. 'We can talk then.'

Annoyed to have been dismissed so rudely in front of the young man, Kate pulled the hood of her duffel coat over her head and went inside the church. She'd sit in there and wait. Intrigued by the stranger, she kept repeating his name over and over in her head. Meeting him was the most exciting thing to happen to her in ages, and she knelt to offer a prayer that he would get the clerk's job.

Suddenly, working for the priest didn't seem such a bad idea. That way, she would get to see Michael again.

4

When Nell returned from work on Friday evening, she lit the fire and opened two tins of soup before picking Róisín up from her neighbour.

'She's been a bit quiet,' Amy said. 'But she's drunk half a mug of buttermilk.'

'Thanks, Amy. Did Kate say she was going to see Father John?' Nell helped Róisín into her coat and picked up her school satchel.

'Aye, she did, and it will be a godsend to you. A couple of hours each day should help, depending on how much he pays. You know what a skinflint he is.'

Nell nodded. 'Thanks for looking after Róisín.'

'We've enjoyed having her. Haven't we?' the woman addressed her five children sitting round the table, waiting for their food to be ladled up to them.

Smiling, Nell placed her arm around her sister and they plodded upstairs. Róisín appeared languid with every step.

'You can have a lie down after you've eaten a drop of soup,' Nell told her.

The child appeared to enjoy the soup soaked in bread, then Nell settled her by the fire, placing a rug across her knees. If only she could get her to a doctor. But they cost money; money Nell didn't have. She was a week behind with the rent and had put it aside to pay the rent man later.

She chopped onions and prepared their meal

for when Kate got home, then glanced across at Róisín. Small at birth, she had defied doctors who said she wouldn't live beyond her fifth birthday. Their mother had lost two babies between Kate and Róisín, and one between herself and Kate. Nell had adored Róisín from the day she was born.

Now, the little girl was staring into the fire, a worried frown on her face.

'What's wrong, pet?'

Róisín pointed to her school bag.

'Do you have homework?' Nell picked the bag up, looked inside and pulled out a letter. 'What's this?'

The little girl bit down on her lip. 'I'm sorry, Nell. I don't know what I've done wrong?'

Frowning, Nell ripped open the letter and read:

Dear Miss Flynn,

Please don't think we are unsympathetic to your plight when we say that we can no longer tolerate Róisín falling asleep in class. Not only is it detrimental to her studies but it is distracting to the other children, who find it amusing.

Please ensure that she gets a good night's sleep. And again, we are sorry for your loss.

Sister Mary Jane,
Head nun

Shaking with anger and frustration, Nell sat down. The nuns had never treated Róisín any differently to the other children, and rarely ever asked about her health. If only she had been able to afford a doctor, things wouldn't have reached this stage. And now she had to deal with the nuns on top of everything else.

'What's wrong?' Róisín asked. 'I haven't been naughty. And I haven't said bad words. Honest, I haven't!'

Nell managed a smile and placed a comforting arm around the little girl. 'Really, it's nothing for you to worry about. Now, I'm going to cook us tripe and onions while you have a nap.'

She filled the rubber water bottle and put it in the bed, then lifted the small girl and placed her under the covers, pulling the blanket over her.

As she prepared their meal, she thanked God it was Friday. But a quick glance at the scullery clock made her frown. Where had Kate got to? How long did it take her to call on the priest and arrange the days he wanted her to work? Nell needed her sister here when Pete Scanlon called for the rent. She didn't like the way his eyes roamed over her body, and she definitely didn't want to be alone with him.

★   ★   ★

Kate stayed in the church until Michael's interview was over. When he came through to the church, as she'd hoped he would, her heart thumped loudly.

He genuflected in front of the main altar, then proceeded to walk down the aisle.

24

'Oh, hello again. Kate, isn't it? I guess he's free to see you now.'

She nodded, her heart doing a somersault. 'Did . . . did you get the clerk's job?'

'Yes, but only after I was grilled in the rudiments of punctuality.' He smiled.

'That's good news.' Kate was pleased she would get to see him again.

'Well, good luck. I hope whatever you need to discuss with him is satisfactory.' Michael added, 'He's a bit cranky. Is he always like that?'

Kate smiled. 'I guess so. Most priests are, aren't they?'

'I hope you don't tar clerks with the same brush.'

'Of course not.' She walked with him towards the entrance. Outside, it was dark and dismal. She glanced down and fiddled with the peg buttons on her coat.

Michael collected his bike, clipped his cycle clips over the bottom of his trousers, then wheeled his bike out of the grounds. 'I'll see you,' he said, and cycled away.

Kate watched him go, her smile fading. She walked towards the priest's house, stepped up to the door and rang the bell, prepared to agree to anything the priest had to offer her.

* * *

When Kate burst into the house, a little breathless, Nell said, 'Well, about time, too. What kept you?'

'Father John had to see someone and kept me

25

waiting ages. But you'll be pleased to know he wants me to clean and dust the house for one hour every day after school. And he'll pay me a shilling a day.' She glanced around. 'I'm starving. Is there anything to eat?'

Nell put her meal in front of her. 'Is that all he's paying you?' she asked. 'Didn't you ask him for more? After all, he knows the situation we're in.'

'Five shillings is not to be sniffed at.' Kate tucked into her dinner.

'No, of course not. It will help pay for a doctor for Róisín.'

Kate's good mood and her willingness to work for such a low wage surprised Nell, but she decided not to press the point for now. They needed money, no matter how little.

'He'll make you work for it, and then you'll have your homework to do,' she added. 'But I'm proud of you for making the effort.'

Kate didn't grumble about the meal for once, and when she'd finished, she pushed back her empty plate. 'What's the matter with Róisín? Why does she need a doctor?'

Nell opened the letter and put it down on the table. 'The head nun sent this letter home with Róisín today. And if she doesn't improve over the weekend, I'll have no choice but to find the money and take her to see a doctor.'

A knock on the door got Nell to her feet.

'That'll be the rent man.' She fumbled in her bag for the money she had separated earlier. When she opened the door, she saw Pete Scanlon standing there, with a huge grin on his face. 'I was hoping to see your father,' she said. 'I need to speak to him.'

He tried to push his way inside, but Nell blocked him and handed over the money. 'Can you give him a message, please? Ask him if he can call up. I'd like a word.'

Just as Nell was about to shut the door, he said, 'Oh, this isn't enough. There's two weeks owing, plus this week. I make that three.'

Nell pulled the door back again. 'No, it's one week owing.'

She was determined not to let him manipulate her into thinking it was more.

'Your mother was in arrears,' he persisted, 'or have you forgotten that?'

'What are you saying?'

'You heard! She owes two weeks' rent on top of what you owe, and you are honour-bound to pay.'

Kate, who was listening to the conversation, glared at Pete but said nothing to defend her sister.

'I know nothing about that,' Nell snapped. 'And that is all I can afford.'

He sniggered. 'The old man won't be pleased with this. But if you come on a date with me, we'll say no more about it.'

Nell pushed the door to, and saw him flinch as he stepped backwards. Her limbs shook as she leant against the door. 'He's lying. Ma never owed any rent.'

'Why don't you go on a date with him?' Kate said. 'He's not that bad looking.'

Nell picked up the tea towel and swiped her

with it. 'You're not a very good judge of character, are you?'

Smirking, Kate lifted her empty plate and took it to the scullery.

★ ★ ★

Kate spent more time than usual washing and preening her hair, ready to go out with one of her friends to browse the shops in Grafton Street. Nell was ironing her work overall and the clothes they needed for the week ahead; her mind was turning over what shopping she could afford with the little money she had left.

Before she headed out, Kate told her, 'I think we should all go to mass on Sunday. It might be good for Father John to see we are making an effort.'

Nell turned round, surprised by her sister's sudden interest in going to church. 'What brought this on? I thought you said you'd never set foot inside the church again, after Ma died.'

Kate shrugged. 'I've changed my mind. And I'm going to ask Father John for more money. I need some new nylons.'

'New stockings!' Nell replied. 'What cloud are you living on, Kate Flynn?' But her sister had already gone out the door.

5

Over the weekend, Róisín had appeared brighter, but Nell hoped it wouldn't put her in a bad light when she asked for an extended lunch hour from work on Monday so that she could visit the school.

When she arrived at her work station, the chargehand was already there.

'Oh, there you are, Nell. If you'd like to take your belongings and come with me.'

Nell's heart thudded as she followed the woman through the factory and down to the floor below, where the temperature was a degree warmer. Nell had been longing to know what the work was like in other sections of the factory, and maybe this was the day.

'Come through here,' the chargehand told her. 'You won't need to wear an apron, but do be careful not to get glue on your overall. It can be a devil to get out.' She gestured towards another woman. 'I'll leave you in the capable hands of Julia.'

Hoping she wouldn't make a mistake, or slow up the production line, Nell swallowed as her stomach churned with nerves.

'This will be your post,' Julia said. 'Don't worry, I'll show you what to do.' More women joined her on the line. 'If you can't find me at any time, you can always ask Ada here.'

Ada had rosy cheeks and a ready smile. She

looked younger than Nell, and the two nodded to each other. Just at that moment, the hooter blasted through the factory and the machines and conveyor belts started up. A mixture of nerves and excitement coursed through her, and she watched carefully as Julia took her through the procedure, which appeared pretty straightforward. Then she was handed a pile of labels and a pot of glue.

Her hands shook as she stuck the labels on the packets as they moved along the belt. Others were doing the same, with the tins Nell had previously washed. All she heard was the sound of machinery and the low chatter of voices.

She was now working alongside twenty other girls, and was fascinated by how quickly their hands moved. Julia explained that the other women were on piecework and, depending on how well she did over the next few days, Nell might well do the same.

Careful at first, in case she stuck the labels on the wrong way up, she soon got the hang of it and found the time passed quickly. Once the packets and tins were labelled, they moved along to another line of women who then filled them with biscuits. The smell of the biscuits, icing, coconut and chocolate made her ravenous, and she wondered if she would manage to work until break time without fainting.

For a few moments, Nell watched another woman hold a small implement to seal round the tops of the tins. Then, at regular intervals, barrow men wheeled away the filled tins — some enormous ones holding as much as ten pounds of biscuits, Ada informed her. They were being shipped over to the UK and other faraway places that she never even knew existed.

One particular barrow boy gave Nell a cheeky wink each time he passed the bench, bringing a blush to her cheeks.

'Watch that one.' Ada nudged her. 'In fact, don't let your guard down with any of them. They think they're God's gift because there's only one of them to every five of us.'

Nell smiled. It felt strange to have this young girl, only Kate's age, giving her advice on men.

When the hooter sounded for their eleven o'clock break, Ada asked if she wanted to go with her to the canteen. But before Nell could answer, Julia was upon her.

'Run along, Ada. I want a word with Nell.'

Nell realised this would be her opportunity to ask for an extended lunch hour to go and see the head nun at her sister's school. But it would depend on what Julia said about her work.

'How are you getting on?' the chargehand asked.

'Grand, I think.' She had been doing her best to keep up with the others.

'We like to encourage our workers, and I've been noticing your work and keeping count of your production. If you carry on like this, you'll be on piecework before long.' She smiled. 'How do you feel about that? I don't want to rush you. But if my calculations are right, your quota is on a par with some women that have been on this section for two weeks.'

This wasn't what Nell had been expecting at

31

all, and her face brightened. 'Thank you. I'd like that very much.' A blush coloured her face. 'I have a request, and I'm sorry to ask.'

Julia frowned. 'A request?'

'Would it be possible to have an extra twenty minutes at lunchtime?'

The supervisor's frown widened. 'You're a good worker, Nell, but you're not that good.' She chuckled.

'I'm sorry. I won't be making a habit of it. I have to see the head nun at my sister's school and there is no other time for me to do this.'

'Well, this is most unusual. Can't your mother do it?'

Nell swallowed. 'My mother died three and a half weeks ago.'

'I'm sorry to hear that, Nell. But you'll have to ask the supervisor. It'll be up to her. You must go to the office on the next floor down.'

★ ★ ★

It had been a good morning, everyone had been kind towards her, and to top it all the supervisor had agreed she could take the extra time, as long as she didn't have a tea break that afternoon. As she hurried towards Róisín's school, it had turned colder and Nell pulled her scarf tighter around her neck, her mind full of what to say to the head nun. The playground was full of screaming children running and playing — all except Róisín, who was crouched behind the wall, shivering.

Nell hurried towards her. 'Why aren't you

wearing your scarf?'

'I dropped it on the stairs this morning and Kate said there was no time to go back for it.'

Nell removed her own scarf and wrapped it round her little sister. 'The head nun wants to see me. You run around and get warm, there's a good girl. You'll be going inside in a few minutes.'

'Am I in trouble?'

Nell smiled. 'No, no, you're not.'

Taking a deep breath, she knocked on the office door of the head nun, Sister Conception.

'Enter.'

Nell turned the shiny brass handle and walked in.

The nun glanced up. 'Oh,' she said. 'Remind me who you are again?'

'Nell Flynn. Róisín's sister, and I'd like to talk to you about the letter you sent me last week.'

'Oh, the letter. Yes, yes. Sit down.' She pushed back her veil and turned her head to look at Nell. 'Róisín falling asleep in class has got to stop.' She folded her arms across the desk, and a stern expression froze on her face. 'It's causing ripples of laughter amongst the other children and makes them lose concentration. I want a reassurance from you, as her guardian, that you will make sure she gets to bed early.' She didn't stop long enough to let Nell get a word in. 'All children require eight hours' sleep to help them perform. Do I make myself clear?'

Nell could barely hold back the rage rising inside her. This nun had no compassion, and it was clear she knew nothing of Róisín's ill health.

'Her tiredness has nothing to do with her not getting enough sleep, Sister. I thought you, of all people, would know that.'

'How dare you speak in that tone, girl? Your sister's health is not my concern. If she is getting enough sleep, why then is she falling asleep in class?'

Nell swallowed. 'I don't know. But it's not her fault.'

'Well, I suggest you find out. And if you can't afford a doctor, take her along to the dispensary, but this situation can't continue. If it does, I'll have no option but to have her removed from this class until we know what's causing her strange behaviour.'

Nell was no longer willing to sit and listen to the nun's uncaring words. 'Surely such drastic measures won't be necessary, Sister?'

'This is not your decision, young woman,' the nun snapped back.

Desperate not to let the older woman see how much she'd upset her, Nell stood up.

'Thank you for your time,' she said. 'I'll not take up any more of it.'

34

6

That evening, all Nell could think about was Róisín. Her instincts were to remove her from the convent school, but would that be fair? Besides, how could she work and leave her alone all day? What would her mother have done? She hated leaving Róisín in a school with nuns who showed little or no compassion. With no money for a doctor, the next best thing was the dispensary, and that meant waiting until Saturday morning and joining a queue of sick people lining the corridor to be seen by the doctor or nurse.

She put Róisín to bed, but she was still awake when Kate breezed in.

'I hope you've kept me something to eat, I'm starving,' she announced.

Nell had been listening to *Dick Barton, Special Agent* on the wireless. She followed the story each evening at 6.45 on the Light Programme. 'You're late tonight, Kate. Has Father John given you extra work?'

'No!'

'Well, where have you been till now?' Nell put her dinner of stew and dumplings in front of her.

'Just talking, you know.' She tucked into her meal.

'Did he say when he'd pay you?'

'No, but I can always ask him, if it will help.'

'What exactly do you have to do?'

'Oh, just the kitchen and the rooms downstairs. I'm hoping he'll ask me to clean the church. There's so much to do in there, it's bound to mean more money.'

Nell couldn't believe her ears. Her sister was looking for more work when she felt domestic tasks of any kind were beneath her? Kate already betrayed a sly and greedy nature, together with a dangerous ambition far beyond her station. There had to be something else behind all this.

She glanced across to Róisín, now fast asleep, before filling Kate in about her visit to the convent school.

'Ma wouldn't stand for that,' Kate said when she'd finished. 'Can't you get her into that small school, St Mary's, just over the bridge?'

Since their mother's death Kate had shown little interest in her younger sister, so Nell was pleased she'd voiced her opinion.

'Umm . . . It's worth a try, I suppose,' she agreed. 'I'll make enquiries tomorrow.'

★ ★ ★

Two days later, during her lunch break, Nell sat in the office of the admissions secretary discussing her concerns about Róisín, surprised at how easily she had got an appointment.

'We might be able to accommodate your sister, Miss Flynn. What level has she reached in her education?'

'She's in second standard at the convent school.'

'I see. Only that class is big, and in view of

what you've told me, I'd like to try and make room for her in our smaller class.' The woman twirled her pencil. 'However, it would mean moving her down a grade.'

Nell, more concerned with her sister's happiness, said she would like to talk to Róisín first.

'Look, I'll show you around our school and you don't have to decide right now,' the secretary offered. 'But don't wait too long. Places fill up fast.'

'Thank you. That sounds grand.'

The building had a clean disinfectant smell, unlike the smell of lavender polish at the convent school, but it was the friendly atmosphere and the happy faces of the pupils which delighted Nell. And she saw no sign of isolated boys or girls lurking in the corners of the playground as she came through the gate. With only three classrooms, it made the school unique.

'We've started elocution lessons, and the children seem to like it . . . some more than others,' the woman laughed. 'Do you think Róisín would like to join us?'

'Yes, I'm sure she would. How many pupils do you have?' Nell asked.

'One hundred.'

'Really!'

'I'm afraid so. We're overcrowded, and it's hard to turn children away. But if you like, I'll put your sister's name down for the lower grade, which has fewer children.' She smiled. 'Once I've spoken with the headmistress, I'll be in touch. How's that?'

'Thank you. You've been very helpful.'
Impressed by what she had seen, Nell went back
to work.

★ ★ ★

On Saturday, Nell took Róisín to the
dispensary. They arrived at 9.30 a.m. and the
place was already heaving. Men with guttural
throaty coughs were spitting into dirty handker-
chiefs, women sneezing and children shivering,
as they each waited their turn. After two long
hours, when she was beginning to wonder if
they should leave, they were called into a room
where a doctor in a white coat sat behind a
desk; he was scribbling on a pad. A nurse stood
by the door.

'Well, young lady, what seems to be the
trouble? You don't appear to have a cough.'

'I'm worried about my sister, Doctor. She has
no energy, and her appetite is poor,' Nell
explained.

The doctor stood up and walked towards
Róisín. A tall, thin man with no hair, he had a
pointy nose on which his spectacles perched. The
little girl edged closer to her sister as he
unwound the scarf from around her neck, felt
her glands, and then told her to say, 'Ah!'
Eventually, he looked in her eyes, and then went
back and sat down.

'What do you think it is, Doctor?' asked Nell.

'I can't find anything wrong with this child.
Give her plenty of milk and chocolate biscuits,
and make sure she gets a good night's rest.'

38

Nell could barely speak. 'Are . . . are you sure?'

His eyebrows shot up. 'There are sick people waiting out there.'

'Aren't you going to give her a tonic?'

His head down, the doctor scribbled something on his desk pad.

'Are you saying there's nothing wrong with my sister?'

The nurse's glare told her the consultation was over.

'Well, thank you for nothing,' Nell muttered under her breath.

As the nurse held open the door, Nell gritted her teeth, put her arm around a sobbing Róisín, and left.

* * *

Nell and Róisín were barely through the door, when Kate pulled on her coat. The fire was lit, and the place swept and dusted.

'I'm off out.' She ruffled Róisín's curly head. 'Hope you got something to perk you up. I'll see you later.'

'Hold on a moment, Kate,' said Nell. 'Where are you going?'

'I've a job to go to, or have you forgotten?'

'What? In your best frock?'

'Sorry, I'm late. Have to dash.' And she flew through the door as if a bat was chasing her.

Nell growled. Father John had never asked their mother to clean at weekends. Perhaps he had given Kate extra work out of consideration for their plight. But if so, why hadn't she said anything last night?

Shaking off her suspicions, she got on with the washing and ironing, with Róisín doing her best to help by putting the clothes on hangers. After a while, because she had been so helpful, Nell let her go downstairs to play with Babs, Amy Kinch's youngest daughter. The chores done, Nell sat down with a cup of tea and Jacob's cream crackers and a slice of Gailty cheese.

Should she take the doctor's opinion, or follow her own instincts? She was convinced something was wrong with Róisín, and she had to find out what it was. Worrying about doing the right thing was getting her down, and Kate behaving suspiciously only made things worse.

With a sigh, Nell rose and went to rinse her cup, when she heard the door handle turn.

Nell glanced round the scullery curtain, and Amy walked in. 'Is Róisín behaving herself?' Nell asked anxiously.

'She's grand. The pair of them are playing with their dollies. Sure, innocence is bliss.' Amy sat down next to Nell. 'I thought I'd come up and see how you got on at the dispensary this morning.'

'Oh, it was awful. A complete waste of time.'

'I wish I could help ye. I hate them dispensaries myself.'

Nell told her what had happened.

'Well, that doesn't seem right,' agreed Amy. 'Didn't he give her a bottle?'

'He dismissed us as if we were wasting his time.'

40

'Oh, lovey.'

Nell shook her head in despair. 'I'm at my wits' end. I don't know what to do.'

'Look, I know ye can't afford a doctor. Sure, what choice do ye have?'

'When can I get time to do that?' asked Nell.

'Leave it to me, I'll find a way. Now, stop worrying.' Amy stood up. 'Go down the town and treat yourself to a pot of tea and a sticky bun, otherwise you'll make yourself ill.'

'Are you sure? I could do with a change of scenery.' She frowned. 'But what about Róisín?'

'She'll be fine. Frank won't be home until midnight, drunk as a lord and shouting the odds.'

They heard Mr Kinch come home drunk most nights, and Nell often wondered how Amy stayed cheerful; she always found time to talk to Nell. At times like this, she really missed Liam. He was a good listener, but she would not put all this on his shoulders. It wouldn't be fair.

How she longed to have him back in her life! But that wouldn't be fair either. She wasn't free like she had been when they first went out together, laughing, joking and having fun on her night off, when she sneaked out of the nurses' home to see him. Now a fully trained mechanic, he was ready to spread his wings and find work outside Ireland, and she didn't blame him.

Nell, on the other hand, had only completed two years of her training. And although the work was hard, some of the nursing nuns were dragons, and the small wage only kept her in nylons and lipstick, she had been determined not to quit.

But that had all changed when her mam died. Liam hadn't agreed with her decision to give it all up, but what else could she do? Abandon her siblings?

Oh, but she missed him. Going downtown on a Saturday afternoon with Joan was a poor substitute, but it was still a blessed release to get out of the tenement and put her worries away for a few hours.

7

The church was bathed in a yellow haze as Kate entered. It was Saturday midday, and the array of lighted candles surrounding shrines to the various saints felt comforting. She was glad to come in out of the cold. At least it was a little warmer in here than outside.

People queued for confession while she positioned herself in a pew nearest the vestry door. She knew what time the clerk came into the church to replace candles and empty the money boxes, and she wanted Michael to see her. As he passed through, wearing a black cassock, he gave her a warm smile. She then moved into the narrow passage leading to the vestry, to wait for his return.

'I'm sorry,' he said, colliding with her and dropping some coins on the floor.

'I didn't mean to startle you.' She bent down and helped him to pick up the money.

When he straightened, she saw a flush rise to his face. He carried on into the room, where vestments were hanging in a neat row, and placed the money in containers before turning to look at her. His dark eyes searched her face.

'Kate, you shouldn't be in here. All the priests are in the church hearing confessions.'

'I'm sorry.' She had no excuse except her need to see him, to talk to him.

He placed his hand on her arm, and her heart skipped.

'You look worried,' he said. 'Is there something I can do for you?'

If she told him the reason she had come to the church this morning, he would think her crazy. Without thinking, she replied, 'No, I'm not worried, Michael.' She played with the toggle on her coat. 'I just wanted a chat with you. Are you free?'

His brow creased with uncertainty. 'Well, if it's a priestly matter . . . I can't help you.'

Kate shook her head quickly. 'No. It's . . . it's nothing like that.'

He knitted his fingers and rolled one thumb over the other. 'I'll be finished here in half an hour.' He cleared his throat. 'I was going downtown for a pot of tea and a scone. Would you care to join me? Whatever's on your mind, we can talk then.'

Kate swallowed nervously. 'Oh, yes, that would be nice.'

'If you wait in the narthex, I'll just finish up here.'

Smiling, she turned on her heel and walked back into the church, thinking how fortunate she was to have met someone as good-looking and clever as Michael. Maybe there was a God, after all. She sat at the back of the church contemplating what they would talk about; there were so many things she wanted to ask him.

She already knew he was twenty-one and lived in Harold's Cross, from a reference she had seen in Father John's study as she dusted. Did he have a sweetheart? Her spirits plummeted at the thought. Did he have a job? She knew he only came to St Saviour's on Wednesday, Saturday and Sunday. What did he do the rest of the week? And in his spare time? She wanted to know every detail about him.

And until her curiosity was satisfied, she would tell no one about Michael. He was hers, and she was determined to keep him.

★　★　★

They walked the short distance to the city, glad to have passed no one she knew.

'Is this okay?' he asked, guiding her inside the crowded cafe. 'Everywhere will be packed; you know what Saturdays are like. I see the shops are already selling Christmas stuff.'

Kate nodded, just happy to listen to him talk. Christmas would be wonderful, after all. Once they were seated, she relaxed, removed her coat, and then drew her long auburn hair over her right shoulder.

The waitress took their order and Kate, oblivious to the chatter and the clatter of crockery around her, couldn't take her eyes off Michael as he removed his grey woollen overcoat. Underneath it, he wore a brown jacket and light corduroy trousers. Even the smell of delicious food sizzling behind the counter did nothing to distract her.

He leant back in his chair and smiled across at her, and she lowered her gaze.

'Now,' he said. 'What did you want to talk

about? I'm not sure I'll be able to help but I'm flattered just the same.'

A flush coloured her face. Should she be honest with him? She wasn't about to reveal she wasn't yet sixteen, and risk him losing interest.

When initially she didn't reply, he coaxed her. 'You obviously need to get something off your chest.'

She swallowed and picked at the edges of her painted nails. 'My parents are dead, and I live with my sisters. I . . . ' Kate stopped when the waitress arrived with their tea and fresh scones.

'I'm sorry, Kate.' She saw compassion in his grey eyes. 'I lost my father a few years ago, so I know how painful it can be.' He set a cup and saucer in front of her, along with a scone, butter and strawberry jam. 'I live with my mother and two brothers. So, we have something in common.'

He poured her tea and asked if she took milk. Kate nodded. Lifting the cup to her lips, she tried to stop her hand shaking. Just sitting here with him gave her a sense of belonging. She had never had tea with a handsome man before. The boys she'd allowed to kiss her behind the bike shed didn't count, and none of them had ever invited her out for tea. She desperately wanted him to like her.

Michael spread jam on his scone and took a bite. Kate did the same, but each time she put the food to her lips, her hand shook, and she quickly put it back down.

'So,' he said, 'you were saying?'

Kate sighed. 'I hate my life. My older sister has

46

given up her career to look after Róisín, our youngest sister, and she thinks she can take my mother's place. But I don't want her telling me what to do. Some nights, I just want to pack a bag and go.' She glanced up and saw a frown crease his forehead. 'You think I'm selfish, don't you?'

He shook his head, wiping the crumbs from his lips. 'No, of course I don't. Your feelings are understandable, considering what's happened. Have you discussed it with your sister?'

As if she would discuss anything like that with Nell, Kate thought. Her sister would go spare.

'No,' she replied sadly, 'that's not possible.'

'Don't you get on, then?'

'Not really. I hate her.'

'Hate is too strong a word, Kate. I don't always get on with my brothers. We fight a lot, and it drives my mother crazy.' He laughed. 'It's natural. When my father died, I had to take his place, and my brothers resented me for a while. Your sister. What's her name?'

'Nell.' Now she wished she'd never mentioned her.

'Well, she's probably grieving, just like you.'

'No, she's not. She never told me my mam had died, and when I got home she had already been taken away. I never got to say goodbye.' A sob caught in her throat. 'My mam was everything to me, and now she's gone.'

Michael reached over and gently touched her arm. 'You need to speak to Nell. Tell her how you feel.'

'No. Never.'

He glanced at his watch. 'I'm sorry, but I have to go. Will you be all right?'

Forcing a smile, she nodded.

'Promise me you won't do anything rash until you've talked about it some more?' He looked into her face. 'Promise?'

She nodded. She would promise him anything.

'Now, eat your scone and I'll walk you back to the church. You live in one of the tenements, don't you?'

Kate glanced down. 'Thanks, I'll be fine.' She didn't want anyone to see her with Michael. Not yet.

'Are you sure? I have a few errands to run before I pick up my bike.'

She smiled. 'Yes, I'm sure, and thank you, Michael. Please say nothing to Father John about what I've told you.'

'Your secret's safe with me,' he assured her. 'And whenever you feel like talking . . .' He smiled as they left the cafe. 'Well, goodbye for now.'

He strode away towards Henry Street, and Kate headed into Switzer's — one of the most expensive shops in Dublin. She strode around the expensive shop as if floating on air, her imagination running wild and picturing the beautiful things they would buy for their home once she and Michael were married.

Now that the ice had been broken between them, she knew she could talk to him again whenever she liked.

8

The sun shone despite the bitter cold as the three sisters, dressed in their best clothes, left for Sunday mass at St Saviour's. Nell was still baffled by Kate's eagerness to attend church when previously she would have said anything to wriggle out of it.

Father John's face brightened as he greeted them in the porch. 'Ah, Nell. I'm glad you've seen sense and come back to the Lord Jesus. Your mother sowed the seed and was a good Catholic herself, God rest her soul.'

Nell had missed the ritual of coming here with her mam each week, but she was unprepared for the guilt that washed over her. Inside, the overpowering smell of incense brought unshed tears to her eyes.

Róisín, dressed in her best red coat and bonnet, with her curls escaping on to her forehead, received admiring glances from parishioners and caught the eye of a neighbour.

'She's a little dote, and a credit to you,' said the woman.

Nell smiled back, and a lump formed in her throat.

Kate, her long hair catching a glint of sunlight from the stained-glass windows, looked around her before stepping into a pew towards the front, drawing her hair over her shoulder. She looked every inch a woman, and Nell regretted the row

49

she'd had with her earlier about wearing lipstick to church. As usual, Kate had won the argument by removing some excess.

Looking sideways at her now, Kate's gaze centred on the altar as the clerk prepared everything in readiness for the service. She looked sincere, devoted even, and there was a glow to her face as she gazed up at the altar. Whatever had brought on Kate's change of heart, Nell sincerely hoped it would last.

★ ★ ★

Monday was a busy day at the factory, with everyone doing their best to get the Christmas orders out on time. The chargehand and the floor supervisor were encouraging them to work faster. Nell, her fingers sticky with glue, struggled to keep her eyes open, having been woken in the night with one of Róisín's nightmares. Taking the child into her single bed, she hadn't had a wink of sleep. All she wanted to do when she got home was to close her eyes and have forty winks before starting on the dinner.

When the hooter went at the end of the shift, Nell emerged with the masses, her mind flitting back to happier times. Not long ago, her life had been blissfully happy. Mam was alive. She had a devoted boyfriend, and a career in nursing. Nell could still vividly recall the events of that terrible day. The knock on the door of her room at the nurses' home, where she and another trainee were sitting on her bed going over their notes during their break. Her shock at seeing one of the nursing sisters standing there with a policeman by her side.

'You're needed at home, Nurse Flynn. The officer here will take you. I'm so sorry, your mother has had a turn. I'm afraid she's dead.'

Her mind blank, she had followed him in a daze. The shattering news had put an end to any ideas she'd had of finishing her training. She recalled suppressing her feelings for the sake of her sisters, never allowing herself to give in to emotion for fear she would cry and never stop. For some reason, tonight she felt vulnerable.

Outside the factory gates, she wrapped her scarf tighter around her neck, inhaling the cold air into her lungs as she walked down Wood Street. She hadn't gone far when she heard a familiar voice behind her.

'I thought I'd missed you in all that crowd.'

She turned round. 'Liam? I didn't expect to see you.'

'Oh,' he smiled. 'So, who were you expecting?'

She shoved him playfully. 'Is everything all right?' she asked.

'No, not really!'

'What's up? Your mam's okay, isn't she?'

He nodded. 'Mam's fine. It's me.'

Nell's face clouded, and her stomach lurched. If anything happened to Liam, she wouldn't want to live.

He touched her arm. 'Nell, I'm not coping without you. I can't concentrate at work. Please don't lose your rag with me. I . . . if I could just see you. I'd be happy with that.'

For an earth-shattering, wonderful moment,

51

his grey eyes looked into hers, in a dark corner of the street. Then he pulled her to him and kissed her — a long, melting kiss that lifted her spirits and filled her with joy. Reluctantly, she pushed him away, embarrassed to be kissing in the open, with people milling past.

'I have to go home, Liam.' If she said what was on her mind, it would break both their hearts and she wouldn't be able to let him go again.

'Come to Bewley's, just for half an hour, please?'

Oh, it was so tempting. 'Róisín's not well,' she told him, 'and I don't like to leave her too long with Kate.'

'Is Kate behaving herself, then?'

'Well,' she smiled ruefully, 'you know Kate. But give her credit, she's cleaning for Father John at the presbytery after school and she appears to have a thing about going to church, even on a Saturday.' Nell laughed.

'It's good to hear you laugh, Nell. Come on, I promise I won't keep you long. You look like you could do with a hot drink.' Putting a protective arm around her shoulder, he led her through the busy rush-hour traffic towards the cosy ambience of the best coffee house in Dublin.

She missed coming here with Liam; he always made her feel special. She couldn't resist savouring every moment of being with him, despite knowing things would never get back to how they'd been before her mam died.

Nell removed her coat, placing it across her lap, while Liam gave their order. 'Tea or coffee?' he asked her.

'Tea, please.' She always relished a cup of Lyons tea as soon as she got home.

As they enjoyed their tea and iced buns, like any normal couple, Liam leant in and took her hand. Nell felt the electricity shoot through her, and briefly closed her eyes. When she opened them, they pooled with unshed tears. Liam reached in his pocket and passed her his handkerchief.

'I know this is hard for you.' He pulled his chair closer. 'It's the same for me.'

'I'll wash this and keep it safe for you.' She stuffed the handkerchief into her bag, avoiding answering him for fear her emotions would spill over in such a public place. The urge to reach out and touch his face, and the pain in his eyes, brought a lump to her throat.

She lifted the sleeve of her navy cardigan and glanced at her watch. 'I should go.' She made to get up, but he pressed her back down.

'Nell, wait, please. Only weeks ago we had plans, and once you had finished your nurses' training we were going to England.'

'Please, don't do this, Liam.' Her voice was barely a whisper.

'Even with my scholarship and apprenticeship at Quinn's garage, there are no prospects for me, or anyone else in Ireland.' He straightened his shoulders. 'And before you say again that you don't want to hold me back, I won't move anywhere without you, Nell.' By now, tears were spilling down her face. 'I understand what you're going through. All I'm asking is that we don't stop seeing each other.'

He reached for her hand, but she snatched it away.

Her eyes flashed. 'Why? What's the point when a future for us is impossible? You must follow your own dream and go to England. It's what you've been waiting for.'

A look of disbelief crossed his face. 'You know I can't go without you. The plan was that we would go together. We can have a good life over there, Nell.'

'Liam, we've gone over this before.' She sighed, and shook her head sadly. 'Even when Kate's old enough, there's still Róisín. Ten years is a long time to be courting.'

She struggled into her coat and hurried outside before anyone saw her tears, but Liam caught up with her and they walked in silence back to Dominick Street.

'I shall keep meeting you after work, until you give me something to hope for,' he told her as they reached the tenement opening. Inside the draughty hallway, he drew her close. 'Don't you think Kate would like to live in England — and even if she didn't, who's to say she won't meet someone and get married? There's nothing to stop us taking Róisín with us.'

She opened her mouth to speak, but he placed his fingers across her lips. 'I love you, Nell Flynn, and I don't intend to give up.'

His kiss was deep and passionate, and she relished having his body close to hers, the feel of his strong arms around her, the smell of his aftershave.

Breathless, and near to tears, she broke away

and dashed upstairs, knowing his kisses would stay with her for a long time.

9

Róisín was curled up in bed, sobbing. Nell rushed towards her, and the young girl flung her arms around her sister. 'I thought you'd gone away, like Mammy.'

'I'm so sorry, lovey. I got held up. I'm not going anywhere.' She glanced around. 'Hasn't Kate come back yet?'

Róisín shook her head. 'I put more sticks on the fire but it kept going out.' She sniffed. 'But I peeled the spuds.'

Nell was struck with guilt. This was all her fault, going off with Liam when she should have been here.

She tucked the girl back into bed. 'You stay where you are until I get the room warm.'

She stoked the fire, placed a few sticks on the hot ash, and scooped up some coal. In the scullery, she scrubbed her hands and prepared the pastry for the rabbit pie. It was almost seven o'clock, and she wondered what was keeping Kate. Her sister would hardly be this long at the presbytery.

She had run out of carrots and was opening a tin of peas when a jubilant Kate burst in. 'Something smells good. What is it?'

Nell came from the scullery. 'Where have you been all this time? I came home to find Róisín upset.'

'I got talking, that's all.'

'It's not good enough, Kate. You'll have to start pulling your weight. I can't do everything. And I won't have Róisín upset. All you have to do is come home after you've cleaned for the priest. Is that too much to ask?'

Kate removed her coat and slumped into a chair. 'Oh, give over. You're not Mam. You can't give me orders.'

Although the remark stung, Nell was determined not to let her win.

'Oh, yes, I can. And as I'm the main breadwinner, the least you can do is look after your sister.' A silence fell between them. 'Can you at least set the table while I mash the potatoes?'

Sulkily, Kate set about the task. 'If you must know, I met an old school friend, Sheila Doyle, and we got talking. You remember, she left school last year? Sorry. I didn't think I was committing a crime.'

'And you didn't think of your little sister here alone and upset, did you?' Even as she said the words, Nell was overcome with her own guilt. Hadn't she just done the same thing with Liam?

When they were tucking into their meal, Kate said casually, 'I'm meeting her again on Wednesday.'

'I don't think so, Kate.' Nell scooped up a forkful of pie and popped it into her mouth, at the same time encouraging Róisín to eat her dinner. 'Leaving Róisín for an hour while you're at the priest's is okay, but you must come home after that. You can meet your friend on Saturday.' Nell raised an eyebrow. 'I mean it, Kate.'

'Oh, don't be so bossy.' Kate scraped back her chair, leaving her dirty plate on the table. Stubborn as ever when she didn't get her own way, she cut herself off from her sisters by reading a book while Nell saw to Róisín's needs, an icy silence filling the room.

* * *

At the end of the week, Nell called at the corner shop on her way home and picked up Róisín's favourite bread — a crusty turnover — a tub of margarine, milk, and a log of briquettes for the fire. They wouldn't last as long as coal, but it was too expensive right now and the alternative would have to do. Over their meal of fried herrings and home-made chips and fresh bread, they sat round the table, their squabble earlier in the week all but forgotten. Nell glanced across to the fire glowing in the hearth and a smile crept across her face. If she was economical and cut back on all but essentials, they might get through until Christmas.

It was rent night and she wondered when Kate would hand over the money she had earned cleaning the priest's house. But for now she said nothing, allowing herself a few minutes to enjoy the food and watch Róisín tuck into the soft bread and eat a few chips. All was serene until Kate bit into her bread.

'What's this?' She spat it out. 'This isn't butter.'

'No, it's margarine, Kate, something we're going to have to get used to.'

'I'm not eating this stuff. I've read what it's made of.'

'You're being melodramatic. And don't forget it's rent night. And if Pete Scanlon thinks he can con us into paying extra rent, he can think again.'

For once, Kate didn't retaliate, and Nell hoped the hint about the rent would remind her to hand over her wages. Instead, Kate pushed back her chair and was about to walk away.

'Where's the money you earned this week, Kate?'

Scowling, she fished around in her bag and tossed three shillings and six pence on the table.

'Is that all Father John paid you?'

'No, but I need the rest.'

Getting to her feet, Nell took Kate aside. Through gritted teeth she said, 'You know we need money for a doctor for Róisín. Can't you think of anyone but yourself?'

'Oh, leave me alone.' Kate glared back. 'You can't tell me what to do with money I've earned.'

Fearful of upsetting Róisín, Nell left it at that. Their little sister needed a warm vest and, most importantly, to see a doctor. She picked up the money Kate had begrudgingly left on the table and put the coins in her purse.

★　★　★

Kate had gone to bed in a sulk and Nell was dozing by the fire, her arm around Róisín, when she heard the rap on the door. Her heart skipped. She picked up the rent book along with the rent money before opening the door.

To her relief, instead of Pete Scanlon at the door, it was his father. 'Oh, Mr Scanlon, won't you come in?'

'It's a cold night to be sure,' he said, stepping inside and rubbing his hands.

Nell handed him the rent and he marked the book, putting the cash into a little black bag.

'I've been meaning to call, but with one thing and another . . . ' he said. 'I had a heavy cold and sent Pete last week. About time that lad earned his keep.' He laughed. 'How are you coping?'

'Sit down, please. I'll make some tea.'

Kate glanced across from the bed but made no attempt to get up.

'It's not easy, but I'm working in Jacob's. I hope you're not thinking of upping the rent?' Nell called from the scullery.

'No, but I do need to have a word,' he replied.

Kate swung her legs from the bed. 'Are you evicting us?' she asked.

'Oh no. No, child. I just need a word with your big sister.'

Nell returned with a steaming mug of tea and handed it to him. 'Do we have to move out?'

He wrapped his hands around the mug. 'The Kinches are moving soon, and that just leaves the three of youse.' He glanced down at his tea. 'Due to the respect I always had for your mother, God rest her soul, I'd be worried about leaving you here in an empty tenement. It's already attracting beggars who sleep in the hallway at night.'

'I know,' Nell said. 'But where can we go?' She

60

sat down next to him at the table, a worried frown creasing her forehead.

'I have a small house in John's Lane, and the couple who rent the top half are moving out in the New Year. How would you feel about moving in there?'

Nell's shoulders relaxed. 'Yes, that sounds grand, but will the rent be more?'

He thought for a moment. 'Well, I'm not sure. There's a few things need doing first. Leave it with me. One thing you'll be pleased about, though. You'll only have to go down one flight of stairs to the lavvy.' He chuckled.

'Well, at least it will be better than this place,' Kate said.

'You can have first choice, and I'll let you know soon.' He got up to leave.

'Before you go, Mr Scanlon,' Nell started, 'Pete was under the impression that Mam was in arrears with the rent. Can you check that for me?' She knew it was a lie but thought it best to clear it up now.

He frowned, then opened his small ledger and ran his bony finger down the last few entries. 'No, indeed, there's nothing owing. I don't know where Pete got that idea from.' He closed the book. 'Your mother never fell behind with the rent. If you follow her example, you'll be grand.'

10

A couple of weeks later, Nell came home for lunch to find both girls still at home. She threw off her coat and walked over to where Kate was sitting by the fire reading a library book.

'Why aren't you at school, and why is Róisín still in bed?' Nell tried to stem her anger.

'She wouldn't get up,' Kate replied. 'I tried, honest I did. I couldn't leave her on her own, could I? So I took the day off.'

'Give me strength! I can't trust you to do anything, can I?' Nell moved to the bed where eight-year-old Róisín lay, tears wetting her long lashes.

'What's the matter, honey?'

The small child looked up. 'My legs hurt. I asked Kate for the chamber pot, but she told me to get out of bed. I'm sorry, Nell. The bed's wet.'

'It's all right, honey.' She glared at Kate. 'Put that book away, warm the soup, and cut up bread. And be quick about it.'

'You can't tell me what to do,' Kate snapped.

'Do it, Kate! I have half an hour to see to Róisín and get back to work.'

Kate closed the book with a thud, uncurled her long legs, and went to the scullery. Nell lifted Róisín from the bed and sat her on a wooden chair while she changed the sheet, then she gave her a bowl of tepid water to wash and helped her

62

to put on dry clothes. 'Show me where your legs hurt, pet.'

'Everywhere.'

'Have you fallen or knocked yourself?' Nell asked.

Róisín shook her head.

'Come to the table and try to eat something.'

But the young girl was so slow, wincing with every movement, that Nell had to carry her. When Kate brought in the soup and bread, Róisín held the bread to her nose, inhaling the smell of the fresh dough.

'Eat it, darling,' Nell urged, 'and try a small drop of soup.'

In no time at all they had finished, and Kate pulled on her school coat and picked up her satchel. 'I'll be off, then.'

'Can you let Róisín's nun know she's poorly?' Nell asked.

Kate nodded, and hurried out.

Taking the sick child in her arms, Nell sat her in the big armchair with a blanket, and stoked up the fire. 'I'll ask Amy to look in on you, and I'll be back as soon as I can.' She kissed Róisín's cheek, then snatched up her coat and hurried down to see her neighbour, who agreed to sit with the child every chance she got.

Nell ran all the way and was out of breath when she arrived at her work bench. She was determined that even if she had to use the following week's rent money, she was taking her little sister to see a doctor as soon as she finished work.

* * *

63

When Nell returned, Amy was sitting with Róisín. 'If we go now,' Amy said, 'we'll just about catch Dr Henley before he closes. It's just off Bolton Street. Dr Henley is a good man, and he doesn't charge as much as some.'

'I'm so grateful, Amy. Thanks for looking after her.' Nell pressed the child into her coat and bonnet and pulled the blanket around her shoulders. 'Are your legs still hurting, Róisín?'

'A little bit.'

'I've given her an aspirin, and it seems to have helped.'

'How will I get her there when she's so weak?' Nell asked.

'I'm coming with you. Our Joan will see to the kids. I suggest we make a cradle with our arms and carry her down the stairs, and we can take her in Babs's pram.'

'Are you sure?' Nell knew Amy's youngest slept in the pram at night.

'Glad I didn't get rid of it.' She laughed. 'You know what they say? As soon as you do, along comes another babby.'

The child was but a featherweight as they carried her down the stairs. Joan was waiting with the pram in the hallway and Nell gently placed Róisín inside, wrapping the blanket around her, pulling up the hood and fastening the front apron across the child's legs. Then Amy and Nell pushed the pram hurriedly past the church, towards the doctor's. The bouncing of the pram soon lulled the child to sleep.

As they turned the corner, Nell thought she glimpsed Kate coming out of a shop further down the street, but her mind was focused on Róisín. Could it be polio? She'd seen many cases during her first year of nursing training, and her fear intensified.

'It's not far now,' Amy said as they turned another corner and crossed the street to a shabby-looking two-storey house on the corner. The door was still open, and they pushed the pram inside.

'We'll have to leave it in the hall and carry her up to the first floor.'

As Amy spoke, Róisín woke up, a red crease of sleep visible down her cheek. Nell lifted the girl into her arms and planted a light kiss on her forehead.

'It's all right, honey, we need to get you upstairs to see the nice doctor.'

On the narrow landing, they stood Róisín on her feet and she leant against Nell's shoulder. The clock ticking on the wall said it was five minutes past six, and there were still three people waiting outside the consulting room. They all looked sickly; one man coughed non-stop. A young woman with a pale face and unkempt appearance stood to offer her seat. Nell gestured to Amy, who sat down, taking Róisín on to her knee.

The door opened and as a patient walked out, Dr Henley popped his head out and removed his spectacles. 'What's wrong with the child?' he asked.

Nell moved forward. 'She's no energy, not eating, and her legs are hurting, Doctor.'

'Bring her inside,' he instructed.

Nell and Amy wasted no time and, ignoring the grumbles of the remaining patients, helped the sick child into the doctor's room. Nell sat Róisín on her lap.

'Which one of you is the child's mother?' Doctor Henley threw a cursory glance towards Amy.

'Neither of us, Doctor,' she replied. 'Her mammy's dead, and her big sister is looking after her.'

'I'm sorry to hear that.' He asked the girl's age and address, then he lifted Róisín and placed her on the couch. He directed the remaining questions to Róisín, and when Nell tried to answer for her, he dismissed her with a wave of his hand. After a quick examination, a few seconds of silence elapsed while Nell held her breath, fearing the worst.

As he turned towards the two women and shook his head, Nell's heart raced. 'What . . . what is it, Doctor? Is it . . . ?' She couldn't bring herself to say the word.

He smiled down at Róisín, then beckoned Nell aside. 'Your sister's very ill,' he said quietly.

'She's not going to die, is she?'

'If it's just her joints, she can be treated with penicillin.'

'And if it's not?'

'It could well be rheumatic fever.' He rubbed his chin. 'I want you to take her across to Cork Street fever hospital and have a specialist doctor do tests. I'll phone them and tell them to expect you.' Nell had a fair idea what that meant, having completed her second year of training. Tears

66

welled in her eyes. 'It's over by the Liberties,' the doctor went on. 'Do you know where I mean?'

'Aye! I know it well,' Amy said.

He turned back towards the couch, lifted Róisín into his arms and carried her outside. The waiting patients glanced up as the doctor carried the frightened child downstairs and placed her inside the pram, the two women following with grave expressions on both their faces.

As Amy tucked Róisín into the pram, Nell opened her purse and took out a ten-shilling note.

'Put that away.' Dr Henley smiled. 'Just get your sister over there as quickly as you can.'

11

Nell recalled her mother telling her never to go within yards of the Liberties because it was a well-known area for prostitutes, but right now all she could think about was getting help for her poorly sister. As they made their way towards the hospital, Nell placed her hand on Amy's. 'Thanks for coming with me. I never expected her to be so sick.'

The other woman smiled. 'I would never let you go alone.'

As they pushed their way through belching trucks and buses, young people on their way home from work were browsing the shop windows decorated with Christmas fare. One smiling couple, their arms entwined, gazed into the jeweller's. For a brief moment, Nell thought of Liam, but she chased the thought away.

Having had little to eat all day, she found the smell of the Jameson's Distillery in Bow Street so potent it almost made her gag. 'Is it much further, Amy?' she asked, and pulled back the pram apron to glance in at Róisín who was sleeping.

'Not far now. It's still quicker this way than waiting for an ambulance.'

They crossed over Merchant's Quay and were now in the Liberties. Nell felt a growing unease. As they were passing the Brazen Head public house, a drunken man was being thrown out by the landlord, who had him by his coat collar. Nell had to swerve the pram to avoid him falling on top of Róisín.

'Sure, the old fella will be in there now supping as if there's no tomorrow, so he will,' Amy said. 'Sometimes, I wish I'd been born a man and could swap places with him for one day, just for the sheer fun of watching him trying to cope.' This made Nell smile.

When they reached Christ Church Cathedral, they cut down Corn Market. Most of the traders had gone, but the smell of fish lingered. The houses along here looked in worse condition than their own, some falling apart at the seams, with gaping doors and boarded-up windows. The women who hung around in doorways were skin and bone, and she wondered when they'd last had a hot meal. Despite their Dickensian state, they laughed and joked with each other, and nodded to Nell and Amy as they passed by.

'Off to the hospital, are youse?'

Nell nodded.

'You're the third one the day wheeling a sick babby to the fever hospital. God love yeas. Yeas are not far now.'

Nell thanked her and they hurried on. 'You'd never believe it was the fifties, would you?'

'It makes my blood boil, so it does,' Amy replied. 'Unscrupulous landlords get away with renting places like these to poor families, and the properties are not fit for a farmyard animal.'

'Don't the Corporation do any checks?'

'Yes, and they promise to get things done but then do nothing. Miserable blithers,' Amy said.

'They don't have to live in them.'

As they turned the corner, a young girl with peroxide-blonde hair, wearing red high heels and an expensive pencil skirt with a slit down one side, stepped into a car. It made Nell gasp. 'She's not much older than Kate.'

'Poor unfortunate one,' Amy said. 'No wonder the kip houses are flourishing, with poverty like this. Who can blame them?'

The Dublin air smelt of soot and smoke, and Nell was appalled by the number of girls hugging the street corners waiting to be picked up. They weren't all dressed as well as the one who had got into the car. Despite her own situation, she could never imagine herself in that position. But these women were victims of circumstance, desperate to feed themselves and their large families.

'It's an eye-opener walking round these streets,' Amy said. 'We're almost there now. Róisín's still asleep. It's just as well she doesn't know.'

When at last she saw the hospital with its foreboding facade flanked by two grey pillars, Nell swallowed back her fear.

'We'll have to leave the pram outside,' Amy told her. 'Can you carry her up the steps?'

Nell nodded, glancing quickly at the older woman. 'What do you think they'll do? Will they keep her in, do you think?'

Amy shrugged. 'I guess they will. But let's wait and see.'

Nell woke the sleeping child and lifted her into her arms. Once inside the large, cold hallway, with its strong smell of antiseptic, a nurse wearing a crisp white uniform and a haughty expression walked towards them. 'Is the child unable to walk?' she asked.

'She's too weak,' Nell told her.

'Take a seat in here.' The nurse opened a door and Nell carried her sister into a small room with two wooden chairs and a desk with a large ledger on top.

Róisín glanced up sleepily, her little face chalk-white. 'Where are we?'

'It's okay. We're at the hospital, honey.'

'Nell, I'm scared,' the little girl whispered.

Nell glanced at Amy, who patted the child's hand. 'It's nothing to worry about, Róisín. You'll be fine.'

They waited only a few minutes, but to the two women it felt like hours. Snuggled down in her sister's arms, the child closed her eyes again. Suddenly the door opened and a tall man in a white coat walked in, a stethoscope dangling from his pocket.

'Hello, I've been asked by Dr Henley to have a look at this young girl.' He smiled kindly at the women, then sat behind the desk and opened the ledger. 'I'll just take her name and a few details.'

When he pulled back the blanket and asked Róisín to try and stand, Nell held her sister's hand to reassure her, but the child cried out.

'Okay, that's fine,' the doctor told them. 'This child is very ill. I'd like to do a few tests and keep her here overnight for observations before saying more.'

He looked directly at Nell. 'I gather you're her

71

big sister? I'm Dr Stapleford. Try not to worry. We'll know more when we get the test results. You can come again tomorrow to see her.' He smiled again.

'Thanks, Doctor.' Nell's heart sank.

Amy placed a kiss on Róisín's forehead. 'You'll be grand, so you will,' she assured her.

'You'll have to excuse me,' Dr Stapleford said. 'I'll send someone to take her to a ward. And it might be best if you don't stay. It will only unsettle the child.'

Her sister clung to Nell when the trolley arrived to take Róisín away.

Swallowing the lump in her throat, she hugged and kissed the little girl. 'Sure, I'll be up to see you tomorrow,' she whispered, then left before Róisín became more upset.

As Nell and Amy walked back home through the Liberties, the empty pram bounced over the cracks in the pavement. In spite of the late evening, young children ran barefoot, their clothes in tatters; young girls went in and out of the kip houses; gap-toothed women in shawls smiled at them from doorways.

A drunk man swayed across the street in front of them.

'Bloody eejit!' Amy muttered.

A girl of about seven ran towards him. 'Come on, Daddy. Come home,' she pleaded.

Nell, her throat tight, felt thankful not to have been brought up in the filth and beer-soaked slums of South-West Dublin.

Neither woman spoke until they reached Dominick Street.

'Sure, she's in the best place, so she is,' Amy said.

Choking back a sob, Nell nodded her agreement, but she couldn't rid her mind of the possibility that Róisín might die.

12

On Saturday morning, Kate helped with the chores, then brushed her hair and applied a coating of pink lipstick. Nell glanced up from sorting through the washing.

'Where're you off to?'

'The Lacys are moving this morning, and I said I'd help. Besides, I want to see where they're moving to.'

Nell's arms dropped to her sides. 'There's plenty to do here, Kate.'

'I won't be that long, and I'll be back to see Róisín with you this afternoon,' she assured her sister.

Nell ran her hand across her brow, wishing Kate could be more helpful. She'd washed a few pots and run the duster over the furniture, but had given no thought to the hundred other things that needed doing. Sick of being left to do everything, she flung one of Kate's jumpers across the room in disgust. It didn't need washing. And if she wanted it doing, she could do it herself. Why should she kill herself washing all this lot in the cold yard while her sister went around as if everything was fine, telling her to stop worrying because Róisín was getting the medical help she needed? It didn't stop her worrying at all.

Nell often wondered what went on inside that head of Kate's. Neither of them had spoken openly about their mother's death, and she wondered if her sister was also bottling up feelings she couldn't speak about. Nell had been forced to stay strong; she knew that any sign of weakness could see her siblings taken into care.

She bundled the washing into a sheet, placed it in the wicker basket, then went down to Amy's. When the door opened, the house was noisy as usual. Babs was crying, and the other children were shouting at one another, which woke Amy's husband. He was swearing and telling them all to shut up as he couldn't get a wink of sleep.

'Joan, sort them two scallywags out, will you?' Amy called into the room, then came out, closing the door behind her. 'Ah, sure they make a holy show of me, they do.'

'I'm sorry to have called at a bad time. Just wondered if you were going to the wash house this morning?' Nell said.

'Yes, I am, and I'll take that for you,' the other woman offered.

'Thanks anyway, Amy, but I must start going there myself. All this is getting too much. Which one do you use?'

'The Iveagh in Lamb Alley. It's the nearest. Hang on, I won't be a minute. We can take it in Babs's pram.'

With the washing inside the pram, the two women bounced it down the stairs.

'I can't say I miss that Purcell woman,' said Amy, 'you know, her who used to live on the ground floor.'

75

Nell pulled a face. 'You mean her that used to lash Jeyes Fluid down the stairs every other weekend?'

Amy held her nose. 'Oh, the smell was terrible.' They both laughed.

When they reached the bottom, Nell said, 'This pram has many uses.'

'Aye, it has indeed.'

'Do you think Róisín would have settled in after we left?'

'She'll be grand, so she will.' The pram bounced along with little effort, and when they reached the end of the street, Amy asked, 'Where's your Kate?'

Nell made a face. 'She said she was helping the Lacys to move house, but there's no sign of anyone moving in the street this morning.'

Amy shook her head. 'Sure, they moved last week, so they did.'

The women turned down Caple Street before Nell replied. 'You know, Amy, she's trying my patience. There'll be another row when she gets back.'

'Wait and see what she has to say first,' Amy cautioned. 'Besides, you have enough to worry about with Róisín.'

It was bitterly cold, and a watery sun struggled to get through the grey clouds. Amy pulled her woolly hat down over her ears. 'I think we'll have snow for Christmas.'

Nell was miles away, glancing into the shop windows as they passed. She couldn't remember the last time she'd had time to do that.

They crossed over Mary Street when she

76

paused, and her heartbeat quickened.

Amy noticed her hesitation. 'What's wrong?' she asked.

'Is . . . is that our Kate? Look, halfway down Mary Street, walking next to a man? Oh, my God, Amy. It is, isn't it?'

Amy gasped. 'Sure, all the young ones dress the same, and it might not be her.'

Nell strained to see as people flocked by, then Kate and the man walked in front of a group of young women. She wanted to follow, but Amy placed her hand on her arm.

'Wait, Nell. If it is her — and we can't be sure, now, can we? — she'll only resent you.'

They carried on walking, but Nell couldn't rid her mind of the image of Kate looking up at the tall young man. Who was he? How could her sister do this and not tell her? Her insides churned with anger as Nell thought of what she had lost in order to look after her two sisters. If it wasn't for Róisín and her love for her, she knew she couldn't carry on.

'Oh, Liam,' she murmured, 'what am I to do?'

They pushed the pram over the Halfpenny Bridge and along the quay, without speaking. It was only as they neared the Iveagh Market, where the wash house was, that Amy said, 'You've got to stop worrying, or you'll run yourself ragged.'

Nell sighed. 'I feel I've wasted my life, Amy,' she admitted, 'and I could murder Kate. Róisín's in hospital because I didn't get help sooner, even though my nurse's training told me there was something wrong. Now Kate's walking out with

77

a man whom I know nothing about.' Tears pooled in her eyes.

'Don't talk such bloody nonsense,' Amy told her. 'You're doing a great job. And you don't know for sure that was Kate. Now, dry your eyes or you'll give that lot in there plenty to gossip about.'

Nell blew her nose, took a deep breath, and followed Amy inside. The wash house was full with women who had brought prams and children and their washing into the steamy room. The floor was soaking wet, and condensation ran down the walls.

'At least it's warm,' Amy said. 'And you don't have to boil the water.'

They found two empty stalls, side by side, and placed their washing into the gas boilers. 'I forgot the washing powder,' Nell groaned.

'There's a woman in the office who will give you a cup of Rinso for a penny,' Amy replied.

Nell made her way through the steamy room, passing women using carbolic soap and scrubbing boards, their sleeves rolled up, their arms red from the hot water. One woman was singing; a few others had joined in. It brought a smile to Nell's face. Yes, she would come here again. It was worth the money, and wouldn't leave her exhausted.

'Sure, it's a grand place to come to cheer yourself up and catch up with the gossip,' Amy said when she returned with her washing powder. 'You're sure to go out with a smile on your face.'

When the washing was finished, they lifted out

the steamy clothes with the wooden tongs, creating a fog of mist around them, and pushed the garments through the wringers.

'Get as much water out as you can,' Amy chuckled. 'Otherwise the load will be heavy going back. I hang mine on the clothes horse. It's warmer in here than back home, but you might not have time to wait for that. Sure, you can leave them here and I'll take them home in the pram.'

'I don't have any woollens, Amy. I'll dry everything around the fire when I get back.' Nell folded her washing and placed it in the basket.

Leaving Amy to gossip with the few neighbours who still came here to do their washing every week, Nell lifted the basket on to her hip, bade the women cheerio, and left. On the rare occasions when she had come here with her mother, they had always found time to browse the nearby second-hand clothes market, but now every penny was accounted for.

On the way home, her fury over Kate returned, and she determined that if her sister didn't toe the line, there would be consequences.

★ ★ ★

Kate had waited by the church railings for Michael to leave the presbytery, and her eyes lit up when she saw him. He walked towards her, a quizzical expression on his face.

'Kate! Is everything all right?'

'Can we talk?'

'Yes, if you don't mind walking downtown with me.'

She was pleased to do just that, and stepped into line with him. A group of women chatting on the street turned to look her way, then continued to gossip. One neighbour beating a rug over the window ledge stopped what she was doing to stare. Aware she was being watched, Kate didn't care. She was with Michael, the new clerk at St Saviour's, and she delighted in giving them something to gossip about.

Smiling down at her, he said, 'I have to call in at the jeweller's at the bottom of Henry Street. They sell banjo strings.'

Kate couldn't hide her surprise. 'You play the banjo?'

'Yes, I do. Has that surprised you, with me being a part-time church clerk?'

'Well, no, not really. Are you good?'

He laughed. 'Few know this, but myself and three other lads have formed a group called The Storms.'

'You play in a group!'

He nodded proudly as they walked further along towards Henry Street, then frowned. 'I'm sorry,' he said. 'You wanted to talk? Is there something worrying you?'

She wasn't at all worried but realised she had to say something. 'It's my youngest sister.'

'Has something happened to her?' He paused to look more closely at her.

Kate's heart skipped. He had the most beautiful brown eyes she had ever seen, with specks of green.

'She's . . . well, they've admitted her to Cork Street hospital,' she explained. 'I don't know what to do.'

'I'm so sorry, Kate. You must be worried sick. Does Father John know about this?'

'No. But, to be honest,' she said, as they walked on, dodging between the Saturday shoppers, 'I'd rather speak to you.'

'I'm flattered, Kate.' He touched her arm, sending a delightful shiver through her body. 'Here we are. I won't be a tick.'

Reluctant to be away from him, she asked, 'Do you mind if I come inside with you?'

He shook his head with a smile, then held open the glass-fronted door to allow her to pass through before following.

While he chatted with the assistant, Kate glanced around at the beautiful diamond rings and watches. She ran her hand over the glass counter, mesmerised by the sparkling array of engagement rings, imagining Michael sliding one lovingly on to her finger.

When they came back out, the street was busy with shoppers.

'I'm afraid I don't have time for a coffee, Kate,' he said. 'We're booked to play at a pub in Blackrock tonight and we have to practise this afternoon. I'll walk you back, though. I've left my bike at the church.'

Kate tried desperately to hide her disappointment. 'Oh,' she said, 'you are lucky, Michael. Before long, you'll be playing in the dance halls.'

He laughed. 'I wish. We're still small fry but, God willing, we're hoping for some lucrative offers in the coming year.' He placed his hand on her arm. 'And Kate, try not to worry too much. I've heard they have some of the best doctors at Cork Street fever hospital.'

She nodded. 'Does your band ever play around here?'

He was walking fast — too fast for her, because she wanted to savour every minute of being with him.

'Yes, we're playing the Father Matthew Hall next Saturday.'

All too soon they were back in Dominick Street. Back to the life she hated and was desperate to change, now she had met the man of her dreams.

13

Nell met Kate on the stairs as she was heading off to visit Róisín.

'You couldn't even get back in time to see your sick sister,' Nell said angrily. 'Where have you been all this time? Or is that a secret? And don't lie, Kate.'

'What's got your goat?' Kate bit back. 'I'm here now. Although I could do with a hot drink before we go.'

'You're unbelievable. We barely have enough time to walk to the hospital before visiting hours are over. Róisín will be looking forward to seeing us.' Nell rushed out on to the street, and Kate followed her.

'Hang on. I'm not walking all that way. Can't we catch a bus?'

Anger ripping through her, Nell snapped, 'What's got into you, Kate?'

'Don't know what you're steamed up about.'

'I saw you earlier.'

Kate's jaw dropped and her face went bright red. 'So, you were spying on me?'

'No, I wasn't. But we'll have this out when we get home, whether or not you like it.'

They walked the rest of the way in silence, Kate pouting and Nell wishing she had someone else's life instead of her own.

★ ★ ★

The ward was bright, with large windows and a shiny floor that made Nell's shoes squeak as they walked on to the ward. There was a strong smell of disinfectant. Róisín, propped up on pillows, saw them straight away and a smile brightened her face. Her bed was halfway down a long line of sick children, some with chronic coughs. She faced a long table with plants and flowers, next to a trolley with small silver utensils. Visitors were still arriving, and Nell gave Róisín a hug, then pulled over a chair and sat close to the bed. Kate remained standing, staring around her.

'How have you been?' Nell asked.

'I don't know, Nell. I woke in the night and my legs hurt. When can I come home?'

'Soon.' Nell brushed her hand gently down the side of Róisín's face. 'You've got a bit of colour. Have you eaten anything?'

'Not much. The soup's horrible.'

Kate said, 'The place is horrible, too.'

Nell turned and gave her a sharp look. 'Be quiet.'

'A nurse took blood from my arm. It hurt.' Róisín pulled back the sleeve of her hospital gown to show a dark bruise.

Nell reached into her bag. 'We're not allowed to bring in any treats, honey. But I'll try to sneak in a few sweets when I come next time, okay? But, look, I've brought up your own nightie.'

Her little sister managed a smile. 'Can I put it on now?'

'Sure, I'll help you.' Nell was about to undo the hospital gown when a nurse rushed across.

'Please, leave it with me,' she said. 'I'll change her later.'

Surprised, Nell passed the garment over.

Kate, looking bored, fidgeted with her hands. 'I need some fresh air,' she said eventually. 'I'll see if I can get a hot drink somewhere. Do you want one?'

When Nell ignored her, Kate walked off in a huff.

'I bet they'll put up decorations soon.' Nell kept her attention on Róisín. 'You'll like that, won't you?'

'Yes. But I want to come home for Christmas.'

'Let's wait and see. Besides, it's a couple of weeks away yet. Have you thought about what you'd like Santa to bring you?'

Róisín looked down. 'Santa won't know where I am.'

'Course he will. When I come up again, I'll help you write your letter. How about that?'

'Okay.' A tear welled up in the young girl's eyes.

'You must be a brave girl, and I promise you'll be home soon.' Nell hugged her close.

Just then, Kate came back without the tea. She came across to the bed and kissed Róisín. 'Don't cry, sure you'll be grand,' she urged. 'A friend of mine says they have the best doctors here.'

Nell stood up. 'Sit with her while I talk to Matron.'

★ ★ ★

She found the woman in a small office just outside the ward.

'Come in, Miss Flynn. Take a seat.'

85

'Thank you. What do you think is wrong with my sister, Matron?'

'We're waiting for the result of blood tests, but we do need to build her up.'

Nell swallowed a lump in her throat. 'I know,' she said quietly. 'I've done my best.'

The older woman nodded. 'We are aware of the poverty outside these walls,' she said. 'But your sister's heart is under great strain.'

Nell knew what that meant, and her hand covered her mouth.

The matron patted Nell's hand gently. 'Try not to worry. As soon as we know more, we can treat her, but for now she must stay in hospital.'

'She won't be home for Christmas, will she?'

The woman shrugged slightly. 'We'll see. I can't say more than that.'

As they walked home, the silence between the two sisters was palpable. Nell wondered how to tackle Kate. She was attractive, and it wasn't unusual for her to have a crush on some boy or other, but they were usually boys her own age. She had even brought one home to meet the family on one occasion. But this was different.

Nell's heart was still heavy at the matron's words, and she felt ill equipped to deal with Kate's secretive behaviour.

Kate reacted immediately to her questioning. 'What is it you think you saw, our Nell?' she said.

'You with a man much too old to be one of your school friends.'

Kate laughed. 'You need glasses. I was on my own. It's not a crime to go window shopping.'

'I thought you said you were helping the Lacys

86

move?' Nell countered.

'Oh, they didn't need me,' Kate replied airily. 'They had plenty there already, so I took myself to town.'

'You're lying, Kate. The Lacys moved last week.'

'So what? I got the day wrong.'

Nell wasn't letting the matter go. 'Why can't you be truthful? And who was the man you were looking up at as you walked down Mary Street?'

'I've no idea what you're talking about. Besides, the town was packed with Saturday shoppers, just like it is now. We were shoulder to shoulder.'

'May God forgive you for telling lies.' Nell had had enough. She walked on, leaving Kate trailing behind.

If her sister was determined not to tell the truth, there was nothing Nell could do about it. She needed to talk to someone. Most people with a family problem talked to their priest. But Nell decided she'd rather talk to Amy first, to ask the older woman's advice.

14

Nell left the factory with a bag of broken biscuits in her shopping bag, her mind flitting from Róisín to Kate. In the weeks since her mother's death, everything had gone wrong, and she felt ill equipped to cope. As she walked down Capel Street, Liam was the last person she expected to see huddled in a doorway of a public house.

'I thought I'd missed you,' he said, stepping out in front of her and startling her out of her dark thoughts. 'I have to talk to you.'

Her immediate reaction was to say no, but seeing him in front of her conjured up happier times. When she hesitated briefly, he took her hand and guided her into the warm smoke-filled pub.

'I promise I won't keep you long. I have news that will cheer you up and put a smile on your face.' He led her to a table in the corner where they had often sat in the past. 'Let me get us a drink.'

Despite the early hour, several regulars were propping up the bar in a cloud of tobacco smoke.

'A pint o' Guinness and a small sherry for the lady, please.' Liam handed the barman half a crown.

Nell removed her coat, and then wished she hadn't; she was still wearing her factory overall. She removed her stained apron, rolled it up and popped it into her bag. With Róisín still in hospital, she felt less guilty about not rushing home. Kate had gone home with a school friend who had moved into one of the new houses in Cabra.

She straightened the lapels on her overall as he walked back with their drinks. He swallowed a fair amount of his, leaving a blond moustache across his upper lip. It always made her smile. He passed over her drink, then removed his grey coat and scarf and settled in the seat opposite her.

'How are things?'

Tears gathered in her eyes. 'Not good, Liam.'

'Oh, Nell. Why won't you let me help?'

She swallowed. 'There's nothing you can do that would change anything.'

He looked away, then picked up a green coaster with the word Guinness written across it, and placed his drink on top.

She had an overwhelming urge to reach out to him. 'I'm sorry, Liam. If only things were diff . . . ' She paused.

He leant in closer. 'They can be, Nell. I can change both our lives, and Róisín's. Kate's, too, if it will help.'

Nell choked back a sob. She wanted that so much, and it delighted her to hear him say it. He reached across and took her hand.

'I've been offered a job in London, looking after a fleet of cars for a motor engineering company in East Finchley. I start in the New Year. They're paying my expenses over, and helping me to find a place to live. Can you believe that, Nell?'

'Oh, my God!' Her hand rushed to her face. 'That's wonderful, Liam.'

But her heart felt like it was cracking. What he proposed wasn't possible. Not now.

Unaware of her thoughts, he pressed on. 'It proves that persevering and getting a qualification pays. When I'm settled, I'll send for you.'

Excitement danced in his eyes. And when a sob choked the back of her throat, he squeezed her hand. 'Don't cry. It's good news, isn't it? Everything will work out, I promise. You will be able to continue your training at St Thomas's Hospital, and we can get married when that's finished.'

Tears cascaded down her face and he wiped them away with his thumb, frowning. 'What is it?' he asked. 'You still love me, don't you?'

'Oh, Liam! It's too late.'

His face clouded. 'What . . . what do you mean?'

'Róisín's been admitted to the fever hospital. She's so sick. And . . . and Kate . . . well.' She refrained from saying more.

He sat back. 'When did all this happen?'

'On Friday. I'll know more tonight once the test results come back.'

He sighed. 'God, Nell. I'm so sorry. You must be sick with worry. Would you like me to come with you?'

'No thanks, Liam. I'd rather be on my own when I find out.'

'She'll get better,' he tried to reassure her. 'It may take a few months, but that's okay. And we can still . . . you know.'

She shook her head. 'I don't want you to be responsible for my family because of me and — '

He cut in. 'I love you. When are you going to get that through your head?'

She swallowed the rest of her sherry. 'And I love you, too. I want to come to London more than anything.' She sniffed. 'But I can't make plans right now.'

He nodded. 'I understand.' His voice was a mere whisper.

She never doubted he loved her, but she couldn't let him take all her family responsibilities on his shoulders; he would only regret it later.

'Look on the bright side, Nell. Róisín will get well again.' And as he held her gaze, she saw the sincerity of his words.

'Oh, Liam.' She reached across and tenderly touched his face. She knew he meant it, but this wasn't just about the two of them any more. Tears filled her eyes and she began to sob.

Realising her distress, Liam stood up, pulled her to her feet and wrapped his arms around her, oblivious to the men staring over at them from the bar.

As he walked her home, his arm around her shoulder, neither spoke, each submerged in their own private thoughts. On the doorstep, when he kissed her deeply, Nell clung to him, wondering what she could do to stop his leaving. But despite her love for him, she would never do that.

When he finally released her, a flush warmed

her face. She pressed her key into the lock and then, smiling, turned towards him. He blew her a kiss before moving away.

* * *

As she tramped up the stairs, a mixture of emotions soared through her. Liam's plans had given her hope, despite her doubts. By the time she reached the third floor, she had composed herself.

Amy had heard her feet on the stairs and came out to greet her, two small faces peering out from behind her skirt. Amy shooed them back inside, closing the door on them.

'Is it tonight you get the results on Róisín?' she asked.

Nell nodded.

Amy patted her arm. 'Don't be fretting now. I'll come with you.'

'You don't have to do that, Amy. You've enough to contend with.'

Amy waved off her protest. 'It'll be fine. Joan's a good girl.'

Nell smiled. 'That's grand. Thanks, Amy.'

'Did you have a word with Kate? About Saturday, when you thought you saw her?'

Nell shook her head sadly. 'I saw her, Amy, but she'll admit to nothing.'

Amy snorted. 'Right, you get yourself something to eat while I sort this lot out, then I'll meet you in the hall.'

* * *

The room felt empty without Róisín, and God only knew what time Kate would be home. Nell hated harbouring suspicions about her sister, but the girl seemed to tell so many lies.

Unwilling to cook for herself, she made do with a cheese and pickle sandwich and a pot of tea. As she sat munching her food, she pondered Liam's words, and the possibility filled her with joy. If Róisín was well enough to come home for Christmas, she might be fit to travel to England. A new life, away from poverty and strife, sounded wonderful.

Nell glanced around the room. It looked dull, and there was no evidence of Christmas cheer. She'd have to put up trimmings, get Kate to help her make paper chains, and scrape together enough money to buy Róisín a doll. The little one still believed in Santa Claus.

Their mother had always made Christmas special, and Nell knew she must do the same for her sisters. Her pride wouldn't let her accept Liam's help, though, and she couldn't let him see how desperate she had become. Not now, when he needed every penny. Most poor families relied on St Vincent de Paul's aid at this time of the year; perhaps she might join the queue.

In a more positive mood, she cleared the table, put a few things in a bag for Róisín, then wrapped up against the cold and went down to meet Amy.

★　★　★

At the hospital, they waited in the corridor until the start of visiting before being allowed on to the ward. Róisín was sitting propped up on a pillow, chatting to another small girl who was out of her bed. Nell and Amy held back, reluctant to interrupt the friendship, until a nurse walked over.

'Come along now, Ann. You may be leaving us tomorrow, but as it's visiting time you need to get back into bed, dearie.'

As she walked away, the girl, who looked about Róisín's age, said, 'Goodbye, I hope you'll be next to go home.'

Róisín waved back, then smiled broadly as she spotted her two visitors.

Amy carefully slipped a bag of sugared jelly sweets on to the bed. 'Put them under your pillow and don't let nurse see them,' she whispered. 'Share them with your friend.' She kissed the young girl's cheek. 'My, you're looking bonny. You'll soon be home at this rate.'

Nell smothered her little sister in a hug and put a clean nightie in the locker. When she turned back, Róisín was watching her every move. 'Amy will keep you company while I have a word with Matron,' she explained.

Her heart thumped as she knocked on the door before walking in.

'Oh, sit down, Miss Flynn.' The matron gestured towards a wooden chair. 'May I say your dedication to your younger sister is admirable.' She placed her arms on the desk and knitted her fingers, her expression serious. Nell had seen that expression before, when parents were about to receive bad news about their sick children. 'Your sister is not in any immediate danger,' the older woman went on, 'but you may get upset by what I have to say.'

Nell swallowed. 'What is it, Matron? What have the blood tests revealed?'

'I'm sorry to have to tell you that Róisín has confirmed rheumatic fever.'

It was what Nell had feared, but hearing it confirmed was much worse.

'Will she . . . will she die, Matron?' She could barely speak the words.

The matron shook her head. 'Not with the right care. Her joint pains concern us, and we are treating that with penicillin. However, we would like a specialist to look at her, to determine if there is any long-term damage to her heart.' She paused briefly. 'If that's the case, I'm afraid it will mean she has to remain in the hospital for the foreseeable future.'

15

Kate took the bus to Cabra. Her friend's dad had just hired their first television set, and she was excited to see it. Tonight, she planned to confide in Teresa Lacy, who was two years her senior, her feelings for Michael.

She had often fantasised about what her first real boyfriend would be like. Someone foreign, the son of a rich businessman, perhaps. But now she'd met Michael, she was sure he was her dream man. She would find a way to his heart. To him, she was still a schoolgirl, but she'd soon change his mind. And besides, he'd never mentioned a girlfriend.

If she'd had the money — money she'd handed over to Nell, she thought grumpily — she would have gone to hear him play at the clubhouse in Blackrock last weekend. It was a lovely place, far removed from the stink of the city slums. She'd been there many times on the train with her mum and dad and Nell, before Róisín came on the scene. They'd enjoyed picnics in the park overlooking the sea, listening to the band play, and watching the trains trundling past on their way to Dun Laoghaire, Dalkey, Killiney and Bray.

But their lovely outings had stopped when Róisín came along, as her little sister was never well enough and Mam wouldn't leave her. But now Kate was older, she could go anywhere she

96

liked on her own, or with friends. Trouble was, she didn't have money.

She hoped that Teresa would accompany her next weekend, when Michael played in the city.

The bus dropped her close to a cluster of houses with fields and open space where building was still in progress. It was dark. Poor street lighting made it so different to life in the city and, apart from a telephone box on the corner, there were no shops. As she walked, her long hair became windswept, and her footsteps echoed in her ears; with hindsight, she wished she'd asked Teresa to meet her off the bus. Unsure which way to turn, she spotted a watchman up ahead, next to a pile of building materials, and walked towards him. He sat in front of a roaring fire that had been lit in an old dustbin punctured with holes. His long hair hung in rats' tails from underneath a battered hat, and he wore a layer of coats that made him appear like a tramp. She paused, unsure whether to approach him.

'Come and get a warm, lass, I won't bite.'

She moved forward. 'I'm looking for St Attracta Road.' She held out her hands to the fire and the heat warmed her face.

He smiled, drawing on his cigarette, showing muddy brown teeth. 'Sure you've come too far up. If you go back and take the third on your left and then a right.'

Thanking him, she plodded back. All the houses were identical, with white doors and windows, pebble-dashed fronts and walled gardens. But Kate thought it would be a dream to live in one of these. If their mam hadn't died, they might have been living in one, instead of the slum she shared with her sisters.

Soon she was walking up the garden path of number eight and knocking on the door with its shiny brass knocker. An excited Teresa opened the door to her. 'Come in.'

Kate stepped into a long, narrow hallway that led to a kitchen at the far end. Her feet made a hollow sound on the wooden floor.

'We've no carpet yet,' Teresa giggled as her mother called hello from the kitchen and her father, who was smoking his pipe, nodded. 'Would you like to look around the house?'

Kate nodded. 'Your mam and dad won't mind?'

'Of course not. Come on. Wait until you see the front room. Mam's had a new Axminster carpet fitted, but you must take off your shoes.'

Kate removed her school shoes, and her toes sunk into the pile. 'Is that the new television?' She pointed to the brown box sitting on a table. It had a screen, with knobs across the front. 'How does it work?' Kate asked.

'Didn't you notice the aerial on the roof as you came in?'

'No, I never looked.'

'This hunky guy put it up for Dad. I watched him go up the ladder from my window. You'll see it when we go out.'

'How do you switch it on?'

'Dad's the only one allowed to touch it, and he'll put it on for the news. Sometimes the picture's shaky; it depends on which way the wind is blowing. And out here it's so open.' Teresa moved towards the door. 'Let's go upstairs to my room. It's grand,' she said, all excited. 'We have three bedrooms. This is mine.' She threw open the door and jumped on to one of two neat single beds covered with pink candlewick bedspreads.

It was everything that Kate desired for herself.

'Who sleeps in the other bed?' she asked.

'I have to share with my sister. The other room is my brother's, and the front one is Mam and Dad's.'

'It seems like bliss, Teresa.'

'We're still settling in,' her friend admitted. 'I bet you've not eaten. Let's go out.'

Kate looked puzzled. 'Out where?'

'We have a fish and chip shop just around the corner. Shall we go there now and get some?'

Chips sounded wonderful, but Kate knew her purse only held enough for her return bus fare and a few coppers. 'I don't have enough money,' she admitted.

Teresa shrugged. 'Don't worry, I have.'

She called to her mother as they left. Round the corner was a row of shops — some occupied but closed for the day, others empty with To Let signs on the windows. A light shone out from the chip shop where a group of boys were hanging around outside. They whistled as the girls approached.

'Hey! Have you got a big sister that looks like you?' The boy, about Kate's age, was looking at her as he drew on his cigarette and blew away the stale smoke. Kate felt a blush rise to her face.

'Take no notice,' Teresa said. 'Sure, he says that to all the girls.'

'No, not all,' the lad said, with a cheeky grin.

Kate's eyes were, however, on the older boy who didn't appear to be one of the group. He sat astride a motorbike, wearing a dingy black leather jacket over a white polo shirt, a colourful scarf tied around his neck. She glanced down at his scratched black boots. His hair was oiled and slicked back. He was eating chips from a paper bag.

'Who's the good-looking one on the bike?' she whispered.

'Don't know, never saw him before.' Teresa linked her arm through Kate's and drew her inside the chip shop.

★ ★ ★

The queue was long and by the time they came out, the boys had gone, apart from the one on the bike. The girls walked past eating their chips.

'I can't remember the last time I ate chips from the chippy,' Kate said, licking her fingers.

'Excuse me,' the boy called. The girls turned their heads. 'I've been racking my brains where I've seen you before.'

'Well, don't wear them out, will you?' Teresa replied. 'Now, buzz off.'

'Is he from round here?' Kate muttered.

'Don't think so. Come on.' They had finished their chips by the time they arrived back at the house.

'So,' Teresa said, when they were back inside

her room. 'Tell us about this Michael that you're so gooey-eyed about.'

Kate curled up on the bed and related all her news to Teresa. 'He's taken me for coffee and I've walked downtown with him a few times. He's gorgeous, Teresa.' She took a breath. 'I can't wait for him to ask me out, proper like. And he's part of a group called The Storms. Michael plays the banjo and the fiddle.'

Teresa joined her on the bed. 'Sounds exciting. Is he good?'

'Well, I don't know, do I? They're playing this coming Saturday. Will you come with me?'

'Where'bouts is it?'

'The Father Matthew Hall.'

Teresa bit her lip thoughtfully. 'It's not one of the big dance halls, then?'

'Not yet.'

'I'll try, but me dad's strict. He forgets I'm seventeen.'

'Oh, please come, Teresa,' Kate pleaded. 'I've never been to a dance, and I really want to see him.'

'I'll do my best.'

'Can I borrow something of yours to wear?' Kate asked. 'That pink felt skirt you bought the other week, with embroidery around the hem? It will go with my sister's black court shoes.'

'Won't she mind?'

'She won't know.'

Teresa frowned. 'Does she know you're going to the dance, then?'

Kate shook her head dismissively. 'She won't care. She blames me and Róisín because she had to give up nursing and her precious boyfriend to look after us.'

'It can't be easy for her, though. I don't think I could do it.'

Kate shrugged. 'So, what about the skirt?'

'Okay, I'll get it. I want it back, mind.' She opened the wardrobe and slipped it off the hanger.

Kate put it up against her slim frame and did a twirl. 'It's lovely.'

'Do you want to borrow my black bomber jacket?'

'Oh, can I?'

'Promise you'll take care of it?'

'Course,' she assured Teresa. Now Michael would have no doubts about how grown up she was.

'If I can get round me dad to drop me in town and pick me up, I'll come.'

'Thanks, Teresa. Do you think your dad will have the telly on now?'

16

Nell switched on the wireless to stop her from becoming maudlin and to break the loneliness that seemed to engulf her. She was still trying to take in the news that Róisín could be in hospital for weeks. And Kate didn't seem to care, which bothered Nell more than she dared to admit.

She sat down with a mug of Camp coffee and mulled everything over in her mind. Liam's proposal for them to follow him to London had uplifted her, but the news that Róisín was sicker than she had first thought had dampened her spirits. Her little sister *had* to come home for Christmas; anything else was unthinkable.

Refreshed after her drink, she considered decorating the room, but her heart wasn't in it. A cardboard box underneath her bed held last year's Christmas decorations. Delving through it, she found Róisín's Christmas fairy, two red paper bells and a few strips of tinsel; not enough to bother. In another box was the crib with the infant Jesus, Mary and Joseph, a shepherd, a lamb and two of the three wise men. If she did nothing else, she would display it on the shelf above the fireplace.

That done, she sat down to wait for Kate, but it was Amy who arrived first. She made her friend a cup of tea and they settled in the scullery.

'I've not made a very good job of keeping the

103

family together, have I?' Nell said sadly.

'Now, you can stop that silly talk. You've given up everything to take your mam's place. Just because Róisín has to have a stay in hospital, it isn't your fault now, is it? And sure, Kate will settle down.' She leant one elbow on the table, looking across at Nell. 'There's been many a young one in the tenement that's gone astray. But they've always seen the error of their ways, because if they didn't, they'd get a walloping off the old man.' She picked up her mug and blew across the top.

'Would you like a drop more milk?'

Amy shook her head. 'Your Kate hasn't a father to keep her in line, and you can't take his place now, can you?'

'I'm not sure she ever took much notice of our dad, Amy, but she adored Ma. And Ma spoiled her until Róisín came along.'

Amy placed her mug on the table. 'Sure, my Frank can have a word with her, if you'd like? When he's sober, I mean.' Laughing, she glanced around. 'Aren't you going to trim up this year?'

'There's no point. Besides, we'll be moving in the New Year.'

'Sure, that's what I said, but the kids insisted on making paper chains and stringing them up.'

'Amy, I meant to tell you before, but I didn't get the chance. Liam wants me and the girls to live in London when he's settled. I've not talked to Kate yet, and Róisín . . . well . . . ' Nell's voice trailed off.

'Sounds grand, so it does. You hold that thought. There's no reason to say it won't happen. Just wait until you hear more about Róisín's condition.' She glanced at the clock. 'The old fella will be home soon and there'll be hell to pay if his dinner's not on the table. Either that, or he'll be too sozzled to eat it.'

★ ★ ★

Nell was damping down the fire by the time Kate got in. 'I was about to send out a search party,' she said, stretching her back. 'How did you get home?'

'Mr Lacy brought me back in the truck. You should see their house, Nell.' Kate was bubbling with excitement. 'It's grand. They have a television and three bedrooms.'

'Teresa has a mum and dad.' Nell's reply was dismissive. 'And when you come to your senses, you'll realise we're lucky to have a roof over our heads.'

'Oh, you! You're always in a mood, these days,' her sister retorted.

Without washing, Kate threw off her clothes, got into bed, and was asleep as soon as her head hit the pillow.

In her room, Nell washed and got ready for bed. Snuggled down under the blanket, she let her emotions spill out. She had wept when her father died, but at the time of her mother's death, her focus had been on keeping the family together and doing the right thing — giving up the man she loved and her career. Now Róisín was ill in hospital, Kate a law unto herself, and soon Amy would be leaving. What was the point of it all, if she ended up an old maid? Her heart aching for Liam, she sobbed herself to sleep.

* * *

Nell was cold and weary when she returned from work. As she trudged up the last flight of stairs, Amy's door opened.

'Hold on a minute, Nell,' Amy cried. 'I've something to show you.'

Nell could hear excited chatter coming from inside the room.

'Look. We got the letter today. We've got a house in Crumlin, and we're moving next week.' Amy thrust the letter from the Dublin Corporation towards Nell, who read it carefully, then folded it and handed it back.

'Oh, Amy, I'm pleased for you.' Nell reached over and hugged her. 'You must be over the moon.'

'I can't imagine it. We'll have our own bedroom, and the kids will share the other two.'

Nell's smile faded. 'You'll be in for Christmas, then?'

'Oh, don't worry. Sure, you'll be moving out yourself after Christmas.'

'Yes, I hope so. And if you need any help, you know . . . '

Amy laughed. 'Well, if you're around, you might look after the three younger ones while we move out the stuff. Not that we've got much, mind.' She returned to her family, still chuckling.

Upstairs, Kate had left a scribbled note on the table to say she would be back after she'd finished at the presbytery. Nell made a pot of Lipton's tea and drank it as she cut up the scrag end for the stew pot. Since their ma died, Amy had kept Nell's spirits up; who could she confide in when the other woman moved out? Being the only family left in the old tenement wasn't something she was looking forward to.

The fire glowed and the stew was almost cooked when Kate walked in. 'I've homework to do tonight,' she announced. 'You won't mind if I don't come with you to see Róisín?'

'What is the matter with you?' Nell snapped. 'Don't you care about your sister?'

'Oh, stop going on. I don't know what to say to her, and I hate hospitals anyway. It's best if you go on your own. I'll come another time.'

Nell spooned the stew on to warm plates and Kate joined her at the table.

'You know, it's freezing in the presbytery,' she said. 'He only lights a fire in his study. And he has plenty of fuel. I almost snatched a few lumps of turf to bring home.'

Nell was shocked. 'Kate, you mustn't. To steal from the priest is a terrible sin.'

Kate shrugged. 'Why not? He wouldn't miss it, the old skinflint.'

'That's not the point and you know it. By the way, I'll be counting on your wages this week. I need every penny. Christmas is not far away, and we need to get toys for Róisín. Have you any ideas?'

'No, I haven't. Anyway, it won't be the same for me without Ma. It never will be.' She got up, took her plate to the scullery and began putting her school books out on the bed.

'Yes, I know that, Kate.' Nell sighed wearily. 'But can't you think of someone else, for once in your life?'

Nell cleared up in the scullery and then got ready to visit Róisín. Before she left, she glanced across at Kate, her head stuck inside the covers of a book. 'Shall I give Róisín your love, then?'

Kate's head popped up. 'Oh, yes. Tell her I'll be up to see her at Christmas.'

Nell frowned. 'Christmas is nearly two weeks away.'

Kate simply shrugged and returned to her book.

On the way to the hospital, Nell recalled her conversation with Kate and hoped her sister wouldn't stoop so low as to steal from the priest. Deep in thought, she turned the corner to the hospital. She hoped Róisín was in good spirits. The child had been looking better of late and eating all the food put in front of her, according to the nurse.

She was about to climb the steps to the hospital when a figure huddled in the doorway, muffled in scarf, gloves and with a flat cap covering his head, turned towards her.

Nell stopped in her tracks. 'Liam! What are you doing here?'

17

Nell stood on the bottom step of the hospital entrance, staring up at Liam before making her way to the top. 'Are you visiting?'

'I'm waiting for you.' He smiled. 'I have a present for Róisín.'

Nell suppressed the urge to throw her arms around him and tell him how much she missed him. Instead, she replied, 'That's really kind of you.'

He took a brown paper bag from inside his coat. 'It's a doll. Do you think she'll like it?'

'She'll love it. Thanks for coming. Would you like to come up and see her? Give her the present yourself?'

'Could I? Do you think she'll remember me?'

'Well, of course she will, silly.' She smiled as he followed her through the door.

'Where's Kate?'

'She had homework to catch up on.'

They walked down the long, windowless corridor, with doors on either side, their feet echoing on the tiled floor. As they entered the children's ward and walked towards Róisín's bed, a smile immediately brightened the little girl's face.

'I've brought someone to see you.' Nell kissed her cheek and sat down on the bed.

'Hello, Róisín. Remember me?' Liam leant down and kissed the top of her head.

'Where've you been? I missed you.'

Liam glanced at Nell before replying, 'I've been busy, sweetheart. How are you doing?'

A nurse was sitting at the nearby table. She glanced over, then continued to write up her notes.

'All right! But I want to come home for Christmas,' Róisín grumbled. 'Nurse says I'm not well enough.' She glanced at Nell, who patted her hand.

'It'll be all right. You keep eating up your food, and we'll see,' she urged her little sister.

The child's face brightened. 'Nurse says Santa's coming to visit us all at Christmas time.'

'That sounds great,' Liam said. 'Look what I've brought you.' He opened the parcel and handed her the rag doll with a porcelain face.

Róisín hugged it to her. 'Thanks, Liam. I love her.' Excitedly, she examined the doll, and the scene brought tears to Nell's eyes.

The nurse in charge, who had been watching them closely, rushed across the room. 'I'm sorry. We don't allow toys to be brought into the hospital,' she said. 'It only unsettles the other children.' She smiled towards Róisín, who had a firm grip on the doll, then prised it from her and handed it back to Liam. 'I'm sorry, but those are the rules. The children will be allowed toys on Christmas Day. You can bring it back then.'

The child began to cry, and Nell glared at the nurse before leaning over to comfort her sister.

Liam placed his hand on the child's shoulder. 'I'm sorry, Róisín. I'll bring it in again.' He glanced at Nell. 'That was uncalled for, so it was.

110

Look, I'll wait outside before I say something I'll regret.'

He stuffed the doll into the large pocket of his overcoat and headed outside. He was halfway through his second cigarette when Nell joined him.

'How is she?'

'Disappointed,' Nell admitted, 'but she knows she can have the doll back on Christmas morning. I'm sorry, Liam. I'd completely forgotten about the rules. So close to Christmas, I didn't think it would matter.'

He threw down his cigarette and snuffed it out with the toe of his shoe. 'I'm sorry to have caused her distress, but she looks well. Shame she can't come home for Christmas, though.'

They walked in silence. The thought of spending Christmas alone weighed heavily on Nell.

Liam reached for her hand, and it felt so good. 'Nell . . . '

'Don't, Liam. Don't say anything. Let's just enjoy this time we have together.' She held his hand tighter. This was what she missed — his touch, his closeness. It made everything bearable.

They continued walking without speaking until they arrived in Dominick Street. 'Thanks, I'll be grand now.' She let go of his hand.

'Let me see you to the door? I want to ask you something.'

Delighted to have more time with him, she nodded, and he pulled her closer as they walked.

'Amy's moving out next week,' she said,

changing the subject.

'Oh!' Liam frowned. 'Does that mean you and Kate will be alone in the tenement?'

'Yes, but Mr Scanlon has a place lined up for us on John's Lane after Christmas.'

'John's Lane? That's good.' He still looked concerned. 'Is it okay? Have you seen it?'

'No. The current occupiers are moving out in the New Year.'

They were outside the tenement. Nell glanced up at the light in the window and hoped Kate had kept the fire on. 'Thanks for coming to see Róisín, Liam,' she said, 'and for walking me home.' She turned to go.

He touched her arm. 'Nell, let's have a night out before I go away? What do you say?'

She swallowed. 'It sounds grand, but . . . ' She was going to say it would make things harder once he had to leave.

'What about next Saturday night, after we've visited Róisín?' he persisted. 'When was the last time you had a night out, Nell?'

She shrugged, unable to remember.

'I need to dance with you, glide around the dance floor holding you close,' he continued. 'It's one of the memories I'll take with me to London until you can join me.' He turned her towards him, and she saw the pain in his eyes, as intense as her own. 'I'll pick you up outside the hospital, okay?' He reached for her hand. 'It will be good for us both.'

Nell nodded. 'All right, I will.'

He pulled her close in a hug. 'Oh, and I almost forgot. Mam wants you all to come to ours on

112

Christmas Day. Please say you will.'

With every fibre of her being she wanted to say yes, but it would send out the wrong signals to his mam and dad. They were fond of the couple, and the break-up had been hard on them. Would it be right to raise their hopes when she and Liam weren't certain how the future would pan out?

He sensed her hesitation. 'Please, Nell. It's only Christmas dinner, for God's sake!'

Drops of rain landed on them and he pulled her into the doorway for cover. As if reading her mind, he added, 'I'll make sure they don't get too carried away. Now, please will you come?' He looked into her eyes. 'Three weeks from now I'll be in London.'

She closed her eyes and he leant in, his hand stroking the side of her head, sending tingles throughout her body. And when he kissed her, she let herself go limp in his arms. When they broke apart, she placed her head against his shoulder, drinking in his scent, and blinked away a tear. How could she bear to let him go?

'Nell, I love you, and I know you love me, too,' he whispered.

'Oh, I do.' This time, his kiss held all the passion she remembered, and it was quite some time later when they drew apart. 'Liam, this is so hard. You'll soon be gone and — '

He kissed her again. 'It's only for a short time. I promise.'

She sniffed but kept hold of his hand. 'Okay. Tell your mam thanks.'

18

At the biscuit factory, Nell enjoyed the banter and singing of the women as they worked. Streamers, balloons, or any form of festive trimming, were all forbidden on the factory floor, but it didn't stop the jolly atmosphere among the workers as Christmas approached. Songs and carols echoed along the factory floor, and when Bing Crosby's popular 'White Christmas' struck up, everyone joined in.

This year, the workers would enjoy an extra day's holiday with pay. Christmas Day fell on a Monday, and Tuesday was St Stephen's Day — another holiday — giving them four days off. Delighted to have a break from sticking labels on tins, she nevertheless enjoyed the cheeriness of her fellow workers.

As she worked, sticking colourful Christmas labels on tins, her mind flitted back to the previous night and Kate's reaction when she had told her about Liam's mam's invitation.

'You back with him, then?' she'd asked.

'Have you forgotten Liam's going to England in the New Year?' Nell replied.

Kate shrugged. 'If I loved someone, I'd go with them.'

'I will, but not yet. Would you come with us, then?'

'With you! I don't think so, but you should go.'

114

Nell gritted her teeth. 'Don't be naive, Kate. I have responsibilities. What about Róisín?'

'She's being looked after, and I can look after myself.'

Nell had struggled to control her temper. 'Don't talk rubbish. You live in a dream world that doesn't exist for the likes of us,' she'd snapped at her sister. 'Besides, where would you live?'

'I'd find somewhere.'

'And where would that be, may I ask?'

'Unlike you, I've got friends I've kept in touch with. So, you've no need to sacrifice yourself for me.'

Nell was furious. 'And how long would they put up with you? You're impossible, Kate Flynn.'

In a huff, Kate had stormed off to bed.

The sound of the siren heralding their afternoon tea break jolted Nell back to the present, and she and Dot trotted off to the canteen. Both girls stood and admired the whole place, festooned with paper decorations, and holly with red berries strewn along the window sills. The women continued to sing as they queued for their hot drink. They whooped with laughter when told they had an extra five minutes to collect a small Christmas cake, courtesy of the firm, before returning to their workbench.

'Oh, lovely,' Dot said. 'Me da loves Christmas cake, and me ma is too sick to make one this year.'

'It's a lovely surprise,' Nell agreed. She had planned to make one herself, but the ingredients cost too much. Her ma used to save coupons at the local store so that when Christmas came round, she could afford what she needed.

When Julia came round with their wages on Friday afternoon, Nell was thrilled to find a bonus of two pounds extra in her wage packet.

'Doing anything nice over Christmas, Nell?' Julia asked.

'We've been invited to Christmas dinner, but my youngest sister is still in hospital, so I'll be spending Christmas morning with her.'

'Oh, I'm sorry, Nell. How long for?'

'I'm not sure.'

'Well, I wish her a speedy recovery anyway.'

★ ★ ★

That evening, Kate was still at the priest's house. Michael wasn't on the rota today, and she guessed he would be busy getting ready for the dance on Saturday night. She was about to ask the priest for her wages when Father John called her into his study.

'What is it, Father?'

'Sit down, Kate.' She hesitated then sat on the chair in front of him just as he swung round in his seat and fixed her with a glare.

'You think I'm blind to what's going on?' he growled.

Her head shot up. 'What do you mean? Are you not happy with my work?'

'Oh, your work is splendid, Kate. But don't take me for a fool. Michael Flannigan might be blind to your wiles, but not me. Not me, my

116

girl!' His face reddened. 'Now is there something you want to tell me?'

'No, nothing, Father.'

'If you'd rather go into the confessional?'

Kate stood up. 'No thanks. I've nothing to confess, and once you've paid me, I'd like to go home.'

The priest snorted. 'Well, well, there's none of us without sin, my girl. And I've watched you commit sin, lusting after the clerk.'

'If you don't mind, I have to be getting back.' Kate struggled to hold her tongue.

'Indeed! And I guess you won't want to work for me once the clerk leaves. You realise he is only covering while Father Whelan is off ill?' Father John smirked. 'We'll be back to normal after Christmas, thanks be to God. In view of that, I've not voiced my concerns to Michael Flannigan, because either way, you'll not be seeing him again.'

Kate remained stony-faced. Yes, she would see him again, she told herself, but next time it would be away from prying eyes.

'Do you understand me, Kate Flynn?' he snapped.

'I understand, Father.'

He stood and handed her the money. 'Now, take it straight back to your sister.'

Rage coursed through her as she stood in the hallway pulling on her coat and stuffing the coins in her pocket. 'Silly old fool,' she muttered to herself, then made her way downtown.

In Woolworths, she bought herself a bright pink lipstick and a pair of Bear Brand nylons to go with Nell's shoes, which she planned to borrow for tomorrow night. She deducted another shilling for her ticket to the dance where Michael would be playing. Nell might be prepared to let Liam go, but Kate was determined she would not let Michael get away that easily.

The traders were selling Christmas toys and decorations along Henry Street, so she spent the rest of her money on a small toy for Róisín — a wooden monkey swinging between two sticks, which she knew her little sister would love. It might be her salvation once Nell discovered she had spent all her wages.

19

Nell could have wept when Kate arrived home empty-handed. 'You foolish, selfish girl.' She threw up her hands. 'It's rent night, and you spent the money on yourself. For that, you can get your own supper.'

In her room, Nell turned up the wireless. What was she doing wrong? How could she get Kate to take responsibility? What had she sacrificed her career for? Then she thought of Róisín, with curls as soft as eiderdown. Why did her little sister have to suffer?

Pulling herself together, she stepped back into the room and found Kate sitting at the table, her eyes red with crying. Rushing to her side, Nell placed her arms around her.

'I'm sorry. I didn't mean to make you cry,' she told Kate. 'But you spending money we don't have makes me mad with frustration.'

'Oh, I'm not crying over the money,' her sister replied.

Nell was puzzled. 'You're not? What is it, then?'

'Nothing, it's nothing.' The priest had upset her, but Kate wasn't sharing that with Nell. She wiped her eyes with the sleeve of her cardigan. 'If you're going to see Róisín tonight, I'll come with you.'

Nell had given up trying to work out what went on in Kate's head. 'Well, sure that's grand. Róisín will be delighted.'

Kate pulled out a bag with the monkey toy inside. 'I got this for her. Do you think she'll like it?'

Nell nodded. 'Yes, she'll love it, Kate, but we're not allowed to bring toys in until Christmas morning. We'll go straight there after church.'

Kate got up and walked to the fireplace, where she held her hands out to the fire. 'Did I mention I'm going to a dance with Teresa tomorrow night?' she said casually.

'No, you didn't. Where?'

'Father Matthew Hall.'

'What time is it on till?' Nell asked.

'Don't know,' Kate replied. 'Teresa's dad is picking her up afterwards, so he'll drop me off, too.'

'As a matter of fact, I'm going out myself.'

'Well, that's grand. Are you going anywhere nice?'

Nell shrugged. 'We've not decided yet.' Kate had assumed that Nell was going out with Joan, whom she used to socialise with before meeting Liam, and Nell didn't correct her; her sister wouldn't understand if she told her it was Liam.

They were interrupted by a loud thump on the door, and Nell glanced at Kate. It was unlike Mr Scanlon's gentle knock, but she hoped it was him. She wanted to ask him about the house on John's Lane.

When she opened the door and found Pete Scanlon standing there, her heart sank. Without speaking, she handed over the rent money, which left her skint — apart from the bonus she had received earlier with her wages. But before she

120

could close the door, he leant in, holding a sprig of mistletoe over her head.

'Get off!' Nell shoved him away and tried to close the door.

Giggling, Kate rushed to help her, and between them they closed it, pulling the bolt across. 'It's Christmas,' Kate laughed. 'He likes you.'

'He's a chancer. Can't you see that?'

Kate made a face. 'He's got money, or at least, his father does.'

'I've no intention of going out with him. So give the scullery floor a mop quickly, or we'll be late for the hospital.'

★ ★ ★

The three sisters had a happy time together at the hospital, but Nell noticed how tired Róisín looked. Although she smiled when she saw them, she found it difficult to keep her eyes open. Kate kept her sister amused with anecdotes she'd overheard between Father John and Father Donald at the presbytery. Meanwhile, Nell had a quiet word with the nurse.

'You mustn't concern yourself so much, Miss Flynn. The bath and hair wash tired her more than usual,' the nurse told her. 'And Matron has asked me to tell you not to come up every night. Twice a week and once at the weekend is sufficient.'

'But, nurse, she's only eight,' Nell argued.

'It unsettles her after you've gone.'

'Oh, I wasn't aware of that.'

'So, leave it until Sunday to come again. I assure you she's in good hands.'

Nell wasn't happy about visiting less, but she had no choice but to accept Matron's decision. When she returned to the bedside, Kate and Róisín were laughing, and Nell felt a rush of love towards Kate.

★ ★ ★

That night, despite Nell's tiredness, it was late when sleep overtook her. Both sisters usually had a lie-in on Saturday morning, but this week Nell woke early.

She washed and dressed quietly, so as not to wake Kate. Her evening out with Liam was foremost in her mind, and she sorted through her meagre wardrobe for something bright to wear. She unhooked her dress with a full skirt from the hanger, held it against her, and did a twirl. It was months since she had last worn it, but her mam had always said the red suited her fair hair. After hanging it back carefully in the wardrobe, ready to wear later, she brushed her short hair and padded in stockinged feet to the living room.

She was startled to find that Kate wasn't in bed. Nell glanced briefly at the mantel shelf as the clock struck nine, then spotted a scribbled note on the table. Thinking the worst, her hands shook as she sat down at the table to read it.

Nell,

Didn't like to wake you. I've caught an early

bus to Teresa's house. *It's best if we go together to the dance. Her dad can take us in the truck. I hope you enjoy your evening out and I'll see you later.*

Kate

Nell sat for some minutes holding the note. The message, although written in a hurry, showed no sign of affection. She swallowed the sob choking the back of her throat, and recalled a time when Kate had been different, at least kinder than she was now. Their mam had always indulged her. And now she wasn't here, Kate appeared to show a bitter side to her nature that Nell hadn't noticed before.

Kate had cried and railed at their mother's death and Róisín had wept for a week, but Nell hadn't grieved. She'd had too much to do and think about, remaining focused on keeping the family together. But now, instead of the three sisters becoming closer, she felt Kate was pulling against her at every turn.

To stop herself becoming maudlin, Nell decided to make up the fire. The rooms were colder now that the tenants below them had gone and the heat from their fires no longer travelled upwards to warm the walls.

She hard-boiled an egg and sandwiched it between two slices of bread, then washed it down with two mugs of tea. Feeling more refreshed, she looked around the room. It was easy enough to keep clean, but there was enough washing and ironing to keep her busy all morning.

She would love to be able to go downtown, like she used to, and buy herself something new to wear for her date with Liam. Sadly, though, those days were long gone. And now Amy, her neighbour and closest friend, was moving on Monday. Nell felt despair cloak itself around her.

She put the ironing away, then pulled on her coat and scarf, ran down one flight of stairs and rapped on Amy's door. She heard Frank roaring at the kids and Amy's youngest, three-year-old Babs, crying. One child opened the door and Amy turned towards her. 'Nell, come in.'

'Can I do anything to help?' she asked.

Amy and Frank were wrapping plates and cups in newspaper and placing them into brown boxes.

'Oh, sure that's good of you, Nell,' Amy said. 'What little we have is nearly packed.'

'Ah, bejapers, if you could shut that nipper up, or take her out of me sight, that would be grand, so it would. She's giving me a headache,' complained her husband.

Amy laughed. 'It's not the child that's given you the bad head and you know it, Frank.'

Nell smiled and picked up the child and gave her a hug. 'She looks flushed.'

'That's because she won't stop howling,' Frank grumbled.

Amy came closer to look at her youngest daughter. 'I'd know if there was ought wrong. Could I trouble you to take her out for five minutes, Nell? Joan's at work, and I'm busy scrubbing the scullery, and the other two are sorting out their stuff. Babs's feeling left out, that's all.'

'Of course,' said Nell. 'Glad to help.' The child stopped crying as Nell unhooked her coat from the back of the door and helped her put it on, then tied a pixie bonnet under her chin.

'Can I come, too?' Jonny cried, glancing round his mam's ample waist.

'Can you manage both, Nell?'

'Are you coddin' me?' Nell smiled. 'Have you got someone to help you move to the new house?'

Amy nodded. 'Frank's got a man with a truck who's coming at nine o'clock Monday morning.'

'That's good. Let's hope it doesn't rain.'

'Ah, sure wouldn't yea know our luck,' Amy laughed, holding down the lid of the box while Frank taped it up.

As they set off, Babs asked, 'Can we feed the ducks?'

Amy hurried into the scullery and returned with a few stale slices of bread, and the trio headed down the stairs. The park was too far for Babs to walk without the go-cart, so Nell took the children as far as the Liffey wall, where there were plenty of seagulls ready and willing to snap up the stale crusts.

It was true that mothers knew their children best, Nell thought, as the little girl skipped along next to her brother. Her own mother had understood Kate, and Nell wondered what she would make of her now.

On Monday night they would be alone in the empty tenement, their future uncertain. But before that happened, she had her night out with Liam to look forward to — and nothing would spoil that.

20

Nell still felt guilty for not visiting Róisín, and prayed she would be all right until her next visit. But tonight she was determined to enjoy her night out with Liam. They'd agreed to meet on the corner of Henry Street at 7.30 p.m., and as she got ready, excitement fluttered in her tummy. Was it only three months since they had been planning their future together?

She boiled water, then lit the oven, leaving the door open to allow the heat to warm the small scullery, before stripping off. If only she'd been able to use the old tin bath in the yard, but without Kate to help her empty it, she would have to make do with a bowl and flannel. She sprinkled on Lily of the Valley talcum powder, then put on fresh underwear, her full-length slip with lace around the hem, and rolled on her fully fashioned nylons, making sure the seams were straight and being careful not to snag them.

Her jar of Pond's cold cream was all but empty and she dug her finger into the crevices to scoop out what remained, smoothing it over her cheeks and forehead, then adding a dusting of face powder. She had run out of mascara, and she knew that if Kate had any, she would have taken it with her. Finally, she coated her lips with red lipstick.

Her make-up complete, Nell sat on her bed and filed her nails. There wasn't a lot she could do with her short wavy bob, so she gave it a vigorous brushing and then eased her dress over her head. Glancing in the mirror, she ran her hand down the red taffeta material, fingered the puff sleeves, and fastened the thin white belt.

For a few minutes, she recalled her first date with Liam. It had been a warm evening. Tonight was cold and frosty, so she would need something warmer than her thin, threadbare coat. Her mother's grey faux fur hung at the back of the wardrobe, untouched since the last time she had worn it. Mam would want her to wear it tonight. Nell carefully lifted it out, took off the cover, and pressed it to her face. Her mother's scent lingered.

She hung it over her shoulders, brought the collar up around her ears, then slipped her arms inside. It was comforting. If her mam was here, she would smile and tell her she looked grand.

Mam and Dad had always encouraged her; they'd been supportive of her chosen career. 'Ah sure, you'll make a grand nurse, so ye will.' Even now, she could hear her father's voice, and her mother's laughter as she agreed with him. 'I've always known it,' she had said.

Their loss touched her more as Christmas approached, but she knew living in the past wouldn't bring them back. Nell removed the coat and placed it across her bed. All she needed now was her high-heeled shoes; even though she'd not worn them since her mother's funeral, almost two months ago, she knew exactly where they were.

But they were not at the back of her wardrobe

where she had left them. Nell looked again, pulling everything out — her work shoes, summer sandals, handbags and scarves, and a shoebox where she kept her trinkets. The treasured high-heeled shoes weren't there. She had to find them. In a panic, she searched in places she knew they wouldn't be, getting down on her hands and knees to look underneath her bed.

Suddenly, her sister came to mind, and fury raged through her as she paced the tiny room. 'Kate, I'll kill you when I get hold of you,' she yelled. 'How could you? You just wait!'

Nell sank down on her bed, fighting back angry tears. Moments earlier, she had been joyful and excited. Now, resentment coursed through her, and she forced herself to roll back her shoulders to ease the growing tension. 'You won't get away with this, Kate,' she muttered through gritted teeth. 'It's unforgivable. You knew I was going out tonight.'

What would she do now? Her flat work shoes would look silly with her dress and her mother's coat, and it was too cold for her light sandals. Her only hope was Amy's daughter Joan, and she wondered what time she got home from work. Running downstairs, she knocked twice before Joan opened the door.

'Oh, sorry, Nell. Come in. I dropped off. Taking advantage of having the place to myself. The others should be back any time now. No doubt they will be excited about the new house.'

Nell stepped inside. 'You must be thrilled to be moving at last?'

Joan nodded. 'Who wouldn't be, leaving this dump? That's a nice dress. Are you going somewhere?'

Nell made a face. 'Yes, if I can find a pair of shoes to wear.' She glanced down at her feet in slippers. 'My black heels have gone missing.' If she mentioned Kate her anger would erupt again, and she didn't have time. 'Have you anything I can borrow?'

'Sit down a minute,' Joan replied. 'I bought a pair in Roches' sale a few weeks ago. They're not black, though. Hang on and I'll get them.'

A few minutes later, Joan came back with a pair of white shoes, size six, with a peep-toe. 'What do you think?' She held them out to Nell. 'The heels are scratched, but try them.'

They were a size and a half too big, but what choice did she have? 'I don't mind the colour if they stay on,' Nell admitted.

'Stuff the heels with cotton wool. That should do the trick.'

'Thanks, Joan. I'll make sure you get them back tomorrow.'

* * *

Nell walked out of the tenement in the fur coat, pulling the soft collar around her face. She felt like a film star. But within minutes, she was stumbling in Joan's shoes. If she took them off to walk in her stockinged feet, she would ruin her new nylons.

Two lads kicking a ball stopped to stare at her, then giggled behind their hands as her shoes clacked against the stone pavement. Every step was a struggle to keep them on, and she was desperate to ditch them. By the time she reached their meeting place, she was mortified and wishing she'd settled for her comfortable work shoes.

Then she saw Liam leaning against the wall by the side of the arcade, his hands stuffed into his coat pockets. She could see by the grin on his face that her predicament amused him. She didn't blame him; she must look a sight.

'Hello, you!' he said as she drew close. 'You look a million dollars.'

'Well, if I had a million, I wouldn't be wearing it,' she laughed.

'What's the matter with your feet?'

They both glanced down at her shoes.

She sighed heavily. 'I can't find my new black heels, so I had to borrow these from Joan Kinch, but they keep slipping off. Are we going far?' She linked her arm through his in her old familiar way, clinging to him for support.

'I thought we'd go dancing at the Metropole after we've had something to eat. But you seem to have trouble keeping your shoes on.' He paused while she adjusted one foot in its shoe for what seemed like the hundredth time.

'I can always take them off once I'm inside the dance hall,' Nell assured him.

'Okay, if you're sure. I hope you haven't eaten?'

'No.' A meal sounded divine, and she suddenly realised she was ravenous.

'Right. What are we waiting for?' He placed his

131

arm around her waist to support her, guiding her through the arcade and past the queues outside the cinema, stopping every time her shoes tripped her up, until they reached the dance hall. Soon they were inside the plush foyer.

'I didn't know they had a restaurant in here,' she said.

'Yes, I hear it's superb.' Liam held open the door for her. 'Shall we?'

The waiter seated them at a table for two and passed them the menu. Nell gratefully slipped her feet out of the offending shoes, wriggling her toes with a sigh, and glanced down at what was on offer.

'Are you sure you can afford it?' she whispered. 'It's pricey.'

He looked offended. 'You think I would take you here if I hadn't been saving?'

'I'm sorry, Liam.' Weighed down by responsibility and money worries, she had forgotten what it was like to enjoy herself and to eat a romantic meal with the man she loved.

'Don't worry.' He smiled to let her know he wasn't upset. 'Let's enjoy every minute we have, Nell.'

She glanced across at him, taking in the way his dark hair had been smoothed down, smelling his familiar aftershave. He wore his best grey suit, white shirt and tie. It was almost unbearable to think this would be their last meal out before he went away. Would he forget her when he lived in England? She'd heard London was an amazing city with many opportunities. If only she was going with him.

Liam ordered a pint of Guinness and her favourite Dubonnet and lemonade, and they both plumped for the steak and chips, with apple pie and custard to follow.

'This is a real treat.' Her mouth watered as she cut into the juicy steak.

'Things will always be tough here, Nell, but once I get settled . . . '

She took a sip of her drink and sat back. 'It will take time, Liam.'

'Yes, I know. Will you wait?'

'You know I will.' She sat forward and he reached across for her hand. Their heads touched briefly, and she inhaled the rugged clean scent of Old Spice shaving cream. Her pulse quickened.

He kissed the back of her hand and sat back. 'You look beautiful tonight, Nell. How can I leave you?'

'Don't say another word, Liam, you'll set me off.' She took a deep breath, determined to hide her sadness. 'Come on, I want to know all your plans before we go into the dance hall. We'll hardly hear ourselves speak once the band strikes up. Have you bought your boat ticket yet?'

'I'm going down the B & I office on Monday.'

She tried to relax and listen to him while the waitress cleared their table and Liam paid the bill. He talked with eager intensity about what he would do once he stepped off the train at Euston Station, gesturing with his hands as he listed the places he wanted to visit once he got there.

She nodded and smiled as he talked. 'It sounds grand.'

'Yes, it will be, once I get to know my surroundings.'

Although she wouldn't be with him, she couldn't help but be caught up in his excitement. She knew deep down that she was envious of his freedom and the new life in England she couldn't share.

21

Kate and Teresa were dropped off outside the Father Matthew Hall, a red-brick building on the corner of Church Street.

'Now, make sure you're waiting by the door when I come back at ten thirty, our Teresa,' Mr Lacy said. 'I won't come looking for you. And that goes for you, too, Kate, if you'd like a lift home.'

Teresa leant into the truck and kissed her dad's cheek. 'Don't worry, Da, we'll be here.'

The two girls stood for a few moments on the pavement, giggling with excitement, before heading inside the building.

'Hey,' Teresa said, 'I can't wait to meet this fella of yours.'

'Me, too. Let's sit here.' Kate hung her coat over the back of a chair and Teresa removed hers, as they both took in their surroundings. Coloured paper chains dangled from the ceiling, and a Christmas tree in the corner added atmosphere. It didn't take Kate long to spot Michael onstage setting up the microphones.

'Well, which one is he?' Teresa nudged her friend, who appeared to be in a trance.

'The tall, good-looking one.'

'You'd better introduce me, then.'

But Kate didn't reply. Her gaze was focused on a young woman with red hair, who was laughing and talking to Michael.

'What's wrong with you? Cat got your tongue?' Teresa glanced into her powder compact and pursed her lips. 'Why don't you speak to him before it gets too crowded?'

'I will, in a minute.' Kate patted her hair into place.

'Look, all the chairs are filling up and they've got a table with soft drinks at the back of the hall,' Teresa observed.

But Kate was still looking towards the stage.

Four musicians, including Michael — all dressed in smart black trousers and white polo shirts — were tuning their instruments. Michael's slender fingers plucked the strings of his violin; one member of the band sounded out the bodhrán; another squeezed and blew into the uilleann pipes. She had always hated the sound of the bagpipes, which reminded her of a bag of cats. Her only thought tonight was to dance with Michael, and she couldn't wait.

'I'll just get us a drink,' she said, turning back to Teresa. 'What do you want?'

'Get me a Pepsi, will you? Although it's not very warm in here.' Teresa ran her hands up and down her arms.

Her eyes still on the stage, Kate watched the red-haired girl lean across to say something to Michael. 'It'll soon warm up once the dancing starts,' she replied.

Pulling herself up straight, Kate walked towards the stage and stood where she knew Michael would see her. She watched him hunker down and whisper to the woman before making his way towards her. 'Kate,' he said. 'How nice to see you. You look different.'

'How?' She brushed her hand over her hair. She had scraped it into a ponytail and wound it into a tight bun. Already the hairpins holding it up were beginning to irritate and give her a headache.

He thought for a moment before replying. 'Well, you look . . . you look lovely.' He smiled. 'Are you on your own?'

'I'm here with a friend.'

He nodded.

'Who's that girl you were talking to?' Kate couldn't help asking.

He smiled. 'That's my girlfriend, Ophelia. I'll introduce you when we have a break.' He placed his hand on her arm and let it linger briefly. 'Must go, we're about to start. Hope you enjoy the music.' Then he was gone.

Numb, she stood transfixed. She could still feel the warmth of his hand on her arm. Her bottom lip quivered, and she bit down hard to stop herself crying.

Girlfriend! She can't be!

Slowly, in a daze, she walked back to her seat and sat down. Teresa had been talking to a group of friends at a nearby table. When Kate sat down, her friend looked curiously at the empty table.

'Well?' Teresa held out her hand.

'Well what?' asked Kate.

'The drinks, silly.'

'Oh, I'm sorry. I got talking and forgot.' Kate was shaking so much she doubted she could have carried anything.

'Don't worry,' said Teresa. 'We can get one later. I saw you talking to Michael. Was he pleased to see you?' Not waiting for Kate's reply, she went on, 'Oh, look, he's back onstage. He's dishy. Perhaps he'll dance with you later. Wouldn't mind a twirl round the dance floor with him myself.' She nudged Kate.

The band struck up with the lively tune 'The Irish Rover'. As couples got to their feet, a boy with ginger hair rushed over to Teresa. 'Come on, Tess,' he said. 'How about it?'

Smiling, she took his hand, and they shuffled on to the floor. Kate, her eyes brimming, rushed towards the Ladies. Once inside the cubicle, she locked the door and let her tears flow. She hadn't cried since her ma died.

She'd thought Michael cared for her. He'd taken her for coffee more than once. Why would he do that if he didn't love her? Kate shook her head. She wouldn't give up, not now. No one would take her Michael away from her. Ophelia! What kind of name was that, anyway? She couldn't be Irish!

Snivelling, she dried her eyes and blew her nose. Well, she would dance with him tonight if it was the last thing she did.

Forcing a smile, she made her way back out of the toilets, just as the tempo changed to a slow waltz. A young man walked across and asked her to dance. Kate was about to refuse when she looked up and took in the dark twinkling eyes that travelled from her face down her body. She ran her warm hands down the sides of her skirt, self-conscious under his scrutiny.

He moved a step closer. 'Do ya wanna dance?'

She hesitated. He was the complete opposite of Michael, in baggy jeans and a black shirt that needed ironing, his greasy hair parted in the middle. But he would do for what she had in mind.

She nodded and followed him on to the dance floor and he placed his arm around her waist.

'I've seen you before.' His breath fanned her ear.

'Have you?' She couldn't place him. 'Where?'

'Yes, don't you remember? Outside the chippy in Cabra.'

If this was the guy on the motorbike, she remembered him all right, but she wouldn't satisfy him by letting him know. She shrugged. 'I'm not sure I do.'

'My name's Jerry O'Shea. What's yours?'

'Kate.'

'Well, Kate, when it comes to the Excuse Me dance, I hope you'll pick me.'

She had to smile. 'Fancy yourself, do you?'

He laughed, throwing back his greasy head. 'Can't blame a fella for trying.' He swung her round and drew her close. The smell of his hair oil repulsed her; it made him look sweaty under the dull lighting.

As they danced closer to the stage, she dropped her head on to his chest and felt him pull her in closer. Glancing up, she caught Michael's eye and he smiled and winked at her. It wasn't the reaction she had hoped for. Furious, she gritted her teeth for the remainder of the song.

Before Jerry could whisk her off for another

dance, she eased away from him and headed to the drinks table and ordered herself a lemon soda. No way was she dancing another minute with that creep. With the drink in her hand, she made a beeline through the centre of the room towards Teresa.

'Two-timing already,' her friend joked.

'You'll never guess who that was.'

Teresa raised an eyebrow. 'Who?'

'It's that fella we met outside the chip shop near your house,' Kate replied. 'Jerry O'Shea. Do you remember him?'

'Oh, him! I'd give him a wide berth if I were you.'

'I have.' Kate sat down, unpinned her hair and flicked it over her shoulder.

At the interval, Michael chatted with a group of young people sitting by the stage. Ophelia was one of them, and Kate felt a stab of jealousy that he hadn't come over to speak to her.

Later in the evening, when he left the stage to allow the accordionist to play the waltzes for the Excuse Me dance, Kate got to her feet. But Michael walked towards Ophelia and swept her on to the dance floor to the tune of 'White Christmas'. Kate watched for a few moments, envious of the way he held the red-haired girl — not too close at first, and then her head was on his shoulder. Spurred into action, Kate shot across the dance floor, winding her way between couples to reach them, then tapped Ophelia's shoulder.

'Excuse me,' she said triumphantly.

Michael looked at Ophelia, who raised an

eyebrow and then unwound her arms from around his neck.

Michael placed his arm around Kate and, keeping her at a safe distance, they waltzed around the floor. His hand on her back sent tingles down her spine, and her heartbeat quickened as she followed his every step to the ballad 'I'll Be Seeing You', hoping the music would never stop.

'You never said you could dance so well, Kate,' he said. 'What do you think of the band?'

'I love it,' she smiled. 'Do you play any other instruments besides the violin, Michael?'

He frowned. 'Don't you like the violin?'

'Oh, yes . . . yes, I do . . . ' she stammered. 'I just wondered.'

'I play the clarinet sometimes. It depends on where we're playing and the tunes we're asked to play.'

Before she could ask any more, Ophelia was back, tapping her shoulder. Kate glared at the girl and kept her arms around Michael, leaning in close to inhale his masculine cologne before slowly releasing him. Her moment of joy was shortlived when he planted a kiss on Ophelia's lips and they glided across the floor to the romantic tune 'That's Amore'.

From then on, Kate danced half-heartedly with whoever pulled her to her feet, all the time pouting and wishing she was dancing with Michael.

'Gosh! You're a bundle of fun tonight,' Teresa said, when she caught up with her between dances. 'Has Michael upset you?'

'Of course not.'

'Come on, I love this one.' Teresa linked arms with her, and they swung each other round to 'Whiskey in the Jar', until they were both light-headed. Teresa roared with laughter while Kate remained sombre.

For the last dance, they played 'Silver Bells'. As the ginger boy came striding across for Teresa, Kate forced herself to ask, 'You dating him, then?'

Her friend laughed. 'Don't be daft, he's an old school friend.'

Kate sat and watched Michael's hand circle the mike as he moved to the centre of the stage to take the lead vocal. She didn't know he could sing like that. What else didn't she know?

★ ★ ★

When it was time to go, Teresa grabbed her coat. 'Come on, Kate, let's get outside. You know what me dad's like. He'll only get grumpy if we're not waiting for him.'

Kate shook her head. 'You go ahead. I'll be grand.'

'Are you sure? Is Michael walking you home?' Teresa asked. 'You could have introduced me.'

'Sorry. He only had a few minutes,' she lied.

When Teresa had gone, Kate lingered while the band dismantled their equipment. Three girls, including Ophelia, went on to the stage to help, and Michael carried the various boxes out the back. Kate went outside, but there was no sign of him.

She pulled her collar up around her neck, dug her hands in her pockets, and walked away, hot tears rolling down her cold face. Nell's shoes had done her no favours, and she wasn't looking forward to facing her sister when she got home. But, after what had happened tonight, she was past caring about Nell and her precious shoes.

She walked along Bow Street, treading carefully along the dimly lit street, ignoring the noise and jibs spilling out from the pubs before turning down a narrow side street. A shiver ran through her body as she hurried down the dark cobbled lane, her heels catching in the cracks. Feeling as if the world had ended, and overwhelmed with disappointment, she didn't hear the footsteps that followed close behind her until she heard her name.

'Hello there, beautiful Kate. Walking home on your own?'

Her heart pounding, she turned and looked into the dark eyes of Jerry O'Shea.

22

By the time Nell and Liam walked into the dance hall, she had blistered feet. She limped her way into the ladies' cloakroom to leave her mam's fur coat, and placed the ticket inside her bag. The staircase looked lovely festooned with Christmas lights, and couples stood leaning over the balcony as the band played festive melodies. Looking down at all the happy faces enjoying themselves, it was hard to believe that more than half the nation was unemployed.

'We don't have to dance,' Liam offered. 'We can stay on the balcony and watch. Should be easier to find a seat, as it's filling up downstairs.'

'Okay. If you're sure you don't mind.'

'Why should I, when I'm with you?'

Nell smiled and linked her arm through his. They found a table with a good view of the floor below. 'I'll get myself a pint. Dubonnet and lemonade okay?' he asked.

Relieved to sit down, she nodded, slipped off Joan's shoes, stretched her legs, and hid her painted toenails underneath the table. For a few moments, she thought back to the first time she had met Liam. They had both been at secondary school, and only started going out together when she was eighteen and he twenty-one. After a year, they had started making plans for their future life together.

She sighed. Liam was everything she'd ever

wanted in a man — jovial and easy-going — and when she was with him, it was like she was the only woman in the world. He was hard to resist, and she had fallen head over heels. Thinking of him leaving was like a constant ache in the pit of her stomach.

As he approached with the drinks, she planted a smile on her face. 'This is nice,' she said, relaxing now that she was free of the offending footwear. Her mam always said you should never wear someone else's shoes, and how right she was.

Sipping her drink, she watched as a couple took to the floor, and Nell longed to be down there with Liam, holding her in his arms and whispering in her ear how much he loved her. Briefly, she wondered how Kate was getting on, and the fury she had harboured towards her sister melted away as she swayed to the band's rendition of 'When Irish Eyes Are Smiling'.

When the lights dimmed for a slow waltz, Liam reached for her hand. She expected him to ask her to dance, but instead he clasped her hand in his and held her gaze. 'I'm not happy about leaving you. You know that, don't you, Nell? You'll be in my thoughts every day.'

She blinked away a tear and nodded. 'Liam, it'll be hard for both of us, but please don't let's talk about it. It won't change anything.'

She had a responsibility towards her siblings, and Liam had to find work wherever that might take him. What saddened her most was the uncertainty of her life. No one could predict what the future held for either of them. The only

145

certainty was what they had now.

'Nell, I'm doing this for us,' he protested, 'so we can have a better life.'

'I know. You mustn't worry about me.' She took back her hand. 'I've got a job and Kate's working part-time now.'

'And why is she still at school when you need her full support?'

'She deserves the chance of a good education, Liam. It's what Mammy wanted for her.' She was being defensive, but she wouldn't let him see how desperate she had become.

'Yes, but . . . ' He stopped when he saw her pained expression. 'I'm sorry.'

'You'll have enough to cope with, changing jobs and moving to England.'

He reached again for her hand. 'If you need anything, promise you'll tell me. God knows, you'll not get much help around here.'

She couldn't answer. There was no point.

'I love you, Nell Flynn,' he went on, 'and that will not change once I go away.' His words took away the bitter regret of how her mother's death had changed her life. 'Come on, dance with me, Nell.' He stood up and held out his hand. 'No one will notice your bare feet.'

The music was slow and romantic as the band played 'We'll Meet Again'. It was so long since they had danced like this, his arms around her, holding her close; their bodies moved as one, in harmony with the music. Nell relaxed into him, her head on his shoulder. His arms tightened around her, caressing her back and sending shivers through her body. They stayed that way

— lost in a world of their own, their arms entwined — until the music stopped and couples vacated the floor. Nell glanced down at her feet, embarrassed, until Liam took her hand and they ran giggling back up the stairs.

★　★　★

On the way home they stopped in shop doorways, kissing and cuddling. By the time they reached the tenement, their passion was high, and they lingered in the empty hallway.

'Oh my God, Nell, I love you and I want you so much,' he moaned.

She felt the same way. She wanted to know what it would be like to lie with him, his skin next to hers, and the notion flushed her face. Her mother's fur coat lay in a heap on the ground and she made no objection as he helped her down and lay next to her. Their feelings were running high, increasing with every loving touch. She knew it was wrong and she was about to lose her virginity in the filthy, smelly hallway, but she was unable to stop herself.

Suddenly Liam pulled back and sat up, his breath visible in the cold hallway.

'What is it?' Nell asked tearfully.

He stood up and pulled her gently to her feet.

'I'm sorry, Nell,' he said. 'Not here, in this hallway stinking of beer and cats.'

Disappointed, then mortified as realisation set in, she moved away and straightened her clothes. He drew her to him but she pulled away, biting her lip. She should have been the one who decided to stop, and the recognition left her confused and wondering.

Liam ran his hand through his hair. 'I've been speaking to Father O'Brien, and he asked me about us and when we would marry.'

She looked at him in surprise. 'What did you say?'

'I told him it couldn't come soon enough. Then he lectured me about the dangers of long engagements.' He made eye contact with her. 'It's hard for both of us, Nell. He wants to see me again before I go.' He smiled. 'No doubt another lecture about keeping the faith.' He reached for her hand. 'I wouldn't be able to look him in the eye, if we . . . '

'I'm sorry, Liam,' she whispered.

'Don't be. You're wonderful, and it will be all the better for waiting.'

She looked into his eyes. 'But we might never again have this time alone.'

'We will. I can promise you that.' He picked up her mother's coat and shook it, then placed it over her shoulders.

She knew he was right. 'I love you, Liam Connor,' she told him. 'I shouldn't have had that extra drink.'

He turned her towards the stairs. 'Now go, before I change my mind and do something we'll both regret in the morning.'

They kissed one last time before she fled up the stairs, the shoes dangling from the strap of her bag.

★ ★ ★

148

She didn't stop to light her way up the rest of the dark, narrow staircase, and was out of breath by the time she reached the top floor. Her body was still tingling from his touch, her Catholic guilt consuming her with every step.

When she reached the landing, the dark shadow of a man loomed in front of her and she quickly raised one shoe in defence. 'Who are you? What do you want?'

A sliver of light shone through a crack in the door to their rooms.

'You must be Nell.' He held out his hand.

She declined and brushed past him.

As she pushed open the door, Kate stood, hands on hips, glaring at her.

'Keep your hair on,' she snapped. 'He only walked me home.'

Nell glanced round at the man, who was still standing there in the shadows.

'I couldn't let the young lady walk the streets alone at this time of night, now, could I?' He smiled at Kate.

Nell didn't like the look of him, and she was furious with her sister for encouraging him. 'Go away and leave us alone,' she said, then hurried inside and bolted the door. 'You stupid girl.' She turned on Kate. 'Don't you realise it's dangerous to bring a stranger home?'

'You can't tell me what to do,' Kate hit back. 'You're not my mother. Besides, you weren't thinking of me a while ago.'

'What do you mean?'

'I saw you coming up the street with Liam. You lied when you said it was over between the two of you. You had your arms draped around him, kissing him.'

Nell sucked in her breath, colour rising to her face. Straightening her shoulders, she glared at her sister.

'This is not about me, Kate. You said Teresa's dad was bringing you home, and I return to find a strange man coming out of our home.' She took a breath, fighting to control her anger. 'Is that the man I saw you with downtown last weekend?'

Kate shrugged. 'Might be. So what?'

Nell walked across and turned up the wick on the oil lamp. Her shoes lay by the fireplace, scuffed and scratched. She picked them up. 'Oh, look at my best shoes! You've ruined them. And you took them without my permission.'

'Would you have let me have them?'

'You knew I was going out tonight.' She turned to look at her sister. 'I'm disgusted with your behaviour, Kate. You can buy me a new pair, and it won't be coming out of the housekeeping.'

'You'll have a long wait,' scoffed Kate.

'I'll ask you again. Who was that man? Have you been sneaking off to meet him?'

'He's nobody. As you said, he's a stranger.' Kate pulled off her clothes, got into bed, and turned her face to the wall.

Nell knew she wouldn't get another word out of Kate tonight, so she gave up and got ready for bed. Worries over her sister and her own indiscretions with Liam kept her awake for hours.

150

23

Kate was subdued on Sunday morning and refused to attend church with Nell or visit her young sister in hospital, so Nell went alone. It had been a couple of days since she'd seen Róisín, and she wondered anxiously how she would find her. As she walked into the ward, the first thing she noticed was a frame in the form of a cage with a blanket over her sister's legs.

Róisín raised her head and smiled as Nell bent to kiss her. 'How have you been, pet?'

'My legs were hurting, but they're better now.'

She made efforts to sit up, but a nurse rushed across. 'We'd prefer it if she remained flat for now,' she explained.

'How long will she have to stay like this?' Nell asked.

'That'll be up to the doctor. But she's comfortable.' The nurse smiled, then went to attend to another child.

'When will I be able to come home, Nell?' Róisín asked.

'Soon, honey. Sure, the place is not the same without you. Amy's moving to a brand-new house and I'm looking out for a better place for us, too. I'll have it all nice for when you get home.'

Róisín seemed to be studying her big sister closely. 'You look sad, Nell,' she said. 'Has something happened?'

'No, what makes you think that?'

'You've not smiled,' Róisín explained, 'and you always smile.'

Nell gave her the best smile she could muster. 'I'm not sad, honey. I just didn't get a wink of sleep last night.' And, she asked herself, who's fault was that? Still guilt-ridden about her conduct with Liam, she knew she ought to go to confession but she couldn't face it.

'Nell. Nell!' Her sister's voice broke into her troubled thoughts.

'Sorry, honey. What was that?'

'Santa Claus is coming to the ward on Friday.'

'Well, that's nice, and it looks lovely in here, pet. It's nice and cheerful with the decorations. And you've got a good view of the Christmas tree from your bed.' Nell sat holding Róisín's hand as she dropped off to sleep. It was something the child did throughout her visits.

Nell took the opportunity to speak with the nurse in charge, who was writing up her notes at the table. 'How is Róisín doing, Nurse?'

The young woman looked up. 'I thought you might ask me that, Miss Flynn. She's as well as can be expected.'

Nell looked puzzled. 'What does that mean? Will she be home any day soon?'

'Dr Mellor is treating her, and he calls at the hospital once a week to check her progress.' The nurse sighed. 'But I wouldn't get your hopes up. Rheumatic fever can vary from patient to patient, and some are with us long term. It all depends on how your sister responds to her treatment.'

'Long term?' It wasn't what Nell had expected to hear.

'As I said, it depends on how she responds to her treatment. It's early days.'

Nell struggled to hold back her distress as she kissed her sister goodbye and told her she would be up on Christmas morning to see her.

'Is Liam coming, too?' asked Róisín. 'He promised.'

'I'm sure he will. He won't break a promise.' Nell forced a smile and kissed her sister again before leaving.

*   *   *

When Amy and her family were packed up and ready to leave the tenement with all they possessed on the back of a truck, Nell felt a lump in her throat. And with Amy's new address tight in her hand, the two women hugged each other. Nell felt hollow inside.

'Don't be a stranger now,' Amy said. 'And if ye can't afford the bus fare, write a letter.'

Both women had tears in their eyes.

Nell's world was growing smaller, and she was going to miss Amy more than she had first thought. Only a few of the tenants who had already moved got to see each other again. With no transport of their own, and the lack of money for bus fares, it was a fact of life.

Amy had become a trusted friend since her mother's death, and Nell knew she could confide in her about anything, even her strong sexual urges towards Liam. Most people in the tenements took their problems to a priest, but Nell wasn't sure she could do that. Father John would lecture her on her morals. She would rather live with the shame. And if she mentioned her concerns over Kate, he would blame it all on her bad example. No, she had to work things out in her own way.

★ ★ ★

Christmas week at the biscuit factory was a mixture of hard work and frivolity. Excitement filtered through the factory at the prospect of having four days off.

Nell was looking forward to spending Christmas Day at Liam's house, but she couldn't get him off her mind, nor how her feelings had run away with her on their return from the dance. And she couldn't shake off her worry that Kate was drifting further and further away from her.

On Friday, three days before Christmas, Nell walked out of the factory with two bags of broken biscuits and her wage packet. With no money, no family, and Amy gone, her life felt empty, and she dreaded how she would pass the four days. She didn't know if Kate would still come with her to Liam's or even speak to her again.

It was damp and foggy as she walked over the Halfpenny Bridge, traffic buzzing in her ears and giving her a headache. She was approaching Mary Street when she heard footsteps running close behind her. Her heart rate quickened as she turned round. 'Liam! Where have you come from?'

'I've only just arrived. I wanted a word . . . ' He paused to catch his breath. 'I know it's cold, Nell, but you don't half walk fast.'

'Is everything okay?'

'I just want to make sure you're still coming for Christmas dinner.' People hurried past them out of the cold, and Liam put his hand on her arm and guided her into a brightly lit shop doorway.

Nell swallowed. What a fool she'd been to worry about her feelings for Liam. It was only natural. After all, they were planning to get married. She looked into his eyes, and he held her gaze.

'Can we walk? It's freezing cold standing here,' she said.

They walked holding hands; her other hand carried the bags of biscuits.

'Nell, I'm leaving on New Year's Eve,' he told her. 'I can't see the point in hanging around. It will give me more time to get settled in.'

She nodded, too emotional to speak, and they walked on in silence.

Eventually, Liam said, 'How's Róisín?'

'She's having new treatment. So, we have to wait and see how she responds.'

He squeezed her hand in encouragement. 'She will get better, Nell. You must believe that. I'll be up to see her on Christmas morning.'

Nell smiled. 'She'll love that. She's expecting you.'

He paused on the corner and touched her

155

elbow, then his lips brushed her cheek. 'I can't trust myself to kiss you,' he murmured, a quiver in his voice that she hadn't noticed before. 'I have to go. I'll see you and Kate on Monday.'

⋆   ⋆   ⋆

Outside her desolate house, she was surprised to see Mr Scanlon with a workman fitting a Yale lock to the scruffy black hall door that hadn't seen a coat of paint in years.

He glanced up. 'Hello, Nell. I thought it best to keep it locked, with you and Kate all alone now in the building.'

'That's grand, Mr Scanlon. We do get the odd tramp sleeping in the hallway at night, as well as stray cats.'

'Well, this will keep out all and sundry. I'll come up in a bit and leave you a couple of keys.'

Kate wasn't at home, so she had to light the fire from scratch. The briquettes didn't throw out as much heat as coal, but it was all she could afford. Now that there was no one but herself and Kate in the building, she hoped it wouldn't be long before they too were rehoused. Too tired to cook, she opened a tin of beans and had it on bread toasted on the end of a long-handled fork against the hot flames of the fire. Where had Kate got to?

Nell changed out of her working clothes and put them in the wash basket. She didn't have to think about them for a few days. As she placed the rent money on the mantel shelf, she glimpsed her reflection in the mirror. Her sallow

156

skin had a tired appearance and she felt much older than her nineteen years. If she had married Liam, she might well be contemplating her move to London with him. Instead, she felt weighed down with worry. She ran her hand over her pale face just as there was a knock on the door, and she rushed to open it.

'Mr Scanlon. Come in.' She moved across the room to pick up the rent money.

'Do you mind if I sit a minute, Nell?' he asked. 'I want a word.' Seeing her anxious expression, he was quick to reassure her. 'Don't look so worried.' He smiled. 'You remember we talked about the house in John's Lane?'

She relaxed. 'Is it still for rent?'

'It will be vacated the first week of the new year, ready for you to move in on the Monday.' He knitted his fingers and placed his elbows on the table. 'So, you won't be here alone for much longer.'

'Oh, that's wonderful news. Something to look forward to.' She brushed her hand over her hair. 'Excuse my manners, will you have a cup of tea?'

'Never say no to that.' He shifted the chair nearer the table. 'Is your other sister, Kate, still living with you?' he called to her as she bustled around in the scullery.

'Yes. She works at the presbytery. You heard that Róisín is poorly and a patient at the Cork Street fever hospital?' She returned with a tray bearing the tea and a few biscuits.

'Yes, I was sorry to hear that. It's a good place, from what I've heard. Will she be there long?'

157

Nell poured the tea and sat down opposite him. 'They don't know yet. I miss her around the place, but she's not been well for some time.'

'Aye. I remember your poor mother worrying about her.' He drank his tea. 'Look, before I forget.' He placed two Yale keys on the table. 'You'll feel safer at night if the front door is locked. Give one to your sister, and make sure she takes it with her when she goes out.' He chuckled. 'Otherwise, you'll have to run down and open it.'

Nell smiled. 'That's grand. Sure, thanks for doing that. We'll feel a lot safer with the door locked.'

He nodded and drained his cup. 'Well, I'd best be off. I'll be in touch again about the new place.'

'What will happen to this building?' Nell asked. 'Only I heard at the wash house that they're being bulldozed to build new flats. Is that true?'

He nodded. 'Sadly, some are beyond repair but a few, including this one, are being bought up by developers who are going to make them into individual flats.'

'Oh, it won't be the same around here, will it?'

'I guess not. It's what they call progress, God help us.' He walked towards the door.

'Here's the rent, Mr Scanlon.' She plucked it from the shelf and passed it to him.

He waved her hand away. 'It's Christmas, love. I'm sure you can find something to spend that on.'

And before Nell could thank him for his

158

generosity, he was out the door and tramping down the stairs.

24

Kate had agreed to meet Jerry O'Shea again to get something she wanted. She hadn't let him kiss her, although he had tried several times, and she'd kept him at the door despite his pleas for a hot drink on the night he'd walked her home. It didn't bother her to let Nell think the worst of her.

Saturday was Michael's last day at the vicarage, and Kate wouldn't let him go without telling him how she felt. She'd make him see she was the one he should go out with, not that mousy lank of a girl, Ophelia.

Once he was no longer clerk at St Saviour's, she would quit school and try to find work. Sitting her final exams was a total waste of time when there was no decent employment. Nell would believe she was doing it for her benefit, but Kate had plans of her own. With little work in Dublin for men, and thousands on the dole, finding employment wouldn't be easy. But Jerry had said he'd find her work and he would have news for her when they next met.

She took a deep breath before walking through the church, where the parishioners were queuing for confession. In the sacristy, Michael was busy sorting through the vestments, and he turned as she came through the door.

'Kate. What are you doing here?'

'I have to talk to you, Michael.'

He turned away before replying. 'I've a lot to clear up here, as it's my final weekend. Can you have a word with one of the other priests?'

Her face fell and her pulse quickened. Kate didn't like being dismissed. She fidgeted with the toggles of her coat while Michael continued to sort through the garments, placing the ones that needed repair and washing to one side.

'It won't take long,' she insisted.

'You shouldn't be in here, Kate. If Father John or any of the priests were to walk in, they would think all sorts.'

That was true. Hadn't Father John already accused her of consorting with the clerk? She shrugged. 'Sure, I won't be working here any more, will I?'

He turned to look at her again. 'What are you saying? You can't give up your job. It's hard out there.'

'That's what I want to talk to you about, if you can spare the time?'

He glanced up and his smile melted her heart. 'I don't know how much longer I'll be, but if you come back in an hour, I'll see you in the church porch.'

★ ★ ★

Kate went home to kill time and found Nell sorting through some small toys she had bought from the stallholders for Róisín.

'You said we had no money,' she said accusingly.

'Well, thanks to Mr Scanlon, we do,' Nell

161

explained. 'He didn't take the rent this week, as a Christmas gesture. Isn't that kind of him?'

Kate brightened. 'Does that mean I can keep my money? I want to buy shoes.'

'No, I'm afraid it doesn't work like that, Kate. You can have a little extra, but we still have bills to pay.' Before she could argue, Nell went on, 'Sure, help me wrap up Róisín's toys, and you can give them to her on Christmas morning.'

Although Kate agreed, she resented her sister making all the decisions. She cut a length of string and wrapped the small parcels, but her heart wasn't in it. 'Anyway,' she said. 'I've got my own present for her, remember?'

She pulled a box from underneath her bed and took out the wooden monkey on stilts. When she pressed the props together, the monkey swung up and over the top. They both laughed.

'She'll love that, so she will,' said Nell.

Kate wrapped it in a paper bag and put Róisín's name on it, as Nell picked up a box of chocolates. 'Who are they for?'

'Mrs Connor. We can't go empty-handed.' Nell wrapped them in coloured tissue paper and tied them with a piece of red string.

Kate sighed. 'We're still going there for Christmas dinner, then?'

'Yes. Liam is coming with us to visit Róisín first.'

Kate paused briefly before asking, 'You still love him, then?'

Nell nodded.

'How can you tell he feels the same?'

Nell smiled. 'I just can.'

'You're a fool to let him go.'

'What would you have me do, Kate?'

'You don't have to stay in Dublin because of me. I can take care of myself.'

Nell shook her head sadly before answering. 'Assuming that to be true, which I doubt, what would happen to Róisín?'

Kate got to her feet. 'I'm going back to the vicarage. Father John's not paid me.' But she already had her wages tucked into her pocket.

* * *

Michael wasn't waiting when she arrived, and the church was empty apart from a man and two women kneeling at shrines. He'd said he would meet her in an hour; Kate hoped she hadn't missed him. Had Father John kept him talking?

Everything she wanted to say to him tumbled around inside her head. She needed to know how Michael felt about her. And if his response was favourable, she'd be ready to run away with him if he asked her to.

She shivered. The church was as cold as their miserable home. She was about to look for Michael when the door to the vestry opened and Father John came out, locking it behind him. He hurried down the aisle, wearing his heavy black outdoor coat, hat and gloves, then stopped next to Kate.

'If you're here for confession, child, you're too late.'

As if she would confess anything to that old goat, she thought.

163

'No, Father,' she smiled. 'I popped in to say a prayer for my mam.'

'Ah, your poor mother, God rest her soul. What are you and your sister doing for Christmas?'

'We're going to a friend for dinner after we visit Róisín.'

'Ah, yes, how's the child doing?'

'Okay, I guess.'

'See you in church on Christmas morning, and the day after.' He nodded and then walked away.

Christmas mass was the last thing on Kate's mind. Her insides churned with fury as questions ran through her mind. How could Michael do this to her? Where was he? Why had he not waited for her?

She got up and hurried outside. After the quietness of the church, the children playing in the street sounded louder than usual. Boys ran back and forth across the road, kicking a ball, while girls played hopscotch on the pavement. Kate hated them and envied them at the same time. Despite their shabby clothes and scuffed shoes, most of them still had parents.

In a local store, she bought a Mars Bar. Coming out, she collided with Michael pushing his bike.

'Kate. I didn't expect you to wait.'

She almost cried with relief. 'I waited. You said an hour.'

He leant on the handlebars. 'I'm sorry. Before he left, Father John kept finding me things to do, including updating the parish records. You look perished. I'll buy you a hot drink, it's the least I can do.'

The tea room was shabby and needed painting; it was not a place courting couples frequented. Michael leant his bicycle against the dusty window and they went inside. Two men sat at separate tables smoking pipes, and a stale, damp smell mingled with tobacco smoke.

'Let's sit by the window, and I can keep an eye on my bike.'

The faded blue tables and chairs were scratched and the floor was covered in tea stains, but Kate didn't mind as long as she was with Michael.

'Sorry,' he said when she wrinkled her nose. 'I've not got much time, Kate. What with Father John keeping me working longer.'

She frowned. 'Have you somewhere else to be?'

'Yes, but after we've had tea.' He leant across the table. 'I wouldn't recommend anything else.'

'Tea is fine, thanks.'

A waitress plodded across and Michael ordered a pot of tea.

'Sure, is that all yeas want?' Her stained apron, with bits of food sticking to it, was enough to put them off.

Kate smothered a giggle and noticed Michael's embarrassment when he said, 'Just two teas, please.'

When it came, it was like thick brown soup served in cracked mugs. Michael paid, telling the woman to keep the change, then glanced across at Kate. 'This wasn't such a good idea,' he said quietly. 'You don't have to drink it.'

'It doesn't matter.' She reached for the cup to warm her hands. It wasn't the kind of place where she'd planned to declare her undying love for Michael, but what choice did she have?

'Michael, I . . . I mean . . . '

He leant across the table. 'What's troubling you?'

'I've met a man who wants to walk out with me. Find me a proper job, like. But . . . ' She hesitated as tears gathered at the back of her eyes.

Michael sat back, a frown creasing his handsome looks. 'A man! What do you mean, Kate? How old is this man?'

'I don't know.'

'Well, have you told your sister?'

Kate hadn't expected that. 'Why? It's none of her business,' she replied. 'What do you feel I should do?'

'Is this the man I saw you with at the dance?'

Kate's spirits rose. Was Michael showing signs of jealousy? Oh, she hoped so.

'Yes, it is. And Nell's met him already.'

'And she approves?'

Kate tried again. 'What do you think, Michael? Do you want me to go out with him?'

He blew out his lips and shook his head. 'Oh, Kate. Sure, I can't tell you what to do. It's not my place, but from what I've seen of the fellow, I don't think he's the one you should go out with.'

'Why?' she pressed.

He made a face. 'I'm aware of his sort. He'll take advantage of a girl like you.'

'What do you mean, a girl like me?'

He hesitated. 'You're a beautiful, innocent young girl, and I'd hate to see you . . . well.'

Kate's heart leapt with excitement and she leant in closer. 'You think I'm beautiful. Do you like me, Michael?'

He looked embarrassed, and glanced around the small cafe as two more men came in. 'Yes, I like you, Kate . . . but — '

She couldn't help herself. 'I love you, Michael.'

His face flushed red. Did that mean he loved her, too?

He gave a little laugh. 'You shouldn't say things like that. Someone might hear you and get the wrong impression.'

'Does it matter?'

'Yes, it does, Kate.'

Her face crumpled. 'So, you don't like me, then?'

He scraped back his chair and got to his feet. 'I can't think what's got into you, Kate.' He wrapped his scarf around his neck and added, 'I must be off.'

Stunned, Kate got up, buttoned her coat, and followed him outside. He didn't speak, just wheeled his bike while Kate walked alongside him, wondering what she had said to upset him.

When they reached the corner, he stopped. 'I have to go, Kate. And I'm sorry if I gave you the wrong impression. The idea is ludicrous. I'm meeting Ophelia in ten minutes and I don't want to keep her waiting.'

Kate staggered slightly, shuffling her feet to

keep upright. His words replayed in her head. He'd said her love for him was ludicrous, and he didn't want to keep Ophelia waiting.

'Will you be okay?' he asked. 'Promise you'll talk to Nell. There's plenty of time to find someone who'll deserve your love.'

'But not you!' she said, pushing her cold hands inside the pockets of her duffel coat and pulling up the hood to hide her distress. What a fool she'd been to think someone like Michael could love her.

'It's lovely to have met you, Kate.' He held out his hand, but she kept hers inside her pockets. 'I wish you and your sisters a happy Christmas,' he added, then threw his leg over the crossbar and cycled away.

Kate turned round in the opposite direction, her heart broken into tiny pieces.

25

It was almost tea-time when Kate got back, a miserable expression on her face, and Nell could see she'd been crying. She placed a couple of carrier bags from Roches Store on her bed, then crossed to the fire and held her hands out to the flames.

'Kate, what's wrong? Are you all right?'

'Course I'm all right.'

'What kept you?'

'Nothing.'

'Did Father John pay you any extra for Christmas?'

Kate took her coat off and threw it over a chair. 'Are you kidding?'

Nell smiled. She had spoken in jest; she knew the priest cried poverty each week from the pulpit. 'So, how much did he give you?'

'Oh, the usual.' Kate glanced into the mirror above the mantel and fiddled with her hair.

Nell gritted her teeth. 'So, where is it?'

'I spent it, okay?' Kate spat out.

'You what?'

'You heard me. I spent it.' She opened her shopping and pulled out a pair of high heels, a dress and new underwear.

'Glory be to God, Kate. Have you lost your senses?'

'It's Christmas. I'm fed up with not having anything nice to wear.'

169

Nell closed her eyes and bit back the anger welling inside her. 'You're not the only one who likes nice things, Kate.' Shaking, she advanced and raised her hand.

'Go on, I dare you.' Kate glared.

The sisters were so different in stature: Kate, four years younger, a curvaceous young woman; Nell, taller and slimmer.

'You selfish girl. How could you?' Nell stood her ground. 'Can't you see how hard I'm struggling. We're barely getting by each week. Have you looked in the pantry? You know the situation. We're lucky to have a roof over our heads.' She paced the room, wringing her hands. 'If you continue — '

'Oh, shut up!' Kate cut in. 'I'm sick of you badgering on.'

'Badgering on, is it? Have you no conscience? I saved you some bread and cheese but now you can go without.' Nell turned to face her sister. 'And, if you'd like to swap places, go ahead. All you think about is yourself, Kate. What about my shoes that you destroyed with scratches? It's all about you, and to hell with everyone else.'

Kate muttered under her breath, and Nell turned away before she said something she would later regret. Fighting with Kate was pointless; the girl showed no remorse. Desperate for air, Nell snatched her coat from the back of the door, made her way quickly down the stairs and walked to the end of the deserted street, tears filling her eyes.

Each window she passed had a red candle burning, reminding her of happier times. She felt inadequate, with no clue how to deal with her wayward sister, and had come close to slapping her. Even Mam had found Kate hard work, but had given in to her from the time she was little, despite their dad's protests that she was making a rod for her own back. How right he'd been. When Róisín came along, she was a sickly child needing a lot of care, so Kate had to take second place in their mother's affections.

But Nell wasn't as soft as their mam had been. Kate would have to toe the line sooner or later.

Sniffing back tears and shivering from the cold, she hurried home. When she got there, Kate was struggling upstairs with a bucket of fresh water. She didn't turn round or speak to Nell on the darkened stairway.

Nell followed her to the scullery, where she scooped water into the kettle and put it on the hob.

'Look, Kate, don't let's quarrel. I . . . '

'Who's arguing? Not me. I'm going out. The market's staying open late.'

'But . . . I thought we'd spend this evening together.'

Kate poured warm water into a basin and stripped off her jumper. 'Sorry.' She glanced down at her legs. 'Oh, darn it! A ladder. What a nuisance. Have you any nail polish, Nell?'

'No, sorry.' She thought about giving Kate her present, then changed her mind.

'Are you meeting Teresa?'

Kate looked round. 'Teresa! No. I'm meeting Jerry.'

'Who's Jerry?' Nell's heart raced.

'Jerry O'Shea. You met him on the landing last weekend. He will help me find work, so you won't have to fret over me for much longer.'

★ ★ ★

Nell would always worry about Kate, and on Christmas Eve when Kate went out yet again, Nell spent it alone. She wrapped up a bottle of lavender water and a pair of Bear Brand nylons for Kate, adding a note: *To my sister Kate. Happy Christmas, with all my love, Nell.* She hid it under her bed to give to Kate on Christmas morning.

It reminded her of past Christmas Eves, when the family wrapped up small gifts for each other. There had always been excitement and laughter, but now the house was too quiet with just herself and Kate. No noisy neighbours, no children crying or family arguments penetrating the walls. The silence grated, and she hoped Kate wouldn't stay out late.

As she sorted through the ironing, she imagined Amy in her new house, with her own kitchen and bathroom, singing as she wrapped up little gifts for each of the children. Nell took a deep breath. Liam was the only brightness in her life, but soon he, too, would be gone. At least she would spend tomorrow, Christmas Day, with him. With that thought, she placed her red dress on the ironing board, taking special care when ironing the pleats. She warmed the heavy black iron on the fire before tackling Kate's dress. It took longer to press, with its full skirt and wide lace collar. When she had finished, she hung both dresses in the wardrobe.

26

On Christmas morning, despite their differences, Nell and Kate breakfasted together on toast and marmalade and wished each other Happy Christmas. The wireless was playing Christmas songs, and the comedian Jimmy O'Dea made Nell laugh.

She passed Kate her present across the table. 'I hope you find these useful.' She watched as Kate ripped off the paper.

'Oh, thanks, Nell. Nylons, just what I needed.' Kate looked thrilled.

Nell didn't expect anything from Kate and when she handed her a small gift wrapped in gold paper, Nell's hand flew to her mouth. 'For me? You bought me a present?'

Kate looked away, crunching the rest of her toast.

As soon as Nell untied the string and opened the box, she gasped. How could Kate afford this sparkling peacock brooch? She knew Kate was observing her as she examined it closely. It wasn't a sixpenny brooch from Woolworths. The thought that her sister had stolen it brought a new fear, and her breath caught.

'Well, don't you like it?'

'It's . . . It's lovely, Kate. How did you afford this?'

'Don't you know it's rude to ask the cost of a present?'

Nell swallowed her concerns for now. Another row would be futile, and would cause an atmosphere that Róisín was likely to pick up on. Forcing a smile to her face, she unclipped the brooch from the box and pinned it to her red dress, then got ready to leave for the hospital.

★ ★ ★

In the long hospital corridor, groups of excited visitors waited to visit loved ones. Nell strained to look for Liam, but it wasn't until the doors at the far end opened and people went to their respective wards that she saw him. He was carrying the doll, unwrapped.

She hurried towards him. 'Liam!'

'Hello, Nell. Happy Christmas, and you too, Kate.'

Kate didn't answer and walked ahead of them into the ward.

'Is it something I said?' Liam looked questioningly at Nell.

'Oh, take no notice of Kate. She hates hospitals.' She smiled up at him as he squeezed her hand. 'It's good to see you.'

Róisín was sitting up in bed and, despite her thin arms and pale face, she radiated happiness. She pointed to the enormous Christmas tree decorated in baubles and tinsel at the far end of the long ward.

'Isn't the tree lovely, Nell?' she cried. 'Look what Santa brought me!' She held up a small clockwork figure of Snow White.

'It's grand.' All the children had received the

175

same toy, and Nell leant in to hug her close. 'We've got presents and sweets for you.' She glanced towards Kate. 'Would you like to give yours first?'

Róisín squealed with delight every time the monkey swung upwards and over the top. 'Thanks, Kate. It's grand.'

Nell was delighted to see a smile brighten Kate's face. She touched Liam's arm. 'Do yours next.'

He moved closer to the bed, and there was no disguising the little girl's pleasure to see the doll again.

'Thanks, Liam. I love her.' She reached up to kiss him, then she brought the doll close in a hug.

'You're welcome.'

'And these are for you,' Nell said. 'They're only little things, but I hope you'll have fun playing with them.'

'I love Snakes and Ladders. Will you play with me, Kate?'

Nell saw the disagreeable expression that crossed Kate's face before she leant down to kiss Róisín.

'I'm sorry, I have to go now, but I'll see you soon, okay?' Kate moved away as the child's face puckered.

Nell caught her arm. 'Where are you going? We've only just got here.'

'I have to make a phone call. I'll meet you outside.'

Nell forced down her anger. She glanced back at Liam as he comforted Róisín.

176

'Where's Kate gone? I want her to stay.'

'Sorry, pet, she had to go somewhere. She'll be back another day.' Nell was furious. How could Kate? She'd been distracted during the Christmas mass, leaving before it was over. And outside, the sisters had exchanged angry words. 'You're a disgrace, Kate. I'm appalled by your behaviour and glad Mammy's not here to see it.'

'I was overcome by the smell of incense and needed fresh air. And don't mention our mam,' snapped Kate. 'You couldn't wait to get rid of her body!'

'Kate! That's not true and you know it.'

'Nell, Nell,' Róisín called, bringing Nell back to the present. 'It's your turn.'

Liam had set up the board game on the table over the bed, and the three of them played the game.

'See if you can get a six.' Róisín squealed each time one of them slithered down a snake. The child was a delight to watch, and when she threw the dice and got the number six, enabling her to have another throw, her laughter was infectious.

If only Kate was as easily pleased, thought Nell.

★　★　★

When visiting was over, Nell and Liam waited by the hospital entrance for half an hour but Kate didn't appear. Liam's arm around her shoulders felt comforting.

'Where the devil has she got to, Nell?' he asked.

177

Nell couldn't speak. Her throat contracted with stifled anger.

'I hope she turns up soon, otherwise it's a long walk to Fairview. I've ordered us a taxi. There won't be any buses today.'

Nell frowned. 'I'd forgotten about the buses.'

Leaving the shelter of the hospital, they walked down the street just as Kate rounded the corner, out of breath.

'I'm sorry. I had to wait ages to get in the phone box,' she puffed.

Nell glared. 'Who were you phoning on Christmas Day?'

'No one.'

'Don't get smart with me, Kate. Who do you know with a phone? You care about no one but yourself.'

'Oh, look. Here comes the cab now.' Liam waved his hand, and it stopped next to them. He ushered the two sisters inside.

Kate sat aloof, across from Nell. Neither of them spoke, leaving Liam to make small talk with the cab driver.

'Business is slow today,' the taxi man said. 'A few runs to the hospitals is all I've had.'

'You'll get home for your dinner, then?' Liam asked.

'Ah, begorrah, I will that.'

When they arrived at Liam's home, Mrs Connor gave them a warm welcome. 'Hello, Nell, Kate. Come in. It's cold enough for snow. And it wouldn't surprise me if we saw the return of that blizzard of three years ago.'

She ushered them into the cosy living room,

where Christmas decorations hung from the high ceiling and a nativity scene had pride of place on the mantel. Mr Connor stood up to greet them, then went to the drinks cabinet and poured two small glasses of sherry and brought them across.

'John! Kate's not old enough,' his wife scolded.

But Kate was reaching out her hand.

'Sure, where's the harm as it's Christmas?' Liam's dad winked at Nell. 'How's your little sister, Nell?'

'She was in good form this morning. Excited with her toys, you know?'

'Ah, sure, happen she'll be home soon,' Mrs Connor commented as she went down the hall towards the kitchen.

Nell sipped her drink. It was just what she needed to help her relax and try to forget her earlier argument with Kate.

'What about you, son? What'll ye have?'

'Mine's a Guinness, Dad, if you've got one in.'

They relaxed over their drinks and chatted until Liam's mother called them into the spacious kitchen. The pine table with matching chairs was set for five, with a lighted red candle in the centre. The smell from the pots bubbling on the range and the turkey warming on the hot plate made Nell's stomach rumble.

'Smells grand, so it does, Ma.' Liam pulled out a chair for Nell, and his dad did the same for Kate.

So far, Kate had said little, and as they sat side by side, Nell hoped no one else noticed her sister's hostility.

Mrs Connor placed bowls of hot vegetable soup on the table, with thick slices of crusty bread. Liam, Nell and Kate picked up their spoons but put them down again when Mr Connor bowed his head to say grace.

Mrs Connor removed her Santa apron and sat down opposite Kate. 'Eat away,' she said, and they all tucked in.

When they had finished, Nell stood and began to clear the soup bowls, but Mr Connor gently pressed her to sit back down. Liam took the dishes to the sink as his mother brought a big dish of fluffy potatoes and green vegetables to the table, while Mr Connor carved the turkey.

Liam passed the dish to Nell and she scooped a spoonful of vegetables on to her plate next to the slice of turkey. Kate helped herself, but Nell caught her looking at the clock and kicked her under the table.

As they all savoured the wonderful food, topped off with rich Bisto gravy, Liam said, 'I'll miss your cooking, Ma.'

'Well, happen you'll think on,' she replied, 'and stay home and help us in the shop.'

Liam glanced briefly at Nell. 'Sorry, Ma, it's not for me.'

Mr Connor paused, with a forkful of turkey halfway to his mouth. 'Sure, hasn't the lad done well for himself landing a job in London?'

'That's right, Da, and I'm going to make something of myself, you'll see.'

'I don't doubt you will, son.' Mr Connor poured more gravy on his dinner and continued to tuck in.

Nell smiled. At least one of them had the freedom to leave their poverty-stricken country and find a new beginning elsewhere.

'Did ye make any cranberry sauce, Mary?'

Mrs Connor sighed. 'Indeed I did. I'd forget me head if it wasn't screwed on.' She laughed and went to fetch the sauce.

'Do you know when you're moving, Nell?' Liam's father asked. 'It's time those places were condemned.'

'We're moving to John's Lane in the New Year.'

'I hate the thought of you in that tenement on your own,' Liam said.

'I'm not on my own,' Nell assured him. 'I have Kate, and Mr Scanlon's had keys cut so we can lock the front door at night. But it is strange with everyone gone.'

Mr Connor shook his head. 'Well, I still think the Corporation should have rehoused you. A little maisonette would have done nicely.'

'We'll be all right, Mr Connor. There's not much we can do.'

'Sure, I'm sorry things haven't worked out for you and Liam,' Mrs Connor said sadly.

'Ma,' Liam interjected, chewing his meat, 'you promised you wouldn't bring that up. Sure, we're planning to be together again once we see how things go with Róisín.'

Again, Mr Connor shook his head. 'Sure, you know your mother can never keep a promise.'

And they all laughed, even Kate.

★　★　★

181

'Ah now, you shouldn't have gone to that trouble,' Liam's mother told Nell when she opened her chocolates. 'Thanks, lovey. Sure, we'll share them later.'

'This is for you.' Liam handed Nell a present wrapped in tissue paper and tied in a small red bow.

She wasn't sure what to say, as she hadn't bought him anything.

'Don't worry,' he said, as if reading her mind. 'Open it.'

Inside the little yellow box was a gold cross and chain. 'Oh, Liam, it's lovely.' Her eyes shone as she fingered the fine gold chain, and Liam placed it round her neck, fastening the catch. 'I'll treasure it. Thank you.'

'This is for you, Kate,' he said. Kate looked up from picking her nails and unwrapped a bottle of Tweed perfume.

'Thank you. I've always wanted some.' She undid the top, brought it to her nose, dabbing a few drops on to her wrist and behind her ears. Despite her pretence, Kate kept glancing at the clock on the mantel, making Nell uneasy.

Mr Connor set up a small table so they could play cards and Liam nudged closer to Nell. 'Are you having a good day, Nell?'

Nodding, she squeezed his arm. They were in the middle of dealing out the cards when Kate got to her feet. 'Please excuse me, I'm meeting a friend in town.'

'Sure there's no bus today, love,' Mr Connor reminded her.

'And there's nowhere open,' Nell added, grinding her teeth.

'Oh, are you sure you'll be all right?' Mrs Connor asked.

'It's not far from here to town.'

Furious with her sister, Nell glared at her.

'I'll see you at home,' Kate said, and hurried out.

Liam stood up. 'Would you like me to walk with her, Nell?'

'I should come too.'

'No, you stay in the warm. I won't be long.' He went into the hall, pushed his arms into his coat, wrapped his scarf around his neck and rushed out after Kate.

Nell turned to Liam's mother, a bewildered look on her face. 'I'm sorry about Kate, Mrs Connor. She's struggling with things at the moment.' Her sister was a devious little madam, and she felt mortified with embarrassment.

'Don't you worry. She's best off with her friends.'

Mr Connor poured the two women a glass of port each, and Nell settled back on the comfortable sofa, to wait for Liam's return. But her mind gave her no respite. Right now, she felt furious enough to wring Kate's neck.

27

Kate was fuming when she saw Liam following her. Why couldn't people mind their own business? She knew Jerry would be waiting for her round the corner, and Liam was bound to tell Nell. He called out to her, but she ran faster and reached the corner first. Jerry was astride the bike, revving loudly and ready to go, grinning when he saw her.

'Up you get, then!'

Kate, who had never been on a bike — let alone a powered one — felt her stomach churn with excitement as she took his hand and he pulled her up on to the pillion. With her arms wrapped tightly around Jerry, she felt the wind blowing through her hair as they sped away. She glanced over her shoulder and saw Liam standing with his arms folded on the deserted street corner before turning away. All she could think about was the excitement of the moment.

'Okay, Kate?'

'Yes,' she yelled above the roar of the engine.

Adrenaline pumping through her veins, she clung tightly to Jerry as they rounded each corner. When he pulled up outside a dingy public house bordering the city, she felt disappointed. Her legs were cold and she couldn't feel her feet.

'Where's this?' she asked, her teeth chattering.

'It's where I live, at the back.' He quickly

added, 'But not for long. Now that I have a pretty girl to impress, I shall be looking for something better.' He pushed his bike through a side entrance, leant it against the wall, then pulled a thick chain round the wheel and locked it.

Kate followed him inside. He had told her she was welcome to stay at his whenever she wanted to, and the way Nell was acting lately, Kate thought she just might do that. Jerry had also promised to find her work, and although she didn't feel for him what she had felt for Michael, she was willing to wait and see what he had to offer.

'Who else lives here?' She glanced around as he guided her through the back door.

'A couple of lads live over the pub, but I have the ground floor to myself.'

The small scullery had a sink and cupboards in need of painting. A fusty smell made her wrinkle her nose. 'How long have you lived here?'

He laughed. 'I've not moved in yet. I've just got the key.'

'So, when are you moving in?' she asked, stepping into the room with its peeling wallpaper and smell of damp.

A square table and four chairs sat in the centre of the room, and there was a scratched sideboard covered in dust and an old sofa with the stuffing hanging out of the back. At least Nell had kept their rooms clean and tidy, but this was far worse than anything Kate had seen at the tenement. There was another room she didn't even want to look in.

'That's the bedroom,' he said.

She couldn't disguise her disappointment. 'I can't move in here, Jerry.'

'I'll clean it up.' He came and stood behind her, placing his hands on her shoulders.

'It's not what I was expecting. And where's . . .'

'The lavvy's outside in the yard. So, what do you think?'

She sat down on the sofa, springs prodding her backside. This wasn't worth leaving home for, and she had no intention of skivvying for Jerry.

'What's up? Not good enough for you?'

Kate sighed. 'If you want the truth, Jerry, it's a dump.'

His eyes narrowed. 'Better than the dump you're living in.'

'Well, at least it's clean,' she retorted. 'It's freezing in here.'

He sat down next to her, placing his arm around her shoulders.

But she edged away. Was this all she was worth? She imagined Michael finding a much nicer place for his Ophelia.

'Don't be hasty, Kate,' he said. 'Look at the bigger picture. You'll be working soon.'

She glanced up. 'You've found me a job?'

'They're looking for a barmaid at the pub. I know the owner and can put in a word. I have an allowance and me dole money, and between us we can make this into a little palace.' He shifted closer. 'What do you say?'

'I'm not working in any pub. I can do better

186

than that. Sorry, Jerry.' She moved away. 'I need to think again about this.'

He shrugged. 'Well, don't think too long. You're not the only girl on the block.'

'So, who else have you been lying to?' she snapped back.

'Oh, I'm only joking.'

But Kate was already regretting taking Jerry at his word. He'd said he would find them a nice bedsit with all mod cons, and get her a clerical job. All lies to get her to this lousy place. And she'd been desperate enough to believe him.

He stood up. 'Look, you know the situation. There's no jobs in this bleeding country. And you should be darned grateful to take what's going.'

She stood up, too. 'I know all about the country's economic situation, Jerry, but I'm not going to live in this dump, or work in a stinking pub.' She pulled her coat tighter around her, desperate to get out of the smelly room.

'So, what are you going to do, then?'

'I don't know yet.'

He pulled her to him.

'Get off me!' She moved out of his reach.

His eyes blazed with annoyance. 'Don't forget, you owe me — and I intend to collect, one way or another.'

'And what do you mean by that?'

'What sort of idiot do you take me for?'

'This was a mistake.' Kate rushed outside.

'Hang on. I'll give you a lift.'

'Don't bother, I'll make my own way back.'

'Don't be stupid, Kate.'

But she was gone, running up Talbot Street towards Nelson's Pillar. He chased after her for a few yards before giving up.

It had turned colder, and she lowered her head against the bitter wind that blew in her face. She knew she had been stupid taking his money to buy clothes and presents when she had no means of paying him back. Darkness was drawing the day to a close and the streets were empty, apart from the occasional pedestrian walking a dog. A shiver ran through her body and she longed to be somewhere warm. Her ruined plans meant she would have to stay with Nell a bit longer.

She arrived in the street to find children playing on roller-skates, wrapped up in knitted scarves and gloves. A taxi stopped at the far end of the street, and she watched as Nell and Liam stepped out on to the pavement. They looked happy, and she envied them. They stood together for a few moments, then Liam kissed Nell before getting back inside the taxi.

Kate felt guilty about earlier and wanted to call out to her sister, but pride stopped her. Her teeth chattering, she hid in the doorway of an empty tenement until Nell had gone inside. It started to rain as she walked the rest of the way. By the time she had climbed the stairs and breezed inside, Nell was putting a match to the kindling in the grate. She turned when she heard her sister come in.

'Where the hell have you been? Look at the cut of you. You're like a drowned cat.' She got up from where she was hunkered down at the fire.

'You disgust me. Do you know that, or even care?'

'Oh, shut up. And no, I don't care, if you must know.'

'You're turning into a right little — ' Nell stopped.

'Go on, say it,' Kate taunted. 'It's what you think, isn't it?'

'You go off on the back of a motorbike and don't say who it is. What else am I to think? And what about Liam's parents? They went to a lot of trouble for us . . . and you.'

Kate placed her hands over her ears to signal she was no longer listening, then she removed her wet clothes and got into bed, pulling the blankets over her head to muffle her tears.

28

The following morning, the air was frosty between the sisters. Nell had planned to take Kate to see a film but that was now out of the question.

Kate was first to speak. 'Is there anything to eat?'

'There's corned beef I cooked the other day in the cupboard, and some of Liam's mam's Christmas cake.' Nell followed her into the scullery. 'You can help me pack some of our stuff. We're moving on the first of January.'

Kate sliced the corned beef, then sliced a tomato and sandwiched it between two slices of Mother's Pride, which she cut into two halves. Nell watched, thinking her sister would offer her one. Once she'd finished off the first sandwich, Kate picked up the second, but paused and looked up at Nell. 'Did you want one?' she asked.

It would choke Nell to accept, knowing that Kate had had no intention of sharing it with her in the first place. She wasn't hungry anyway. Her insides churned with frustration. She wanted to know who Kate had been with, but refrained from asking. Instead, she said calmly, 'Well, I'll start on the packing, then, shall I?'

Kate shrugged and finished the rest of her sandwich.

Using old newspapers she had saved, Nell

began to wrap a couple of brass candlesticks and put them into a box, while Kate filled the kettle and placed it on the hob.

'Can't we see inside this place before we move?' she suggested. 'It might be worse than this.'

'Well, hardly,' Nell scoffed. 'So, let's stay positive. 1951 might be a better year for us.'

'Well, I'm not that sure.'

'We don't have a choice, Kate. This building is being sold. We can't stay here.'

Nell unhooked the photos and the religious pictures from the walls and wrapped them in lots of newspaper.

'Just so you know,' Kate said, leaving the scullery, 'when I'm sixteen, I'm quitting school. And I won't be working for Father John any more, either. I'm looking for a proper job.'

Nell was kneeling on the floor, sticking tape across the wrapped pictures. She stopped what she was doing and looked up at her sister. 'Are you mad? You haven't finished your leaving cert, and without good qualifications you have no chance of finding a half-decent job.'

'I don't care any more,' Kate replied airily. 'I want to earn proper money, get my own place.'

Nell could hardly believe her ears, and sat back on her heels. 'You can't be serious. There's nothing out there! What makes you think you'll be lucky when the dole queue is growing day by day, and hundreds are taking the mail boat to England every night?'

Kate placed her hands over her ears, but Nell wasn't finished.

'You're coming to the new house with me, if I have to drag you there kicking and screaming.' Furious now, she got to her feet and pulled her sister's hands from her ears. 'Has this got something to do with the person you met yesterday? Who was it? Have they put this stupid idea into your head?'

Kate pulled away from her sister. 'You may have missed your chance with Liam Connor,' she spat, 'but don't think for one minute that I'm going to do the same.'

Nell swallowed the hurt and frustration, and bit down hard on her lip. 'Why are you being like this? What I did was for us. For God's sake, Kate. We've only got each other, and Róisín needs us both. Talk to me.'

'I wouldn't talk to you if you were the last person on this earth. So, leave me alone and get on with your own lonely life.'

Kate's words stung, but Nell couldn't give up. 'Have you spoken to Father John or anyone else about your plans?' she asked.

'The priest! Are you codding? And yes, I have talked to someone, and who that might be is none of your business.'

Defeated, Nell sank into the big armchair, her thoughts in turmoil. Neither girl spoke, and the only sounds were the ticking of the clock and the fire crackling in the grate.

What was Nell to do? If Kate refused to support her and Róisín, she'd have no choice but to talk it over with Father John — to get his opinion, for what it was worth. With Liam about to leave the country, who else did she have?

On Wednesday, everyone who was lucky enough to have a job returned after the holiday. Kate wasn't due back at school for another few days, and when Nell left that morning, she scribbled a note telling her sister she was sorry if she'd upset her, and that she only had her best interests at heart. She finished her note by saying she would always love her.

At work, though, she couldn't concentrate, and Dot asked her if she still had a hangover. Chance would have been a grand thing, she thought. She was desperate to speak to someone, but she wasn't close enough to anyone at work. Liam was the only one who would understand her frustration with Kate, but they had already said their goodbyes and she certainly couldn't go through another emotional farewell.

At the end of her shift, the thought of returning to the lonely room felt daunting, and she went into one of the nearby coffee houses to revive her drooping spirits. She had almost finished packing away their few belongings, and all she had to do now was find someone to move the beds and furniture. But the excitement of moving had gone. It all seemed pointless, without Kate and Róisín.

Kate's words kept resounding in her brain, and she was worried that her sister would be stupid enough to leave.

Nell ordered a coffee with milk and sugar. When the waitress — an older woman, with tired eyes — brought it across, she smiled. 'You look like you need this.' And she placed a biscuit on the saucer.

Smiling, Nell thanked her. 'Do you by any chance have any vacancies?'

'Is it for yourself, like?'

'My sister.'

'Well, to be honest, I could do with an extra pair of hands on a Saturday, but I can't pay much.'

Nell's face brightened. A few hours was better than nothing. 'Thank you, I'll let her know.'

When Nell reached Dominick Street, she noticed the gradual changes taking place. Houses had been torn down, leaving unsightly gaps between tenements. Outside her own building, an enormous billboard was attached to the railings, announcing the sale of the property, and she wondered who would live here after they'd moved out. Using the Yale key Mr Scanlon had given her, she let herself into the dank hallway. A stack of letters lay on the stone floor. As usual, most were for tenants who had left ages ago, but her face brightened when she discovered one for her, written in Amy's uneven handwriting. She shoved it into her bag and left the rest with the ever-growing pile in the corner. With no electricity, she made her way carefully up the dark stairway. Every little sound echoed in her ears in the corridors of the empty building, and she was glad to reach the top floor. Once inside, the room was cold, and there was no sign of Kate. She sat at the table and eagerly opened Amy's letter.

194

Dear Nell,

I haven't had a minute to write but hope you're all okay. We are nearly straight and there's so much room I can't believe our luck. The neighbours on one side of us are friendly enough but the other side are a bit stuck-up. Not like the grand neighbours we had in the tenement. You'll have to come over when you can afford the bus fare. It will be great to see you. How is little Róisín? Give her a hug from me and Joan.

Have you heard when you're moving to John's Lane? It must be soon now. Me cousin, Tommy, who moved our stuff for us will do the same for you. He's got one of them phone things installed. I ask you? And you can ring him. He's a good sort and won't charge you. But a packet of ciggies will put a smile on his face. I've scribbled his number on the back of this letter.

Let me know when you're settled. I want to hear all your news.

Amy

Nell read it again. She was so pleased to hear from Amy. She really missed their chats and had felt very isolated since Amy and her family had moved. Without Kate's support, things were about to get even harder.

29

The next morning, after Nell left for work, Kate braved the frosty pavements. She headed towards the dole office, her stomach knotted with apprehension. When she arrived in the city, afraid of bumping into Jerry, she changed her mind and instead decided to spend the morning looking for work. She was determined to prove Nell wrong, faking her age if she had to. Trams were being phased out and a few buses were at a standstill, one behind the other, in gridlock. From where she stood, her hands deep inside her pockets, it would be quicker to walk across to St Stephen's Green where she was sure she had seen employment agencies.

After two hours of traipsing from office to office and being turned down, her enthusiasm was waning and her heels were blistered. Wearily, she called into a small cafe in George's Street for a hot drink, spending the last of her money on a mug of tea and a sticky bun. It was a noisy place, with customers shouting their orders at the frazzled woman behind the counter, and the clatter of crockery along with the hissing urn made her headache worse. She sipped her drink, wrapping her cold hands around the mug, and bit into the iced bun, savouring the taste and licking her fingers. When she'd finished, she used the convenience out the back and left.

Kate was in no hurry to get home and

couldn't resist one last attempt to find work. She called at Gestetner, a printing office on Dame Street. They appeared impressed until they asked her how many words a minute she could type. Lying, she told them she could manage fifty, but she hadn't expected them to give her a test. Her fingers shook, and she made too many mistakes.

'I'm sorry,' said the older woman who interviewed her. 'I'm afraid your typing skills are almost non-existent.' Kate was about to plead her case, but the woman was already showing her the door.

Wishing she had taken a typing course instead of staying on at school, she gave up and made her way home. She hated to admit it, but Nell was right about jobs; they were like gold. Those lucky to be in employment stuck to them for life.

Back home, the room was freezing, but she couldn't be bothered to light the fire. Nell had left vegetables on the table for her to prepare for their dinner, but Kate wasn't interested. Pulling her red suitcase from underneath her bed, she gave it a dusting, then put her few clothes inside along with two history books borrowed from the library. Her mam's words tumbled into her head: *Education is the key to getting anywhere in life; without it, you'll be on the scrap heap.*

'I'm sorry, Mam. You're not here, and I'm doing what I have to do,' she whispered into the empty room. 'Nell seems happy to wallow in poverty, and I can't be what she wants me to be.'

She pushed the case out of sight and glanced at the clock. Another hour before Nell got home. Kate knew there would be another row if she didn't get a fire going. The coal scuttle was empty, as was the kindling basket. Sighing, she lifted them both and made her way down the dark staircase to the backyard. She'd been afraid to go down since she saw a rat scurrying across the concrete yard.

As she passed down the stairs, she recalled the faces that had once been a familiar sight to her as she grew up, all gone to better homes. If their mam hadn't died, they would be in a nice house like Teresa's. But what was the point of ifs?

Carrying back a few briquettes, with kindling on top, she felt a shiver run through her body. How she hated this place. She could barely see her hand in front of her by the time she reached the top landing, where a figure suddenly loomed in front of her.

Startled, Kate let out an expletive before a match was struck and held over her head, revealing the portly figure of Father John.

'Taking the Lord's name in vain is a disgrace, Kate Flynn,' he scolded, panting from exertion.

'Sorry, Father. If you'll allow me to get in with the firewood, we can talk.'

She pushed open the door and dropped the heavy basket by the hearth while the priest followed, chuntering to himself.

He flicked the light switch, but the room remained in darkness. Kate picked up the matches and lit the candle Nell had left on the mantel. 'Sit down, Father, I'll light the fire and make you a cup of tea. It won't take long.'

'Well, it's the least you can do after the climb up here,' he grumbled. 'It's enough to give me a heart attack. I want to know what's going on. Why's the electric turned off? I heard from Mrs Cassidy that you and Nell are moving, and I'm the last to know about it.'

Her hands shaking, she twisted two sheets of discarded newspaper tight, releasing some of her frustration, then put a match to it and placed the kindling on top. Standing up, she hurried into the scullery to put on the kettle. While the priest watched her every movement, she came back into the room and threw a few briquettes on top, crossing her fingers it would ignite.

'I asked you why the electric is turned off?' he persisted.

'The tea won't be a moment.' If only she'd stayed out longer, she would have missed the priest and his interrogations.

'Are you deaf? I asked you a question. Wasn't the bill paid?'

'I've been out all day looking for work,' she replied.

The fire crackled, and the priest got slowly to his feet, He walked to the fireplace, holding his hands out to the heat.

'The very fact that you're not answering me tells me you never gave that money to your sister. Did you?'

She could see irritation flicker across his face, in the same way it did when he gave his sermon from the pulpit. Still ignoring his questions, Kate brought one of the two remaining mugs that had not been packed to the table, along with two Marietta biscuits, hoping to sweeten him up.

Father John came and sat at the table, sipped

the tea and crunched the biscuits. But he hadn't finished his tirade. 'If you've taken money from me on false pretences, you've committed the sin of theft and will need absolution. Are you listening? I'm trying to save your immortal soul, child.'

Kate sat opposite him, holding her hands tight in front of her to stop them shaking. 'I'm . . . I'm sorry, Father. I am. But the truth is I wanted to buy something nice for Róisín for Christmas. And I didn't have the money.' She sniffed.

He put his mug down with a clatter, and she was sure he'd cracked it. 'So, you stole it?'

'No, not really, Father.'

'Don't lie, Kate. You think a toy is more important than paying the electric bill? My, you have a lot to learn. I shall have words with Nell. I said nothing to your sister about you flirting with the clerk, because I thought you'd mended your ways.' He took a deep breath. 'Now he's no longer with us, I dare say we won't be seeing you at the presbytery, or at church on Sundays, will we?'

Kate bit back her annoyance at the priest bringing up Michael's name.

'I'm sorry I'm such a disappointment to you, Father,' she said quietly, 'but you'll have to excuse me, I have the dinner to get ready before Nell comes home.'

He snorted. 'Aye! And if you imagine I believe that, you don't know me as well as you think.' He got up. 'Now you listen to me, Kate Flynn. You had better be at the presbytery tomorrow.'

'I've been out all day looking for work,' she

200

repeated. 'But I'm not coming back to the presbytery.'

'Your sister needs your support to keep you both off the streets.' He took a deep breath. 'Tell Nell I need a word with her urgently. Do you hear me?'

'Loud and clear!' she muttered.

'I'll bid you goodbye.' He moved towards the door, leaving it swinging behind him.

She heard him clattering down the stairs and couldn't help hoping he'd fall and break his neck. He certainly knew how to rock the boat. She wanted to run out and never come back.

As Kate lit another candle and brought it to the table, a tear trickled down her cheek and she brushed it away. Thoughts of Michael came flooding back. He knew how to treat a girl. Whenever he spoke to her, or said thanks, he said it in such a lovely way, with his eyes. It had been such a shock to discover that he didn't feel about her the way she felt about him.

Shortly before Nell was due home, she threw another briquette on the fire. With a last look around the room, she pushed her arms into her coat, wound a scarf round her neck, then picked up her handbag and the suitcase she'd packed, and left.

30

It was bitterly cold as Nell hurried through the streets, cheerful and excited to tell Kate her news. Her sister had shown little interest in the Saturday cafe job when she'd mentioned it, so Nell hoped she would be more enthusiastic about a vacancy that had come up for a junior clerk at the biscuit factory. They needed someone good with figures, and she'd immediately thought of Kate. Her supervisor had advised Nell that her sister should put in her application straight away.

'You know, Nell, these kinds of jobs are not vacant for very long. They don't have to advertise them,' she'd said. 'Word of mouth and they're snapped up.'

Nell couldn't wait to tell Kate. The job would be the making of her, if she applied herself. And she intended to help Kate all she could.

It was pitch black as she entered the stark hallway, and there was an eerie feel to the building as she took the stairs two at a time. At the top, she stopped to catch her breath and then went inside. The place was in darkness but the fire was still burning.

'Kate! Kate, are you in?'

She struck a match and lit the candle on the table. It had burned down, leaving a small stump and a pool of candle wax in the saucer. Her heart sank. Where could Kate be? She'd clearly been home, but why hadn't she peeled the spuds? In the scullery, she saw crumbs and bread on the chopping board, and the ham had been left uncovered.

'Oh, Kate! What am I to do with you?' Nell placed her head in her hands. She had sausages in her bag for their meal, but her appetite had gone. She put them under the grill, hoping Kate would be home any minute and she would have everything ready before telling her about the office job.

When everything was cooked and she had made Bisto gravy, there was still no sign of Kate. After she'd eaten her own meal and put Kate's to keep warm, she couldn't rest.

It was getting late and, worried about her sister, Nell felt she had no choice but to call on Father John and ask his advice. One of the priests opened the door to her.

'I'm sorry to intrude at this hour,' Nell told him, 'but could I speak to Father John urgently, please?'

The priest's eyes narrowed. 'Father John's resting in the study. Step inside and I'll ask him if he'll see you, but it is rather late, you know.'

Nell shivered, rubbing her hands together, her pulse racing. Yes, it was late, but she knew she wouldn't sleep a wink until she had spoken to someone about Kate.

She heard mutterings before she was admitted further into the house and told to wait in the refectory with the door ajar. The room was spotless, and she wondered if Kate had changed her mind and cleaned for the priests today.

When Father John tottered in, he was yawning, and Nell quickly apologised for disturbing him. He gestured for her to sit on one of two high-backed chairs by the grand stone fireplace, while he eased himself into the other one.

'It's all right, child,' he said. 'I wanted to see you. At least your sister passed on the message.'

Nell was confused by his words. 'No, I've not seen her all day and she's not at home now. What can I do, Father? I'm worried sick about her, on top of everything else . . . and Róisín.'

He leant forward and placed his hand on her shoulder. 'I know, child. You've a lot on your plate. But this business of Kate is serious, very serious indeed. We must nip whatever is going on with her in the bud, or lose her immortal soul.' He stood up. 'Would you like a cup of tea?'

'No, thanks, Father. Don't trouble yourself. I couldn't drink it.'

'When do you move?'

'In a few days, Father.'

He made his way to a mahogany cabinet and poured a smidgen of whiskey into a tumbler and a fair dollop into another one, then carried them across. 'Sip this. It will help you sleep. Medicinal, you understand.' He smiled and sat back down. 'Are you aware of your sister's sexual awakening?'

Nell felt a flush to her face at the priest's use of words. 'What do you mean, Father?'

'I caught her. Positively flirting with the clerk, Michael Flannigan. If she becomes promiscuous, God knows where she'll end up.'

Nell turned the glass round in her hand, then brought it to her lips and sipped it slowly. It burned her throat, and she wrinkled her nose. 'No, I ... Are you sure, Father?' She immediately regretted her words when his eyebrows shot upwards. 'I'm sorry, Father. I had no idea. It's no doubt an innocent crush.'

'Aye, well, you can believe that if you want.' He swallowed a good measure of his drink. 'That temptation has gone now. Sure, when he came for interview, he told me he was courting and soon to be married. So you can understand my concern.'

'Yes, of course, Father. Thanks for telling me.'

He got up and poured himself another drink and offered the bottle to Nell, but she declined. Her mind was still trying to unscramble Kate's actions in her head. It made sense now why Kate had suddenly stopped going to church. Could the clerk have been the tall, well-dressed man she had seen her sister with a few weeks back, in Mary Street?

Father John sat back, relaxed now, with the drink. 'Look, sure try not to worry. She'll be back. If it will help, we can talk to her together.'

Nell sipped the remainder of her drink and felt it warm her insides. She hadn't yet told the priest why she had come to see him. Kate had been distant since she went off on Christmas Day, and Nell had her suspicions about this lad she had been seeing. She needed to share her concerns with someone, for Kate's good and her own sanity.

'There's something else, Father ... ' she

began. 'I might as well tell you.'

It was half an hour later when Nell left, with Father John calling on all the saints in heaven to save Nell's sister from the evils of the flesh.

31

Nell woke, surprised to have slept. Her talk with the priest had definitely helped, although she wished it hadn't been necessary. Her feet touching the cold floor, she pulled on her dressing gown and went into the living room, hoping that Kate had crept back in while she slept. But the bed hadn't been slept in. Nell closed her eyes in a silent prayer that nothing untoward had happened to her sister. If only she had Amy to talk to; she vowed to write back to her tonight.

Struggling to eat, Nell cut a slice of bread and spread it with marmalade. She made a mug of tea, then got herself washed and dressed for work.

Worry nagging at her, she worked mechanically all morning, smiling at her colleagues as if nothing was wrong. How could she tell anyone that her sister had gone missing? They would blame her.

She was glad she didn't bump into the supervisor and have to explain that her sister couldn't, after all, apply for the office junior position.

★ ★ ★

At lunch break, she ran most of the way until she reached Dominick Street. *Please*, she prayed, *let*

207

Kate be home. But as soon as she went into the room, she knew her sister hadn't been back, and her heart sank deeper. The place was freezing, and a shiver ran through her body.

Nell made a hot drink to warm herself, then noticed the door to Kate's wardrobe lying slightly open. When she pulled it open further, it was empty. Neither of them had many changes of clothes, but Kate's best frock and other stuff had gone. Nell looked underneath her bed; the suitcase was missing. Oh, dear God, surely she hadn't left without telling her? She scanned the room in search of a letter or a note, but there was nothing.

Anger coursed through her. 'Kate, how could you?' she screamed into the empty room, then picked up Kate's pillow and flung it across the bed.

There was nothing for it now but to strip Kate's bed. It would have to be done anyway, when Tommy came to move all their stuff to the new place.

As she pulled the sheet away from the straw mattress, an envelope floated to the floor. Picking it up, Nell sat on the bed. The envelope had the name *Michael* written across the front, and was covered in kisses. It was lightweight and sealed . . . and the urge to open it was strong. It might reveal some answers to the question of Kate's weird behaviour, but it wouldn't be right.

Why had Kate kept it under her mattress? Had she written the letter and then decided not to give it to this Michael? If only she knew what was going on in her sister's head. Had she failed

208

in her duty to look after her? A tear escaped down Nell's cheek. Did Kate really love this Michael? If he had rejected her, it would explain why she had now picked up with this other lad. Why had she not taken the letter with her? Had she left it so that Nell could see it? Nell sighed heavily. It would certainly explain a lot about her sister's behaviour of late.

Her hot drink forgotten, Nell got to her feet, her cold hands shaking. Thank God it was Friday and she would get to see Róisín at the weekend. If Kate had decided to go her own way, Róisín was all Nell had left to live for. She would concentrate her energy on getting her little sister well and home with her, where she belonged.

* * *

That evening, there was still no sign of Kate, and Nell wondered if she should get the Gardaí involved, but her gut feeling told her that her sister hadn't been abducted and she had gone wherever she was of her own free will.

She forced herself to eat the fish she had brought from the market, with mashed potato and mushy peas. Then, to stop herself from dwelling on her worries, she finished emptying the chest of drawers and wrapping the remaining cups and plates. The room now looked as bereft as she felt.

She needed to keep busy, so she made a few trips down to the cold hallway with what she could physically carry on her own. Later, she made more tea and then huddled by the fire, her thoughts straying to Liam. He would be leaving for London at the weekend, and she wondered what he would think of it. Was he already missing her? He had promised to write and tell her everything as soon as he got settled. But what if she never heard from him again? Half of her wished she had gone with him, and the other half couldn't wait to see Róisín and give her a big hug.

In the silence, she could hear every creak and movement of the old house, and she thought she heard footsteps on the stairs. She moved to the door to listen, but realised she had probably imagined it. If it were Kate, she would throw her arms around her and plead with her to come with her to the new house.

She was about to sit back down when she suddenly heard the stairs creak. Mr Scanlon had said he wouldn't collect any more rent from her until she was resettled, so a rap on the door startled her. Who could it be at this hour? No one had a key to the front door — apart from Kate herself, and Mr Scanlon.

She swallowed and tentatively walked back to the door, her heart racing. 'Who is it?' she called nervously.

'It's Pete. My dad's asked me to come and check if you need any help?'

'No. I'm grand, thanks.'

'Can you at least let me in? It's freezing.'

'I'm sorry, Pete. It's late, and I've an early start tomorrow.'

'I've brought empty boxes and brown wrapping paper to wrap your wall pictures.'

'Thank you. Just leave them at the door.'

It went quiet, and Nell's shoulders relaxed. 'Please, please go away,' she murmured.

She heard him shuffling his feet. 'Come on, Nell. If you don't want my help, that's fine. But I'm not going until I get a warm drink after coming all this way. It's the least you can do.'

What should she do? He was likely to keep knocking until she opened the door. And if his dad did send him, what would he think?

'Just a minute.' She checked she had enough milk, and put a light under the kettle. She wanted this hot drink to be over as quickly as possible so she could get rid of him. There was something about him that gave her the creeps.

She slid back the bolt and opened the door. With his shoulders hunched against the cold, he pushed his way past her, lugging two big boxes and old newspapers under his arm.

'For God's sake, Nell. It's not like you to be so inhospitable. It's cold enough to freeze brass monkeys.' He stomped across to the fire, rubbing his hands together.

He had on a woollen hat, scarf and military-style winter coat and boots. She'd never really looked closely at him before. He wasn't good-looking, not in the way Liam was. His bushy eyebrows hid his eyes, making it hard to read his expression.

Nell didn't reply or attempt to defend herself. She went into the scullery to make just one mug of tea with milk and brought it to the table.

He glanced around the room. 'I see you're all set to go, then. Where's your Kate?'

'She'll be back soon.' It was what she hoped and wanted to believe.

He wrapped his hands around the mug, then took a sip and made a face. 'Yuck, there's no sugar.'

'I don't have any.'

He put the tea back down. 'Look, Nell. We appear to have got off on the wrong foot before. I like you, and want to let you know that I might be going away. That's if there's no chance for you and me.'

The idea revolted her, but she didn't respond.

'Can I just ask if you're still courting?'

'Yes, I am, Pete. And now, if you'll excuse me, I still have things to do for the morning.'

She walked to the door and opened it. She could see by his face that he wasn't pleased, and she didn't want to antagonise him, so she added, 'Thanks for the boxes. It was good of you to think of us.'

He walked to the door. 'Well, if you change your mind.'

As soon as he was out on the landing, she closed the door quickly and pushed the bolt across. Her heart racing, she stood with her back to the door until she heard his heavy boots tramping down the stairs.

32

Kate had stayed the night at Teresa's. Her mam had glanced down at her case when she arrived, so Kate said she was going away to stay with an aunt for a few days but her train wasn't until the following morning. When the girls went upstairs, Teresa bribed her younger sister with a Mars Bar to leave them alone for a while.

'What are you up to, Kate Flynn?' she asked. 'You never said you had an aunt.'

'I don't. But listen, we're moving and I don't want to live with Nell.'

'But she's your sister. She's all you've got.' Teresa looked at Kate as if she was mad. 'Where will you go?'

They both sat on the bed together. 'I don't know yet, but no more education for me. I've signed up and I'm looking for a job.'

Teresa shook her head. 'Kate Flynn, you are impulsive, but I guess that's what I like about you. What if you don't get one? I'm in work only because my dad put a word in for me at the gas works.' She looked down at the floor. 'What's with the case?'

Kate turned to face her friend. 'Do you think I could stay with you just for a couple of nights?'

'Yea, of course you can. I'll have to let Ma know, though.' She stood up. 'What then?'

Kate ignored the question. 'I'm starving,' she

213

said instead. 'Can you get us anything to eat?'

'Look, Kate, I'll help you because we're friends, but I don't agree with what you're doing.' Teresa sat back down. 'What happened with that guy Michael?'

The mention of his name sent Kate's pulse racing. She lowered her head. 'He doesn't feel the same way as I do. He's got engaged to that girl we saw at the dance, Ophelia.'

'Where's she from?'

Kate shrugged. 'How do I know?'

'I'm sorry.' Teresa placed her hand on Kate's arm. 'Someone else will come along.'

'Get me something to eat, will you?' Kate smiled. 'And I'll tell you all about Jerry O'Shea.'

★　★　★

By Saturday morning, Kate's feet were sore traipsing around offices in the city with no luck. It was the same story everywhere; they didn't have any vacancies. Finally, she tried all the big shops and stores, but they didn't want her either. By then, she was fit to drop, and with only coppers in her purse she was glad to see Teresa waiting for her under Clery's clock. A shake of her head was all Teresa needed to know she hadn't been successful.

'Come on, I'll treat you to a tea and a bun.' Her friend ushered her inside the store.

Kate was beginning to wonder if she had been hasty in leaving home, but she wouldn't go crawling back and give Nell the satisfaction of knowing she'd failed.

When they were seated in the crowded cafe, with steaming cups of tea in front of them, Teresa said, 'You should forget that Jerry O'Shea and go to England instead. Your sister's boyfriend's gone. Maybe he could get you in somewhere?'

Kate made a face. 'I have thought about that, but with no qualifications . . . '

'There's plenty of jobs in England where you don't need certificates.' Teresa leant her elbow on the table. 'I'd come with you myself if I hadn't been so lucky in getting a job.'

'Dead-end jobs,' Kate replied dismissively.

'What do you mean?' Teresa sipped her tea, as Kate bit into her iced bun.

'I want better than that.'

'Well, stay and finish your exams, then,' her friend suggested. 'It'll give you more choice. Giving up is daft, if you ask me.'

'I didn't.' Kate pouted, then apologised.

Teresa smiled. 'Look, you can stay at ours for the weekend. Is that any help to you?'

Kate glanced up. 'Thanks, Teresa. That's grand. But what about your sister, and your mum and dad?'

'They're grand, so they are. We'll push the two beds together; there'll be plenty of room. But I'll have to warn you, my sister snores.'

Kate sighed. 'I don't deserve you as a friend.'

'You'd do the same for me, eh?'

Kate gave her a lopsided smile.

'Come on, let's get back.' Teresa stood up. 'If there's nothing much on the television tonight, we could go to the local picture house.'

On Monday morning, Kate thanked Teresa's parents for having her to stay, then caught the bus back to the city. The amount of people, including children, begging on the streets didn't surprise her. She saw nothing but poverty everywhere she looked. Up until now she had been protected from it all, but now she was one of the homeless.

She had intended joining the dole queue and signing on, but she'd forgotten the offices were closed for the New Year Bank Holiday. She'd have to come back and speak to a clerk about her situation later in the week. If she didn't get some money soon, she would not only be homeless but destitute.

There was no sign of Jerry hanging around, and she was glad to have more time to consider whether or not to take him up on his offer. In two weeks' time she would get a few shillings dole money, but that wouldn't get her far. And what would she do in the meantime?

She couldn't impose on Teresa's parents again, and she wanted to try everything before she went cap in hand to Jerry. Her conscience began to prick. Maybe she should go back and leave a scribbled note for Nell, just to let her know she was okay. She couldn't remember what day she said they were moving.

To ease her conscience, she walked back to Dominick Street. It was still early, and she might get there before Nell made any plans for the day. Kate's case was beginning to irritate her, banging against her legs as she walked. It wasn't heavy, and if she didn't need the few belongings she had she'd dump it somewhere.

She was halfway up the street when she saw the familiar sight of their furniture being loaded on to a horse and cart; Nell was passing boxes to the driver. To Kate's surprise, her eyes filled and a tear dropped on to her cold cheek. Her pride wouldn't allow her to go home now, so she immediately turned round and headed in the opposite direction.

She wasn't sure how she felt. Teresa had advised her to swallow her pride and go home, but she couldn't do it. Instead, she made her way back into town, then walked in the direction of Talbot Street and Jerry O'Shea's.

Her hands shook with a mixture of nerves and the cold as she knocked on his door. There was no reply. The curtains were partly drawn, and she peered through the grimy window. She couldn't see much and wondered if Jerry had done all he'd said he would to the place, or if he had just lied to her. If only she could get inside out of the cold, but the door was firmly locked.

Kate couldn't see the point in carrying her case any further, and placed it in the outside lavvy. Feeling hungry and tired, with her handbag slung across her shoulder, she made her way back to the tenement. Nell would be gone now, and she still had a key.

Making sure no one saw her, she let herself into the cold, silent hallway. As she made her way up the stairs, she felt a mouse brush against her legs. Shuddering, she tried the doors on each landing but they were all locked. But when she found the door to their room open, she hurried inside and bolted the door. The room was bare, and there was no sign that they had ever lived there.

The ash in the grate was still hot so she threw on a few sticks that lay about the hearth and crossed her fingers it would take. The scullery was also bare, apart from a pot of stewed tea. An envelope was stood up against it with her name written across it. She tore it open.

Kate,

I've written down the address where I've moved to in John's Lane.

Please, come and join me. Whatever's troubling you, we can work it out together. I've really missed you and hope you are all right.

Nell x

Kate's eyes filled with tears; angry tears. She scrunched the note tightly in her fist and threw it to the floor. She had hoped there might be money in the envelope, but no, Nell was too frugal to part with money. How did she think Kate was going to get there? She drank the remaining milk from the bottle, then moved back to the miserable fire and warmed her hands. A few sparks flew up the chimney.

She glanced around the stark room, taking in the paper peeling from the walls and ceiling.

From the day her ma died, this had never been home to Kate. Now that nothing of the family remained, it was what it was — a stark, damp, miserable room.

When the heat faded from the makeshift fire, she pulled her coat tighter around her thin body and made her way wearily back to Jerry's.

33

That morning, as she waited for Tommy to arrive with the cart, Nell kept a vigil for Kate. When her sister didn't put in an appearance, she ran into the church to say goodbye to Father John.

'You're off, then?' he asked.

Nell felt a lump form at the back of her throat and could only nod.

'Ah sure, happen Kate will come to her senses and follow you. If I get wind of anything, I'll come across and let you know.'

'Thanks, Father,' she replied and turned to leave.

'Don't neglect your Catholic upbringing,' he called, 'and I hope Róisín comes out of the hospital soon.'

Her emotions running high, she hurried into the church to light a candle and say a hurried prayer that Kate was somewhere safe.

Her worries were soon pushed to the back of her mind as she helped Amy's cousin load their belongings on to the cart. Everything went on easily, so there would be no need to return. Before finally leaving the room, she scribbled a note for Kate, then glanced around the empty room. Finally, she picked up her mother's wicker sewing basket. Inside, she fingered the many buttons, cottons and coloured threads, the odd remnants of wool, and needles and knitting pins. A warm tear wet her cheek and she dashed it away, then she carried the basket out of the room as if she was taking her mother with her. There was no need to lock the door, so she left it ajar.

She climbed up on to the cart next to Tommy, who pulled on the reins, and the horse went off at a trot. A cheerful soul, he chatted incessantly while Nell's mind gave her no rest. She felt a pang of regret and sadness to be making the journey across town without Kate and Róisín.

'You're as well out of the old tenement, Nell. Some of them aren't fit for animals, let alone human beings. Your Kate not with you today?' They moved across Capel Street Bridge with bus fumes blowing in their faces.

'No, she had to go somewhere,' she replied quickly. She knew by his face that Amy had filled him in on Kate's wanderings, but she left it at that.

The tenement was where she had been brought up, and she had to admit it had become shabby since most of the neighbours had moved out.

'What do you think they'll do with the building?' she asked.

'Luxury flats, is my guess. And they'll charge the earth for them as well.'

'I'd like to see that.'

'Oh, it will happen.'

When they reached her new home, Tommy pulled the reins tight to stop the horse. 'Here we are. Not a bad little place,' he said. 'You'll not be too far away from the city.'

Nell smiled and climbed down from the cart. To her surprise, Mr Scanlon was there waiting for her. 'Is everything okay?' she asked, her brow furrowed in concern.

'Sure, I thought I'd come over and give you a hand,' her landlord replied. 'Come on in while Tommy is untying the cart. Would you like to take a look upstairs?'

'Oh, yes please.'

She followed him up one flight of stairs. Three doors led off the landing and she stepped into each one in turn, excitement lifting her spirits. If only Kate was here to see it. She felt sure she would love it, too.

The landlord ran his hand over his face. 'Well, what do you think? Will it do you?'

Nell smiled. 'Yes, it's grand.'

'It's up to you if you want to double up and use one as a living room. The front room here is big enough to take two beds.' He shrugged. 'But it's up to yourselves how you arrange things.'

Nell swallowed. It was perfect, but she still had no idea how much all this was going to cost, and now that she had seen the place she was frightened to ask. The room at the back overlooked an unkempt garden.

'I'm afraid none of my tenants are gardeners,' he said when he saw her glance outside.

Nell smiled, then followed him into the small kitchen. It had fitted cupboards and a Formica table and four chairs, a black gas cooker, and a small sink with running water. What a godsend, she thought.

'This gadget is one of them new geysers. It heats the water,' he explained.

'It's lovely, Mr Scanlon, but — '

She was interrupted by Tommy, edging along the landing with one of the bedheads. 'Where would you like me to put this, Nell?'

'Can you put both beds in the larger room, Tommy, and the table and chairs in the other, please? I'll come and help you with the boxes.'

'Not a bit of it. I can manage well enough.'

'Are you sure?'

Tommy laughed. 'It'll be a doddle compared to all them stairs at the tenement.'

Nell and the landlord moved back into the small kitchenette.

'How about a cuppa to celebrate you moving in, Nell?' he said.

'Tea!' She looked around. She couldn't see how he was going to make tea without a kettle or even a saucepan to boil water. 'But how?'

'Sit down, please, Nell. I brought a flask of tea and a few mugs, and picked up a pint of milk from the shop.' He opened a shopping bag on the counter. 'So,' he smiled, 'how do you like your tea, Nell?'

'As it comes, thanks.' Truth be known, she could murder a cup and now was as good a time as any.

Pouring hot tea from the flask, he looked at Nell. 'Your sister's not with you, then? Is she coming over later?'

She wasn't sure what to say as she reached for the mug he offered her. If she told him the truth, he might think twice about letting her rent the place on her own. Eventually, she replied, 'She's got a few things to do first.'

'Well, get that down you. Do you take sugar?'

'Please, if you have some.'

Smiling, he took a small bag from his inside pocket and held it up. 'I've come prepared.'

As Tommy came upstairs with a pile of boxes, he called to him, 'There's a cuppa here for you, Tommy, when you're done. If you need a hand, just give us a shout.'

Nell sipped the tea, amazed at how nice it tasted from a flask. She hadn't had time to make herself one earlier; her mind was still on Kate and where she had spent the last few nights.

'Is everything all right, Nell, only you . . . well, seem a little distracted. You are happy to move in?'

She straightened her shoulders. 'Oh, yes. I'm sorry. I was miles away. It will be strange at first, having spent so many years in Dominick Street. Memories, you know?'

'Of course. I know. But I guess you'll be wanting to know about the rent.'

Now he had mentioned it, it saved her the embarrassment of having to ask.

'How about we say you pay me the same as you did at the tenement?'

Nell leant forward and put her mug on the table. 'I don't want any favours, Mr Scanlon. I'll pay the going rate.'

He nodded. 'That's it. It's what I'm prepared to let you have it for.'

She wasn't sure how to respond.

'Look, Nell, I'm not one of them unscrupulous landlords. I'm sure your mother told you that.'

That was true. Mr Scanlon had always treated

224

them fairly, but this place was so much better than the tenement, and Nell didn't want to feel indebted to him in any way.

'I just want to see you and your sisters all right, Nell,' he explained. 'Your parents always paid the rent on time, not like some others that were always falling behind.'

Nell smiled, unable to hide her relief. 'I don't know what to say, but thank you. Of course it's lovely.'

Tommy tapped the door. 'All done. Is that cuppa still going? I've a thirst like an elephant.'

Despite the banter she exchanged with the two men, Nell's heart was heavy, and she felt very much alone when they'd left. She wandered from room to room, emptied a couple of boxes, and made the beds. But all the while she couldn't stop thinking about Kate, and how much her sister had changed since their mother's death.

34

Starved and cold through, Kate knocked once and the door flew open. Jerry stood in front of her, grinning broadly.

'I thought you'd be back. You're white as a ghost. Come in.' He stood aside to allow her access.

She could smell fresh paint as she stepped into the untidy kitchen, and when she walked into the room the first thing that caught her eye was the glowing fire in the grate. Jerry pulled over a chair and told her to sit and get warm. She hated being dependent on him, but now that she had cut herself off from Nell, she had no other choice.

He poured her a mug of tea, stirred in sugar, and passed it to her. She wrapped her hands around the warm drink and sipped. Then he made her a slice of toast and marmalade.

As feeling returned to her hands, and the glow of the fire warmed her face, she finally found her voice. 'What do you mean, you knew I'd be back?'

He smirked. 'Well, I found your suitcase outside in the lavvy.'

She glanced around.

'I've put it in the bedroom.'

She got to her feet and went into the bedroom that led from the living room. It was nothing special: a bed, with a crumpled yellow candlewick bedspread, none too clean, and one pillow; a wardrobe and a small chest of drawers. The walls had been painted yellow. When she turned round, he was right behind her.

'Do you like it?'

It was better than sleeping on the street, and he had clearly made an effort, but she had no intention of sleeping in that bed with him.

'You'll need to open a window to get rid of the smell,' was all she said.

He sat on the bed and patted it for her to sit next to him, but Kate turned on her heel and walked back to the fire. After a few minutes, Jerry followed, then pulled a chair over and sat next to her.

'You're not going to mess me about, are you?' he asked.

'That depends on what you mean?' She shrugged. 'For one thing, I'm not sleeping in that bed with you.'

She noted his jaw drop. 'Well, where are you going to sleep?'

'In here, on the floor.'

'Don't be daft.'

She glowered at him. 'Look, Jerry, I'm grateful. Really I am.'

He made a face. 'Well, that's something, I suppose.'

'One other thing, Jerry. If this arrangement works, I want you to know that I won't be subservient in any way. We'll share the cleaning and cooking — and you'll have to do your own washing.'

He laughed. 'What arrangement? I thought you liked me.'

'I do. But you have to give me time.' She didn't want him to throw her out. But liking him didn't mean she would entertain doing his washing.

'So, what do I get out of helping you?'

'You'll have to wait and see, won't you?' She began to button her coat. 'But if you'd rather I left . . .'

'No, no,' he replied quickly, 'of course not. This is frustrating, Kate. I don't know where I stand with you.'

'Don't forget, Jerry, I'm educated and I can pick up a reference whenever I need to. I still have something to show an employer.'

'Well, I wish you luck with that. Reference or no reference, it won't get you a job.'

'We'll see.' She was determined not to let him get the better of her.

'Did you sign on this morning, then?' he asked.

She nodded. 'For all the good it did me. The stupid woman asked me to fill in another form. And was I married, and did I have any dependents? It's degrading what you have to go through for a few bob.'

'It's just how the system works.' He cleared his throat. 'Have you given any more thought to working at the pub?'

She bit her bottom lip. She wasn't going down that road, not until she had explored other avenues first. She wanted her independence, and if she did what Jerry wanted, it would only tie her in with him all the more. Anyway, she still hadn't given up on her quest to find work.

'Pub work is not for me, Jerry.'

He sighed. 'Look, Kate. If we're going to keep this place, we need money coming in.'

'Yes, I know that, Jerry. I'm not dumb. How much is the rent?'

'Twelve and sixpence.'

'And how much dole are you drawing?'

'Fifteen bob.'

She paused briefly. 'Two and six won't buy much food.'

He nodded. 'That's what I'm saying. I want to be able to take you out from time to time, and I won't be going without my nights down the pub. Don't you see, Kate? I'll be there to keep an eye on you. You've no idea what some of the punters can be like.'

She flicked her hair to one side. 'I can look after myself. Besides, I need another week to look around. If nothing comes up, then I'll think about it.'

'You're a fussy little madam, aren't you?'

'You'd better believe it. I intend to pay my way, but not in the way you're thinking.'

He put up his hands in mock surrender. 'Okay, okay. You win. We'll see how things go.' He smiled. 'I like you. Otherwise I wouldn't put up with your demands.'

'You agree, then?'

He ran his hand over his unshaven face. 'Hmm, but in no time at all, I'll grow on you and you won't be able to resist me. And once we have money rolling in, we can rent one of the latest televisions. And you can fix the place up how you like.'

She had to hand it to him, he was trying. But despite the fact that she was dependent on him for shelter, she wasn't going to make things easy for him. And she didn't feel anything but friendship for him. He didn't make her face go red and her heart race in the way Michael had by just walking next to him.

He stood up. 'Right, I bet you're still hungry. I'll nip out to the shop and pick up some food. Is there anything you fancy?'

'Food,' she smiled back. 'I'm not bothered.'

'Okay, you fill the kettle and get out the mugs. I won't be a tick.'

★　★　★

It was dark outside and there was no sign of Jerry. Kate switched on the light and immediately heard the bulb ping. She searched around for a candle, and eventually found matches in a kitchen drawer that was littered with what looked like unpaid bills. She lit the stub of a candle in a cup on the kitchen window sill, then boiled the aluminium kettle for the third time and made herself yet another mug of tea. The milk was running out. Apart from the toast earlier, she hadn't eaten all day. What could possibly be keeping him?

She returned to the now ashy fire and looked around for more wood to keep it going, but there wasn't any. Kate went outside but there was no firewood there, either. After using the toilet, she came back in. Her only consolation was that she was inside, as the night had turned bitter.

Where was Jerry? Had he met someone and gone off somewhere? She wouldn't put it past him. As she huddled over the fading embers, the sudden realisation of what she was getting herself into dawned, and she once again regretted her decision not to stay with her sister.

By eleven o'clock — cold and hungry — she had no choice but to lock the door and go to bed. She lay on the bed fully dressed and eventually fell asleep, only to be woken by a loud banging on the back door. It took her a few minutes to realise where she was, before she got out of the bed and went into the kitchen. She could hear Jerry shouting and swearing at her to open the door, and it was obvious by his aggressive tone that he was well and truly drunk.

She unlocked the door and he staggered inside, slumping heavily into the old armchair.

He glared up at her. 'Why'd you lock the door?'

'Why do you think?' she snapped. 'I didn't know if you were coming back.'

'Of course I was bloody well coming back.'

This was a side to Jerry she hadn't witnessed before. She remained standing, her hands deep inside the pockets of her coat. 'You went out for food, remember?'

'Yeah, I bumped into O'Brien . . . sure, and he dragged me . . . into the pub for a few jars. He . . . he knows where . . . there's plenty of work.' He made a grab for her.

She flinched and moved away. 'You stink of Guinness. Have you got any coffee?' She moved into the kitchen, where she found tea but no

231

coffee. With the remains of the milk, she made him a cup of tea, but by the time she brought it in he was snoring his head off.

She wrapped her cold hands around the mug and sipped until the dark brown liquid was gone. This wasn't what she had expected, but he was the only friend she had right now. Frustrated tears ran down her face as she set the cup down, then went back into the bedroom, closing and locking the door behind her.

35

Nell lay awake listening to the different sounds in the house. She heard the young couple below arriving home late, and hoped it might be Kate. When she finally drifted off, she slept soundly, having spent the rest of Monday sorting out the rooms and putting everything in its place.

Tommy had kindly put the heavy stuff where she had instructed him to, and she hoped her sister would be happy with the arrangement when she finally came home.

She had ironed her work clothes for the following morning, and made a plan to visit Róisín after work.

With all the fuss of moving she'd forgotten to get any groceries, and made do with bread and cheese and several cups of tea to keep her going. Having hot water on tap was a godsend, and she decided to worry about the bill later.

★　★　★

When she arrived at the hospital, the youngster looked fine on the surface and appeared to be happy. She was now allowed to sit out at the side of the bed and talk to the other children. She held up her arms when she saw Nell and they hugged.

'How've you been, pet?'

'We played Snakes and Ladders this morning.

I kept sliding down the long snake.'

Nell smiled. 'How is the pain in your legs?'

'It's okay but, Nell, can I come home soon?'

'I hope so, darling.'

Róisín glanced back up the ward. 'Where's Kate?'

Nell pulled a chair over and sat down next to her. 'You know we moved yesterday, and there's still so much to do. Kate sends you her love.' She hated lying to the child, but what was the point of upsetting her when Kate might be home tomorrow? 'I'm sure you'll love the new place, Róisín. We have hot water and a separate kitchen for cooking. And when you're well enough to come home, you can sleep in my bed.'

Her little sister beamed. 'Oh, I want to see it, Nell. Can you have a word with Matron? She might let me. Please, Nell.'

'Okay, I'll have a word with her before I leave.'

★   ★   ★

The Matron was firm with her response.

'The child is not ready to leave the care of the hospital yet, you should know that, and any disruption from the routine could set her back.'

Nell felt a knot twist in her stomach. 'How long will it be before she can leave hospital?'

Matron opened a file in front of her, glanced at the contents, then looked up. 'The doctor has recommended she be sent to the Cappagh Sanatorium for sick children, to continue her

234

treatment . . . ' The woman paused. 'He will review her again in six weeks, after she's settled in.'

'Six weeks!'

The Matron nodded. 'I'm afraid Róisín's heart has been damaged. She'll never be strong.'

Nell knew that, but she had hoped her sister wouldn't have to go into a sanatorium. The realisation that Róisín was sicker than she had first thought concerned her and she swallowed to hide her distress. 'When . . . when will she be moved?'

Matron consulted her file again. 'She's a very fortunate little girl. It looks like there's a bed available for her immediately. She'll be moved in the morning.'

Nell nodded, but her mind was a jumble of thoughts. Cappagh! That was at least five miles away, and she wondered how Róisín would take the news.

'Are the visiting hours flexible?' she asked.

'Weekends and evenings only, I believe, and strictly by appointment. She'll attend school during the week, so her learning won't be affected.'

Well, that was good news, as Nell had been worried that Róisín had had little schooling since she took ill, but she couldn't help the sadness that crept over her. 'Thanks for being frank, Matron.'

'Try not to worry,' the woman replied, her tone a little gentler. 'These places have amazing healing powers — the fresh air, you know?'

Nell nodded. That was easier said than done.

As Nell moved towards the door, Matron turned to face her. 'Miss Flynn. It might be best if you leave the staff nurse to explain to the child. We don't want her getting upset before the move.' She smiled kindly. 'Your sister will get better, you know. Rheumatic fever takes time. Try and stay positive.'

'Thank you, Matron.'

As Nell passed Róisín's ward, she glanced in and noticed her little sister was back in bed and appeared to be asleep. Nell walked back to John's Lane with a heavy heart. She couldn't shift the gloomy feeling that filled her. Her chances of joining Liam in England were now slimmer, to say the least.

★　★　★

Nell made a pot of tea and crunched the last apple she had been saving for Kate. Although she didn't have much in the way of food, the house was warm; she had electricity and hot water, as well as an electric fire that fitted into the open grate. It was luxury after their life in the tenement, but she couldn't shake off the sadness that hung over her.

Stepping out of her shoes, she tucked her legs up under her and played with the fine gold cross and chain Liam had bought her at Christmas, before he went away. She wondered if he had arrived in London, and how he would settle without her. She couldn't wait to hear all his news. Idly, she thumbed through a copy of last week's *Woman's Own*, left behind by the previous tenants, when suddenly she was overwhelmed by loneliness and she began to cry. It was something she hadn't done in a while, but shedding tears released the bitter resentment she felt at the way things had turned out. Loud sobs wracked her body, and she hoped the people who lived beneath her couldn't hear her distress.

After a while, she blew her nose and had just got to her feet when she heard footsteps on the stairs. Her heart raced. Hoping it was Kate, she threw open the door.

'I'm sorry. Have I called at a difficult time?' Her landlord was holding a box with vegetables, cereal, milk and bread in front of him.

'No, no, of course not. Come in, Mr Scanlon.'

He walked in behind her and placed the box on the kitchen table. 'I bought too much on Friday and, as Pete's gone, I won't use it all.'

'Gone! What do you mean?'

'He's gone to England to make his fortune,' he chuckled.

'Really!' She tried not to sound too pleased, but she had never taken to the landlord's son. 'Soon, we won't have any young people left in the country.'

He nodded.

She glanced again at the groceries. 'Are you sure you can spare all this?'

'Sure, what am I to do with it?'

'Well, I guess you'd like a cup of tea, so,' Nell said.

He sat at the table. 'Did you sleep last night?'

'It felt strange.'

'Aye, you'll get used to it.' He glanced around. 'No Kate?'

'Kate likes to please herself, Mr Scanlon.'

When the tea was ready, Nell brought it to the table and opened a packet of fig rolls she had brought home from the factory.

'Me favourites.' He bit into one and then supped his tea. 'How did you find Róisín?'

Nell sat opposite him, leaning her elbow on the table. 'Well, on the surface, she looked all right, but they're sending her to a sanatorium for more treatment.'

'Well, sure that's a step in the right direction.'

'Is it?' She glanced up. 'But isn't it where they send really sick people and children?'

'Yes, but I've known children recover very well from a stay at one of these places. Which one is it?'

'Cappagh! She'll be there for some time.'

'Well sure, you'll see a difference in no time.'

'I hope so, I really do, Mr Scanlon,' she replied. Glad to share her concerns with someone.

'Have you heard from your young man yet?' he asked.

'It's early days, and Liam's hardly settled in yet. We were planning to follow him over, but that's not possible now.'

Her landlord nodded. 'In the meantime, you need to stop worrying and get out a bit more. You're a young woman and on your own too much.'

'Well, that's more difficult now, Mr Scanlon, and by the time I pay the bills . . . ' She paused.

238

'Once Kate finds work, we'll be fine.' She played with her teaspoon, clinking it against the side of her cup.

'Nell, why don't you drop the Mr Scanlon and call me Joe? Sure, we've known each other a long time.'

'Oh, I couldn't do that, Mr Scanlon. It's hard to change old habits.'

He stood slowly and scraped back his chair. 'Well, I'll be off, then. Would you be offended if I was to call in now and then, apart from rent night? Just to make sure you are all right?'

Nell wasn't sure how to respond. Without Kate and Róisín, she was lonely. And talking to another adult might be just what she needed. 'Thanks,' she said. 'That would be nice.'

36

Kate woke to the sound of a plane overhead. She put on an extra jumper, brushed her hair and then tied it back. She pulled on her coat, wrapped her scarf around her neck and, picking up her case, crept into the room where Jerry was still asleep, his breathing easy, his upper body hanging over the arm of the chair. She held her breath, as if to breathe would wake him. Quietly turning the key in the back door, she let herself out. In the entrance she manoeuvred around Jerry's motorbike and hurried out into the cold, deserted streets. She didn't know what time it was, but the sky was getting light. No one else was up this early, and she thought about Nell, all safe and warm in her new home.

With hindsight, Kate wished she hadn't been so hasty. Jerry had let her down big time, and if last night was an example of how he would treat her she wasn't having any part of it. She kept glancing over her shoulder as she hurried along.

Music blared out from a room above a shop, and the shadowy figure of a man stood in the doorway. He moved into the light, his shoulders hunched against the cold, and glanced down at her case. 'If you're going for the ferry, sweetheart, you're going in the wrong direction. The docks is that way,' he pointed.

Kate shook her head.

'You look frozen, love. Why don't you come in

for a bit and get a warm?'

Ignoring his advances, she walked faster. The sooner she got rid of her case and found something less conspicuous the better. She turned down Marlborough Street. The Pro-Cathedral loomed in front of her, flanked by large protective columns. It was too early for the heavy brown doors to be open, and she perched on her case by the front entrance to wait.

She should go home, but she couldn't bring herself to admit defeat to Nell, who might not welcome her. Her feet were numb and she felt faint from hunger.

Huddled into herself, her eyes closed, the stillness around her was suddenly punctuated by someone shouting abuse at her. An older woman, dressed in rags, her grey hair tangled, reared up from behind a recess and threw her grubby blanket aside, then glowered at Kate.

'Be on your way, girlie. This is my patch. Now feck off.'

Kate got to her feet and, without a word, went round to the other side of the church wall, where she sheltered under the canopy of a side doorway. The woman, still shouting abuse, lay back down under a mountain of old coats.

Gulls flew overhead, their harsh piercing cry breaking the silence. They came inland with the trawlers at this time of day; they were hungry, like her, and looking for scraps. It started to rain, and Kate brought her legs up under her. Her head and belly ached.

She thought of her mam — a proud woman who would turn in her grave to see her in this state — and the quarrel they'd had about her staying on at school. Wishing now that she had listened and finished her exams, she recalled her mother saying, over and over, to herself and Nell, 'I want youse to be educated so you can have a future.' She had insisted they all went to the convent school, even though she had struggled to buy their uniforms. 'Oh, Ma, why do I keep making the wrong decisions?' Aware that her ma wasn't going to give her the answer, she prayed for the doors to open so she could get inside before she died of the cold and starvation.

Footsteps, voices, and coins falling on to the step next to her, told her people were arriving for mass and she got to her feet. Light-headed, she swayed and dropped to the ground, hitting her head.

When she came to, it took her a few seconds to realise she was in the presbytery. She sat forward on a chair. A woman in a tweed coat and headscarf had just finished wrapping a bandage around her head, and Kate winced.

'How are you feeling now?' the woman asked.

'I'm fine, thank you.'

The woman stood back. 'You're not like the usual beggars we find on the church doorstep.' She picked up Kate's case and handed it to her. 'I guess you're heading for the boat?'

'No, I'm not. And I'm not a beggar. I was on my way to visit my sister at the fever hospital when I felt giddy and sat down outside the church to rest.' She told the first lie that came to mind.

'I see.' The woman gave her a quizzical look. 'I

hope you don't have a wasted journey. Few come out alive from that place.'

Kate took a sharp intake of breath at the woman's remark, then gripped her stomach.

'Haven't you eaten?'

'I didn't have time. Can I have more water, please?'

'Look, wait here and I'll get you a hot drink, then you can be on your way. And don't steal nothing, do you hear me?'

Kate was hurt. Did the woman think she'd steal the candlesticks? A dish with money sat on the counter; Kate felt the woman had left it there to tempt her.

* * *

A few minutes later, Kate hugged a warm mug of tea as she crunched several Marietta biscuits. The woman hovered around as she did so.

Once the feeling returned to her hands, Kate stood up. 'Thanks, I'll be on my way.' She placed the empty mug on the counter.

The woman snatched it up and rubbed at the offending mark. 'Well, don't forget this.' She lifted the few coppers and a silver sixpence from a side table, passing them to Kate. 'It must have fallen from your pocket when you fell. If you hurry, you'll be in time for the next mass.'

Kate thought she ought to go in and thank God for her good fortune, but the woman's condescending attitude was everything she disliked about the Church. Instead, she walked away, fingering the cold coins inside her pocket.

The city was coming to life now, with pedestrians hurrying towards their destinations. Carts and horses clopped their way down O'Connell Street, past the closed shops. It was bitterly cold as she walked along Henry Street and down Moore Street, where she knew she'd find fruit left behind from the previous day; but the smell of rotten vegetables made her gag. She picked up a squashed orange and squeezed the juice into her mouth, hoping no one would see her. A plump brown rat ran from one side of the street to the other, sending a shiver through her.

Was this what her life had become, a beggar on the streets? A tear rolled down her face and she dashed it away with her hand, then she bit into the good side of an apple and sat in a shop doorway. It was a long wait for the first bus to Cabra where she was sure her friend, Teresa, would find her something proper to eat and give her a bed for the night.

37

On Wednesday morning, Nell phoned the sanatorium and was told that Róisín had settled in and was comfortable. At work she struggled to stay focused, and came home at lunch-time to find two letters for her lying on the mat. She recognised Liam's handwriting immediately; the other letter was from Amy. Holding Liam's close to her heart, she made tea, then sat down to read Amy's letter first, saving Liam's for later.

Dear Nell,

How's things? I hope Kate has settled down and is behaving herself. And how is poor Róisín? Have they said yet when she will be home?

We are settling in here, although I miss the tenement and the neighbours. It's not the same on a big housing estate. Some of them are stuck-up and wouldn't give you the time of day. Too busy polishing the brasses and cutting the lawn. But our next-door neighbour, Mrs Cooney, is friendly enough. Give you a cup of sugar, she would, if you ran short, more than I can say for the rest of them. The kids love it, though, and drive me mad running up and down the wooden stairs and in and out of the rooms on bare floorboards. Sure, I'll be glad when the novelty wears off, so I will. Not sure when, if ever, we'll be able to afford lino to cover all the rooms.

I'd love you to come and visit us, but I expect you're busy moving and visiting Róisín. Give her a kiss from me when next you visit.

Don't forget to write back and tell me all the news.

Love,
Amy

Nell missed Amy. She used the back of her hand to wipe away a tear that was sliding down her face. How nice it would be to visit her friend. But apart from the money, where would she find the time?

She made herself toast and jam and crunched one of the apples she had bought from a stall in Moore Street on the way home. Then, her fingers trembling and her heart almost bursting out of her chest, she carefully slit open Liam's letter.

Dear Nell,

This letter is brief, as I know you'll be wondering. I arrived okay and am settling into a well-equipped bed-sitting room. Bathroom and toilet upstairs. It's only a stone's throw from the factory. I've started work alongside three other chaps. I miss you like mad. Last night I went to the pub with *the lads, otherwise I'd be sitting in alone, thinking of you and driving myself insane.*

I'm determined to save as much as I can so that you, Róisín and Kate can join me. It can't happen soon enough.

Love and kisses,
Liam x

Nell smiled, kissed the letter, then folded it back in its creases and placed it in the envelope, bringing it to her lips, too. She'd write to him that evening, after work. Choking back a tear, she put both letters into her bag, used the convenience, and hurried back to the factory.

★   ★   ★

Having spent the night at Teresa's, Kate joined the dole queue and went through the motions of signing on. She pleaded poverty, along with the masses, but received the same response. 'After you've signed on for two weeks, we'll review your situation again. Next.'

Kate had no choice but to walk away empty-handed. By the time another week passed, she could be dead from starvation. But by the snooty look on the clerk's face, she clearly didn't think that was her problem.

Kate sighed wearily. Maybe she should go home. See what kind of reception she got. She could build up her strength there, continue to sign on, and look for work. Despite how wretched she felt, when she glanced down at her untidy appearance, her pride stopped her.

As she left the building, she almost collided with Jerry. Kate quickly turned away, but he took hold of her arm.

'Let go of me,' she hissed.

'Not until you explain to me why you went off without a word. You can't mess me about, Kate.'

'You've got a nerve. You showed your true colours on Monday night, and I don't want any part of it.' She shrugged him off. 'Now, leave me alone, or I'll call a garda.'

He smirked. 'Go ahead. They'll take one look at you and tell you they're not interested in domestic squabbles.'

That, at least, was true. Kate knew the Gardaí never interfered in fights in and around the tenements, unless someone got murdered.

'Look. Watch my bike, will you? I'll only be a few minutes and we can go somewhere and talk. Give us a chance to explain . . . please.'

Before she could think of an excuse, he had gone inside the building. Kate stood next to the black and silver bike, running her hand over the shiny petrol tank. He certainly kept it clean, and he always had money to buy petrol. Sober, Jerry was definitely a charmer, but she didn't have any romantic feelings for him, and for that she was glad. Michael had spoiled her for anyone else. But he was in love with Ophelia. For all she knew, they could already be planning their wedding. She had to know if there was the tiniest chance of him changing his mind. If only she knew where The Storms were playing next, she could go and see Michael play, maybe talk to him.

As she was daydreaming, Jerry came out. 'Come on,' he said, 'I'll buy you a hot drink. You look cold.'

It was an offer she couldn't afford to turn down. On Monday night, he hadn't cared that she was starving while he spent money on drink. She certainly wasn't going to forget that.

He pushed his bike until he came to O'Connell Street, where he parked it up and paid the attendant. Then, taking her arm, he crossed the street into the nearest tea shop. It was still early, and there was no one else inside. Taking a seat at one of the plastic tables, he ordered her a hot cocoa and an iced bun, and tea for himself. He sat quietly as she devoured the cake.

'Kate, I'm truly sorry about that night. How was I to know that O'Brien was lying? He said he knew where there was work, and after a few jars he admitted the work was in Birmingham. Say you'll forgive me, and we can start again.'

She didn't speak. Keeping her anger under wraps, she stayed silent until she had finished eating. 'What kind of idiot do you take me for? I might be down on my luck, Jerry, but that doesn't mean I'm prepared to accept the crumbs you offer me.'

Glancing around him, he leant in close. 'So, what then, Kate? You've obviously not gone back to your sister's. Where are you sleeping tonight?'

She glared at him. 'Where I slept last night.' She went to get up.

But he pressed her to sit. 'Kate, come on. I'll change. I promise.'

She glanced away.

'Let's try again, and if it doesn't work and you want to go, I'll not stand in your way,' he went on. 'What do you say?' He dug into his pocket. 'Here, go downtown and get yourself something nice. Come back later and I'll have a meal ready for you. Come on. You know you want to.'

No, she didn't want to, but the one shilling and sixpence he had put down in front of her was tempting. She snatched it up. 'Okay,' she said reluctantly. 'But I have to pick up my case.'

'I won't let you down again, I promise.'

Then, as they left, Kate watched him walk away, his hands deep inside his jacket pockets, and she knew exactly where he would go as soon as the pubs opened.

Kate took a stroll down Henry Street. As she passed the shop she had gone into with Michael to have his guitar string replaced, she wondered where he was and what he was doing. No doubt he was at work. Men like Michael would never be out of work, despite the recession. Men like Jerry, on the other hand, would never work if they knew they could get by without it.

She didn't want to end up like Jerry, and vowed to keep looking until she was one of the employed working class. But she couldn't do that looking as she did. Her mind made up, she decided she would go home, see if Nell would help her to get back on her feet, then find a job. She didn't want to be dependent on a man she knew could never give her the security she craved. And as for Jerry O'Shea, she had no intention of ever going back to him.

38

Kate spent the next hour window-shopping, then went into Woolworths, where she bought a warm headscarf before going to pick up her case. Teresa's mother insisted she had a bowl of stew before she left. It tasted delicious, unlike the poorhouse stew that had a peculiar odour you could smell streets away.

She felt awkward carrying a suitcase through the streets when most people doing so were heading for the ferry and a new life in England. Having made her mind up to find Nell at the new address, she caught a bus in O'Connell Street that took her along Dame Street into Lord Edward Street. Here she got off and cut down a side street next to Christ Church, a medieval church of particular interest in the history books.

She walked towards John's Lane, hoping that Nell was home from the biscuit factory. She was in desperate need of a good wash and a change of clothes. She was also hungry and tired, and missing her own bed, despite the lumpy horsehair mattress. Unsure of the reception she might receive from Nell, though, she was decidedly nervous.

There was no response to her first knock, and she stood staring at the black door, willing it to open. When it didn't, she peered through the window. The net curtain twitched. She knocked again. The door opened, and a young man of about eighteen stood for a few seconds staring at Kate.

'I'm sorry,' she said. 'I must have the wrong address.' She was about to move off.

'Who is it you're looking for?'

'My sister, Nell Flynn. I thought she moved into number sixteen.'

'This is eighteen,' explained the boy. 'I think someone recently moved in next door, you could try there.' She saw the colour rise up his neck and brighten his pale face. He looked posh in cords and a cable-knit crew-neck jumper.

'Thank you.' Smiling, she moved to the blue door at number 16, and again she had to knock twice before it was answered by a young man.

'Yes, can I help you?' He glanced down at her case. 'The rooms upstairs have already been taken . . . if . . . '

'I'm looking for my sister, Nell. Nell Flynn.'

'Oh, the young lady upstairs. I think I heard her come in. You can go straight up.'

Kate slipped past him and hurried up the stairs. She tapped the door. The wireless was on. Nell always listened to the wireless; she said it made her feel less lonely. She knocked louder, and the door flew open. Nell's eyebrows shot upwards and she stood back.

'Kate, oh, Kate. Is it really you? I've been so worried.' She took her sister's case and ushered her inside.

'Can I stay with you for a few nights?' Kate's eyes flicked around the place.

'Well, of course, you silly goose. It's your home, too.' Nell made to hug her.

But Kate shifted sideways. 'What have you done with my bed?'

Nell opened the bedroom door and showed her inside. 'It's in here, Kate, next to mine. We have two rooms, plus a proper kitchen, come and have a look.' She pulled Kate behind her into the kitchenette. 'Sit down. I'll make you something to eat. I'm sure you're hungry.'

'Thanks. I could murder a cup of tea.'

The sisters sat opposite each other, sipping their hot drinks.

'Do you like the place, Kate?'

'Anywhere has to be better than the tenement.'

Nell lowered her head. 'Yes, I suppose so. How have you been?'

'Okay, I guess. I've been looking for work and I've signed on the dole, but I've not received a penny yet.'

'That's because you've not worked before and have no credits. Are you happy for us to share a bedroom, only if you like?'

'No, it's fine. You've done a good job.' Kate stood up and opened the cupboards. The food was sparse. 'How much is Scanlon charging you for this?'

'The rent's the same. It's for both of us, and Róisín when she comes home.'

'The same! Well, that's good of him.' She sat back down. 'How is Róisín?'

Nell sniffed. 'She's gone to a sanatorium for her health.'

Kate kicked off her shoes and crossed her legs. 'How long is that going to take?'

'I don't know, Kate. I honestly don't know.'

254

For the next few days, Kate appeared to settle down. While Nell was at work, she took advantage of the hot water to wash her hair and some undergarments. Nell's sense of relief at having her back stopped her from asking too many questions, though she was curious to know where Kate had spent her time away. Kate made no effort to enlighten her, and at times Nell felt like she was walking on eggshells around her sister, frightened of upsetting her in case she took off again.

When Mr Scanlon called for the rent, he made a special fuss when he saw Kate was back. 'Ah, sure it's grand to see you both together again. I hope you'll be happy here.'

Kate's response was a nod of her head. Nell offered him tea, after which he left.

'You could have at least shown some gratitude,' she told Kate. 'If it weren't for Mr Scanlon, we might not have a roof over our heads.'

Kate shrugged with disinterest. 'Well, he's not doing us any special favours. He's getting his rent, isn't he?'

'Not for much longer, he won't be.'

Kate glared at Nell. 'What do you mean?'

'Well, unless you start putting some money in the pot, I can only pay the rent by foregoing decent food and heating, which is what I'm doing.'

'Oh, don't start. I'll be getting dole money soon. And,' Kate added, 'I'm walking my feet off looking for work.'

'You missed out on a job at the biscuit factory that would have brought in good money,' Nell couldn't resist reminding her.

In response, Kate sulked for the remainder of the day.

★ ★ ★

One morning, Nell was at the biscuit factory, leaving Kate to her own devices. When she finally unravelled herself from the bed, there was no milk on the kitchen table. She pulled on her coat and went out to buy some. She didn't have to go far, and on her return she bumped into the young man from next door. He had a satchel under his arm.

'Hello, again,' he said. 'I gather you found your sister?' His face reddened and he glanced down at his brown polished shoes.

Kate took advantage of his awkwardness. 'Yes. So, I found her, then.' She shifted the milk into her other hand. 'Do you have a name?'

'I'm William Brennan. What's yours?' He offered his hand.

Kate took it; it felt cold. She could smell his musky aftershave. 'Kate Flynn. What do you do for fun around here, then?'

'Well, I'm . . . I'm studying for a diploma in social history. I want to teach, so I don't have time to go out much.'

'Well, good luck. A lot of good it'll do you in this country.' She turned away, leaving him standing.

Kate was secretly jealous. She resented having

to abandon her own studies. She could have done better; she knew it, and her teachers had told her that she had the ability to go far. But she had been so cheesed off with Nell taking over and nagging her to take responsibility that she'd acted without thinking. And Jerry O'Shea hadn't helped, with his empty promises.

Back in the kitchen, she made toast and then spread it with strawberry jam, wishing she could turn the clock back. Without Nell, she was scuppered, out on a limb. But she couldn't live with her sister's nit-picking and fussy rules. Maybe she should open up to her, tell her how she felt. How losing their mam had affected her, and how she begrudged Nell taking over and letting Mam go before she'd had time to say goodbye. Deep down she couldn't forgive her sister and still felt a bitterness towards her that festered inside and hurt.

Their mam had wanted her to finish her education and get a good job, like Nell. But look how that had turned out! Nell had given up nursing, Liam had gone to England, and Róisín was sick. So much had changed, and Kate just wanted to run away from it all. Then there was Michael. Michael loved someone else, not her.

She stood up and took her cup and plate to the sink. It was heavenly to have running hot water when they needed it, and she knew she should try and help Nell. After all, she had managed to keep a roof over their heads.

With renewed effort, Kate decided to give job hunting a bit longer. If she were lucky, she could give half of what she earned to Nell. Then, when the moment was right, she would talk to her about returning to her studies. Meeting William had prompted her to rethink her future. Without that important piece of paper, she knew she would never be offered a decent job in Dublin, the only place she'd ever known, and would end up like all the rest . . . on the boat to England.

39

The following week was Kate's sixteenth birthday. Nell baked a cake with chocolate icing, and searched the secondhand bookshops to find Kate's favourite book, *Wuthering Heights* by Emily Brontë. She signed it with love.

Kate's expression was one of surprise when she opened the package. 'Thanks, Nell. That is grand.'

For tea that evening, Nell brought out the cake decorated with candles, just as someone knocked on their door.

'Who's that?' asked Kate. 'Are you expecting someone?'

'Don't worry,' Nell assured her when she saw Kate frown. 'It's probably her from downstairs run out of sugar again. That husband of hers has a sweet tooth.' She opened the door, surprised to see a young man standing there holding a bill.

'I'm sorry to disturb you. This came next door by mistake.'

'Thank you, won't you come in?' Nell held open the door. 'We're celebrating my sister's birthday. Stay and have some cake.'

Kate scowled, and Nell hoped she would be civil.

'Hello, Kate. If I'd known it was your birthday, I'd have got you a card.'

'You know each other?'

'Not really,' Kate muttered.

Nell passed him a slice of cake.

He bit into it and then licked his fingers. 'This is delicious.'

Nell gestured for him to sit.

'I'm in the middle of my studies so I must get back.'

'Oh,' Nell said. 'What are you studying?'

'Social history. I want to be a teacher one day.' He glanced towards Kate, who was sitting picking her nails. 'Are you doing anything special this evening, Kate?'

'I might be, don't know yet.'

'Well, I'll be off, then. Thanks for the cake. And Happy Birthday, Kate.'

★　★　★

Each time Kate signed on at the dole office, she was fearful of bumping into Jerry. She still owed him money from Christmas, and if she hadn't been so desperate she would never have taken the one and six he'd offered her, the last time they met. When she didn't see him, she sent up a silent prayer, hoping he'd gone away to find work; if so, she could breathe easy.

Now that she was sixteen, Kate was determined to find work, and she took extra care over her appearance. Her hair was neatly pinned up and secured with a tortoiseshell slide. She wore a black knee-length skirt and a cream jumper. Checking the advertisement again that she had cut from the newspaper — for a trainee hair stylist — she made her way down Henry Street.

When she arrived at the salon, she removed her coat and patted her hair into place. Her knowledge of styling ladies' hair went no further than arranging her own, but she'd take what was offered, even if it meant sweeping floors.

The salon was busy. A row of women sat reading magazines, their heads underneath large hairdryers. The hum of a wireless muttered in the corner. The woman behind the counter looked up as Kate walked in. Her hair was expertly styled, heavily lacquered, and flicked out to the sides. Her expression was as stiff as her hair.

'Do you have an appointment?'

'An appointment?' Kate swallowed.

'Yes. What time are you booked in for?'

'I'm not. I'm here about the vacancy.'

The woman came out from behind the counter and looked Kate up and down.

'Well, it's hardly an appropriate time,' she sneered. 'Why didn't you write in the first instance, like my advert stated?'

Kate's shoulders sagged. 'I'm sorry.'

'Well, as you're here . . . ' She called to the surly girl sweeping up around the washbasins. 'Get a move on, girl. The stylists are parched and want their tea.'

Kate took an instant dislike to the woman but followed her towards the back of the shop and through the coloured strips hanging in the door frame. She gestured for Kate to sit at the table, then plucked a notebook and pen from the drawer and sat opposite her.

'Well, before we start, I'll take your name, age and address?'

Kate straightened her shoulders and sat back before answering. If she got taken on here without qualifications, that would show Nell.

'So, what experience do you have, Miss Flynn?'

'None, I'm afraid.'

'So, why apply?'

'I need a job and I saw your advertisement.'

'Can I see a reference?'

'I don't have one, but I can get one.'

The haughty woman stood up. 'I'm sorry. You're just wasting my time and yours. You've no experience in the business, and not even a reference. Goodbye, Miss Flynn.'

Kate flounced out, leaving the door swinging behind her.

The response was the same everywhere. And by the time she walked home, she was furious with the world, humiliated, every ounce of confidence knocked out of her.

As she approached the house, William was coming in the opposite direction. She lowered her head. With no good news to impart, she didn't want to talk to him.

He paused alongside her. 'Hello, Kate. Do you fancy coming to the cinema with me this evening?'

After so many rejections, she wouldn't enjoy sitting next to William, listening to his successes when she had none of her own. 'I'm sorry, I can't,' she muttered.

'Another time perhaps.'

* * *

262

Inside, she sat brooding over her situation. Nell had done well getting this place, and it was luxury compared to their life in the tenement. No Father John breathing down their necks; no coal to lug up flights of stairs. But it all had to be paid for. And Nell wouldn't want her here if she didn't contribute towards the bills.

She had tried. Tried her best. No one was prepared to give her a job without experience, or that important piece of paper to prove she wasn't an idiot. It wasn't too late for her to do something about it. But, for it to work, she needed Nell's approval. First, she had to get her sister in a good mood. There was little food in the store cupboard: bread, Stork margarine, jam and marmalade. She made herself a jam sandwich without the margarine, because it made her sick. After she had eaten, she found two links of sausage and a slice of bacon, covered with a plate inside the oven. She washed and peeled the spuds and cut up a small turnip. And just before Nell arrived, she mashed the potatoes and turnip together, keeping it warm underneath the grill. With the table set, she made the tea.

'What's brought this on?' Nell remarked when she walked in to the whiff of something cooking. 'Have you found a job?' She whipped off her coat and sat down while Kate poured the tea.

'No.' Kate took in a deep breath. 'I've been out all day. They all want experience and qualifications, not to mention references — none of which I've got.'

'Something will turn up,' Nell said kindly. 'Did you try the glove factory?'

'I told you before, Nell, I don't want a factory job.'

'I've had to take a job I don't like. Why can't you?'

Kate dished up the food and Nell tucked in. 'This is lovely, Kate. I'm starving.'

They ate in silence. Kate, doing her best to impress her sister, had given Nell the bigger portion, along with the two sausages. Kate scooped up a forkful of the mash, then put down her fork. 'Have you heard any more from Liam?'

Nell shook her head. 'No, I guess he's busy settling in.'

'So, he doesn't know about Róisín being moved? Are you still going to England?'

'If you mean will I leave Róisín, the answer is no.'

'Teresa Lacy knows someone who was in there for years. What if that happens to Róisín?'

Nell put down her fork. 'Stop talking like that, Kate. Everyone is different, and Róisín will get better.'

'Well, I'm just saying.' Kate pouted.

'That reminds me.' Nell reached for her handbag and plucked out a small envelope with 'Michael' written across the front. 'I found this underneath your mattress when your bed was dismantled.'

Kate blushed and snatched the envelope from Nell. 'You've no right to touch my things.'

Nell laughed. 'What did you want me to do?'

'I'm sorry,' Kate muttered, and stuffed it into the pocket of her cardigan.

Nell finished the last of her potato and pushed

back her plate. 'Who's Michael?'

'He's no one. He's not important any more.'

'But he was, wasn't he, Kate? Michael Flannigan, Father John's clerk?'

'Father John's been talking to you.' Kate looked at her sister defiantly.

'What happened?'

'Nothing. Like I said, he's nobody.' She pulled her chair closer to Nell. 'I want to talk to you about something important.'

Nell sat forward, picked up her mug and placed her elbows on the table. 'What is it now? You're not thinking of running off again, are you?'

Kate stood up and lifted the plates. 'Depends.'

'This sounds ominous.'

'I want to go back and get my qualifications.'

Nell gasped. 'Why now?'

'I'm fed up of those snooty women looking down their noses at me.'

'Who?'

'The women who interview me. I want to show them I'm just as good if not better than any of them. It'll only be for six months, just until I qualify.'

Nell sighed. 'I never wanted you to give up your education, Kate, but can't you see how impossible that is now. I can't do this alone for another week, let alone six months. Besides, you're sixteen and should be working.'

Kate slammed the plates down. 'I don't know why I bother. I knew you'd be like this. You just don't want me to get on.'

'Oh, shut up, Kate. There's work at the biscuit

factory if you really want it.'

'Oh, shut up, yourself.' Kate tossed her hair over her shoulder and glared at Nell.

Nell took the dirty plates to the sink and plunged them into hot water, scrubbing them more than she needed to. 'Take some responsibility. How many times must we go over the same ground?' She turned to face Kate. 'It was your choice, remember, and you who messed things up at the vicarage.' Nell held out her wet hands. 'Look at us. There's not enough money to pay the rent, gas and electric, never mind food. I'm at my wits' end.'

'Oh, you're like a broken record.'

'Right, this is the situation, Kate. I can put a roof over your head but I can't feed or clothe you. You can take it or leave it. I'm exhausted and I can't do any more.'

'Well, if that's how you feel,' Kate snapped, 'I'll pack my bag and leave tomorrow.'

'Don't be an idiot. You can't storm off every time we disagree.'

'Why does it have to be what you want, all the time?'

Nell glared at her. 'Well, I'm happy for you to step into my shoes, because I sure don't know what to do any more — ' The knock on the door interrupted them. When Kate startled, Nell walked to the door. 'Who do you think it might be, Kate?'

Her sister shrugged. 'How should I know?'

Both girls lowered their heads as Mr Scanlon walked in. 'I appear to have picked a bad time,' he mumbled, 'I couldn't help but overhear.' He buttoned his jacket, fumbling in embarrassment. 'Is there anything I can do?'

'No, it's fine,' Nell assured him. 'I'm sorry. We were having a discussion.' She could tell by his face he knew it was more than that.

'You don't have to say sorry to him. It's none of his business,' Kate snapped.

Nell, her face hot with suppressed anger, turned to her sister. 'I'm ashamed of you, Kate. Apologise to Mr Scanlon.'

'No! Why should I?'

'Because without him we would be on the streets.'

'Why don't we all sit down?' he suggested.

Nell sat and so did Mr Scanlon, but Kate remained standing. Still defiant, she glared at them both.

'Sit down, Kate. Let's talk this through calmly.' He cleared his throat. 'Your sister is trying her best, why can't you see that?'

'And what would you know? I hate her. I hate you both. I can make my own decisions.'

'Now you listen here, young lady. Nell has provided for you and Róisín, fed and looked after you. But for her you could be in the workhouse. Don't you understand? If she had been half as selfish as you appear to be right now, she would have continued her nursing training and gone to England with her young man, but she didn't. She sacrificed it all to care for her sisters, and what thanks does she get?'

Kate shrugged. 'Oh, poor Nell. Well, I didn't ask her to do any of it.'

'No,' he agreed. 'You didn't have to. But she

did it anyway. She did it because she loves you. You think about that, why don't you?'

Despite Mr Scanlon's lecture, Kate wasn't interested.

The landlord stood up. 'I will leave you both now,' he said and, turning to Kate, added, 'I want you to think hard before causing your sister any more heartache. She deserves none of it.'

40

When Kate decided to leave the following morning, no amount of pleading or coaxing from Nell made the slightest difference.

'At least give me an address where I can get in touch with you?' she asked in desperation.

'I don't know where that'll be yet,' Kate replied airily.

Nell gripped her arm. 'Don't be ridiculous. You can't just roam the streets, you've already tried that. Wait a while longer.' How could she let her sister go again? She'd only lie awake at night worrying.

But Kate shrugged her off. 'Wait for what? Nothing will change.'

'Well, you don't know that. If Éamon de Valera gets back into power, you don't know what may happen. Mam believed in him.'

Kate continued to ram stuff into her case. 'And if you believe that, you're a fool, our Nell. Government don't care about the likes of us. Why do you think the ferry's full, night after night?'

By the determined jut of her sister's chin, Nell knew she'd already lost the battle.

'At least give me Teresa's address,' she urged. 'Is that where you're going?'

'I'll let you know when I find out.'

'Kate, for God's sake . . . '

But she pushed past Nell, the door slamming

shut behind her. Nell rushed to the window and held back the net curtain. Kate was talking to William next door; he had on a waterproof jacket, with a knapsack on his back.

Nell knew that William was fond of Kate. Could she be going off with him? Nell watched them walk down the street together, the boy carrying Kate's case. She thought about going after them, to see where they were going. They paused on the corner, talking for a few moments, then William passed the case back to Kate and they headed off in opposite directions.

Nell ran outside and tried to catch up with her sister. She called out her name above the noisy traffic. Kate rounded the corner just as a bus, heading for the city, pulled to a stop, and she stepped on to the platform. Nell stopped to catch her breath and wished she had tried harder to persuade Kate to stay.

Turning away in frustration, Nell decided to go and see Róisín at the sanatorium that afternoon. At least she had that to look forward to.

★ ★ ★

The sound of birds twittering delighted Nell as she went through the entrance and walked up the long driveway, admiring the peaceful setting of open grassland and trees. Her gaze settled on the impressive building in front of her, with tall sash windows, all of them open. A workman digging the flower beds raised his cap to her, and Nell inhaled the clean, frosty air.

270

She stepped inside the open front door and stood in a vast hall with black and white tiles. The apple-green walls reminded Nell of the convent school, with a statue of Mary and the Sacred Heart on either side of the door. A smell of lavender hung in the air, and the mahogany staircase gleamed as if it had just been polished. Her eyes were drawn to a gigantic rocking horse on the landing, but she doubted the children ever played with it; it looked brand new. There was no enquiry desk. Instead, she noted a side table with fresh flowers and a chair on either side. Impressed by what she had seen so far, Nell wasn't sure if she should sit, or remain standing, when a nun walked towards her.

'And what brings you here, child?'

'To visit my sister, Róisín Flynn.'

'Well, you'd better go round to the proper entrance, then.'

Nell felt a flush rise to her face. 'I'm sorry, Sister. I didn't realise.' Her blood boiled. Why did nuns have to be so cold and sanctimonious? It made her wonder what the rest of the nursing staff were like. Towards the back of the building, it didn't surprise her to see a wide veranda on the second floor, with a row of beds occupied by sick children enjoying views of the open countryside. She quickly found the entrance and made her way inside.

A nurse in a neat white and blue uniform walked towards her. 'Can I help you?'

'I've come to visit my sister, Róisín Flynn. She's a patient here.'

'There's no visiting today.'

'Oh, no! I must see her, please.'

The nurse sighed. 'I'm afraid that won't be possible.'

'Please, can't you make an exception this once.'

'I can't promise you'll get to see her today, but take a seat and I'll make enquiries.'

Nell glanced around her; with no one else waiting, she wished with hindsight that she had phoned before turning up. Now that she was here, she so wanted to see Róisín.

The nurse's shoes squeaked on the polished floor as she returned. 'If you follow me, please.'

When Nell stepped on to the ward, she saw no other visitors. Just a line of empty beds. And her anxiety heightened when the nurse took her into an office at the end of the ward.

'Please sit down.' A nurse glanced up from the desk. 'You must be Nell, Róisín's sister.'

Nell nodded. 'Is . . . is she all right?' Her pulse raced.

'Yes, she's as well as can be expected. The move here set her back. She's outside, resting on the veranda.'

'Can I see her?'

'I'm afraid not. You see, the visiting rules are strict. At this stage in Róisín's treatment, visiting is once a week, by arrangement.' She handed Nell a sheet of paper. 'This is a timesheet that will apply to your sister, and your visiting times are highlighted.'

Nell scanned the sheet of paper with a list of treatments and activities taking place throughout the day, including school and rest time. An hour was allocated on Wednesday, from 5 to 6 p.m., for visiting.

'But, I can't come then. I have to work. Can I come at the weekend?'

'I'm sorry, weekends are out of bounds to visitors.'

'But why?'

'I don't make the rules, Miss Flynn.'

'Please, can I see her?' she pleaded.

'Your sister's resting. Now, please come back on Wednesday.'

'Please. I've come a long way.'

The woman sighed. 'I'm sorry. You'll have to leave now.'

Deflated, Nell walked away. How could she go home without even a glimpse of Róisín? On impulse, she hurried up the stairs. She felt the fall in temperature as soon as she stepped on to the veranda, and she would never understand how a draughty corridor and open windows would improve her sister's health.

A row of beds faced the open windows. Some children were sleeping, and one was crying. Róisín saw her from her bed at the end of the row and Nell waved to her. Róisín was lying fully dressed on top of the bed, her feet and ankles swollen. Her eyes brightened and she tried to sit up. But as Nell ran forward and placed her arms around her in a big hug, the sister in charge rushed towards them.

'We'd prefer it if you didn't touch the patient. She should be resting. And what, may I ask, are you doing here?'

Nell felt her hackles rise, but she refused to

apologise to this sour-faced nun who had probably never had a cuddle in her life. Smiling at her sister, and ignoring the nun, she asked, 'How are you, sweetheart?'

'Can I come home, please, Nell?' Tears gathered in the child's blue eyes.

She'd have loved nothing better than to scoop her sister up into her arms and carry her home, but she knew it wasn't possible.

'I'd like you to leave, this instant,' the nun said.

Nell touched Róisín's hand. 'I'll be up to see you every chance I get, I promise.'

The child sobbed.

'You should leave right now.' The nun's face reddened. 'Can't you see you're unsettling the child and the rest of the children.'

Nell knew if she went against the nun's wishes, it could jeopardise her chances of seeing Róisín again. So, turning away, she threw her sister a kiss, told her she loved her, and left before her emotions spilled over. She couldn't help wondering when she would get to see Róisín again.

41

The following week, Nell received a letter from Liam. She curled up on her bed to read it. She scanned it quickly to assure herself that he still loved her and then slowly read every word twice.

My darling Nell,

It was so good to hear from you, and I'm so sorry to hear about poor Róisín. Give her a hug from me when you see her. Reading between the lines of your letter, I sensed your anxiety, sweetheart, but you must believe she will get well and that you both will come and live in London where we can be together again. I know it's hard for you and worrying over Kate isn't helping. Once she gets a taste of what it's like out there on her own, she'll come running back. In the meantime, try not to blame yourself. You've done more than your best.

I'm sure you'll love London as much as I do. Life is very different here and the people I work with are friendly enough. However, from what I've been hearing, the unskilled Irish and West Indians are finding it lonely and unwelcoming. But, don't worry, I love the work and, as you know, I love tinkering with cars. But these are not old bangers. They're well-maintained company vehicles, with everything I need for repairs at my fingertips. My salary will be reviewed after three months, but I'm already getting twice as much as I got back home. At this rate, it won't be long before I can send you money to put by for your flight.

One good thing, there's no one breathing down your neck about going to mass, and some people even work on Sundays.

Mam wrote and said to tell you you're welcome to pop round any time, they will always be glad to see you.

I miss you more than words can say and can't wait to see you, hold you in my arms, and show you how much I love you. Write back as soon as you can.

All my love,
Liam x

It relieved her to know he was happy in his job, and she wondered what it would be like when she got to be with him again. Oh, Liam! If only. She held the letter to her heart, then sniffed it for the scent of him and blinked back tears. How wonderful it would be to go to London and be with him. But Róisín's recovery could take months . . . possibly years. She would have to stop torturing herself with dreams that might not come true. She rolled off the bed and made herself a mug of tea in the kitchen. Although Liam's letter had uplifted her, it had also made her longing for him more intense.

In the living room, she sat on the sofa with her

276

thoughts. With no word from Kate, Nell wondered how her sister could go off like that and not get in touch. She should be here searching for work and helping her with visits to Róisín.

On Wednesday, Nell tried to get time off work, but as they were behind with orders, they refused her request. And for the rest of the afternoon all she could think about was Róisín's disappointed face.

That evening, she wracked her brain for a solution to her problem. But apart from risking her job, there was none. How had it come to this? With no one to talk to, she felt totally alone. And, before she knew it, she was choking back sobs. She had made several friends at the biscuit factory, but no one brought their personal problems to work. Most of the women talked about boyfriends, clothes and going out dancing. Nell often felt old and staid in comparison.

A loud knock on the door cut through her racing thoughts and she sniffed loudly before drying her eyes. She was in no mood to let anyone see her in this state, so she waited a few moments, hoping whoever it was would go away. On the third knock, she ran her hand over her hair, straightened her shoulders, and went to open the door.

Father John stood there, a worried expression on his face. Nell took a deep breath as he plodded inside.

'What took you so long?' the priest asked. 'I thought I'd had a wasted journey.'

She lowered her head. 'I wasn't expecting anyone.'

'Sure, when I didn't see you at church, or hear

a word from you, I thought I'd better come over here myself.' He removed his hat and placed it on the arm of the chair. 'Have you been going to another parish?'

'John's Lane Church is on the doorstep.' She hadn't attended mass there yet, but if she didn't say something, he would keep nagging.

'That's up to you, as long as you're keeping your faith.'

Nell didn't reply. He followed her into the room, slipped off his coat and flopped down in the armchair as Nell sat back on the sofa.

'Where's Kate? I gather the wanderer has returned?'

'Yes, but she's gone again, I . . . '

'And didn't you try to stop her?'

'Well, of course I did.'

'Where in the name of God is she, then?'

'I don't know, and she wouldn't say.'

'Holy Mother of God. That's a nice how do you do.' He shifted and sat forward. 'Sure, her soul's in mortal danger.'

Nell bit back an angry retort. It was always about Kate. He never asked her how she was managing, and she didn't need the priest to tell her what she already knew. Wasn't she worried enough? Inside she was screaming, but she wouldn't let him see her distress. 'Kate tried for work but became impatient.'

'Well, she'll get nothing decent without her leaving certificate.'

'She knows that, Father.'

He cleared his throat. 'Sure, there's a parish priest not far away looking for a full-time

278

housekeeper. And I foolishly thought of Kate.'

If only he'd come a week ago. 'I'm sorry, Father. It was good of you to think of her.' She sat forward. 'I could do it, Father. After I get home from work.' It would stop her feeling lonely in the evenings.

'Ah, no, sure it'd only be pocket money. And he'd want you there in the mornings when the priests are away saying mass.'

He stood up and looked around him. Nell did the same, hoping he was about to leave. 'It's not a bad little place you've got here. Are you settling in okay?'

'I'm doing my best, but without Kate . . . ' She swallowed.

'Well, wherever she went last time, that's where she'll be now.' He glared at Nell. 'Don't you even know that?'

He wasn't helping her mood, and she was sick of talking and fretting about Kate. She folded her arms as angry words swirled around inside her head. If she let them free, she knew she'd regret it, and the priest might die of shock, so she said, 'No, I don't, Father. You know how stubborn she can be.' Then she changed the subject. 'Did you know Róisín's out in Cappagh?'

'Ah, is she now? Well, sure there's many a one that's come out cured from there.' He sat back down. 'Well, am I going to get a cup of tea? Me throat's parched, so it is.'

'I'm sorry, Father. I'll put the kettle on.'

Then, over tea and biscuits, she told him about Liam's offer to pay for them all to go to London.

'Ah, sure, he's a young fella with his head full of dreams, so he is.'

'What's wrong with that? There's nothing wrong with having a dream, Father. That's all some of us have.' Heat flushed her face.

He swallowed the tea, making slurping sounds. 'Now, you're a level-headed girl, Nell. Your place is here. And with a good man to take care of you; someone who won't run off to England and leave you to cope alone.'

She put down her cup with a clatter and glared at him. 'You know nothing about Liam, Father. He's gone away to work and make money. As soon as Róisín can travel, we'll be joining him in London.'

'Well now. Glory be. That's one of the most idiotic ideas I've heard in a long time.' Picking up the last biscuit, he crunched it meditatively. Then he picked up his hat and coat and, to Nell's relief, he ambled towards the door. 'Sure, the world's gone mad. Gone mad, I tell you.' And grumbling to himself, he headed out the door.

* * *

The next day, with still no word from Kate, Nell took it upon herself to call on the boy next door whom she'd seen walking down the street with Kate on the day she left.

'Yes, what is it?' The burly man who opened the door to her looked annoyed that she had interrupted him.

'I'm sorry to intrude, but I'd like a word with your son, please.'

'What's your business with my son? He's upstairs studying, and we don't like to disturb him unless it's urgent.'

'This is urgent.' Unflinching, she stared at him. She hadn't expected her neighbour to be unfriendly.

A boy of about seventeen, with a fringe of thick fair hair falling across his forehead, leant over the balustrade. 'It's all right, Dad.' He bounded down and paused on the last but one step.

Nell wondered if he had been expecting Kate. She moved forward. 'Hello, I'm Nell, Kate's sister from next door.'

He stepped down and shook her hand. 'Pleased to meet you. Is ... is something wrong?'

His father shuffled his feet. 'William, remember your time schedule.'

The boy glared at his father, then opened the front door and guided Nell outside, closing the door behind him. 'I'm sorry about that.' He shook his head. 'Parents! Who'd have them?' Although said in jest, the remark stung. 'How can I help?'

'I wouldn't have called, only I'm worried about Kate.' She gripped his arm. 'Is there anything you can tell me about where she might be?' Feeling desperate, she released her grip. 'I'm sorry.' She folded her arms. 'If there's anything at all you can tell me ... '

He frowned and flicked back his hair. 'Why? What's wrong with her?'

'I haven't heard from her since I saw you walk

down the street with her, days ago. I hoped you might throw some light on where she went?'

He ran his hand over his chin. 'I understand how worried you must be, and I wish I could help.' He leant against the window sill. 'We just passed the time of day. I was off to a study seminar and she said she would stay with a friend.'

'Did she say who the friend was?'

'No! Don't you know?'

A stab of guilt rendered her speechless. She *should* know, but that was Kate all over: closed and secretive.

She shook her head. 'I'm sorry to have disturbed you, William. If she gets in touch, you will let me know?'

He shrugged. 'That's very unlikely.' He dipped his gaze. 'I like her, I like her a lot, but she's not interested in me.'

'Does Kate know about your feelings?'

Colour tinged his face. 'No, I doubt it. You . . . you won't say anything, will you?'

Nell shook her head.

'I asked her out, and she refused.'

Something else Kate hadn't mentioned. What else was she keeping from her?

282

42

The weather had turned warmer, but it made little difference to Nell. She felt unable to cope or concentrate on anything, and she dreaded coming home to the empty flat. She still fretted that she hadn't managed to see Róisín, and life in general was a drudge, day in day out, with no respite.

The repetitiveness of her job bored her, and today, when the buzzer went for the mid-morning break, she was first to down tools and remove her apron.

'Nell, can I have a word?' Julia, the chargehand, drew her aside from the stampede of women rushing towards the canteen.

Nell's heart somersaulted, and she knew by the other woman's expression that all wasn't well.

'Come into the office a minute.' Julia closed the door and then turned to face Nell, who remained standing. 'I've been observing your performance over the past week or so, and it's not good. You've made quite a few mistakes of late. And I wondered if there was something troubling you?'

Nell bit her bottom lip. 'I . . . '

'Your mind's not on the job.'

Nell knew she was right, and felt ashamed to have let her family problems impinge on her work. 'I'm sorry, Julia.'

'Is it something you feel you can share?'

Nell didn't see the point of bringing her troubles to work, and shook her head.

Julia frowned. 'I see. As you're here, there is something I've been wanting to say to you, and your poor performance has made it necessary.'

Nell's head jerked up. She was ready to beg to keep her job. She'd leave her troubles behind the next time she came to work.

'You may feel it is none of my business,' the other woman went on. She sat down by the table and gestured for Nell to do likewise. 'However, for what it's worth, I'll speak my mind. I think you're wasted here, Nell, and that you would be better served doing the job you were trained for. There's no satisfaction doing a job you hate.'

Nell gasped. Had she made it that obvious?

Julia rested her elbow on the table and cupped her chin. 'Why not return to nursing?'

Puzzled, Nell sat forward. 'I only wish I could. But it's not possible, especially not now.'

'Sure, why is that, then? How old are your sisters? The older one . . . ' She turned to Nell.

'Kate's sixteen.'

'And the younger one?'

'Róisín's nine in a few months, but she's in a sanatorium for her health.'

Julia looked contrite. 'I'm sorry, Nell. Do you know how long for?'

'No, but most children stay for anything from one year upwards.'

'I'm not being unkind, Nell, but you can't put your life on hold, it's not fair. I only say this because . . . well . . . I did something similar and

284

lived to regret it. And it was years before I was promoted to where I am now. I've learnt to live with it, but there's not a day goes by that I don't think about what my life would have been like, had I gone with my friend to America. I stayed to nurse my father until he died, and by then it was too late. I'd hate to see the same thing happen to you.'

Nell was staring, her mouth slightly open. 'I'm sorry, Julia,' she managed to say eventually. 'I'd no idea.'

'Well, I've said what's on my mind. The rest is up to you. If you hurry, you'll just have time to grab a brew.'

★   ★   ★

That evening, Nell scanned through the bills, hoping that Kate might have dropped her a line. It wasn't as if she didn't know the address. But there was nothing. She was worried sick, and Father John hadn't helped by blaming her for Kate's disappearance. He was right, she *was* responsible. But what else could she have done, apart from locking Kate in a room? Even so, guilt hung heavily on her shoulders.

She switched on the wireless and, sick to the teeth of eating beans and tinned corned beef, she made herself a cup of tea and nothing else. Settling in the big old armchair where her father used to sit, she wondered what he would have done. How she would love to take Julia's advice; the more she thought about it, the more it began to make sense. If it was possible, she could work

285

shifts to fit in with visiting Róisín.

Then reality set in and the pipe dream faded. Her mother had scrimped and saved to pay her fees. Would the hospital still honour them? There was no way she would get a bursary or a scholarship in the current economic climate. Tears stung her eyes. If she followed her heart and went back to nursing, it would help when Róisín was finally allowed home. But what about Kate? She felt trapped, with no way out of her desperate situation.

The gentle knock on the door alerted her, and she uncurled her legs. She stood up and quickly glanced in the mirror; her eyes were red with unshed tears. It could be William from next door, with news about Kate! As the knocking continued, she rushed to open the door.

'Mr Scanlon!' She lowered her head and turned back into the room.

He followed her into the kitchen. 'What is it, lass? Has something happened?'

She didn't answer at first; she needed time to compose herself.

'Can I do anything?' He looked around. 'You've not eaten. I'll make some coffee.'

She sat at the table, embarrassed to have been caught at a disadvantage. Although she had known her landlord for most of her life, she didn't want him to see her like this. He brought the steaming drinks to the table with a plate, then opened his bag, took out a slab of fruit cake and began to slice it. 'Eat something, and then if you feel like talking, I'm a good listener.'

She sniffed and rubbed her eyes. 'There's

nothing anyone can do to make any difference.'

He sat next to her. 'A trouble shared and all that.'

She sipped the coffee and bit into the cake. It tasted good. 'You didn't bake this?'

'Are you kidding? It's shop bought, and well you know it.' His remark brought a smile to her face. 'I was passing and wondered if you had managed to convince Kate to stay.' He shifted in his chair. 'And by the looks of things, I guess not.'

Nell looked up. 'It's not my fault. I tried my best.' But as she began to talk about it, her tears started again.

'Don't, lass. Don't upset yourself. It's hard, but if Kate is determined to leave, there really isn't a lot you can do about it. Take my Pete!'

Nell didn't want to think about him. Any encounter she'd had with him was best forgotten.

'Well, I tried everything to get him to straighten himself out. But he chose to take the boat to England, same as many a young one. Bad 'un all as he was, I miss him. Living alone is never easy. Pete, well, he's who he is.' He glanced down at his hands. 'His father was a rough diamond.'

Nell was surprised. 'Really! He's not your son, then? I didn't know.'

'Not many do.'

As she sipped her coffee, she found herself telling him about the sanatorium and the strict visiting timetable. It felt good to share her troubles with someone who didn't believe she was to blame for what had befallen them.

He studied the timetable carefully. 'It's a very tight ship they run there, Nell. She won't get bored, though. Sure, according to this, there's something going on all the time, apart from attending school.' He sat back, crossing his legs. 'Every activity is timed, and the breathing exercises, medicines and treatments take place early in the morning. And I see they allow time for playing quiet games, jigsaws, reading and drawing. She'll love that.' He paused to look at Nell. 'I think your Róisín will settle into that, and in no time at all, you'll see a marked improvement in her.'

Relaxed in his company, Nell saw no reason not to call him by his first name. He had shared private information with her, and she had known him for most of her life.

'Thanks, Joe. I know all that, but five o'clock visiting? I don't finish work until six. I'll never see her.'

He smiled. Then he put the schedule down and sat forward. 'How about if I was to visit her in your place?'

'You? But . . . I couldn't let you do that. It's such a long way.'

'I've nothing much on, most days. You can always write a letter for me to read to her. What do you think? I'm a familiar face; she knows me.'

'Oh, Joe. Would you do that?' His concern for Róisín and the interest he had shown listening to her worries brought a lump to Nell's throat and she choked back a sob. When he pulled his chair closer and placed his arm protectively around her, her head tilted on to his shoulder. She could smell the cigarette smoke on his jacket. It had been so long since she'd had a hug, and it felt good to unburden herself to someone. Within seconds, she sat upright. 'I'm sorry, Joe. It's . . . well . . . '

'Think nothing of it, Nell. If an old family friend can't give comfort to someone he admires, then the world is indeed a sorry place.' He got to his feet. 'I'd better be running along. If you need anything . . . anything at all, Nell, I can bring it over next time I call.'

She smiled. 'Goodnight, and thanks, Joe.' She closed the door behind him.

43

Teresa's mother had been kind when Kate told her she had nowhere to go and allowed her to stay a few nights. And Teresa had put Kate's name forward for a junior office position at the Electricity Supply Board before it went to the press. But it all came down to qualifications in the end, and Kate had none, leaving her once again regretting not finishing her secondary education. Fearful of outstaying her welcome, she thanked Teresa's mother and left, leaving them to believe she would return to her sister's.

As she made her way back into the city, Kate recalled how stupid and humiliated she'd felt after her interview at the ESB. And when she glanced down at her school shoes and ankle socks, it was obvious why the woman had told her she wasn't suitable. Determined no one would treat her like that again, she headed for the dole office where she picked up her money, then she shopped for a pair of nylons and picked up navy court shoes at the second-hand market.

If she were to survive on the streets alone, she would have no choice but to swallow her pride and take any old job. And she had better do it while she still looked clean and tidy. A few more days and she'd be struggling for somewhere to wash herself.

Kate bought a newspaper and a Mars Bar, along with a brown paper carrier bag. Fed up with people staring at her case and assuming she was going away, she stopped by the park, where she emptied her belongings into the paper bag and then flung the battered case into the bushes. After using the park toilet and changing into her nylons, it surprised her to find them warm next to her skin. With the newspaper spread out along the park bench, she traced her finger down the situations vacant column. A live-in job would be ideal, but looking after children wasn't something she would relish. And everything advertised wanted experience.

Then she spotted a silk-screen printer in Gardiner Street looking for young girls to start immediately. The job wasn't explained, but by now she didn't much care as long as she got enough money to look after herself. She jotted down the address, noting that it wasn't far away. She had on a navy pleated shirt and a green jumper, which was fine for an interview and, as the weather had turned milder, she removed her coat and folded it over her arm.

When she walked down the row of shabby houses, nerves made her insides churn. She just had to make a good impression this time. Her well-being depended on it.

The screen printer operated out of one of the old tenement houses, newly revamped into offices for small businesses. Kate walked through the open door into the spacious hall and knocked.

When the door opened, a stout grim-faced woman peered at her over thick-rimmed glasses. 'Yes?'

Kate straightened her shoulders. 'I've come about the vacancy in the paper.'

'Which one?'

'The silk-screen printer.'

'Upstairs.' And the door closed before Kate could respond.

Despite the blue-painted walls and the posters of tropical birds, a faint odour of damp and decay hung in the air. On the first floor, a man resembling a beer barrel with short stubby legs opened the door to her. Kate was sure that the slightest push would send him rolling across the floor.

'Can I help?'

'I'm here about the vacancy?'

'Oh, yes, come in.'

There was a strong smell of ink and paint, and several posters hung on the walls. A man and a woman wearing aprons and rubber gloves were stretching fabric over heavy wooden frames. Another man was washing paint brushes and hanging them on hooks below a shelf of dripping paint pots. She followed the little man to a desk behind a partition in a corner of the room. Aware of him staring at her, his scrutiny made her face hot.

'Sit down, miss.'

She sat, as directed, straightening the pleats of her skirt. A wireless mumbled on a shelf above the man's head. He leant back, filling an enormous chair that took up most of the area. 'Shall we start with your name and address?'

'Kate Flynn. Number sixteen, John's Lane.'

'That's the other side of the Liffey. You sure

you can get here on time?'

'Yes, sir.'

'What kind of experience do you have in this work?'

Her heart skipped. Not again. 'I . . . well, I . . . The advert said nothing about experience, otherwise I wouldn't have come.'

'Well now, dearie, that's a complete cock-up, then. We don't have time to train anyone,' he said, scratching his head. 'I need experienced operatives.' He shifted forward in his chair. 'We're expanding the business and we need people who know what they're doing.' He ran his hand over his cleanshaven face. 'I'll get on to them. Incompetent idiots. They must rerun my ad.'

'I'm sorry to have wasted your time, sir.' She stood up. 'But I'm desperate to find work, any kind of work.'

'How old are you?'

'Sixteen.'

He nodded. 'You look like a bright young woman. I'm surprised you're unemployed.' No one had said anything like that to her in ages. He spoke English, but she couldn't place his accent.

'My family have fallen on hard times and I'm forced to find work, sir.'

He pulled at his bottom lip, and she hoped he was reconsidering.

'With no experience, are you happy to do menial tasks and a few deliveries? Our delivery boy is off sick.'

'Yes, anything.'

'We print designs on to T-shirts. Whatever the

customer wants. So, are you still interested?'

'Well, yes, I am.'

'When can you start?'

'How much will you pay me?'

This made him chuckle and his body wobbled like jelly. Kate wished she hadn't asked. Would he change his mind? He pulled his chair forward. 'Yes, I like you. You've got pluck. How does thirty shillings a week sound?'

'I'll take it. Thank you, Mr . . .'

'Schneider.'

'You're not Irish, then?' Kate asked, then bit her tongue, wishing she hadn't been so outspoken.

'God, no! Would it bother you to know that my greatgrandfather was a German?'

She swallowed. Why had he come here? Six years since the war ended, and people still hated the Jerries. But she didn't care where he originated from as long as he gave her a job. 'No, not at all, Mr Schneider.'

He stood up and shook her hand. 'Don't be late. Be here tomorrow at eight sharp.'

Delighted to have secured a job, even if it wasn't what she had first hoped for, she decided to learn all she could about the job. She'd move up the ladder sooner rather than later. Outside, she swapped her court shoes for her comfortable school ones. It was only as she walked down the street that the smile slipped from her face. Where would she sleep tonight?

She crossed over O'Connell Bridge, where the stench of the Liffey made her gag. Further along, the smell of food floating out from the cafes and confectioners made her drool. She bought a penny liquorice, saving what little money she had left. There was a shelter for homeless men attached to the Iveagh wash house, but did they take women in as well? She wasn't sure.

As she paused by the General Post Office, where street urchins were begging, a thought came to her. She had seen women going into a hostel somewhere on Mountjoy Street; she'd passed it many times, never thinking she might need refuge there one day. As she made her way in that direction, it was growing dark and the alternative — a bench in a city park, before it was locked for the evening — made her stomach wobble in panic.

She hastened through the city, and it started to rain as she turned down Dorset Street, bypassing Dominick Street, taking short cuts down alleys and side streets until she came to Mountjoy Street. The paper bag she carried containing her possessions was now sodden and about to give way, and she held it closer to her body. The green door of the hostel looked in better condition than the rest of the houses on the row. Cold and damp, her hair dripping, she pressed the bell. As she waited, she closed her eyes and prayed she would find a bed for the night.

A nun dressed in navy attire was the last person she expected to see when the door opened. 'Can I help you, child?'

'I hope so, Sister. I'm homeless.'

'Come in and we'll see what we have available.'

Kate stepped inside, her teeth chattering.

'I'll get you a towel to dry your hair. Wait in here.'

Surprised to have been treated so kindly, Kate stared around the basic room with its shabby furniture. The nuns were everywhere; there was no getting away from them. Right now, though, she didn't care, as long as she had somewhere to lay her head. She removed her wet coat and hung it over the back of a chair just as the nun returned with a well-worn towel in one hand and a sheet of paper in the other. Kate rubbed her hair dry.

'One and sixpence a night, and I'll need you to fill in this form.' She placed the paper on the table. 'When you've done that, I'll get someone to show you to the beds. There is a kitchen if you need to cook and make a drink, and a washroom and toilet facilities. God bless you, my child,' she said and left.

Kate had never experienced a nun who didn't shout, and she wondered what order of nuns the sister belonged to.

A short time later, the nun returned with a girl of about Kate's age. She lifted the form, and the money. 'Miriam will show you where to go. She'll inform you of the rules and tell you anything you need to know.'

Kate followed the timid girl through the building until they came to a door. Miriam never spoke, just pointed at the door and left.

An argument was already going on, with two women quarrelling over beds.

'Get out me way, you stupid bitch,' one

296

woman said, flinging a bag from her bed. 'I was here first.'

'Oh, shut your gob.' The older woman grabbed the other's hair, and a screaming match took place. Kate stared at the scene in front of her. This was no youth hostel; it was more like a place for drunken women off the street. Unsure which bed to take, she was about to try one of the other rooms when a woman, her bedraggled hair hanging down over her eyes, came in and yelled, 'What's going on here?'

'That old crab tried to pinch me bed, and God knows what else, once I turned me back.'

'Youse don't own the beds! Now, put a sock in it, or it'll be Sister Alphonsus you'll be dealing with.'

The two women looked daggers at each other before putting their belongings into closets, then sat with their backs to each other.

The woman with the wet hair glared at Kate, who was beginning to think she should have slept on a park bench, after all. 'You can sleep in the middle bed for tonight.'

As she stood by her bed, Kate couldn't describe her feelings — nervous, panicky, aware of sidelong glances, eyes watching her every move. She wouldn't close an eyelid in this place tonight. The bag she had been carrying her clothes in suddenly split and she discarded it, placing her belongings in the bedside locker. She couldn't afford to lose anything.

She removed her shoes and, too cold to undress, got into bed, placing her damp coat over her feet. Keeping a tight hold on her handbag, she lay down on the straw mattress and pulled the smelly grey blanket up around her shoulders. Within minutes, the lights went out. The windows were curtainless, and light from the street shone through.

Her body shook from the cold, and she feared that she could be murdered in the night. She was no better than any one of these destitute women, but her trouble was of her own making. Was this what she'd become? Throughout the long night, she could hear women shouting abuse, some even sobbing in their sleep. This was the worst night of her life and she couldn't wait for morning. As she lay there, wide awake, she wasn't sure if she was safer in here than out on the streets of Dublin.

44

She must have slept, for when Kate woke she was alone in the room. Taking her bag, she went into the washroom. It was empty. Apart from the smelly toilet, there was no sign that anyone had washed in here this morning. Kate wallowed in the luxury of having the place to herself as she got ready for work. She piled her hair on top, just in case it rained again, and apart from a small ladder running up one leg of her nylons, she was ready to face the day. She paused by the kitchen, intent on helping herself to a drink of water and whatever else she could find, then she heard a row erupt over who owned the bread. How she would love to tear a strip off these two; they had kept her awake with their stupid arguments and foul language. Instead, she gritted her teeth and forced herself to leave them to get on with it. She couldn't afford to be late on her first morning.

She went back to collect her belongings, and found that her warmest jumper was missing, along with her socks. If it had been one of the two women in the kitchen, they would hardly have hung around. Furious, she complained to the woman in charge, who merely shrugged and told her to keep her belongings with her in future. Frightened of being late for work, she left without so much as a drink of water.

Kate stepped out on to the pavement. The rain had stopped and the chill of the wet street seeped into her bones. She pulled her coat tighter for extra warmth and set off, glad to see the back of the place, and vowing not to return. She bought a bottle of Pepsi Cola and a bag of crisps, and sat on a bench to eat them.

She arrived at the screen printer's a few minutes before eight, just as Mr Schneider was unlocking the door. 'Ah, there you are.'

'Good morning, sir.' Kate followed him inside and smiled as he wobbled across to his small office in the corner of the room.

'Before we do anything else, get the kettle on,' he announced. 'I'm parched. Mine's the big mug — milk and four sugars.'

Did that mean she, too, could have one? She hoped so. She found the makeshift kitchen behind another partition, in the far corner, with a table full of dirty mugs and a sink. She had no trouble finding his mug, with his face printed on the front. There were more dirty dishes on the table. She filled the kettle but realised there was no gas ring on which to boil it. She held up the kettle.

He lifted his head. 'Oh, be a dear and go downstairs. Ask nicely and Mrs Schneider will boil it for you.' He bent his head over his work.

Mrs Schneider! Now it made sense to her why the grim-faced woman had given her the evil eye yesterday, and she wasn't looking forward to another encounter. But what choice did she have?

The door opened on her first knock. 'You again.' The woman's eyes fell to the kettle in Kate's hand. 'Look here, I've told him before to

get his own gas ring. Just because we were . . . '
She paused. 'This has got to stop.'

'I'll get on to it for him.' Kate pushed the
kettle towards her.

The woman's eyebrows shot up and she glared
at Kate. 'You can wait outside.'

The man and woman who worked upstairs
passed Kate in the hall, without speaking. Later,
when the tea was made, she took one to Mr
Schneider and he clasped his hands around it as
if he was cold. She told him what Mrs Schneider
had said, and he shook with laughter.

'I can organise that for you, sir,' Kate offered.
But her response made him laugh even louder,
until he was choking and spluttering, his tea
spilling all over his paperwork.

She rushed to get a cloth to mop it up, while
he got up and wandered over to the sink and
emptied out the remains of his tea. She
wondered what sort of boss she was working
for.

The two other employees didn't speak when
she brought them their tea. They were hanging
T-shirts on a rail above their heads, and hardly
acknowledged her.

She was still mopping up the spilt tea when
her boss returned. 'Make me another one, will
you?'

'But . . . but the kettle's cold now, sir.'

'I know.' He rubbed his fat little hands
together and chortled.

It was then that she realised she was going to
be playing cat and mouse with these two. She
gritted her teeth and then went to do his

301

bidding. Squirming, she knocked tentatively on the door.

'Yes, what is it now?'

'I'm sorry to bother you again, Mrs Schneider, but — '

'Don't you dare call me by that name!' the woman yelled, in a distinctive Irish accent.

Kate held up the kettle and flinched when the door was shut in her face. She went back up to find her boss pouring himself a steaming mug of tea from his flask.

'I can tell by your face what her answer was.' And he chuckled again. 'She has a right temper on her does Mrs Schneider.'

Kate was fuming. She didn't want to be part of whatever was going on with these two strange individuals.

'I'd appreciate you not sending me on a wild goose chase, sir. What other menial tasks do you have lined up for me?'

Her sarcasm didn't go unnoticed.

'Now, now, Miss Flynn. You did agree to this at your interview.' He shifted from side to side in his chair. 'You can just as soon turn around and walk out. The choice is yours.'

The urge to do just that was strong, but with only pennies in her purse, she swallowed her pride. 'Yes, I'm sorry.' The apology almost choked her.

'That's better. You know as well as I do, jobs don't fall from the sky.' He laughed. 'At least not here in dirty Dublin.'

'You don't mind working in dirty Dublin, then?'

302

'Wit I can take,' his tone was sharp now, 'but disrespect me again and you're out.'

Kate swallowed and found herself apologising again. What an odd little man. If only she wasn't so desperate.

'Now, we've got work to do. I have a little job for you. The order will be ready in a minute and I want you to take it to this address.' He scribbled it down on a piece of paper and passed it to her. 'Do you know it?'

'Yes, I know Parnell Street.'

'I'll time you. I know how long it should take.' He smirked.

Kate glanced down at her court shoes. 'I'll expect bus fare.'

'For that, you can walk.'

This wasn't at all what she had expected. She had intended to walk anyway, and save the money he gave her for food. Her stomach already thought her throat had been cut. Mr Schneider was a nasty old fool with a split personality, and she was regretting having agreed to work for him.

Knowing he was timing her, she ran all the way there. But on the way back, her energy spent, she called at the newsagent's for a packet of Tayto Crisps and a Mars Bar. She sat on a bench for five minutes to eat them, fearful of getting the sack, before hurrying on.

She was just crossing over Talbot Street, in the direction of Gardiner Street, when she spotted Jerry O'Shea walking with a swagger along the pavement, as if he hadn't a care in the world. She hadn't seen him around for a while, and he was

303

the last person she wanted to meet. She dodged into the doorway of a confectioner's, where the mouth-watering smell of cakes and fresh crusty bread made her stomach rumble.

'Kate!' Jerry called, weaving through the traffic towards her. 'I hardly recognised you with your hair like that.'

Turning, she gave him a withering smile. Caught at her most vulnerable, and owing him money, she felt like a rabbit caught in headlights. Then an idea pinged in her mind like a light switch. Jerry was the lesser of two evils, and he could be her refuge for a few nights.

She feigned reluctance when Jerry offered to take her to a nearby cafe for a hot drink and something to eat. But the temptation proved too much, and she allowed herself to succumb. She reckoned she was entitled to a lunch break, and she knew a couple of short cuts she could take on her way back to the printer's.

The fact that she had work pleased Jerry. 'You could do well there, Kate. Learn all you can,' he encouraged her.

For the first time in days, Kate felt herself relax. She was relieved to find Jerry in such good humour — and apparently delighted to see her. And how could she resist his offer of a bed for the night, or for as many nights as she wished?

'I've sold my bike and I have a driving job,' he told her. 'So try and get back to my place before six, as I have to leave then.'

'That will depend on the mood old Schneider is in,' she explained, the memory of her boss puncturing her good mood.

When Kate returned to work an hour later, she received a rollicking from her boss.

'You're on your first and last warning,' he told her. 'I can get ten of you on the streets, who'll jump at the chance of work.'

'I'm sorry, sir. I'll make up the time.'

She'd no sooner said it than he chuckled. 'You most certainly will, Katie, starting tonight.'

She hated when he called her that, but when she took him up on it, he said he would call her what he damn well liked. For the remainder of the day, she washed every paintbrush in the room and hung them up to dry, made tea three times, took the flak from Mrs Schneider each time she asked her to boil water, ran three miles there and back with two more deliveries, and stayed behind when everyone had gone home. Schneider had left her a stack of folders to sort and leave ready for him first thing in the morning.

By the time she left work, it was too late to catch Jerry before he left. Thinking she'd blown it, she took her time getting back to the flat. She wouldn't be able to get in, but there was always the outhouse, which was better than the streets. As she entered the yard, she saw an envelope pinned to the door. She tore it from the nail, and the door key dropped out.

Relieved, she let herself in and was taken aback to see the table set and a cold meal waiting for her, with a note. She kicked off her shoes and flopped on to the chair. She ate the food first

— ham, pickle, tomato, plus two slices of bread and margarine; it tasted divine. Then she picked up the note.

What kept you, Kate? I told you I had to leave at six. Won't see you now until eight in the morning, by which time I guess you'll have left for work. I can make you happy but, Kate, don't even think of messing me about. You can sleep on the settee. It pulls out into a bed. Sleep well and cook me a hot breakfast in the morning before you go. Leave it under the grill to keep warm.

Jerry x

She was pleased he hadn't suggested she sleep in his bedroom. The pull-down bed would suit her fine. A peaceful night's sleep was what she craved after her experience at the hostel.

Before she got ready for bed, she looked in the kitchen cupboards and prepared everything for Jerry's breakfast. His driving job must pay well, she thought, when she found the cupboards well stocked. He never spoke about his parents, and she doubted he received an allowance.

She took a packet of fig roll biscuits to bed with her and listened to the small wireless Jerry kept on the shelf. The news of continued food rationing in England was of little interest to Kate, or indeed, most of the people of Ireland, who were struggling to make ends meet. It was reported that over 500,000 Irish, desperate for work, had emigrated to England. She had no

306

family in England, and she was reluctant to go where she knew no one but, if things carried on as they were, she might well be joining them.

45

Nell tried to forget that she had found comfort in Joe's hug, but she missed Liam so much, and she felt vulnerable and lonely now that Kate had abandoned her. The sooner she made a decision regarding her future the better, and she would mention it to Joe next time he called. Some days, her landlord was the only person she had a meaningful conversation with. To return to nursing was a big decision, but she could see no point in struggling to pay for a flat on her own.

With each passing day, she worried more about Kate. If she reported her sister missing, the Gardaí wouldn't take it seriously. She reminded herself that Kate wasn't a child, and she had left home of her own free will. Nell missed her, though, and longed for her to walk through the door, or just to get in touch.

Nell wondered how Kate was managing, when she only had beans on toast herself some days. If she was back at the nurses' accommodation, she'd be warm and well fed — and she'd still have a small wage to call her own. She'd always found the work satisfying, and had enjoyed every aspect of nursing — even the not so nice bits. But she knew that if she gave up the flat, her sisters would have nowhere to call home. They were still her responsibility, despite what she wanted for her own future.

Next time she saw Joe, she'd get his opinion.

He was like a father figure to her, someone whose judgement she trusted. So the following day, when he called round, she put her idea to him over tea and cake.

'Sure, that's a great idea, Nell. It's about time you thought about yourself.'

'I need to consider my sisters, too, Joe. But I'm struggling to keep this place going, without Kate for support. And it's hard work at the biscuit factory. I'm bored with it. I could be finished with my training by the time Róisín comes home.' Her voice rose with enthusiasm. 'What do you think?'

'If you're sure it's what you want. True, you could be a fully qualified nurse by the time young Róisín is well enough to come home. You must do what you feel is right for you now, Nell.'

'You really think so?'

He nodded in agreement.

She smiled wistfully. 'It's what both Mam and Dad wanted for me.'

'They saw the caring side to your nature, Nell.'

She lowered her head. 'If only I knew where Kate was. That she was safe. What if she comes back and I'm not here?'

'You can leave a letter with your neighbour,' he suggested. Draining his tea, he stood and took the mug to the sink. 'And you have no idea where she might have gone?'

'None whatsoever. She was friends with Teresa Lacy and, as you know, they moved to the new housing estate in Cabra. But I don't have their address.'

'Would you like me to see what I can dig up?' he offered.

'How?'

He blew out his lips. 'Leave it with me. I can but try.'

★ ★ ★

Later that evening, Nell opened the door to find William hovering uncertainly on the other side. 'I'm sorry to disturb you.' He looked embarrassed.

'Please, come in. How can I help?'

Fidgeting with the cuffs of his jumper, he stepped inside. 'I . . . well . . . I wondered if you'd heard from Kate?'

'No. Have you?'

He shook his head. 'I just wondered, that's all.'

Nell smiled. 'You're fond of Kate, aren't you, William?'

He went bright red. 'I only spoke to her a few times.' He hung his head.

'Thanks for asking after her. She's probably still at her friend's, but if you do hear anything, anything at all, you will . . . '

'Of course.' He moved towards the door. 'I'd better be getting back.'

Nell couldn't help wondering whether a studious young man like William would have got on well with Kate, had she finished her education. Now, with hindsight, Nell wished she'd given her another chance.

Foreboding settled in her stomach like an abscess, her mind plagued with thoughts of what

310

might have happened to Kate. Sleep was her only release, but sleep wouldn't come.

★ ★ ★

On Saturday morning, Nell sat mulling over Liam's latest letter, then read it again. A smile creased her tired face.

Darling Nell,

I miss you so much and wonder how you are coping from day to day. Any news on how long Róisín's confinement might last? Has Kate found work yet? I hope she's supporting you.

I've been to the cinema a few times, not really caring what's on, and wishing you were sitting next to me with your head on my shoulder. I love the job and the lads I work with are friendly. They all call each other 'mate'. Strange! I've joined the company's social club and enjoy a game of pool most evenings. By the way, I've opened a savings account with the Post Office.

I can't wait for you to join me. It gets lonely at times, and I don't know how long I can stay away without seeing you or hearing your voice. I've been checking out accommodation nearby, suitable for the three of you, and as soon as you know when Róisín will be well enough to travel, I'll book the flights. It's so easy to save here, Nell. I've nothing to spend my money on.

I know you'll love it. So let me know as soon as you can and I'll start the ball rolling to get you over here to be with me, where you belong.

Love and miss you more than words can say.

Your ever loving,
Liam x

She kissed the letter, folded it and pushed it back inside the envelope, which had SWALK written across the back. It took her a few minutes to work out what it meant: Sealed With A Loving Kiss. Tears gathered in her eyes and the pain of loss deepened. Liam was the only one who could save her from the black pit of despair, and she would fly to him right now if she was free to do so. Sadness gripped her, and a feeling of foreboding settled in her stomach.

Liam was a homely lad at heart, and she sensed his isolation being away from the people he loved. Reading between the lines, she wondered if he really was happy, or just sticking it out because he expected she would be joining him soon. She guessed the latter.

Everything hinged on Róisín's progress. But what if Liam met someone else? It was possible, if he stayed away too long. The English girls were smart, sophisticated, and Liam was attractive, kind and caring. He could charm the birds down from the trees. The ache of losing him was growing stronger with every day that passed.

Before bed, she wrote him a letter, pouring out

her innermost worries about Kate's disappearance and Róisín's health, as well as her own desire to be with him. She signed it with kisses then sealed the envelope with a loving kiss. In bed, with the bedside light still on, she lay awake, staring at the crack in the corner of the ceiling, her mind racing with dark thoughts. Sleep still wouldn't come.

★　★　★

She didn't see Joe all the next week and when he called on Friday, she was glad of his company. She was anxious to know if he'd managed to get to see Róisín, and what news he might have to tell her.

'Hello, Nell. How've you been?'

'I'm grand.' She dipped her hand into the jar where she kept the rent. She didn't want to assume he had been to see Róisín, and despite her eagerness to know, she refrained from asking. 'Have you had a busy week, Joe?'

'Very busy. But don't you want to know how I got on at the sanatorium?'

Her face brightened, and she joined him at the table. 'You saw her, then?'

'I did.'

'And?' She cupped her face. 'How was she?'

'She looked bonny. Filled out since I last saw her.'

'Did she recognise you, Joe?'

'Not at first. You see, she wasn't expecting me, now, was she?' He chuckled. 'Her little face puckered up and she glanced over at the nurse,

313

who gave her a nod and a smile before she raised herself in the bed. I told her, 'I'm Mr Scanlon, the rent man, remember me?' She nodded and then asked where you were. So, I explained as best I could. Her face scrunched up, and I thought she was going to cry until I took out your letter.' He laughed again. 'I offered to read it to her, but she was quite indignant. 'I can read it meself,' she said.'

Nell smiled at this.

'I watched as she read, Nell, and a big smile lit up her little face. What you said certainly cheered her up.'

'Oh, that's so good to hear, Joe. I can't thank you enough.' She got up to make the tea and brought it to the table with a plate of custard creams. 'I'm sorry I've nothing better to offer you.'

'These are nice.' He crunched one into his mouth. 'I went to see the nurse in charge before I left. Thought it best to get her used to seeing me.'

'You did? Did Matron have a word, or did they say anything about Róisín's progress?'

'Well . . . ' He let out a deep breath. 'I didn't think they would discuss her health with me as I'm not family, so I said I was her Uncle Joe. It was the only way I was going to get anything out of Matron.'

'What is it, Joe? What did she say?' She leant in closer. 'Tell me, please.'

'Nell, it's good news that she's making steady progress. However, you're not going to like the fact that Róisín will have to stay at the

314

sanatorium for three years.'

'Three years! Oh, my God! Does she know?'

'Not at all. It wouldn't help her to know that now, would it?'

Nell sat back and placed her hand across her forehead. For a few moments, a silence filled the space around them.

Joe stood up and pushed back his chair. 'Nell, I take it you haven't eaten?'

'I'm fine, Joe, honest.'

'Let me take you out somewhere. I'll nip home and change, and pick you up in an hour.'

'No, no thanks, Joe. I couldn't let you do that. You've done enough by visiting Róisín. It's taken a weight off my mind.'

'Where's the harm? Come on, if only to keep you from fading away. You'll be no good to anyone if you don't eat.'

She shook her head. 'I couldn't.' She picked up the rent money. 'Before I forget.' She handed it to him. 'Goodnight, Joe, and thanks for everything.'

'If it's that young man of yours you're thinking about, do you think he's sitting in night after night without a social life? If he's worth waiting for, he won't condemn you for doing the same. I'm only looking out for you, Nell.'

'I know that, Joe, but I've things to do. Maybe another time. Oh, would you mind popping this letter to Liam in the box on the corner?'

After he left, Nell sat in the living room, curled up on the old sofa. She had plenty to think about. She was fond of Joe. He was the father figure she missed so much, the only person she could open up to with Liam so far away. The offer of a meal out in a restaurant had been tempting, but who knew where that might lead? Joe was getting too close, and they were both lonely. If she didn't take charge of her life now, she might end up doing something she would regret for the rest of her life.

She thought again about what Julia, her supervisor, had said. Terrible as it was, Róisín's predicament helped to sway her decision. She wrote another letter to Liam, telling him of her decision to return to nursing and her reasons for doing so. All she could do now was hope that he would understand and wait for her. She fell into bed and slept soundly for the first time in months.

46

Liam didn't reply immediately, but when his letter came it infuriated and upset Nell.

Dearest Nell,

I can't say how hurt and disappointed I was to receive your letter. That you would prefer to finish your nursing training in Dublin, rather than London, where we could be together. Have you considered the benefits you are turning down? What about us? Have your feelings changed? Is there someone else?

If this is the case, I'd rather you just came out and said so.

Liam x

Nell cried for days, and kept going over and over in her mind what she had said to upset him so much. All she had done was to point out to him the dire situation she found herself in. And she'd assured him of her love, so why did he think her feelings for him had changed? When, finally, she had recovered enough and rid herself of the anger she felt towards him, she wrote him a letter.

Dear Liam,

I'm sorry that my letter disappointed you. I

317

assumed you would want to know what my life was like here without you. I was being honest. I have never stopped loving you and I never will, whatever you believe. I did what I had to do to keep myself from going under. And I thought you, of all people, would understand. Was I wrong?

Did you really expect me to leave Róisín alone in Dublin and finish my training in England? You know I couldn't do that. If that's what you expected, then we never really knew each other.

As much as it hurts me to say this, Liam, if you want to finish our long-distance relationship, I'll try and understand. I don't expect you to stay faithful, but rest assured that I won't be going anywhere without Róisín — and Kate, if she ever returns.

I will always love you.
Your Nell x

The week before Nell moved back to the nurses' home, she wrote two more letters to Liam. Joe offered to post them for her. It saved her walking to the post office, and she was grateful to him.

Each day, she checked the post and found nothing, and as the days turned into weeks, she felt numb inside. Why had he stopped writing? Could there be someone else? She had been so sure she knew him. Could she have been so wrong? Her heart was broken. She couldn't sleep or eat; she just wanted to give up. It was only her sense of pride, and the thought of Róisín with no

318

one to care for her, which brought her to her senses. But it became a challenge to get up and face each day, knowing that Liam was no longer in her life.

★   ★   ★

Focused now on her nursing career, Nell felt a sense of relief when she discovered that her original fees were still valid. With no worries about rent or food, she managed to put a little by from the small wage she received. On her day off, she got to visit her sister, and on occasions she met Joe for a coffee at Bewley's. He continued to visit Róisín when he could, but so far had drawn a blank in finding out where Kate's friends, the Lacy family, lived.

Having been through so much in her life already, Nell was determined not to let her personal life get in the way of her work. She had been really nervous on her first day back, and was surprised at the welcome she received from Sister Amelia.

'Nice to have you back, Nurse Flynn,' Sister told her. 'Every week we are losing our nurses to England. I hope you'll stay with us. As you know, training is costly and time-consuming.'

'It's nice to be back, Sister.' And Nell really meant it.

She shared a room with two new trainees, and had to take a refresher course to make sure she was up to scratch, but she didn't mind. The work was hard but, weighed against her life at the biscuit factory, she found it rewarding.

Those first few weeks back, she didn't have time to think about Liam, or to dwell on Kate and where she might be.

A month later, Nell was in the sluice room when the tutor sister announced, 'I think you're ready to start working on the wards, Nurse Flynn.'

Up until then, she had practically lived in the sluice, cleaning bedpans and dirty trolleys. However, the nun's next words made her heart race.

'Your first task will be on the geriatric ward. You're to give the patient in bed number four a blanket bath.'

Alarmed, Nell dropped the bedpan she was cleaning.

'Don't worry,' she was told, 'I'll explain the procedure as we go along. An ill patient will appreciate a wash.'

When she arrived on the ward, it was cold, and she was mortified to find four trainees sitting in front of an elderly woman, waiting to observe how Nell performed. She tried to stop her hands and legs from shaking, not least because of the cold ward and the prospect that began to present itself.

Sister Amelia arrived. 'Now, Nurses,' she said, standing next to Nell but addressing the trainees. 'Blanket baths are one of the most important treatments we give to elderly patients who are bedridden. Nurse Flynn will show you how it's done, under my supervision.' She smiled towards Nell, reviving her confidence.

How hard could it be to wash the poor old dear?

No one addressed the patient, and Nell felt sorry for the old lady lying in the bed, a blank expression on her white face. A giggle was heard coming from one of the younger trainees.

'Merely a matter of common sense,' Sister continued. 'First, we strip the bed with as little discomfort as possible to the patient.'

She gestured towards Nell, who proceeded to remove the counterpane as carefully as she could. When the patient let out a little moan, she said, 'I'm sorry, dear.'

'Now some hot water . . . ' Sister Amelia signalled to the assistant tutor, who rushed out with two large jugs. 'Always have the patient's toilet requisites ready.' She nodded, and Nell rummaged in the bedside locker.

The water was poured, one jug at a time, into the bowl.

'You must undress your patient completely,' instructed Sister Amelia.

There was a stifled gasp from the trainees.

Nell swallowed, her face hot and her legs shaking, as she tried to stay confident. She had looked after her mother when she was ill, but this was a complete stranger and she felt protective of the old lady's dignity. But the lady, who still remained nameless, showed no signs of distress. Nell pulled the nightgown gently over her head to reveal a paper-thin', wrinkly body, but the woman didn't try to retain her modesty, and Nell guessed that this wasn't her first blanket wash.

Using a flannel, she proceeded to wash the woman carefully, frightened her tissue-like skin might break if she rubbed too hard. As Nell washed the patient thoroughly, Sister pointed out the areas of greatest importance. Ears and armpits had to be washed twice and powdered.

'Patients with bedsores must be treated every four hours.'

Luckily for Nell, this woman did not have bedsores yet. Nell didn't dare look at her classmates, but as she finished washing and drying the patient's legs, she turned to give them a weak smile. The whole thing was like a cooking recipe, she thought.

After that, everything else came naturally to her, and in between her studies she worked on the geriatric ward. Some of her patients were cantankerous but they were also funny, and she was never short of someone to talk to. Her hope was to be moved to the children's ward and gain experience of how to care for Róisín when she was finally released from the sanatorium.

For now, though, she was happy to work hard, pass her exams, and keep Liam tucked away in a special corner of her heart.

47

After Kate's first night back at Jerry's place, he couldn't do enough for her. She made sure she kept the house rules, while Jerry respected her privacy. She wasn't naive enough to believe it would last, though, and she caught him glancing sideways at her on numerous occasions.

He told her about his job, driving cargo to and from the docks, and the good wages he was receiving. They settled into an easy routine together.

One evening, before setting off for his night shift, Jerry surprised her by declaring, 'A few months from now, I'll have enough money saved to get us a better place, a little terraced house close to the city.'

She glanced up from the magazine she was reading. 'Really?'

'Yeah!' He grinned. 'But you and me, you know, we'd have to be together like.'

She glanced away. She wasn't sure how to reply. As far as she was concerned, they were all right as they were. 'I'm sorry, Jerry. I'm not ready for anything serious. And if you feel you want to look elsewhere, I'll move out. I don't want to hold you back.'

'No, it's not that.' He turned to face her. 'We get on, don't we?'

'Well, yes, but . . . '

'Sure, in time you'll grow to like me as much as I like you.'

'I don't want to just *like* you, Jerry.'

His face clouded.

Fearful of burning her bridges, she added, 'Give me a bit more time, eh?'

Smiling, he jumped up and grabbed his heavy coat. 'I'd best be off. I'll see you tomorrow. And, Kate, I'll have porridge in the morning.'

At first, he was generous, leaving her money for food. It suited her, and he made no demands on her, but she agreed to keep the place clean and have a hot meal ready for him every evening before he set out to work. Kate was happy enough, but she could see the frustration on Jerry's face, especially at the weekends when they were thrown together. She had a roof over her head and money to spend on clothes. She hated cooking, but it was the least she could do, and Jerry hadn't complained when she charred the meat and overcooked the potatoes more than once. She continued to work for the printing firm, while Mr Schneider continued to treat her like a dogsbody.

★ ★ ★

The turning point came when Jerry lost his job. He was caught drinking while working and given a warning, but when it happened again he was out on his ear. Kate was shocked to find him slumped in the armchair when she returned from work.

'Jerry, wake up, you'll be late for work.'

He muttered a few expletives and turned over. She could smell alcohol on his breath.

She made him a hot drink. 'Here, drink this. What's the matter with you? Why are you not at work?'

'Oh, shut your mouth.' And he lashed out with his arm, knocking the hot coffee to the floor, scalding the back of her hand.

She cried out, but he was too drunk to care and turned on his side and went back to sleep. She ran her hand under the cold tap, something she had seen her mam do when she burnt herself on the hot iron. Then she got out of her work clothes, which were covered in paint and coffee, and put on a pleated skirt and fresh blouse. She had to get out of there.

Kate pulled on her new green jacket and, after rifling Jerry's pockets, headed out. Most people in employment were still winding their way home after a hard day's work, and the evenings were growing lighter. She went into a tea room on O'Connell Street and pondered the situation with Jerry as she waited for her order to be taken. What would he do next? If he didn't find work immediately, she knew what road he would go down, and she didn't want to be around when that happened. And if he was still snoring in the armchair when she got home, how was she to sleep in the same room with him smelling of alcohol?

The waitress took her order of egg, chips and sausage, and Kate settled back in her chair, removing her jacket. There were only a handful of people dining.

Then she saw them at the back of the tea room. A little gasp escaped her lips and she

325

turned away, lowering her head and feeling colour flush her cheeks. She covered the side of her face with her hand.

Suddenly, he was standing next to her, his slender hands folded in front of him. 'Hello, Kate. I wasn't sure it was you at first. You look well. Are you alone?'

'Hello, Michael. Just treating myself, you know.' Her heart pounded in her ears and she thought he must hear it.

'How are things? Are you still working for Father John?'

'No. No, I'm not.' Her voice trembled.

'How is your sister, and the little one?'

'Fine. Róisín's still in hospital.'

'I'm sorry to hear that.' He was rubbing one hand over the other, then he glanced round. 'Well, I'd better . . . ' He smiled in that wonderful way that made her knees go weak. 'It's nice to see you again, Kate.'

'Michael?'

He paused.

'Are you . . . I mean . . . are you married now?'

He smiled. 'Not yet. June next year.'

As she watched him make quick strides back to Ophelia, the waitress brought her food, but she had lost her appetite. She turned her head and glimpsed him helping his fiancée on with her jacket, smiling and whispering into her ear, before they walked from the tea room without a backward glance, his arm firmly around her waist.

'Oh, Michael,' she murmured. Seeing him

326

again brought back all the lovely memories she had of him, and it made her sad — and sadder still to think that she was shacked up with the likes of Jerry O'Shea. She nibbled some of her meal, sipped her tea and then left the tea room.

When she got back, Jerry had gone, and she hoped he had changed his mind and gone to work. Although in her heart she knew exactly where he would be.

48

As the months passed, Nell knew she had made the right decision to return to nursing, but it didn't stop the loneliness she felt. Occasionally, she went to the cinema with Kelly, one of her room-mates. The other girl was quite laid-back in her approach to life and managed to put the smile back on Nell's face.

She liked Kelly and had confided in her about Liam. But Kelly had been out with several boys, and tried to encourage Nell to do the same.

'Men are like trams,' she giggled. 'You miss one and, before you know it, along comes another.'

Nell had shoved her with her elbow and told her not to be so flippant. 'Besides, it's buses now. Trams will soon be a thing of the past.'

'Anyhow, this fella of yours. How can you be sure he's the right one unless you've tried a few?'

Nell smiled. 'I knew early on, before we even kissed, that Liam was the one.'

But, secretly, she was no longer that sure.

* * *

One warm summer evening, Nell returned to the nurses' home with a pint of milk and was surprised to see Joe standing outside.

'Joe! This is a surprise. Nothing wrong, is there?'

'Oh, not a bit of it, Nell. I have a couple of tickets for the Theatre Royal and wondered if you were free tomorrow evening to come with me.'

Taken aback, she held the bottle of milk to her chest. 'Come into the hall a minute. I'm afraid I can't invite you up, as one of the nurses is having an early night.'

'I understand. Can you come?'

'It's good of you to think of me, Joe. Why not? It'll be a nice change. What time does it start?'

'If I pick you up here at, say, seven o'clock, that should give us enough time.'

★ ★ ★

The following evening, after her shift on the wards, Nell wanted nothing more than to fall into bed and sleep. Getting ready for the theatre outing with Joe, she realised he hadn't told her who was on. It was usually a bit of drama and variety, which would make a change from the cinema.

'Oh, you're a dark horse,' Kelly said as she watched Nell get ready. 'Thought you said you only had eyes for one man.'

Nell laughed. 'Oh, it's not like that. He's a family friend who just happens to have a spare theatre ticket.'

'Pull the other one,' Kelly said, rolling off the bed. 'Next you'll be looking at rings.'

'Don't be daft, Kelly. He's old enough to be my father.'

In some ways, her friend reminded Nell of

Kate. Unfortunately, Kate didn't have a sense of humour.

Joe was waiting outside to help her into the car, and he was the perfect gentleman throughout the evening. Nell found herself laughing more than she had done in months, and it lifted her spirits.

As they walked towards the car, at the end of the show, she thanked him for inviting her. 'I'd forgotten how good variety at the Royal was. The last time I was here, Mam and Dad took Kate and me. My dad loved the theatre.'

Joe paused outside Mulligan's. 'Well, I'm glad you enjoyed yourself tonight, Nell. Would you like a nightcap before I take you back?'

She shook her head. 'I'd say yes, only I don't want to be locked out.'

'Don't worry, it'll be fine.'

Normally, she would have insisted on getting back. But Joe had been so nice, and she didn't want to seem rude by refusing, so they slipped inside the noisy city pub. The music and banter were loud, and they could hardly hear each other speak.

'There's a quieter room upstairs,' Joe shouted. 'You go ahead and I'll bring the drinks. What would you like?'

If she had her favourite — a Dubonnet and lemonade — she might oversleep in the morning, and she was on early shift. 'Just a lime juice, please,' she decided.

When they were seated, there was only the pleasant murmur of conversation from those around them who just wanted a quiet drink. The noise from below drifted upwards, but it wasn't intrusive.

Nell slipped off her coat and took a sip of her drink. 'Nice and cosy in here, Joe. Is this your usual haunt?'

He shrugged. 'I've been here a few times. It's better than sitting alone at home.' He put down his beer. 'Nell, I take it you've heard no more from Kate? Do you think she'll ever come back?'

She lowered her head and swallowed. 'I don't know, Joe, that's the truth of it.'

'She's not been back to the flat,' he told her. 'I've asked.'

'You will ask again, next time you're there?'

'Of course.' He sat forward, placing his elbows on the table. 'I'm glad we came up here, where it's quieter. I have something I want to ask you.'

'What is it, Joe?'

'Are you . . . well, are you still communicating with . . . ?'

She took a deep breath, annoyed that he couldn't, or wouldn't, say Liam's name. 'His name's Liam.'

'Yes, of course. Liam.'

'You did ask at John's Lane if there was any post for me?' she questioned.

He nodded.

She frowned. 'Why do you want to know, Joe?'

'Oh, nothing.' He sat back.

Still peeved that he couldn't remember Liam's name, she was nevertheless curious to find out what he was going to ask her. 'Joe, what is it?'

'I don't want to step on anyone's toes, Nell, but I was wondering if you were free, that's all.'

331

He paused and supped his beer. 'I like you, Nell. I like you a lot.'

'What are you saying?' Shocked by his remark, she sat back. 'I've looked on you as a father figure, a friend. But this changes things . . . I . . .'

He lifted a hand in apology. 'I'm sorry, I shouldn't have spoken my mind.'

'I may not have heard from Liam in months, but my feelings for him remain the same,' she replied, and stood up.

He pressed her to sit down, and she did so reluctantly. 'I can offer you a home and a good life, if you were to give me a chance. And what about when Róisín comes home? She will need a stable home. Have you thought about that?'

'I've thought of nothing else, Joe.'

'I hate to see you waste your life on someone who . . . well.'

Nell bit back an angry reply. 'I can't talk about this now, Joe,' she told him. 'Please, take me home.'

49

Nell threw herself into her nursing studies, and barely noticed the changing seasons as she focused on building a future for herself. As autumn approached, the days grew shorter, and soon it was the anniversary of her mother's death. Nell planned to take flowers to the grave and say a prayer for her mother's soul once she finished her shift on the men's ward.

She had become attached to one patient, in particular. At fifty, he had been diagnosed with lung disease, and she pitied him, especially when his breathing was bad.

'I hate it when your shift finishes, Nurse,' he told her. 'But don't tell nurse Hatty I said that.' He was wheezy, a terrible rattling coming from his chest.

Nell laughed. 'Get away with you. Now behave, and don't exert yourself.'

'Ah, sure I miss you when you go.'

'You get more attention than all the rest put together.' She smiled and tucked him in.

'Nurse, would you be an angel and bring me back a packet of Woodbine?' He pressed a silver coin into her hand.

She shook her head. 'You know I can't do that, Leo. It's against the rules.' She placed the silver coin on the bedside cabinet.

He placed his hand on his chest. 'Sure, it doesn't matter now, does it?'

'Of course it matters. I'm sorry.' She walked away, feeling dreadful to have denied his request, but she had already been in trouble a few weeks back for bringing him in cigarettes.

It had rained for most of the morning, and she went back to the nurses' home to wait for it to ease before setting off for the cemetery. A year ago, it had been a cold but bright and sunny day when they laid their mother to rest. Today, it looked like there would be no let-up with the rain.

Early afternoon, Nell picked up her red umbrella and hurried down the street to the florist's to pick up flowers, then caught the bus out to the cemetery. She wondered if Kate was remembering, too. It had been nine months now since she'd walked out. And not a day went by that Nell didn't wonder where she was and wish she'd get in touch.

Nell shivered from the cold as she made her way up the long pathway towards her mother's grave, a bunch of flowers sticking out of her shopping bag, her umbrella dripping on to her legs and shoes. At the graveside, she was taken aback to see a small bunch of freesias — their mother's favourite flower — muddied and splashed with rain, lying across the top of the unmarked grave. She glanced about her, but the graveyard was empty. No one would come here in such weather unless, like her, they had good reason.

If Kate had money to buy flowers, she must be working. Nell hoped so. She placed the flowers for her mother — a bunch of lilacs — on the wet

334

earth next to Kate's. A choked sob snagged the back of her throat and she straightened up, looking furtively about her in case Kate was sheltering beneath a tree.

If only she'd come straight here and not gone back to her room, she might have seen her sister. 'Oh, Kate. Where are you? I miss you so much.' A cry escaped her lips but there was no one near enough to hear.

Nell murmured her regrets to her mam. Wishing she had done more to keep the family together, she hoped her ma would understand that she'd done her best, even if it hadn't been enough. She pleaded with her to help find Kate, and filled her in on Róisín's progress.

All the while she stood there, her eyes scanned the vast cemetery in case Kate was still around. Eventually, she murmured a short prayer and left.

* * *

Earlier that morning, Kate had been sent on a delivery and had asked Mr Schneider if she could take an extra half hour to visit her mother's grave. At first, he pondered her request, tapping his fat fingers on the desk, keeping her waiting for his response.

'It's a year today since I lost my mother, and I won't be able to concentrate until I've been to her grave . . . I — '

She was going to say she'd make the time up, but he seemed to be in one of his rare good moods and interrupted her.

'Well, I suppose so, but don't take all day. We have a large order to get out.'

By the time she arrived at the cemetery, she was shivering and soaked through, despite wearing a raincoat. She only stayed a minute to place the small posy of flowers on her mother's grave.

'I'm sorry if I've disappointed you, Mam, and I'm sorry we rowed,' she whispered to the grave. 'And I'm sorry I couldn't get on with Nell. Why did you have to leave me? I miss you so much.' A tear mingled with rain and trickled down her cold face. 'I've got a job, Mam, so I have to go.' She made the sign of the cross and left.

She made her way to North Earl Street, where she dropped off the delivery, wrapped in a waterproof bag, and picked up instructions for another order. She thought more about Nell and Róisín these days, and today as she walked, she wondered if Nell still worked at the biscuit factory and if Róisín was out of the sanatorium.

The anniversary of their mother's death brought back unhappy memories of the last time she had seen her, the row she'd never told anyone about, and her disagreements with Nell. If she'd bumped into her at the cemetery, Kate wouldn't have known what to say. She hated her job, but the thought of getting a place of her own kept her focused.

50

Sharing a small flat with Jerry was not ideal, but unbeknownst to him Kate had been saving half the money he gave her for housekeeping. Another week or two and she would have enough money to put down a deposit on a rented bedsit of her own.

Since Jerry had lost his driving job, she dreaded going back to what had now become a slum. He did nothing around the place, and left dirty mugs and plates all over the floor; that went for his washing, too, but that was one thing she wasn't going to do for him. When she got home every night, she cleaned up before she could think of cooking anything. Gone were the days when he would have a warm meal waiting for her. Even without a job, he still had money to spend down the pub.

Tonight, when she arrived back, Jerry was out. The place was like a pigsty, but luckily there was a tin of stewing meat. She peeled a few carrots and made an appetising meal, leaving his to keep warm over a saucepan of boiling water that she had to keep topping up.

Kate watched television until the news finished, then washed and got ready for bed. No sooner had her head hit the pillow than she drifted off into a deep sleep.

She woke sometime later, when Jerry stumbled into the room. The air immediately soured with the smell of beer. He switched on the light and she sat up, rubbing sleep from her eyes. 'Keep the noise down, I'm trying to sleep.'

He mumbled, 'Sorry,' and sat on the end of her bed to remove his boots. They made a loud thud as they fell to the floor.

'Go into your own room and do that.' Kate turned away, pulling the covers up over her shoulders.

'Hey, I've got something to tell you.'

'You're drunk. And unless you've got a job, I'm not interested.'

'I've only had a couple of jars, and I've been offered work.'

She pulled herself into a sitting position. 'They're not letting you drive again, are they?'

'Loading and unloading down the docks.'

Well, that was a relief. 'When do you start?' she asked.

'The morrow night.'

The less she saw of him, the better she liked it.

'The money's not bad, and as long as the work continues, we'll be able to find a better place. You'd like that, wouldn't you, Kate?'

He'd moved further up the bed, and the smell of beer wrinkled her nose.

'Go to bed, Jerry. We'll talk about it tomorrow. Some of us have work in the morning.'

'Have you any idea how it feels, Kate?'

'What are you on about?' She knew exactly what he was getting at. It wasn't the first time he'd tried to get her onside, but she was having none of him. He was just a convenience as far as she was concerned.

'For months now I've tried to keep me hands to myself, but it's not natural. You know how I feel about you, and you owe me.'

'You said that debt was clear!' she snapped.

'Well, I've changed me mind.' He moved closer and placed his hand around the back of her head.

'Get off me.'

She pushed him away, but he grabbed her wrist.

'Let go of me, you drunken sod.' She leapt from the bed and ran into his bedroom, but the lock was broken.

The smell in there was vile. Smelly socks and dirty washing lay everywhere, and the bed was no better. He hadn't been to the launderette in ages. She couldn't stay in there, and within minutes she stepped back out.

He was lying across her bed, his eyes closed. It was much too early for work, but she wasn't going to stick around for Jerry to start his litany of pathetic apologies. She couldn't stay here any longer. She put some food into a bag, and her personal stuff and a few clothes in another. But before she could manage to get dressed, Jerry shot up.

'Where do you think you're going? It's the middle of the night.'

Holding her belongings tight to her chest, she said, 'I'm leaving, Jerry, and you can't stop me. I've never given you any reason to think I had feelings for you. It's all in your stupid head.'

'You bitch! After all I've done for you. You think you can just swan off?' He pinched the top of his nose. 'Do you have any idea what it costs to keep this place? You wash a few dishes, cook a few meals, and you think that's all there is to it.' He was on his feet. 'Well, I've got news for you. You're going nowhere until I've been paid.'

His eyes grew wild, and she made a dash for the door. But he grabbed her arm, and her belongings scattered to the floor.

'Let me go, you dumb idiot.'

His grip tightened, digging into her thin arm.

'Leave me alone, I tell you!'

She lashed out with her hands, scratching his face, but he held her fast. His arms around her waist, he carried her kicking and screaming to the bed. Before she could recover, he had her arms pinned.

'What are you doing?' She was becoming increasingly afraid. 'Stop, I tell you. Let me go.'

Holding her with one hand, he clamped the other over her mouth, leaving her gasping for breath. His foul breath fanned her face and she turned her head, struggling to free herself.

'If you'd just been a little kinder, Kate, this wouldn't be happening.'

As his hand groped her body through her nightgown, a silent scream scratched the back of her throat and her head shook violently from side to side. She kicked and thrashed, then felt his weight on top of her, knocking the breath from her lungs. Squirming beneath him, she continued to struggle against him, but he was determined.

Looking upwards, she cried out to her mother to help her. Her stomach twisted into a knot until she thought she'd be sick, but still his hand covered her mouth. He showed her no mercy as he penetrated her, and searing pain wracked her body like she'd been stabbed.

When he finally released his hand from over her mouth, her cry of agony echoed through the flat. He drew a shuddering breath and rolled off her, then quickly got to his feet, pulling his clothes together.

He glanced down at her. 'God, Kate. Why did you make me do that?' And he went out, leaving the door swinging on its hinges.

Kate curled up into a ball and wept as if her heart would break. Sobbing and shaking uncontrollably, she grabbed the sheet that now smelled of his sweat and her blood. Oh, dear God. What had he done to her? She tried to leave the bed, but pain kept her rooted to the spot. She felt dirty, used and violated. She screamed out in anger. How dare he do this to her! Her heart pounded in her ears and the adrenaline coursing through her veins paralysed her.

She stayed where she was, motionless, her mind a fog.

★ ★ ★

Dawn had given way to daylight when she crawled from the bed, leaving a blood-stained sheet behind, to close and lock the door. Sobbing and shivering, a trembling she couldn't control took over as she scrubbed herself clean in the small tin bath, knowing she would never feel truly clean again.

How could she go to work and pretend she was fine? The girl who had gone to the silk printing works the previous day wasn't the same any more. How could she face people, knowing what Jerry had done to her? But she knew no one would believe her. She would be to blame. She'd be shunned, treated as an outcast, a fallen woman.

Kate took a deep breath and squared her shoulders. Nobody would see the pain she was going through, she decided. And she vowed never to trust another man as long as she lived.

She let the water run over the bruises to her arms and legs. Bruises would heal, but what Jerry had done to her would live with her for a very long time.

51

Nell wrote again to Liam, first checking his address and making sure her room number at the nurses' home was correct, then she took it to the post office in her break. If she didn't get a reply this time, she wasn't sure what she would do. So far, nothing had turned up at the nurses' home. It was so long since she had last heard from Liam that she wondered if he'd had an accident at work. And if she hadn't been so busy at the hospital, she would have gone out of her mind with worry.

It wasn't like Liam to be petty. He knew her situation only too well. And he had vowed his love for her, as she had for him. So, what had changed?

Between her shifts at the hospital and visits to the sanatorium, she didn't have a lot of time to spare. She didn't want to worry his parents unnecessarily, but if she didn't hear from him soon she would have no choice but to go and visit them. And if they had heard from him, her hopes and dreams would come crashing down.

The first thing she did each morning was to look through the post in the community hall, but there was never anything for her. Not even Kate had any time for her.

Since her theatre outing with Joe, back in the summer, she had declined his subsequent offers of a visit to the cinema, or to the dog track. She didn't approve of greyhound racing, despite Joe telling her it wasn't cruel.

She would have loved to say yes to the cinema but, knowing how he felt about her, she didn't want to hurt him. He was a genuinely nice man, and his constant visits to see Róisín were a comfort to her.

On Friday night, the city was cloaked in fog and it was unusually mild for November. As she walked through the grounds of the hospital towards the nurses' home, she wasn't looking forward to another night in while her two roommates were out with their boyfriends. She had boring medical stuff to finish writing, and sometimes the small print in the textbooks made her eyes ache. But at least it might stop her from brooding over Liam. 'Dear God, if you're there, please let him get in touch,' she murmured.

When she reached the main door, she spotted Joe pacing up and down outside.

'Joe. What are you doing here? Is . . . is something wrong?'

'Nell, I thought I'd catch you before you went inside. Is there somewhere we can talk?'

'Come inside. If there's no one in the kitchen, we can use that.' Her heart raced and she hurried ahead of him, up a flight of stairs and along the landing. The small communal kitchen was empty.

'We can talk in here.' Nell removed her nurse's cape and sat down, pulling the chair in closer to the table. 'What is it, Joe?' The thought that Róisín's health had deteriorated panicked her.

She should have made the effort and gone up herself this week.

Joe sat opposite, slowly unbuttoning his coat. He knitted his fingers.

'For the love of God, Joe, what is it?' Annoyance furrowed her brow.

'Calm down, Nell, Róisín is fine.'

Nell placed her elbows on the table. 'You've seen her, then? How was she?'

'Yes, she's fine. She's coming on nicely, and they think there's a possibility she could be home within six months.' He sucked in his breath. 'What do you think of that?'

The anxious look slipped from her face and she smiled broadly. 'Oh, Joe.' A tear threatened, and she swallowed. 'That's the best news I've had in months.'

'The specialist is taking a look at her tomorrow. So, you might know more when you go up.'

She nodded. If he'd brought her bad news, it would have broken her already fragile state. But now, thanks to Joe, she had hopes that her baby sister would be home soon, and she felt the weight of the world lifting from her shoulders.

'Well, I'd better be off.' Joe got to his feet.

'I'm sorry I can't offer you a cup of tea.'

He waved his hand.

'Before you go, Joe, did you post the two letters to Liam that I gave you?'

He paused. 'Why do you ask?'

'Well, it's been ages since I heard anything back from him, and it's not like Liam.' She picked up her cape. 'Well, thanks for coming all

345

the way over to let me know about Róisín, Joe. I appreciate it.'

'It's no trouble; I knew you'd want to know. Besides, I was on my way to see that movie, the one with Bette Davis. *All About Eve*. It's got a good plot, and I love Bette Davis.'

Bette Davis had been her mother's favourite actress, and Nell had been waiting for a chance to go and see it. 'Is it still on?'

'Yes, it's been doing the rounds for months. You wouldn't care to come with me, would you?' He rolled back his shoulders. 'That's if you're not doing anything?'

She glanced down at her uniform thoughtfully. It was just the pick-me-up she needed after the trying day she'd had on the ward.

He wrapped his scarf around his neck and started for the stairs. 'Well, goodnight, Nell.' He cleared his throat. 'I'll catch up with you another time.'

'Joe, wait. I love Bette Davis, too.'

He turned, smiling. 'Good. We'll have to hurry, though, there's bound to be queues.'

'Give me five minutes to change and I'll come with you.'

⋆ ⋆ ⋆

Nell had become engrossed in the film, and they'd been lucky to get two seats together.

When Joe walked her back to the nurses' home, the fog still hovered over the city. They could hardly see where they were going.

'If anything else comes along with Bette Davis,

346

I'll let you know. And if you're free, we can go together.' He added quickly, 'No pressure.'

'Thanks for a lovely evening, Joe, and for the news about Róisín.'

'That's all right. I'll see you safely inside and then I'll be off.'

She was about to put her key into the lock when a figure stepped out from the side of the building, startling her.

Joe reared up, shielding her. 'Who the dickens are you? And what are you doing hanging around the nurses' home?' he yelled. 'Clear off, or I'll report you.'

Shocked, Nell steadied herself against the door post. 'Liam! Oh my God, Liam.' Her eyes filled with tears of relief, and she reached out to him.

But he held up his hands to ward her off.

'What's wrong?' she asked.

He moved away and shifted the knapsack that was slung over his shoulder, avoiding her eyes.

'Liam. I've been so worried about you.' She fumbled with her key. 'Come in. Please, come in.'

'I thought you said you'd wait.' His voice was hollow. 'But it looks like I got that wrong.'

'No. No, you didn't.' She turned to Joe for support, but he was nowhere to be seen. 'Come in and let me explain,' she pleaded.

'I won't, Nell. I need to get my head around seeing you with another man.' He looked down at his boots. 'I've come straight from the boat because I couldn't wait to see you.'

'It's not what you think,' she replied.

'Don't try to defend what you've done. I

347

should have known when you didn't bother to answer my letters.' He turned away.

'Liam, don't go.'

But he strode away into the fog, leaving her filled with rage, gritting her teeth, and choked with emotion.

She screamed inside. Why, oh why, tonight of all nights? If she hadn't gone to see Bette Davis, she would have been here when Liam called. She raged at herself, and at Joe for asking her out. Fate had a way of cutting her down at every turn.

Upstairs, her room-mates were chatting as she entered, but Nell, unable to face their questions, feigned a headache and went to bed.

It must have looked suspicious to Liam, her arriving home with a man in tow. She buried her head in her quilt to stifle her sobs.

52

Nell couldn't stop thinking about Liam. Why had he come home? Had he come to end their relationship, and seeing her with Joe made it easier for him to walk away? Why wouldn't he let her explain? And if he had sent her letters, why had she not received them? So many questions she couldn't answer.

Her whole world had turned upside down, and she was at sixes and sevens to know what to do. She would have to find him, to try to explain. Her heart told her to go straight to his parents' house and, if he was there, beg him to forgive her.

All weekend she kept replaying the awful scene on the doorstep of the nurses' home, over and over in her head. What could she have done differently? And why had Joe not defended her? She could only imagine what had been going through Liam's mind.

Nell did her best to stay cheerful as she joined her team of nurses on Monday morning. Matron was in full flow as she issued their duties for the early morning shift.

'Nurse Flynn, I want you on women's primary care. I'll pop along later to see how you're doing.' Nell was about to shoot off when she called, 'And Nurse Flynn? The patient in bed five needs her medication at eight a.m. sharp.'

'Certainly, Matron.' As Nell walked away, she

could hear the remaining nurses being set tasks on other wards. She still hoped she would be put to work on the children's ward, but so far that hadn't happened.

The ward she had been assigned to was mainly made up of older women, with a row of beds on either side of the room. It was a little more cheerful than the men's ward, with large vases of flowers on the centre table and on some of the patients' bedside lockers.

Most of the women were still asleep, and Nell sat at the table in the centre to speak to the nurse she was relieving.

'Everything all right, Nurse?' It was the rule always to address staff by their title and not their Christian name, no matter how well they were acquainted.

'Pretty quiet, apart from her in bed number four.' The other woman grimaced. 'Kept on complaining that her in bed number five was keeping her awake snoring.' Smiling, she gathered up her belongings. 'Good luck, Nurse. She'll be as grumpy as hell when she wakes up.'

Nell smiled. 'Thanks for the warning.'

She hated the early shift, and in particular having to wake patients from their sleep to take their temperatures. As she walked along the row of beds, it was still only seven fifteen. Most looked up, bleary-eyed, but accepted that checks had to be done. But there were always patients, like the woman in bed four, who grumbled and called her names.

'You and your silly rules at this ungodly hour,' she mouthed when woken. And Nell got the same reaction when she brought the tea round just before eight.

Today, she was finding everything a chore. Her mind flitted to Liam every time she was idle: his face when he looked at her; the distrust in his eyes that had once held such love for her. By the time breakfast came round, she was relieved to see a change in the patients, who were all sitting up, eager to see what was in store for them.

It was then she remembered Matron's instructions, and she hurried along to bed four. 'Before you start eating your porridge, can you pop this pill on to your tongue for me, please?'

The woman glared at her. 'What's that for?'

'Your angina.' Nell unscrewed the bottle top and popped two pills on to her palm.

'I don't have bloody angina, whatever that is. I want to see the Sister.' The woman was yelling and waving her arms about.

Matron had just entered the ward and walked brusquely towards the bed where Nell stood trying to calm the woman.

'Nurse Flynn!'

Nell jerked round.

'I'll see you in my office now. And bring that medication with you.' Matron turned on her heel and walked from the ward.

Frowning, Nell retrieved the pills and followed her, wondering what she had done wrong.

Matron sat behind her desk and rolled back her shoulders. 'Hand me those pills, Nurse.'

Nell passed them over. 'You've not administered any, have you?' Her face had that stern expression that meant Nell was in deep trouble.

'No, Matron.' Her voice was barely above a whisper.

'Just when I was about to commend you for all your hard work since you returned, you go and do something like this.'

'I . . . I'm sorry, Matron.' Nell still had no idea what she had done wrong.

'Are you deaf as well as incompetent, Nurse? I distinctly told you to give this medication,' she held up the bottle, 'to bed number five. Had you succeeded in giving the wrong medication to bed number four, there could have been serious consequences.'

Nell's hand flew to her face. 'I'm so sorry . . .' She attempted to apologise again. Tears sprang to her eyes.

'Whatever your personal problems, Nurse, you can't bring them into the hospital. If this happens again, you will be seriously repri-manded and possibly thrown off the course. Do you understand?' Matron's voice rose a pitch.

Nell felt the blood drain from her face. How could she have let herself down in this way? Her mind had been so full of what had happened with Liam, she had almost made a serious error. 'It won't happen again, Matron.'

'I think you should go back to the sluice room for the remainder of this week until I can trust you again.'

For the rest of her shift, Nell put her back into cleaning sticky trolleys and scrubbing bedpans until they shone. No one noticed her tears as she worked, and the empty feeling in the pit of her stomach grew with each passing hour. There was no concentration needed, only hard graft.

With hindsight, this was Matron's way of getting her to work through her personal problems. She had lost all her family, apart from Róisín, and now Liam had walked away. Was she such a wicked person to have chased off everyone she loved?

What had happened on the ward that morning could have landed her in serious trouble. Her only consolation was that she still had a job.

53

Disorientated, her mind in turmoil, Kate regretted the bad choices she had made. Since leaving Jerry's, she had found a cheap bedsit on the south side of the city. Each time she ventured outside, she felt as if the whole world knew her secret, especially when men looked her way. She imagined that women stared and whispered, talking about her and guessing her guilt.

The little money she had only lasted her a few days. The food she had taken with her was soon all but gone, and she needed to go in search of work. She couldn't face going back to the printing works, and imagined Mr Schneider's anger erupting. But she couldn't worry about him; her mind was still confused by what Jerry had done.

In another few days, when she felt stronger, she vowed she'd go out and find a new job. Each day she told herself the same thing, and each day she stayed where she was, away from prying eyes.

If she signed on the dole there was every possibility she would bump into Jerry, and she never wanted to see his face again for fear of what she might do to him. The longer she sat going over the nightmare in her head, she feared for her own sanity. Each day she told herself she would take charge of her life again, but each morning she couldn't muster up the courage to even get dressed.

She had a terrible secret she would have to bury within her, and she daren't tell a soul for fear she would start to cry and never stop. She had been in the lonely room so long, she could barely remember what street she was on. She had only a vague recollection of the landlady giving her the key once she had handed over the required deposit. But she had been so traumatised that she hadn't cared about the bedsit's shabby state. It had a bed, and it was somewhere for her to lie down.

She couldn't remember anything, apart from the fact that the house was close to the canal. At one point, she had walked along the pathway, wrestling with the urge to throw herself in. But she hadn't had the courage, and had continued towards the house and knocked on the door. The landlady hadn't questioned her strange wanderings, and the house was quiet. Kate had locked the door of her room, dosed herself up with aspirin to ease her pain, then kept falling in and out of sleep. Sometimes she wasn't sure if she'd dreamt it all, but the pain in her abdomen was a sharp reminder.

For the first time in a long while, she thought about Nell. She had treated her sister badly, and this was her punishment. But Nell was so righteous that she would have the priest send her to one of them homes, if she knew what had happened to her.

She had heard of that kind of thing happening to other girls. 'For their own protection,' it was said. No, she couldn't go crawling back to Nell and give her the satisfaction of being right.

Kate had cried more than she had ever done in her life. When it was morning, she longed for night, and then longed for daylight again.

Today, she felt more positive despite the frost that formed on the window. She forced herself out of bed. She wouldn't let Jerry win. From now on, she would take charge of her life, and trust no one. She dressed in warm clothes and ventured to the corner shop, bought milk and a newspaper, and went back to the room before anyone saw her. Over a cup of tea, she scanned the situations vacant.

She wasn't hungry, and hadn't eaten in days, but the tea was soothing, with sugar, something she had never taken before. Most of the work advertised wanted qualifications and experience, neither of which she had, so her choice was narrowed down to the more menial jobs.

Then she spotted a notice. Clery's department store on O'Connell Street was looking for shop assistants for the Christmas rush. That would suit her nicely. But before she got to grips with the idea, her confidence ebbed. How could she work amongst decent people when she was tarnished? And what if Nell, or her friends, or even Jerry O'Shea, walked into the store. She couldn't handle that. Her spirits waned. However, they were also looking for kitchen staff. She could cook at a push. And if she was lucky, she would get fed and be safe from public scrutiny. It was probably the best she could hope for.

Taking heart, she smartened herself up, washed her hair, and applied a small amount of make-up to her pale face. Then she rolled her hair into a coil, held it together with her best slide, and placed a peaked cap on top. A little overdressed, maybe, but it helped boost her confidence. It went well with her tweed suit and brown court shoes. If Jerry was nothing else, he was generous, and she had been able to buy nice clothes. Now she hated having to wear them when she wanted to cut them to shreds.

If she got the job, she would burn everything that had been paid for with his money. She hated herself for her naivety in thinking that everything he had done for her — giving her a roof over her head, food, and money for nice clothes — was because he loved her. In reality, he had been biding his time to do that to her. Perhaps if she'd been nicer to him, it wouldn't have happened. It was her own fault, and that's what Nell would tell her if she ever saw her again. But she missed her, despite her infuriating wise words.

She finished dressing and took a last glimpse at herself in the wardrobe mirror. Pulling on her gloves, she picked up her handbag and fought the urge to change her mind. She had to do this if she wanted to survive on her own. Straightening her shoulders, she took a deep breath and left her room, locking the door behind her, then walked with purpose towards the bus stop.

* * *

Kate was nervous as she walked towards the back of the store and through an entrance that led her inside the shop. Two smartly dressed girls teetered on high heels in front of her, and she was glad she'd made the effort. She lingered a while until a man in a brown coat, who was sweeping the floor, came to her assistance.

'Go up them stairs there, miss, and through the door marked Staff.' He smiled. 'Is it a job you're after?'

Kate nodded.

'Good luck,' he said, as she hurried up the stairs.

She walked along a long corridor with many doors, and knocked on the first one. When she was told to enter, she gingerly opened the door.

A tall, thin man was looking out of the window, with his hands behind his back. He pushed his specs further up on his nose. 'Can I help you?'

'I'm . . . I've come about a job.'

'You'll be wanting Personnel. Last door on the left.'

Apologising, she closed the door. Her courage was fading as she walked further along, looking for Personnel. She knocked and went inside, where a row of women and girls were already in front of her, sitting on chairs. She forced a smile and stood against the wall when one girl was called in. An older woman nudged up, so she sat down.

'I wasn't expecting there'd be so many,' Kate whispered.

'Aye, well. It's the same everywhere you go. You'll probably have a better chance, looking so smartly dressed. I couldn't afford a decent pair of shoes.' She glanced down at her feet and pulled at her clothes. 'Worked in retail before, have yea?'

Kate swallowed, feeling extremely nervous now. She didn't feel much like talking so she just nodded. It would be silly to admit she hadn't, and she didn't want to say she had come about the kitchen work, especially the way she was dressed.

As each woman came out and she moved along a chair, her nerves grew. It was like going to confession, only this was worse. She felt a fraud sitting amongst decent people. The woman before her came out with a face like thunder.

'Next!'

Kate stood up. Her legs felt like jelly. The queue of women waiting had doubled.

The office she entered was small, with a tall filing cabinet, a table with a telephone, and two chairs, one on either side of the desk. It was nothing like the one she had seen earlier, with carpets and an almost panoramic window. She sat, as directed, her knees knocking together, and folded her hands in her lap.

The woman behind the desk reminded her of Nell, with short, curly fair hair and bright blue eyes. It put Kate off immediately.

'Where is your application form, miss?'

Kate was about to stand up. 'I didn't know about any form. I'm sorry to have wasted your time.'

The woman put up her hand. 'Sit down and tell me your name.'

'Kate Flynn.'

'Well, Kate. I'm Miss Montgomery. How long have you worked in retail?'

Kate cleared her throat. 'I'm . . . I'm sorry. I've come about the vacancy for a kitchen assistant.'

The woman frowned and sat back. 'You're looking for kitchen work?'

Kate nodded and lowered her head.

'Don't you want to work on the shop floor at one of the biggest stores in Dublin?'

Kate shrugged. 'I don't have any experience.'

'You don't? Well, for someone dressed as smartly as you are, I'm puzzled. What kind of work do you have experience in?'

Kate wasn't above telling a lie. She had to make this work or she'd soon be out on the streets again. She straightened her shoulders. 'I managed a small silk-screen printing business until it went bust. But I'd be quite happy to work in the kitchen, if you think I'd be suitable.'

'Well, of course, Miss Flynn. But you'd be wasted there.' The woman sat back, and Kate felt her eyes as she studied her. Then she leant forward. 'We do a certain amount of training, but if you've already been in business, you shouldn't find it difficult. We do expect you to follow rules and to be good at basic adding up.'

Kate glanced up, her confidence returning. 'Thank you.' She'd always got top marks for her arithmetic, so she had no worries on that score. Besides, it was the first time any employer had shown her any respect as a prospective employee, so maybe things were beginning to look up.

'Now, go further along the corridor and pick up a form from the main office,' she was instructed. 'Fill it in and do a simple test, and we'll take it from there.'

54

Two days later, with no word from Liam, Nell was in despair. Had she lost him for good? Had he already gone back to London? She couldn't let him go out of her life like that, without explaining the situation. But would he believe her? He had looked pretty aggrieved that night, but surely he would understand her need for a visit to the cinema? Questions swirled around inside her head, driving her mad. She knew it must have looked bad, her arriving home late at night with an older man. What must Liam have thought? How could she stand another day of misery, wondering if she'd lost him?

When her shift finished, she hurried back to the nurses' quarters to change. The morning had started grey, and clouds still hovered overhead, threatening rain. Dressed in a warm belted coat and black heeled shoes, her brolly dangling from her wrist and her bag across her shoulder, she caught the bus to Liam's parents' house. She felt embarrassed, not knowing if Liam had confided in them about the other night. But she had to know one way or the other.

She arrived dead on one o'clock, and the little grocery shop with Connor & Son above the door looked inviting, with fresh green vegetables and rosy apples displayed in crates outside the shop. Nell swallowed and tentatively went inside. Mrs Connor was serving a customer, counting the change into her hand. She glanced up and smiled.

'Nell, you're a sight for sore eyes. Go through to the back. I'm just closing for lunch.'

Nell went through the narrow passage to the cosy parlour. It was almost a year since she and Kate had been here and enjoyed a wonderful Christmas dinner, cooked by Liam's mother, and she felt bad not to have called sooner. She glanced around for signs that Liam was still here, but saw none.

Mrs Connor bustled in. 'Well, you timed that well, Nell. I was just about to make a drink, and we can chat. The shop's quiet at this time of the day. It's later on I get rushed off me feet.'

Nell smiled hesitantly. 'I hope you don't mind me calling unexpected like?'

'Sit down, love. Why would I mind? You're welcome any time. I hear you've gone back into nursing. And how is little Róisín?'

'Much better, thanks.' Nell removed her coat, hung it over the chair, and sat down. She was glad to find Liam's mother alone. It would be doubly embarrassing if his father was here. 'Yes, and getting stronger every time I see her.'

'That's good news.' The woman carried the tea tray with the fruit cake to the table. 'I'm afraid it's shop cake. I don't get much time for baking my own, what with the shop to run and Liam away in England.'

Nell's heart almost stopped beating. 'Hasn't he been to see you?'

The older woman stopped pouring the tea and glanced at Nell. 'What do you mean? Is he home?' She sat down and unwrapped the cake, sliced it, placed it on the plate, and passed an empty plate to Nell.

Nell shifted, pulling her chair nearer the table. 'You haven't seen him?'

'Not since he left after Christmas.'

Nell felt the blood drain from her face. He'd gone back then, and she might never see him again. Tears welled in her eyes.

'Whatever's the matter, Nell?' his mother asked gently. 'Why would I have seen Liam?'

Nell had no choice but to tell her the whole sorry tale. When she'd finished, they sat in silence. Nell was embarrassed and reluctant to look into the eyes of her once-to-be mother-in-law for fear of seeing disappointment and, worse, blame. She lowered her head and closed her eyes. 'It was innocent. I couldn't resist an opportunity to see Bette Davis . . . '

Liam's mother patted her hand. 'It's all right, love. Sure, you must get lonely.'

'I did nothing wrong.'

'You need to tell him that. Where in God's name can he be? You don't think he's gone back without calling to see his mother, do yea?'

'I don't know what to think, Mrs Connor. He turned up out of the blue, and I'd not heard from him in months.'

His mother frowned. 'That's peculiar. He mentioned that he hadn't heard from you.'

'But I've written to him regularly. What's going on?'

'Well, I've had letters from him. But you know what the post can be like.'

So he had written to his mother, but not to her. Sadly, she sipped her tea. 'I don't understand. I love Liam with all my heart, Mrs Connor.'

'I know that, and if he had any eyes in his head, he'd know it, too.' His mother looked thoughtful. 'I can't think of anywhere he might have gone. And if he's not gone back to England, he'll be somewhere licking his wounds.'

Nell pushed her cup away. 'I've got to find him.' She stood up and pulled on her coat. 'If you do see him, please ask him to call at the nurses' home. And thanks for the tea and cake.'

* * *

Nell had no idea where to start looking. It was very likely Liam had gone straight back on the boat the same evening. And the only way she could be sure of that was to call at the B&I office and hope they would check their passenger list.

She joined the end of a long queue. Young people were still filling the boat, night after night, to find a better life in England, and she didn't blame them. Things were not improving in Ireland, and she felt lucky to have returned to nursing. It was a respected profession, and as long as she didn't break any more rules or make any silly mistakes, she would be back on the wards soon. She missed the banter as well as the grumpy patients.

As she moved up the queue, she wondered if the harassed assistants behind the counter would have time to check log books; she kept her fingers crossed.

After Nell explained her dilemma, the clerk told her to wait and he would see if someone in the office could help her. As she waited, she couldn't help but notice the relief on people's faces as they left clutching their sailing tickets.

'How can I help?' A young man called her into the office. 'Please take a seat.'

'Thank you.' She swallowed, feeling a little silly to be checking up on her boyfriend. 'I was wondering if you have any way of knowing whether a particular passenger travelled on a particular sailing?'

'When are we talking about?'

'He arrived from the UK on Friday night, and may have returned the same night or days later.'

'Well sure, if he bought his ticket in England, we wouldn't have any record of his return date here.'

'Of course. How silly of me. I'm sorry to have taken up your time.'

'If you need more information, you could call down to the docks and see if they know anything there. But it's unlikely.'

Embarrassed to have wasted everyone's time, she thanked the clerk and walked out into the cold afternoon. It was too far to walk to the docks and back, and it would make her late for her visit to Róisín. The town was busy with shoppers, and with Christmas only six weeks away, many were browsing the shop windows rather than spending their few pounds.

On the way back to the nurses' home, she

stopped for a coffee and a bite to eat, then bought a few groceries and a newspaper and took them back with her. She could only hope that Liam would have second thoughts and come back to see her.

★ ★ ★

Nell found Róisín in good spirits. She had now taken to sitting out of bed and walking around the ward. Nell was thrilled to see she'd put on a little weight and had a rosy glow to her face.

'My, you're a sight for sore eyes, our Róisín. At this rate you'll be home very soon.'

'Oh, I hope so, Nell. But where will we live if you're still at the nurses' home?'

'Don't worry, sweetheart, I'll find somewhere once I know when you're coming home. I'll speak to the Sister on my way out.'

'Have you . . . have you heard from Kate?'

'I'm afraid not, love. But this year you'll be home for Christmas, and we'll have a wonderful time. Won't that be nice?'

The child's face clouded. 'It won't be the same without Kate and Liam. Can't you find her and bring her home?'

Nell sat next to her and held her close. 'I don't know where she is, pet. If I did, I'd go and see her. Don't you worry, she'll come home when she's ready.'

The little girl looked confused. 'Why'd she go away? Doesn't she love us any more?'

As Nell wasn't sure herself, she wondered how

to explain. 'Of course she does. She went to find work.'

'Has she gone to England like Liam?'

Nell had wondered that herself. 'The truth is, pet, I don't know. But look, we'll be together again soon and you can help me decorate the new place, and we'll buy a Christmas tree.' That brought a smile to the child's face.

Nell kissed her goodbye, and left her chatting to another girl who was learning to knit with one of the nurses. It brought a lump to Nell's throat to see her little sister recovering so well. She walked down the corridor and knocked on the door of Sister's office.

'Your sister has made excellent progress since she's been here with us, Miss Flynn, and we can't see any reason why she won't be home by Easter of next year.'

Nell was shocked. 'But that's months away. I was hoping . . .'

'She will be allowed home at Christmas and other times, for short visits only, until her full release.' The woman smiled.

'Thank you, Sister. That's good news.'

★ ★ ★

After a busy few days, Nell had Sunday off, and spent the morning chatting and catching up with her two new roommates, Marian and Stella.

'What plans have you made for when your sister comes home?' Stella asked. 'You'll have to find alternative accommodation, won't you?'

'Yes, I've been saving for a place. Ideally,

368

somewhere close to the hospital. It won't be easy. If either of you hear of anything, let me know.'

Both girls were visiting family for Sunday dinner and had invited her to come with them, but she declined. She wasn't in the mood to socialise.

'You think he'll come back, don't you?' Marian said.

'I hope so.'

'Sure, he will if he loves you.'

That was the problem, she didn't know if he did any more.

Nell curled up with yesterday's newspaper, but by four o'clock she felt peckish and went to the kitchen to make herself something to eat. She placed ham between two slices of buttered bread and wondered yet again why Joe hadn't stayed around to defend her that night.

Now that she had more positive news on Róisín, she intended to ask him about accommodation. He had contacts that might find her a suitable place rather than scouring the newspaper. It wasn't too soon for her to start looking at a few places, and she was determined to make it nice and cosy for when her sister came home. She was still hopeful that Kate might return, too.

But after Joe's reaction when he saw Liam, she wasn't sure about getting him involved; she didn't want to be beholden to him in any way. If only Liam had stayed around a bit longer, things wouldn't have ended the way they had. If he'd just let her explain.

To stop herself becoming maudlin, she switched on Radio Luxembourg, to listen to the Top Ten, and munched her sandwich while staring out at the rain running down the window in little rivulets. A loud knock on the front door alerted her. She switched off the radio and heard the knock again. If it was Joe Scanlon, she would give him a piece of her mind.

She went running downstairs and threw open the door.

55

'Liam.'

A gush of wind and rain wet her face. All she could do was stare, her heart thumping, her ears woolly. She felt a flush to her cheeks. Rain dripped from his hair and she wondered how far he had walked. He wore the same clothes he'd had on the other night. 'Come in. I'll . . . I'll get you a towel.'

'Is there somewhere we can talk, Nell?'

This sounded ominous, and she wasn't sure what to expect.

'Sure.' She opened the door to the kitchen, opened a drawer with her name on, and handed him a towel.

He patted his hair, pressed the towel to his face, then placed it on the table.

'Would you like a hot drink?' she offered.

'No thanks.' He sat down and removed his knapsack, placing it on the floor. She could smell his wet jacket as he undid the zip. He placed his elbows on the table and ran his fingers across his forehead.

She wanted to throw her arms around him and tell him how sorry she was, but instead she swallowed the lump forming in her throat. Her heart raced. What was he about to tell her? She wanted to speak but the right words wouldn't come.

Eventually, he glanced up. 'Seeing you with — '

'It wasn't what it looked like . . . ' she began. 'I tried to explain.'

'Yes, I know.' He linked his fingers.

She leant across the table. 'You know? Then why?'

'I hadn't heard from you in ages. That's why I didn't write to the nurses' home, and decided to come home.'

She shook her head, confused at his words. 'But I wrote several times, Liam. Didn't you get my letters? And why did you stop writing to me? I haven't heard from you since I told you I'd returned to nursing.'

'I don't know what's going on, Nell. I thought you wanted to finish with me.'

'You know I'd never want to do that. I returned to nursing because it was the only way I could survive.'

He hung his head. 'I'm sorry, I should never have gone away and left you to cope. I thought I'd lost you.'

Her heart leapt. 'You haven't lost me . . . that's if you still love me?'

'I've never stopped loving you, Nell. That's what I came home to tell you.' He cleared his throat. 'Ma's told me everything.'

'You've been to see her, then?'

He nodded. 'I feel ashamed for walking away. When I saw you with Joe Scanlon, I almost died. I assumed he was the reason I'd not heard from you.'

Nell felt defensive now. 'I thought you trusted me, Liam. Joe is just a friend. It gets lonely here on my own.'

'I don't begrudge you a life, Nell. But Joe Scanlon? He's . . . '

She looked away, fighting her tears, then turned back to face him. 'At times, Joe was the only person I spoke to. He's been good about visiting Róisín when I was working, but he's nothing more than a friend to me. I'm shocked that you jumped to the wrong conclusion, without waiting for an explanation.'

'Forgive me. I'm truly sorry. Now, can we forget Joe Scanlon and concentrate on us?'

He smiled that wonderful smile, melting her heart, and she reached for his hand. It was cold, and she cupped it in her warm one.

'Where have you been staying?' she asked.

'At a bed and breakfast in town.' He stood and pulled her to her feet. 'Nell, I can't live without you. I know you can't leave Dublin without Róisín, and I wouldn't want you to.'

His hold grew tighter around her, and she stroked the back of his neck, drinking in the familiar whiff of his cologne. How long she had waited to hear his voice, to feel his lips kissing her neck, her face. A tingling sensation raced through her as his hands ran up and down her spine. His arms drew her even closer. She never wanted this moment to end.

'Tell me you feel the same, Nell,' he whispered in her ear.

'I do. You know I do.'

He turned her round, holding her in front of him as he kissed the back of her neck. Her heartbeat quickened. Right now, she would have done anything to keep him with her. She couldn't let him go. And as his kisses caressed her face and found her lips, she responded eagerly until he pulled away.

Her face clouded. 'What's wrong?'

He sat down and pulled her on to his knee. 'I can't live like this any more. I want you with me.'

It sounded like an ultimatum, but maybe that's what she needed.

'It's what I want, too.' She smiled. 'And it might be sooner than you think.'

'What do you mean?' He couldn't hide the excitement in his voice. 'Is Róisín . . . ?'

'She's doing really well.' And she gave him an updated report.

'Well, that's grand news, so it is. When she's fit to travel, we can all be together.'

'A few more months, Liam, that's all.'

He nodded, a smile creeping over his face. 'What about Kate? Has she come home?'

Nell's enthusiasm faded. 'No, and I feel as if I've failed. I've let her down.'

'You know that's not true, Nell. In the meantime, if she comes back, she can come with us, too.'

It was all she needed to hear. She placed her hands on either side of his face and kissed him. 'I love you, Liam Connor.'

'Well, I'm glad to hear it.' Their kisses were full of passion, and when they drew apart, he glanced at his watch. 'Before I go, Nell, there is one other thing I want to ask you.'

She wrinkled her nose.

'What's to stop you coming over to London for a weekend?' The old sparkle returned to his

374

eyes. 'I'll make the arrangements. You must be due some holiday?'

Nell was thoughtful. Now that her baby sister was getting better, maybe she could have her life back.

Liam frowned. 'Well, will you come?'

'Oh, I'd love to.' She threw her arms around him. 'I'll speak to Sister, first thing tomorrow.'

56

Kate had been training on the handbag and scarf counter for a week. The job kept her so occupied, and she had no time to dwell on what had happened. It was the first time since she had started looking for work that she felt appreciated. Miss Montgomery told her she was a quick learner, and the woman's encouraging words had boosted her confidence.

Today she was working alone, and she enjoyed arranging the bags to show them off to their best advantage, alongside a variety of silk scarves. Kate had never seen such an array of handbags, some made of crocodile, suede and patent leather. There were clutch bags, beaded evening bags, even linen string bags, which were beautifully crocheted.

Rich women with fur-collared coats browsed and handled the bags, some asking questions as to their durability. 'This kind of accessory will last a lifetime, madam, if cared for,' Kate assured one customer.

'I'll take it,' the woman said, and handed over what Kate thought was an excessive amount of money for a handbag.

'If you'd like matching shoes, madam, you can find them in our shoe department just across the way, just past the haberdashery counter.'

'Thank you. I'd like that.' And the customer made her way in the direction Kate had told her.

Men seldom came within yards of the handbag counter, leaving that to their women-folk. But now that Christmas was approaching, there was every possibility they would browse Kate's counter for gifts for their wives or girlfriends. The thought of coming face-to-face with any man caused her anxiety and panic attacks.

It was almost lunchtime when a man who at first glance resembled Jerry O'Shea walked into the store. Her heart raced and she ducked down just as Ann, one of the assistants, turned up to relieve her for lunch.

'What are you doing down there?' she asked, when she found Kate hunkered down behind the counter.

Kate got to her feet. 'I heard something drop. I think it was a sixpence but I can't find it. I don't want my takings to be down.'

'I'll make a note just in case,' Ann said. 'You'd better be off, I'll see you later.'

Kate lowered her gaze, picked up her bag, and hurried from the store. Outside, she glanced furtively about her, as she did most days. Fear of bumping into Jerry O'Shea was foremost on her mind; the thought of him conjured up a deep hatred of the man, and she vowed to one day take her revenge.

She spent most of her lunch breaks in the church, as there wasn't enough time to go back to her bedsit, and it was too cold to sit about in the park. It was also one place she knew Jerry would never go. At first, it was just a place to hide and weep for what might have been. But today, she felt stronger, more confident. She had sold four leather bags and three silk scarves, and the only thing holding her back now was her feeling of unworthiness.

She would have settled for the kitchen assistant's job, had she been offered it.

Sometimes the smell of the food coming from the kitchen made her stomach rumble, but her appetite was sparse. Some days she felt hungry, but other times she didn't feel at all like eating. Like now.

If she worked in the canteen, she would have been out of sight, without the added worry of bumping into someone who might recognise her. The possibility that Nell, Teresa, Amy Kinch or her daughter Joan could walk into the store at any time unsettled Kate, and the constant anticipation made her nervous. She wasn't sure how long she could keep it up. As she walked, she reflected on her life before this terrible thing had happened to her. It appeared to belong in another world.

Inside the church, which had become her refuge, she hung her head and a tear dropped down her cold face on to her hand. A shiver of regret raced through her. When she should have been grateful for Nell, she had treated her sister with contempt. It was only now that she could look back and see what she had thrown away.

Jerry had turned out to be a false sense of security, and no matter how much she enjoyed her current job, it didn't stop her feeling used and worthless. Her punishment was what had happened with Jerry and the guilt she carried

378

around with her every day.

People were coming into church for the lunchtime mass. She glanced up at the clock; it was time to be getting back. As she entered the store, she rushed up to the Ladies and the smell of the food coming from the kitchen made her queasy.

When she got back to the counter, Ann was finishing serving a well-endowed woman with some knicker elastic.

'Are you sure it's strong enough?' the lady asked nervously.

'Certainly, madam.' Ann glanced at Kate, and stifled a giggle. After the woman left, she turned to Kate. 'I've not made any mistakes, so if you're short, it will be the money you dropped under the counter earlier.'

Kate smiled. How could she tell her the true reason she had been crouched behind the counter?

As the day wore on, the store was a hive of activity, with people hurrying in to do some Christmas shopping after they had finished work. It was almost closing time when a young man stopped by Kate's counter. She could feel his eyes boring into her. Embarrassed, she placed tissue around a brown crocodile bag, then slipped it into a carrier bag before turning to the man.

'Kate, is that you?'

She drew a quick intake of breath. For a split second, she didn't recognise the light stubble along his jawline. Her heart almost stopped, and she thought she was going to faint. She gripped the counter.

'Kate, it's me, Will.' He reached to touch her arm, making her flinch.

Trying to act normally, she smiled. 'William Brennan . . . what can I get for you? I take it you're here to make a purchase?'

'Yes . . . I . . . I'm just surprised to see you. You know your sister's been worried sick about you? She's been looking high and low to find you.'

Kate swallowed. She knew she shouldn't have taken this job. She glanced around her as the bell rang out to signal the store would close in ten minutes. 'I'm sorry,' she replied, 'I can't talk here. What can I get you?'

'Of course. I'm looking for a silk scarf for my mother. Have you any suggestions?'

Kate quickly placed a few alternatives along the glass countertop. She had never met his mother and had no idea how old she was. 'This is our full range. Do you know her favourite colour?'

He looked uneasy as he pondered the line of plain and multi-coloured items. 'I'll take the red one, as it's for Christmas.'

Kate put the others away and proceeded to wrap the scarf. She was aware of him watching her.

'How have you been?' he asked eventually.

'Grand. I'm grand, thanks.' She handed him the wrapped scarf and took his money. His hands were white, as if they'd never seen the sun. Too long indoors studying, she guessed. She looked up

His face was tinged pink. He made to walk

380

away, then turned back. 'Kate, can we meet up after you've finished?'

Kate swallowed a lump in her throat. He was bound to tell Nell he'd seen her. 'I don't think that's a good idea,' she said.

At that moment, Miss Montgomery walked down the store, checking that everything was turned off. 'Switch off your lights, Kate.'

She reached underneath the counter, and the area where she worked dimmed. Miss Montgomery quickly ushered her customer out of the store.

Kate's hands shook as she finished tidying the glass counter and prepared to leave for the night. Christmas was almost here, and she wasn't looking forward to it one bit. The store would be closed, and she would be alone in her room, with only her wireless for company.

In the staffroom most of the women were chatting excitedly about what they were planning for the forthcoming holiday, as she pulled on her coat.

'Going anywhere over Christmas, Kate?' Ann asked.

'Not sure yet,' was all she could think of to say.

The staffroom emptied as Miss Montgomery walked in. 'You should get off, Kate, before the weather worsens.'

Kate nodded. What did she have to rush home to?

'I hate it when people leave it to the last minute like that, don't you?' Miss Montgomery said. 'Still, you did well to sell another silk scarf so late in the evening. Let me know what you

381

need reordering tomorrow.'

'I will, Miss Montgomery.' Kate finished buttoning up her coat and they both left by the staff entrance, to go their separate ways.

The fog was coming down thick as Kate sauntered towards her bus stop. At the newspaper stand she bought a copy of the *Evening Press*, and when she glanced up, William was standing in front of her.

'I hope you don't mind, Kate, but I had to talk to you.'

In spite of the fog, she was in no hurry to get back to her flat, but talking to William was risky. She wanted nothing to do with her past, and he was bound to tell Nell where she worked. She wasn't ready for anything like that. She pulled at the strap of her shoulder bag and dug her hands deeper inside her pockets. She couldn't look at him. He reminded her of Michael, honest and good, while she was —

'Kate.' He touched her arm. 'Are you all right?'

She walked on and he walked next to her. 'I won't keep you long. We can go somewhere warm. The buses are all held up due to the fog. There's a pub round the corner.'

She didn't reply but let him guide her inside, where it was packed in spite of the early hour. She hesitated until William took her hand and led her through a fog of smoke and the smell of spilt beer, to the back wall of the pub, where there was a high shelf with two stools underneath.

'Sit here, I won't be long. What would you like?'

At sixteen, she hadn't a clue what to ask for.

The noisy atmosphere drowned her inner turmoil and she was sitting, facing the wall in a world of her own, when he returned. He put a small sherry and a pint of Guinness on the shelf and sat down.

'Here, drink this.' He pushed it towards her. 'It will warm you up.'

The smell of the beer reminded her of her ordeal with Jerry O'Shea and she swallowed the bile rising in her throat. 'I didn't know you drank, William.'

'I don't, but we both need something to put a bit of colour in our cheeks.' He took a sip and made a face. 'Can't say I'd ever get used to it. Try yours?'

She gave him a half smile, fingered the glass, but refrained from drinking any of it.

'I can see you're not comfortable here,' he said, 'but it's warmer than standing waiting for a bus in this weather.'

She nodded.

'Kate. I like you. Have done from the first time I saw you.'

She closed her eyes. She didn't want to hear him talk this way. Not now.

'Where have you been, these past months? Where are you living?'

If this was what he'd asked her here for, she wasn't impressed. She pushed the drink away. 'I have to go.'

He placed his hand on her arm and saw tears form in her eyes. 'Oh, Kate. What's wrong? Whatever it is, you can tell me.'

'I can't.' A sob caught at the back of her throat. 'And you can't tell anyone you saw me. If you really are my friend, you have to promise?'

'I promise. Please, sit down and finish your drink.'

The noise in the packed pub made her head ache and she didn't want to be here, but he pressed her more and she sat back down. She cupped the small glass, turning it round on the beer mat.

'If you were to breathe a word to Nell about seeing me today, I'd have to find another job. Can you understand?'

He reached out and touched her hand. 'Kate, I haven't seen Nell in months. She's gone back to nursing. She came to see me before she left, worried that you'd come back and not know where she was.'

Kate swallowed. She felt hot and her stomach clenched. She had to get out of here. As she stood up, her body swayed and she gripped the edge of a table, her hand landing in a pool of beer.

'Kate, are you all right?' she heard him say.

'I'm grand.'

William got to his feet.

'No!' she shouted above the noise. 'Don't follow me.'

She hurried through the smoky pub and ran out into the misty fog outside, reaching her stop as a bus came into view. The crowd surged forward, and she climbed on board, her mind in turmoil.

57

Nervous about her first flight, Nell hadn't slept a wink. Eventually, she concluded that she was going to see the man she loved, and what could go wrong?

Her hands shook with excitement as she packed her suitcase. She had bought herself a few new items of clothing to take with her. Her old red jumper had little fluffy bits along the sleeve, so she invested in a new one and a warm straight skirt to go with it.

Liam had sent on her tickets for the flight, and although she was nervous about flying for the first time, she would have gone up in a rocket to be with him. Besides, he would be there at the other end to meet her, and she couldn't wait.

Liam had written and told her how magical London was at this time of year, with displays of Christmas lights everywhere and shops full of fashionable clothes. She couldn't wait to see it all. Her mind flitted back to last Christmas, when she and Kate had gone to Liam's parents' house for dinner, and how her sister had disappeared on the back of a stranger's motorbike. Nell wondered if the man had enticed her away from home and, if so, was she with him now? If only she knew where he lived, but he remained a mystery, along with Kate.

She had thought about asking Joe to take her to the airport, but decided against it, especially now that she knew how he felt about her. He hadn't put in an appearance since that night when they had been to the cinema, which puzzled her, but she was too happy to dwell on it.

Her case packed, she made her way across the grounds to the main hall of the hospital to call for a taxi. As she was crossing the path of the hospital, she could just make out the shape of a man coming towards her.

'Joe! Where have you been hiding lately?'

'Sorry, Nell. I've been busy sorting out some new properties.'

'Oh, I thought you were going to start taking things easy.'

'Well, it was too good an investment to miss.' He shifted, pulling the lapels of his warm coat up around his neck. 'Anyway, I was just coming to see how you were.'

Nell smiled. 'I'm that excited, Joe. I'm going to London for a few days and I was just going to phone for a taxi. You can walk over with me if you like.'

He pressed her arm. 'What? It's a strange time to be going away, and besides, have you seen the weather?'

'I've been listening to the radio and some flights are still going out.'

'Well, if you're sure, I'll take you to the airport.'

'Sure, I'll be grand. You must have other things to do.'

'It's no trouble.'

She only had on her warm cardigan and began

to shiver. 'Well, if you're sure, let's go back inside where it's warm.' He followed her down the path towards the nurses' quarters and into the kitchen, where she made them both a cup of tea.

'Are you sure about this, Nell? Where will you stay?'

She nodded, her eyes shining with excitement. 'Liam's sorted everything.'

'What about Róisín? It's almost Christmas,' he said, frowning.

'She'll be fine. I've had a word with Matron. She'll have a wonderful time at the hospital, and I'll be back to go up with her presents.'

He seemed to ponder her words as she rinsed out her cup, dried it and put it away.

'By the way, Joe,' she went on, 'I need to find somewhere to rent, cheap and not too far from the hospital. Can you let me know if you hear of anything?'

He nodded, but there was something different about him and she couldn't put her finger on it. Nell didn't like to press him, but he wasn't his usual smiley self. Come to think of it, Róisín had said he hadn't been to see her for a while.

★　★　★

Dublin Airport wasn't far but even though the fog was lifting, Joe struggled to see his way. Inside the terminal building, there was a lot of confusion about which flights would take off, and the noticeboard showed a number of flights that had been cancelled. When Nell arrived at the check-in desk, she was told to wait for confirmation before they could take her case.

They found a seat in the crowded lounge, and Joe raised an eyebrow. 'I really don't think your flight will take off today, Nell. It's a busy time of year. Would you not have been better to go after the Christmas break, like?'

She was already nervous about the flight, and Joe was beginning to irritate her with his negativity. She smiled tightly. 'Thanks for the lift, Joe, but there's no need for you to wait.'

'How will you get back if the flight's cancelled?'

'I'll be fine.'

He looked uneasy as he stood up, fidgeting with his hands.

'What's the matter?' Her voice was louder than she intended over the hum of activity.

'I have a confession.'

'What are you talking about?'

'I have to do it now before I weaken.' His words only added to her nervousness.

'Why would you need to confess to me, Joe?'

He reached inside his pocket and took out a small bundle of letters.

Nell gasped, and her hand covered her mouth. 'Are they what I think they are?'

'Yes, they belong to you.'

An even louder gasp escaped her, and she reached for them. 'Where have they come from?' She flicked through them: two of the letters were ones she had asked him to post to Liam; the others were all from Liam to her.

He lowered his head. 'I'm ashamed, and really sorry.'

In the chaos that surrounded them, she got to her feet, anger surging through her. 'You mean . . . ? How could you? How dare you do this to me? I trusted you.' People were glancing their way, but she didn't care. 'You saw how broken I was, yet you kept these from me.' She waved the letters in front of his face before tears gathered and she slumped down into her seat. 'Just go. I don't need you here.'

'I was jealous,' he almost whispered.

'I don't want to hear your excuses. It was a despicable thing to do.'

'I'm an old fool. I let a lovely young girl get under my skin.' He shifted his feet. 'I hope, in time, you'll forgive me. I've already confessed to the priest, and he suggested I make my peace with you by returning your property.'

She glared at him, trying to control her anger.

Then he turned and walked away, leaving her with the letters clasped to her chest.

58

When Joe left, Nell's anger was slow to dissipate. How could he have classed himself as a friend and do this? Barely aware of the hustle and bustle going on around her, she stood up and paced, going over the occasions when she had asked him to post her letters to Liam. It had never entered her head he could be deceitful. Now, everything made sense. He had called at the old address to check if Liam's letters had gone there by mistake, shaking his head when he returned empty-handed. But all the while he had been picking them up and keeping them from her.

Choking back tears, she placed the precious letters inside her bag to read on the flight. Liam's words would, she hoped, steady her nerves. However, when it was announced her flight to London would be delayed for a further hour, she knew she couldn't wait that long to read them.

The noise in the airport was still manic as people fought through long queues to find out what was happening. She moved around, lugging her case, looking for a quiet spot to sit and read in private. It was near impossible. People were milling around everywhere she went. She overheard a family of four saying they had had enough and were going back home, but she wasn't going to miss an opportunity to be with

Liam. She hoped he wouldn't tire of waiting.

She bought a cup of tea and a slice of fruit cake wrapped in cellophane from the tea bar, found a quiet table in a corner and sat down to read Liam's letters. As she read, a feeling of happiness spread through her; at the same time, sobs caught at the back of her throat. Liam's letters were filled with love and longing, and even worry that he hadn't heard from her.

One letter, dated the end of August, was full of exciting news about the Festival of Britain.

You would have loved it, Nell. I paid five shillings to go into the Dome of Discovery. It's full of interesting things, even has a 3D cinema and a theatre. Remember how we used to talk about London? Well, it's every bit as exciting as we thought, only more so. How I wish you had been here to have experienced this wonderful event with me. People came in from all over the world to see it. It was amazing. There will be more amazing things for us to share together once you make up your mind to join me. Please write back so I know you are all right . . .

She read his words over and over, tears trickling down her face. She thought about the times Joe had consoled her when she was upset that there was no word from Liam, yet he had the letters all the time. It made her sick to her stomach. What else had he kept from her? Had he really tried to find Kate? Did he know where she was and had kept that from her, too? How could she ever trust him again?

★ ★ ★

When, at last, her flight was called, her animosity towards Joe Scanlon was replaced by a tight, heavy feeling in her stomach. If she wanted to see Liam, she had to board that plane, no matter how nervous she felt. She blew her nose, placed the letters inside her handbag, and went to the Ladies to wash her face and retouch her make-up.

She joined the queue for the Aer Lingus flight, checked in her case, and was directed to the boarding area. Nerves kicked in, and her stomach tightened. She rubbed one hand over the other and wiped her sweaty palms down the side of her coat as she followed the crowd outside and across the tarmac towards the waiting plane. With a mixture of expectancy and dread, she found herself seated next to a mother with a small girl of about five who was crying while the mother tried frantically to pacify her.

Nell smiled at the child, but she continued to cry. 'You're a nurse,' she told herself. 'For heaven's sake, keep calm.' Opening her bag, she took out some chocolate and offered it to the child's mother. 'This might help,' she smiled.

And for the duration of the flight, all was well. Nell found herself enjoying the experience of flying, and it wasn't until the plane's wheels touched down that her heart lurched.

Excited, she followed the other passengers into

392

the arrivals hall. It was growing dark but the air was clear. Would Liam be waiting? Oh, she hoped so. All she had to do now was collect her case. She stood next to the excited group waiting for the conveyor belt to start up and the luggage to roll along the belt. She had attached a bright red label to her grey case, and she identified it straight away, reaching over to snatch it from the moving carousel.

She had heard about customs and excise and wasn't looking forward to it, although she had nothing worth declaring. She watched as a couple of men were pulled over and their bags searched, the entire contents pulled out. Trying not to show how nervous she was, she placed her case on the low table and swallowed as the officer placed his hand on top of her case.

'Anything to declare, miss?'

She shook her head and he moved on to the next passenger. With an inward sigh, she lugged her case through to the arrivals hall.

The airport was much bigger than Dublin and she was quickly swallowed up in the throng. There was an air of Christmas joy, as people greeted and hugged each other, some carrying coloured parcels. Her heart raced as her eyes searched for a sighting of Liam.

At first, she couldn't see him and her heart plummeted. She stood still, unsure. Then . . . there he was, waving both his arms in the air. Her stomach fluttered as they made their way towards each other, and she dropped her case and ran into his open arms. He smothered her in kisses before she could say a word.

Finally, catching her breath, she smiled. 'Oh, Liam, sure, it's grand to be here at last.'

'I know. The waiting was torture. But you're here now. You look lovely.'

She wasn't sure how she looked, but she was happy to be here.

'I'm starving. Let's get out of here.' He picked up her case, his other arm around her shoulder, and they walked outside, laughing and chatting.

They caught a bus to Victoria coach station. On the journey, in between kisses, they talked about their plans for the next few days.

'Well, what do you think of London, so far?' he asked.

'I've not seen much of it yet.' Truth be known, she hadn't taken her eyes off Liam, linking her arm through his, inhaling the scent of him, and watching his twinkling eyes as he told her of his plans.

When the coach pulled in, Nell asked, 'Where am I staying?'

'With me.' He gave her a cheeky grin. 'I've managed to get you a room at my lodging house. The woman upstairs moved out, and I persuaded the landlady to let you stay for a few days.'

'So, we'll be together, then? That's grand. Sure, I was hoping you wouldn't be too far away.'

'You don't mind, then?'

'No, of course not. We'll be married soon and then we'll be together all the time.'

'I can't wait, Nell,' he grinned.

They left the coach and caught a taxi.

Mesmerised by her surroundings, Nell took in the sights, sounds and smells of a city she was looking forward to exploring. 'I've never seen a red bus before.' Her smile turned to a frown at the bomb sites they passed. 'Hitler has a lot to answer for,' she commented.

Liam shook his head. 'Beautiful buildings destroyed, some never replaced. London still bears the scars of the Blitz.' Liam took her hand. 'It was hit many times, remember. Even Buckingham Palace got bombed.'

'Gosh! We were lucky in Dublin, then. The houses on North Strand were never rebuilt, either.'

He squeezed her hand gently. 'The war's been over for six years now, so let's not dwell on it. There's so much of London I want to show you.' He leant across and kissed her, their happiness apparent to anyone who saw them.

Nell said nothing about the letters; there was plenty of time for that later. For now, they were both caught up in the joy of being together.

59

The cab pulled up outside a three-storey house in Finsbury Park, and Liam jumped out and paid the driver. Carrying her case and holding her hand, he led her up the steps to the property. Inside, the hall was long and narrow.

'I'll show you your room first. Mine is on the ground floor towards the back.'

She followed him upstairs, where he pulled back the mat and found the key.

'Someone is trusting?' Nell said.

'Mrs Cooney told me where I'd find it. But I wouldn't recommend you doing that.' The door swung open and he handed her the huge key.

She glanced down at it. 'I'm not likely to lose it.'

Liam grinned. 'These old doors all have big keys.' He moved further inside and placed her case on the single bed, while Nell glanced around her. The room had a wardrobe, dressing table, and a bay window overlooking the street.

'It'll look better in the morning,' he said, drawing the heavy brocade curtains.

'It's lovely, Liam.' She removed her coat and placed it on the bed. 'Who lives above this?'

'Her nibs. But she's okay.'

Nell bounced on the bed. 'I don't think I'll have any trouble sleeping tonight.'

'The bathroom is along the corridor, the kitchen's downstairs. So I'll get to eat all the food first.' He laughed.

She nudged him. 'I hope you have tea? I still prefer it to coffee.'

He laughed. 'Don't worry. I'll have a fresh brew and a cooked breakfast ready for you in the morning. So, no sleeping in.'

Unable to contain herself, she threw her arms around him. 'Liam Connor, have I told you how much I love you?'

'Yes, but you can tell me again.'

His kisses were urgent and passionate until a tap on the door startled them, and they pulled apart. Liam's landlady stood in the room.

'Just checking you arrived okay. Nell, is it?'

'Yes . . . nice to meet you, Mrs Cooney.' Nell extended her hand. 'It's a lovely room.'

'Well, yes, this is only for a few days, you understand.' The woman turned, directing her next words at Liam. 'And just so you both know. There'll be no hanky-panky in my house.'

Liam winked at Nell, then guided his landlady towards the door. 'Mrs Cooney, whatever do you mean? The very idea!' And he went out, closing the door behind them.

★   ★   ★

Liam was knocking on Nell's door at nine o'clock on Saturday morning. 'Can I come in?'

She had only just finished dressing, and her hair was still damp. 'Just a minute.' She ran her comb through her short hair and wrapped a towel around her shoulders. The bed had been so comfortable that she had slept through until

397

eight, had a soak in the bath, then got herself dressed in her first pair of jeans with a white roll-neck sweater.

She imagined Liam pacing up and down on the landing, and hoped Mrs Cooney wouldn't spot him. She reached for the key and unlocked the door.

He was inside in a trice, and sweeping her into his arms. 'You smell good enough to eat.'

'Stop messing and put me down,' she scolded him, with a smile. 'What if Mrs Cooney sees you?'

'She's gone to the shops. I've just seen her go.' He kissed her again.

She pushed him playfully. 'Behave! Just let me finish doing my hair and I'll be ready.' She rubbed her hair dry and combed it into place, aware of him looking at her.

'I thought I wore the trousers?' he laughed.

'Don't you like them?'

He whistled. 'You look fantastic, Nell. Most of the women over here wear trousers and jeans, so you're right up to date with the fashion.'

Her smile returned. 'That's okay, then. They've just arrived in the Dublin shops.' She slipped her feet into her ankle boots, smeared on some red lipstick, and pulled on her coat.

Liam pulled up the wide collar and wrapped her scarf around her neck. 'It's nippy out, this morning. Can't have you catching cold.' He waited as she picked up her shoulder bag and checked inside. 'Make sure you've got everything you need,' he added, 'as we'll be out most of the day.'

'Where are we going?'

'I want to show you as much as I can, so you won't be able to resist coming here to live.'

* * *

The air was fresh but dry, though last night's frost still clung to the rooftops as they walked, hand in hand, down the street towards the bus stop.

Once on board, Nell gazed through the bus window at buildings and crowds of shoppers hurrying along the pavements. 'Is that the latest fashion in hose, then?' she asked, when she saw two girls gazing into a shop window, wearing high heels and black fishnet stockings.

Liam laughed. 'You're asking me?'

'I thought you knew all about London fashion?'

'Stockings I know nothing about. If you want shops, we'll do that later, but first I want you to see the waxworks at Madame Tussauds.'

'Oh, grand. I've heard about it.'

They got off the bus in Marylebone Street and joined the queue. Excitement bubbled inside her when she saw Charlie Chaplin. 'He's even smaller than I imagined. They all look so realistic,' she said. 'Especially Winston Churchill. I've seen his picture in the newspaper.'

From there, they visited the Tower of London, where the story of the two princes fascinated her. And later, they walked along the South Bank, watching the riverboats pass up and down the Thames.

Christmas was everywhere, and hope hung in the air. 'Oh, isn't it lovely, Liam?' She'd lost count of the number of times she had gasped in wonder.

Liam took a photo of her sitting on the wall outside the Houses of Parliament, and asked a passer-by to take one of them together in a bear hug. Later, as they sat in Trafalgar Square huddled together against the cold, pigeons pecked around their feet and then flew up to perch on the ledges of buildings.

'Can you see yourself living here, Nell?' he asked nervously.

'You try stopping me.' She snuggled up closer to him.

When it started raining, they ran for cover into a cosy Lyons tea shop, where the smell of food made her mouth water, and ordered sandwiches and mugs of tea.

His thirst satisfied, Liam sat back. 'I can't live without you much longer, Nell. I've saved three months' rent to put down on a terraced house. A few more months and you'll be finished your final year in nursing, and when you come over permanently, we can be married.' He leant in close. 'What do you think?'

'Haven't I said so? It's all I ever wanted, Liam.' She touched his hand. 'Are you still happy to help me raise Róisín?'

His eyebrows shot up. 'You know I am. As soon as she's well enough and you can bring her over, I'll have everything ready.'

A tear threatened, and she bit her lip. Could this really be happening? She snuggled in closer, a warm glow filling her being, despite the cold.

He stood up and pulled her to her feet. Outside, a crowd had gathered around a shop window.

'What's going on?' she asked. 'Is it a sale?'

'They're watching the lunchtime news in pictures for the first time,' he explained. 'Not everyone in London has a television.' They tried to squeeze in, but the crowd was too thick and all they could hear was Churchill's name repeated by the newsreader. 'Come on, there's so much to see yet.' Liam took her hand and they moved along, stopping now and then to look into shop windows.

'Do you miss Dublin, Liam?' Nell wondered.

'I miss my parents, and you, of course. But it's a good life here. What about you, Nell, will you miss it?'

She shrugged. 'What's to miss?' She took a deep breath. 'I'll miss Kate.'

'Still no word from her?'

'No, and if I knew where she was, I'd get her to come home.'

'What about that guy on the motorbike? He might know where she is.'

She shook her head sadly. 'He's a mystery. No one knows where he lives. Do you think I should report her as missing?'

He looked doubtful. 'She's sixteen, so the Gardaí won't bother.'

She sighed. 'This is the first time I've felt relaxed in a long time. If I just knew Kate . . . well, if I knew she was safe.'

Liam stopped walking. 'Nell, you can't hold

yourself responsible. But I understand. If she was my sister . . . well, I'd worry, too.' He put his arm round her shoulder and pulled her closer. 'I'd like you to be happy in your mind about Kate before you come away. When did you last see her?'

'Not since January. But she was at Ma's grave in October and left flowers. I just wish I'd got there earlier, and I might have seen her.'

'So, she's still in Dublin?'

'Dublin's a big place,' she replied. 'She could be anywhere.'

It was late when they returned to the lodging house. Liam had taken her to see Buckingham Palace, and now she was exhausted and her feet blistered.

'Look, you're bushed. I won't come in.' He kissed her. 'Get a good night's sleep. I've something special planned for tomorrow.'

60

Kate couldn't stop William Brennan from meeting her after work, her insults appearing to go unheeded. On the Saturday before Christmas, she was glad to leave behind the happy smiley faces wishing each other compliments of the season; all she wanted to do was go to bed and sleep until it was all over.

'I don't know why you keep hanging about,' she grumbled, when she found him huddled in a doorway. 'You're stalking me, and I don't like it.'

'I'm just looking out for you.' He grinned. 'And besides, I like you.'

'Well, I don't want you to.' She pulled her scarf closer around her neck. He wouldn't want to spend time with her, if he knew the truth. 'I don't need you. I don't need anyone.'

He fell into step alongside her. 'No one's an island, Kate. What are you doing on Christmas Day?'

'Just go away.'

'I can tell you're not happy, just talk to me. You know you can trust me, don't you?' He went on and on, until she felt her head would burst.

'What do you want from me?' She had nothing left to give.

'Just to be a friend.' He touched her arm and felt her draw back. 'And for the record, Kate, if I was stalking you, I would know where you live. But I'd rather you told me.'

'Why? So you can tell Nell?' She paused and glared at him. 'How many times do I have to say it? Leave me alone, William, or I'll call a garda.'

He looked away, but not before she saw the hurt in his eyes and regretted her outburst. He was the only friend she had, but she couldn't afford to let him get close. Not now.

'Okay, I'll go. But I'll be standing under Clery's clock at three thirty on Christmas Day, and St Stephen's Day, in case you need to talk.' With that, he walked away.

Tears stung her eyes as she sat on the bus, with her face to the window. Four days with no one to talk to. Time would drag, but if she could sleep it might go more quickly. She had borrowed a book from the library, and that helped to pass the time of an evening. She was halfway through reading *The Canterbury Tales*.

Kate knew she couldn't go on as she was, hating herself for what had happened to her. Sooner or later she would have to tell someone, even if that someone never wanted to look her in the face again. For now, though, it had to remain her secret.

She got off the bus and went into a corner shop, where she picked up milk, tea, a loaf of bread, butter, biscuits, a tin of beans and a box of headache tablets, along with a large red Christmas candle.

Once she'd let herself into her room, she put down her shopping and looked around. It was the first time she had properly taken notice of the shabby room. She placed the candle into a holder in the centre of the dusty, scratched table, with its two chairs. The bed was against the wall, and there were no sheets, just two well-worn blankets. A gas fire in the grate swallowed her money if she was to turn it on, and the wallpaper was peeling away from the damp wall. In the corner there was a shelf with a small gas ring, and underneath a bucket for water. The area was cordoned off with a floral curtain, which was badly in need of a wash.

This was far worse than the tenement. At least there, Nell had always kept their rooms spotless. What would her mother say if she saw the conditions she was living in? She glanced over at the candle on the table. She would light it on Christmas Day in memory of Ma.

Weary and cold, Kate longed to light the fire. Instead, she got into bed with her clothes on. For the next four days, she never set foot outside except to be sick and to use the privy. At night, she swallowed extra pills to help her sleep. The outside world could be as merry as it liked, but she was determined to stay put until things returned to normal and she could go back to work.

61

On Sunday morning, Nell was up early, determined to make the most of her last day with Liam and excited to know what he had planned. She had barely finished applying a light coating of lipstick to her full lips before he was knocking. They were catching the early mass at the local Catholic church.

'Ready?' he said when she opened the door.

She nodded.

His kiss brushed her lips before he helped her on with her coat. 'Let's get church over with and then I want to take you somewhere.'

'Where?'

Placing his arm around her shoulder, he didn't reply but ushered her outside.

'Oh, Liam,' she complained. 'You don't half keep a girl in suspense.'

He winked. 'You know your trouble, Nell Flynn? You've no patience.'

'That's not true, and you know it.' She shoved him playfully.

The day was grey and overcast, and the streets were empty apart from a few parked cars and someone walking a Great Dane towards the park. 'Is it far to the church?'

'Just a couple of streets away.' He took hold of her hand and they walked fast.

'Where's everyone?' Nell was used to lots of people toing and froing to mass on a Sunday morning, but here it was quiet, peaceful.

'They've got more sense. Still tucked up underneath the blankets. For most people over here, Sunday is really a day of rest, doing what they like to relax.'

'So, we'll be the only ones at mass, then?' Nell laughed, and Liam tightened his grip around her waist until she giggled.

To her surprise, the church was packed and no one took any notice of them. Afterwards, people hurried back to their homes; it wasn't a day to stand about chatting. Nell and Liam hurried towards the Underground.

'Where are we going?' she asked.

'We're catching the tube to Brixton.'

'Brixton! Why?'

'Just wait!'

'Liam Connor, you're impossible!'

The Underground was busy and they stood crushed close together on the train. In a short time, they emerged from the station and found themselves walking down streets with rows of Victorian houses, some in a bad state of repair, with windows boarded up. Children from different communities played together in the streets and it reminded her of the streets of Dublin.

'What are we doing here, Liam? Oh, go on, tell me?'

He shook his head, with a self-satisfied smile on his face, until they finally came to a halt. 'I believe some Irish families, as well as people from the Caribbean, emigrated to this area.' He placed his arm around her. 'The area has been rundown since the war, but we might be able to buy it cheap in a few years' time.'

Nell glanced up at a billboard with the words 'To Let'. None of what Liam said made sense to her. She pulled nervously at the sleeve of her coat, barely able to speak.

'But . . . you . . . I mean . . . What's going on, Liam?' She leant against the garden wall.

'I'm renting number nineteen from the end of February,' he announced. 'Admittedly, it needs some work and a lick of paint, but it's close enough for work, and it will be our home once we're married.'

'Really! Oh, Liam.' Tears gathered and she blew her nose. 'That's grand, absolutely.'

He stood next to her. 'I've already put down a holding deposit for when you come over with Róisín — and Kate, too, if need be.'

She saw a twinkle in his eye. How she loved him. Liam was big-hearted, and his generosity, especially towards Kate, made her emotional again.

'Come on, don't cry,' he said. 'Unfortunately, we can't go inside.'

The Victorian house, set in the middle of a row of shabby bay-windowed terraces, still bore traces of scars from the war, but it was a dream come true for Nell. And she couldn't stop gazing at it, taking in every angle of the house.

Liam pulled her close. 'Are you happy?'

'Oh, Liam, it's wonderful. A whole house.'

'It's got three bedrooms.'

She glanced at the scratched blue door and the windows with net curtains. 'I think I'm going to cry again.'

Just then, the curtains twitched and a black face stared out at them.

Liam took her hand. 'We'd better move, or the people inside will think we're peeping Toms.'

★　★　★

Later that day, they strolled through Petticoat Lane, where Nell experienced different cultures and a melting pot of people, all Londoners, working side by side together on the stalls.

'A market on a Sunday,' she remarked, her eyes shining. 'Isn't it brilliant?'

Liam smiled back as he watched her eyes light up with every item of clothing she bought. A red jumper for Róisín, a cream one for Kate. The clothes were good quality and cost only pennies. She tried on leather boots, and held a tweed skirt against her body. 'What do you think?'

'Very nice,' he agreed. 'And what about this pretty white blouse to go with it?' Liam insisted on paying for it. 'We'll have time for a bite to eat before we have to get going,' he said, looking at his watch.

Her face clouded. 'I don't want to think about going.'

'I know.' He took the bags from her and guided her away from the market and into a coffee shop.

Nell, already feeling the nerves about flying, chose a light cheese omelette, while Liam had a thick cheese sandwich with pickled onions. She watched him bite into the sandwich and crunch an onion, and wrinkled her nose at the vinegar smell. How was she going to say goodbye to him? It would be months before she saw him again.

When they had finished eating, Liam surprised her when he asked, 'Did you ever throw any light on what happened to our letters, Nell? It's been puzzling me for weeks.'

She lowered her gaze, then opened her handbag, taking out the letters. 'I'm sorry, Liam, I didn't want to spoil our time together by telling you.'

He sat forward. 'I don't understand.'

'Joe Scanlon kept our letters from each other. He came clean at the airport.'

'The dirty, rotten scoundrel. Why?'

Nell shrugged. 'It doesn't matter now.' She handed him the letters she had written to him and put Liam's back inside her bag.

'Please don't tell me that he read them!'

'No, of course not. He ... well, I'll never speak to him again.'

'If he comes anywhere near you ... I'll be on the next flight over and I'll knock his block off. I mean it, Nell.'

She leant in and kissed him, regardless of who saw them. Liam pushed his letters down inside his jacket pocket.

★ ★ ★

'I've had a lovely day, Liam,' she said when they returned to the digs. 'I've all this,' she glanced at the bags, 'to pack.'

He passed over her shopping. 'Okay, but I'm

410

coming to the airport with you. And if Joe Scanlon puts a foot wrong, you promise to tell me?'

'Don't worry, he won't.' Nell couldn't remember the last time she had felt so completely happy, and her arms went around his neck as she planted little kisses on his lips and face. 'I love you, Liam Connor, and I can't wait for us to be together in our very own house.'

'Sit down a moment.'

They sat together on the stairs.

'Me, too,' he said. 'It can't happen soon enough. And once Róisín's home, you won't need to search for suitable rooms, you can both stay at Mam and Dad's before you leave for London.'

Nell made to protest.

But Liam silenced her with a kiss. 'I've already written to them, and they're happy to help.'

Nell's heart leapt. 'Are you sure they won't mind?'

His eyebrows shot up. 'Of course not. It makes sense. I'll make all the arrangements this end.'

Nell cried, sobbing into his shoulder, occasionally blowing her nose on a tissue. Everything was coming together. Leaving Liam was more bearable now she had so much to look forward to. She glanced up into his kind eyes. 'Not long now before we are husband and wife. I'm counting the days.'

Nell's sobs grew louder, just as the landlady stepped into the hall.

'Now what have you done to upset that poor girl?' She glared at Liam.

They jumped to their feet.

'Oh, it's nothing,' Nell said, smiling up at Liam. 'They're tears of happiness.'

62

Kate was one of the first to arrive at the store after the holidays. The sales were about to begin, so there was plenty to do in preparation.

'Oh, there you are, Kate. Nice and punctual.' Miss Montgomery smiled. 'Did you have a nice Christmas, dear?'

Smiling, Kate nodded.

'I'm afraid I overindulged,' the older woman said. 'Here, I've brought you in a piece of my home-made cake to have with your tea later on.'

'Thank you, Miss Montgomery.' The smell of the fruit cake with white icing made her mouth water as she put it away under the counter. Her mind flooded with thoughts of her mother and the wonderful Christmas cake she used to make. She missed her so much.

Kate liked her supervisor; she was the only one she could relate to. Maybe it was because something in the woman's manner reminded her of her mother, even though they didn't look alike.

As she returned from her tea break, Kate bent down to recover some labels that had fallen to the floor, when she felt the taste of sour bile rise at the back of her throat. She rushed from the shop floor to the Ladies, just in time, and was sick in the toilet bowl. She wiped her mouth. Miss Montgomery's Christmas cake hadn't agreed with her.

At that point, her supervisor rushed in. 'Are you all right? You can't just leave your post.'

'I'm sorry, Miss Montgomery. I couldn't help it.'

The older woman came closer. 'You're as white as a sheet. Have you been sick? You ought to go home. I'll get someone to cover your station.'

'I'm fine now, really I am.' The thought of going home after spending days in the flat alone didn't appeal to Kate one bit. A few more minutes and she'd have gotten away with it.

The supervisor patted Kate's arm. 'We can't take chances, dear. It might be catching, and we'd have no staff left. No, you go home and keep warm.' She opened the door. 'I'll get your handbag while you fetch your coat. I'll let Personnel know.'

Reluctantly, Kate caught the bus home. At least she wouldn't have to see William. She wished she hadn't eaten the Christmas cake. It was quite rich, and no doubt Miss Montgomery had baked it with the finest of ingredients. Kate hadn't tasted anything that good in a long time.

* * *

The following morning, she sat at the table with a pot of tea and buttered toast. No sooner had the bread touched her lips than she felt queasy, and she reached the back door just in time to vomit into the yard. Oh, dear God! What is the matter with me? she wondered.

She remembered hearing the married women

throwing up many times back at the tenement. But they were having babies!

'No, no, no,' she cried. This couldn't be happening to her. Her periods had always been erratic, but she'd never needed to keep track of them. Until now.

What was she going to do? Jerry had done this to her! To have his seed growing inside her revolted her, and she heaved some more.

She sat on her bed. How would she cope if she couldn't work? How could she admit this to anyone? If it got out, she would have to hide away. Shut out the world.

She picked up the bottle of tablets and held them to her. Tears streaming down her face, she swallowed enough to make her sleep.

Day ran into night, and when she woke she wasn't sure what day it was. Her head was fuzzy, but she was still alive. Perhaps she hadn't taken enough tablets. She dragged herself from the bed and made a hot drink. The room was icy, and she crawled back under the covers with a mug of tea.

Somewhere far away someone was knocking, and for a while she didn't realise the banging was on her door. Fearful of who it might be, she stayed where she was. If it was William, she couldn't face him.

Was it rent night? When the knocking continued, she pulled herself from the bed, draped a blanket around her shoulders, and stood where she was, unsure what to do. When the knocking grew louder, she had no choice but to open the door. She peered through the crack, squinting into the bright daylight.

Miss Montgomery stood there, an anxious expression on her cold face, holding a bag full of groceries.

'My Lord. You look ghastly.'

Kate drew backwards, her stomach churning. She couldn't speak. She was shocked to see her boss looking at her, her expression grave, and Kate made no objection when Miss Montgomery stepped past her into the room. The woman placed the shopping on the table, then fished two single shillings from her purse and dropped them one at a time into the gas meter. They made a tinny, hollow sound.

Kate pulled the blanket tighter across her chest. Why had she opened the door? All she could do was to stare at the woman in front of her and wish for the floor to open up and swallow her where she stood. For her boss to find her in this state — in such a cold, miserable room that she wouldn't invite a dog to — was humiliating.

'I'm sorry, Miss Montgomery,' she managed. 'You don't have to do that.'

The older woman glanced around her, then placed a chair next to the fire and beckoned Kate to sit. 'I'm sorry to have called uninvited, Miss Flynn. Please, do forgive me.' She rubbed her gloved hands together. 'When you didn't phone in like we'd arranged, I waited another day before calling.'

'I'm sorry . . . I wasn't . . . ' Kate swallowed.

'Have you seen a doctor?'

Kate shook her head. Doctors cost money and she didn't need a doctor. As kind as Miss Montgomery was, Kate was desperate for her to leave.

416

'Looks like I did right to follow my instincts. I'll warm up some soup for you before I go, and as soon as you're dressed you must see a doctor, as you don't look at all well.'

Thoughts of soup — in fact, food of any kind — made Kate want to heave. She looked up to where the older woman was taking food out of the shopping bag. 'Please, Miss Montgomery, if it's all the same to you, I'd much rather sleep. I'll be fine in a day or so.'

The woman turned round with the soup tin in her hand. 'Well, if you're sure. Do try and eat something later, then.'

Kate nodded.

'Keep the fire on low and it will last you for a few hours.' She crossed her arms and rubbed them. 'Good Lordy! It will take a box of shillings to warm up this ice box.'

Kate stood and moved towards the door. 'Thank you, you're most kind.'

'I'll call again on Tuesday. It'll be early, on my way to the store. That will give you the weekend to recover. In the meantime,' she urged, 'please see a doctor. These kinds of things can escalate if not treated.'

Kate nodded, desperate for her to leave. 'I will. And thank you.'

Miss Montgomery picked up her handbag and made her way to the door, where she paused briefly. 'By the way,' she said, 'I thought you'd like to know that you had the most sales on your floor for December, and we would like to see you back soon.'

63

After her guest had left, Kate turned down the gas and crawled back into bed. Miss Montgomery's news that her sales had been good had lifted her spirits and taken away the sting of being seen at her most vulnerable.

That night, Kate slept without taking tablets and woke the next morning feeling refreshed. Already feeling better, she washed and dressed and looked through the groceries Miss Montgomery had left. Milk, bread, real dairy butter, tins of soup, a jar of Chivers mixed-fruit jam, a packet of Lipton's tea and some grapes.

Kate couldn't remember when she had last seen so much food, or when anyone had been this kind to her. Not since her mam. She put her head in her hands and cried. Sniffing and wiping her nose, she filled the kettle and sliced some bread, spreading on the creamy butter until it stuck up like tiny peaks on a Christmas cake. Her mouth watered in anticipation.

No sooner had she taken her first bite than she had to run out the back. Kate brushed aside the most obvious reason for her sickness; it wasn't something she was prepared to contemplate — not now. Not ever.

Her focus was on getting back to work, and she prayed that another day would ease her discomfort.

On Tuesday morning, Kate ate all she wanted and managed to keep it down. She washed the cups, tidied the room, and made her bed, then dropped her last shilling into the gas meter, hoping it would last. She washed and put on her best grey woollen dress. Her auburn hair, still damp, hung down her back.

Apart from the wobbling feeling in her stomach, which she put down to nerves, Kate was confident she would be able to persuade Miss Montgomery to allow her to return to work after the Bank Holiday. She was smiling when she opened the door to her boss and invited her in.

'Well, you look tons better, Miss Flynn. I'm glad you took my advice to see a doctor. Once these things take hold, they can lead to all sorts of problems.'

Kate smiled and asked her to sit while she made tea. This time, Miss Montgomery removed her coat and gloves. 'You know, that young man I saw you speak with once, outside the store? Well, he's been asking after you. So,' she smiled, 'it seems you have an admirer.'

Kate stiffened. 'You didn't ... I mean ... I ...'

The other woman waved her hand. 'No. I'd never give out confidential information about the staff, Miss Flynn. When did the doctor say you'll be fit to return to work?' She lifted the mug to her lips and sipped her tea, grimacing slightly. 'Do you have sugar?'

Sugar! Kate had never bought any. 'Sorry, no. Would you like me to go and get some?'

'No, it's sweet enough with a biscuit,' Miss Montgomery assured her. 'So, when can you return to work?'

'Oh, tomorrow.' Kate smiled. 'I can't wait to get back.'

The supervisor looked relieved. 'Well, if you're sure, we certainly could do with the help. January sales and all that.' She got to her feet. 'I must get to the store and keep the wheels rolling.'

Kate stood. 'Yes, of course. It was kind of you to come and see me. Thank you for the groceries you brought the other day. You must let me pay you back next week.'

The woman waved her arm. 'I wouldn't dream of it. See you on Wednesday morning, bright and early, Miss Flynn.'

★ ★ ★

Once she'd left, Kate blew out her lips, relieved at the way things had gone. Miss Montgomery had put her illness down to nothing more than a nasty infection that had run its course, and as far as Kate was concerned she would do the same.

Her body had looked no different when she had washed it this morning; her tummy was flat, as it always was, with hardly an ounce of fat to pinch.

She was looking forward to standing behind her glass-topped counter again, now that she was feeling better, and if she felt queasy at all — and

420

she hoped it wouldn't come to that — she would make sure no one saw her. She needed her job more than ever, and this thing trying to grow inside her wasn't going to hold her back. When her stomach showed the slightest bulge, she would bind it as tight as she could bear. She had a job, with people who respected her, and money in her pocket. For the foreseeable future, Kate was determined that's how it was going to stay. If she was careful and didn't get too close to anyone, no one would suspect a thing.

As she washed the tea cups at the sink, her thoughts strayed to William. In different circumstances, she might have walked out with him, but not now. He deserved better. Even she wasn't heartless enough to land him with Jerry O'Shea's bastard.

64

The next few months flew by, and Nell had so much to do and think about that it didn't matter how many times the sister in charge told her off, inside she was smiling. She was expected to give the hospital a month's notice, which suited her as Róisín was due home at the end of March. But Nell was worried about breaking the news to Sister Amelia.

At first, she thought the nun, who had trained her in all aspects of her nursing career, was disappointed in her, but once she explained her reasons for moving to London, the nun's face softened.

'Well, I see you've thought this through, Nurse Flynn.' She sat back and folded her arms. 'Now, this boyfriend. Are you sure of him, that he won't desert you once you've made the journey?'

Nell smiled. 'I'm sure, Sister Amelia. We love each other. We'll be married in London.'

'Well, famous last words, Nurse, but I'm thinking of your reputation and the well-being of your young sister, should things go wrong.'

Nell fingered the edge of her starched white apron. 'Of course, Sister. I understand your concerns, but I'm looking forward to a new life with the man I love.'

'In that case, I'll take your month's notice as from today.'

Nell felt her shoulders relax.

'Well, Nurse Flynn. Make sure you take the good name of St Vincent's with you, and congratulations on achieving Staff Nurse status. You will, in the future, need to do your probationary year.' She stood up, and Nell got to her feet. 'All that remains is for me to wish you all the best for the future.'

'Thank you, Sister Amelia.' Nell shook the proffered hand, and left to return to her duties with a huge smile on her face.

A month from now, she would be on her way to London.

* * *

Humming a little song to herself, Nell arrived at the convalescent home to bring Róisín home and the child was as excited as she was. It was fifteen months since she and Amy had taken her to the city's fever hospital, thinking the worst. But her prayers had been answered, and her sister was now a much healthier ten year old, with a future ahead of her. For that, Nell was grateful. She still thought about Kate every day, but so far her prayers had gone unanswered.

Nell's dreams were about to come true — living and working in London, with the man she loved. Her priority now, though, was her little sister.

Róisín was sitting on her bed with her little case packed, and she had the biggest smile on her face. Her blonde curls bounced on her shoulders as she ran into Nell's arms. Tears of joy ran down Nell's face as she wrapped her in a bear hug.

'You look wonderful, sweetheart,' Nell told her. 'And that blue coat and bonnet suits you.'

A nurse came to her side. 'Well, don't you look nice? We'll miss you, Róisín,' she said, bending to give the child a hug. 'These are her instructions,' she told Nell. 'If you have any concerns, you know where we are.'

'I'm going to England to live,' Róisín said.

'Really! Have you relatives there?' She looked to Nell.

'Yes, I'm going there to be married to my fiancé.'

The nurse smiled and shook Nell's hand. 'Congratulations.'

Outside the hospital, both girls took a deep breath of fresh air and then walked slowly, hand-in-hand, to the bus.

'Where are we going, Nell?' The little girl glanced out of the bus window, taking in everything she hadn't seen in a long while.

'We're going to Liam's mum's. Everything will look strange at first, but you'll soon settle back in.'

'Will you be staying with me?'

'I'll have to sleep at the nurses' home until we leave, but I'll see you every day. I promise.'

* * *

Róisín soon settled into the warm, welcoming fold of the Connor family, and appeared to be enjoying her new-found freedom. The colour had

424

returned to her face, and Nell was pleased to see her little sister was putting on weight and eating better; her once spindly legs finally had some shape. It was a load off Nell's mind to know that Róisín was well looked after while she was working, and being spoiled with sweets and treats. Mr Connor often took her to the park to play on the swings and feed the birds.

'Sure, the child's a grand help to me, so she is,' Liam's mother told Nell. 'She's good at totting up as well, and sure, the customers love her.'

'When are we going to London?' Róisín asked Nell.

'As soon as I work out my notice at the hospital. It won't be long now.' She hugged Róisín. 'Are you looking forward to seeing Liam again?'

'Yes. Will we have a house to live in, Nell?'

'We certainly will, honey.'

'Will we ever see Kate again?'

Nell's happiness dimmed slightly. How could she tell Róisín that Kate obviously didn't care about them, otherwise she wouldn't have stayed away? She knew the child was finding it hard to understand their sister's absence.

'Will we, Nell?' she persisted.

'I hope so, honey. I'll leave our address so she can get in touch.'

65

Kate's attitude to her pregnancy was to ignore it. Burying her head in the sand was the only way she could cope. But four months after that terrible night at Jerry's, she noticed the changes to her once slender body. Lying in bed at night, she ran her hand over the slight bump, realising now was the time to take action. Whatever happened, she was determined that no one would find out. If Miss Montgomery got wind of her predicament, it would be the end of her career. She was doing well; she enjoyed working at the store and the extra responsibility entrusted to her.

Each morning, she bound her stomach as tight as she could bear, so that nothing showed under her shop uniform. It was only when she stripped off for bed and unbound herself that she was aware of the small bulge growing.

So far, she had kept her secret safe from William, who continued to meet her after work. On Sunday, he had taken her to Blackrock on the bus for the afternoon, and she had enjoyed the chance to breathe the fresh air into her lungs.

She never spoke about her family, and William appeared happy just to be with her. She realised she was beginning to enjoy his company, too. Her address remained a secret, and William knew not to pry.

A recent pay rise meant she could buy

whatever she needed, but she rarely bought enough food to keep a cat alive. She reckoned if she didn't eat, she wouldn't get fat. Her pregnant state had not, so far, disrupted her life, and that was how she intended to keep it.

One day, while she was serving a customer, she felt the baby move, and it startled her.

'Are you all right, dear?' the customer asked. 'You've gone quite pale.'

'Oh, yes, I'm fine, thank you.' Smiling, she passed over the neatly wrapped package.

Kate had just got back to her counter when Miss Montgomery called her into the office. When she saw the expression on the supervisor's face, Kate's mind went into overdrive.

'Close the door and sit down, Miss Flynn.' The abrupt formality startled her.

Kate fidgeted, straightening her skirt, picking at an imagined piece of fluff.

'When is the child due?'

Kate's head shot up. The question had caught her off guard.

'When were you going to tell me?'

'I'm sorry, Miss Montgomery. I was hoping no one would find out. How did . . . ?'

'These things always come to light. I've guessed for some weeks, waiting for you to approach me. Is he going to marry you?'

Kate swallowed and dropped her head.

'Hasn't he asked you yet? He seems very fond of you.'

'William is not the father.'

The ticking clock above Miss Montgomery's head seemed louder, and seconds passed before anyone spoke. A serious expression creased Miss Montgomery's face, and she shuffled her pen between her fingers. A tight knot formed in Kate's stomach.

'I had thought it was a slip between you and William, and I was going to offer my suggestion. However, this puts your reputation in a whole new light.' She stood up. 'I'll have to let you go immediately. To keep you on another day would be more than my job's worth.'

'I was raped!' Frustrated tears rolled down Kate's pale face. 'I was raped!'

There, she had said it. There was no going back.

Miss Montgomery lowered her head and knitted her fingers, then looked up at Kate. 'My dear girl. Have you reported him? Do you know him?'

If she admitted to knowing him, having lived with him, and that it was all her fault, it would gain her no sympathy from her boss. She knew she didn't deserve sympathy, but she did need a friend.

'No . . . no, I didn't report it. I was in shock for weeks. I don't want anyone to know. I feel so ashamed. Please don't tell anyone, especially not William.' Kate was sobbing now.

'If you didn't report him then, it's too late now, and the Gardaí wouldn't believe you.' Miss Montgomery smiled for the first time. 'You're not the first girl to get into trouble, and you won't be the last. Unfortunately, you are the one who has to pay the price.' She stood and came round to where Kate was sitting, her whole body trembling. The woman placed her hand on her shoulder. 'I can make some recommendations, but I have no choice but to dismiss you immediately.'

'Oh no, please don't, Miss Montgomery.' Kate wept. 'I won't let it interfere with my work.'

Miss Montgomery sat back down. 'Be practical, Miss Flynn. How would you feel when others found out? The cruel jibes? People can be insensitive to unmarried mothers. It's happened before in this very store, and I'd hate to see you go through the same thing.'

'But what will I do? I never asked for this. I don't want this baby.'

Her supervisor pursed her lips before answering. 'The reality is you have to deal with it. What about family?'

'I have no family. My parents are dead.'

Miss Montgomery pulled her chair closer to Kate's. 'In that case, you must let the good nuns take care of you until the baby is born. They will have the child adopted, and then you'll be free to get on with your life again.'

Kate had heard about the Magdalen laundries and the strict religious regime, and she knew it wasn't as simple as Miss Montgomery made out. But what choice did she have now?

'I must get back to the shop floor. I'll have your wages sent on to you. Now, if you can collect your belongings, I'll make your excuses. Goodbye, Miss Flynn. I hope things work out for you.'

★　★　★

429

Humiliation, a feeling far worse than she could ever have imagined, washed over Kate. She couldn't get away from the store fast enough, and she battled the strong March winds to return to the safety of her bedsit. To go begging to the nuns was the last thing she planned on doing. She'd do anything rather than that.

When was the baby due? She hadn't given much thought to that. All she knew was when this terrible sin had happened to her. It had been shortly after the anniversary of her mother's death, towards the end of October. Next week would be the first week of April, and she was grateful to have kept her secret this long.

How hard could it be to give birth anyway? Women were having babies all the time. Once it was delivered, she would take it to the nearest convent and leave it at the gate, she decided. Then she could get on with her life.

The following weeks were lonely. Kate hid away from public view, only going out for essentials and avoiding eye contact with anyone. If she died from taking too many tablets, so much the better. It would save herself and her family any embarrassment. She supposed it wasn't really the baby's fault — it was as much a victim as she was — but she couldn't conjure up any feelings for the child whatsoever.

One morning, in the middle of April, she woke in excruciating pain. When she could bear it no longer, she screamed out. With no idea what to do, she crawled from the bed, dragging the blanket with her out into the street for help, where she collapsed.

66

Nell had just finished her last day at the hospital. It had been an emotional day, with the nurses and staff, and even the patients, saying their farewells. Kelly had organized a collection amounting to ten pounds, and presented it to her in the canteen along with a good luck card and a bunch of daffodils. Nell was overwhelmed, and really touched at their thoughtfulness. She would miss them all very much, but not in the way she had missed Liam for such a long time.

Róisín was waiting for her when she arrived at the Connors' shop. Mary had a lovely tea of poached salmon, baby potatoes and peas ready for her, and they all sat down at the table.

'I'm eternally grateful for all you've done for us, and especially for Róisín,' Nell told Liam's parents. 'I could never have managed otherwise.'

'Get away with you,' his mother scoffed. 'Sure, aren't ye practically family.'

'In a few days we'll be in England.' Nell's eyes shone with happiness. 'I can't believe it's happening, Mary.'

'I'm pleased for you,' the older woman said. 'Although I'll miss you both.'

'Will you come over and see us, Aunty Mary?' Róisín had taken to calling Liam's mother aunty, at her request.

'Wild horses couldn't keep me away.' She

laughed. 'As soon as you and your sister are settled, we'll be over.'

Her comment was seconded by Mr Connor, who lowered his newspaper. 'I'd better get measured for a new suit, then,' he said, winking at Nell.

'And I'm going to be a flower girl at the wedding, Aunty Mary,' Róisín giggled.

'You'll be a bobby dazzler.' Mr Connor folded his paper and pulled his chair closer to the table. 'I'll arrange an hour off work and drop you at the airport, love.'

'Thanks, Mr Connor. That's grand.'

'You can drop the Mr Connor. I'm John to you, love.'

'Well, thanks, John. That'll be lovely.'

Róisín put down her fork. 'I can't wait to see the Queen's palace. And I keep trying to remember what Liam looks like.'

They all laughed.

'Well, you'd better eat up all your dinner.'

'Oh, I will. Will we have salmon in England, Nell?'

Again, they all laughed. And Róisín picked up her fork and tucked in.

Nell couldn't remember a time when she had felt this happy. And to see her little sister with a healthy complexion, after all she'd been through, was more than she could have envisaged over a year ago. Now, she was going to marry the man she loved and live in a proper house. She had the flight tickets, sent by Liam, tucked inside her new handbag, and she couldn't stop her excitement mounting.

★ ★ ★

Nell was woken in the early hours by voices downstairs. Hoping nothing had happened to Mary, she slipped out of bed and pulled on her dressing gown, careful not to wake Róisín. On the landing, she heard low whispers and wondered if she should be eavesdropping.

At that moment, Mary came upstairs. 'Nell, one of the nurses from the hospital is here to see you.'

Nell rushed down. 'Kelly, what is it?'

Kelly placed her hand on Nell's arm. 'A young girl has been admitted to the women's ward. She's asking for you, and I wondered if it might be your sister Kate.'

'Oh, my God! Is she all right?'

'Look, you get dressed and go,' Mary said. 'I'll watch over Róisín.'

★ ★ ★

The Dublin streets were eerie, with shadowy figures lurking in doorways as the two girls hurried back towards the hospital. 'Thanks for coming, Kelly.'

'One of the other nurses was going off shift and gave me a lift.'

'I'm glad you didn't have to walk on your own. Do you think it's Kate? Did she say her name?'

'Well, I've never met her but you talked a lot about her, Nell, about her going missing, and from your description, I think it might be.'

They were both panting as they ran. Kelly

433

stopped briefly and put her hand on Nell's arm.

'Listen, Nell, I didn't like to say before, but she's having a baby, and having a rough time of it —' She broke off.

'Oh, my God, is she going to be okay?'

They were rounding the corner to the hospital when Kelly said, 'She's in maternity. I have to get back, because I'm still on duty. I had to beg old frosty knickers to let me go.'

'Thank you for this, Kelly.' Nell hugged her and half ran, half walked through the gates.

★ ★ ★

Kate had been sedated by the time Nell got there. The baby was stillborn, weighing less than two pounds. Nell wept as she sat by her sister's bed, overwhelmed by guilt. She had let Kate down in so many ways. If only she had gone to the Gardaí, they might have found her. She wondered who had taken advantage of her sister. The boy on the motorbike came to mind; Kate had been friendly with him. But where had she been living? How had she managed? So many questions, but Nell knew she would have to tread carefully so as not to drive her sister away again.

The nun in charge was abrupt when she looked at the sleeping patient. 'Well, she got off lightly,' she told Nell. 'Just as well the baby died. The child is better off.'

Nell was on her feet in a flash, tears coursing down her face. 'How can you say that? You don't know anything about my sister, or what she's been through.'

434

'It's all self-inflicted.' She turned away and walked to the far end of the ward.

Nell had often wondered how nuns, with no experience of life or real hardship, could be so judgemental. Unmarried mothers got no sympathy from nursing staff, and she was grateful to Kelly for coming to get her.

Nell sat by Kate's bed, longing for her sister to wake up so she could give her a hug. Her eyes were starting to close just after daylight crept into the room, when William turned up, concern written all over his face.

'William, what are you doing here?' Nell got to her feet.

'I've just heard that Kate's been brought to hospital. How is she?'

She took him aside. 'We need to talk. We can go to the waiting room.'

William followed, a frown creasing his handsome face.

When they were seated opposite each other, Nell asked him outright, 'Are you the father of Kate's baby?'

He raised his hand. 'I don't understand . . . '

Nell glared at him. 'Don't you? Then why are you here?'

'I've befriended Kate over many weeks, but she never said anything about a baby!'

'So, you're not the father?'

'The father!' He got to his feet. 'Of course I'm not. This is a complete shock to me.' He slumped back down. 'But it won't change how I feel about her.'

Nell rested her head in her hand. 'I'm sorry,

William. Do you know where Kate has been living?'

'No, she never divulged that either, and she never spoke of another man. We had the odd drink together and occasionally went for something to eat, but she never took me home, wherever that is.'

'Did she have a job?' Nell asked.

'Oh yes, until recently she worked at Clery's. That's where I first saw her again, last Christmas. But she swore me to secrecy.' He glanced up. 'I'm sorry, Nell, I couldn't betray her trust. She seemed on edge all the time, always glancing over her shoulder.'

Nell sighed. 'Thank you, William. It's good to know you were there for her.'

'She didn't want me around, but I kept turning up outside the store because I was worried about her.' He gave a little chuckle. 'She even called me a stalker.'

'She did?' Nell touched his arm and smiled gently. 'I need to talk to Kate alone when she comes round. Would you mind, William? But I'll tell her you were here.'

His brow furrowed with concern. 'She will be all right? Have they said anything?'

'Not really. But Kate's lost the baby!'

67

Nell was dreading Kate waking up and finding out that she had lost her baby, and her stomach churned when she eventually saw her sister's eyes flicker and slowly open. Would she want her here? Despite Kate calling her name when she was delirious and first admitted, Nell feared she might push her away. But when Kate pulled herself up in bed and threw herself into Nell's arms, relief washed over her and the two sisters wept.

'It's all right, Kate,' she soothed. 'I'm here.'

'Nell, I'm so sorry. Please, please don't let them send me away. I don't want to be a Magdalen.' She sobbed. 'Please, Nell, I'll do anything.'

Nell, sniffing back her own tears as she perched on the side of the bed, gently took both Kate's hands. 'Listen, sweetheart.'

'What is it? You've not signed the papers for them to take me away, have you? Please, Nell. They've already taken the baby. I want to come home with you.'

'Of course I haven't. Kate . . . the . . . the baby didn't live. I'm so sorry.'

Kate took a few seconds to process this. 'It's my fault. I didn't look after myself. I didn't ask for it, and I didn't want it.' She sobbed again. 'I didn't want anyone to know.'

Nell held her sister in her arms until she calmed down.

Then Kate whispered, 'Get me out of here, Nell.'

'Keep the noise down,' a passing nurse muttered. 'There's God-fearing women trying to rest.'

Nell, her heart aching for her sister, patted Kate's hand and went in search of the sister in charge. She found her writing at the table.

The nurse didn't look up when Nell approached her.

'I'm Kate Flynn's sister. I'm a registered nurse and I'd like to take her home.'

The nun continued what she was doing as she replied, 'As much as it pains us to have *her* here amongst decent women, she's lost a lot of blood and needs to stay at least another day.'

'My sister is seventeen years old, and as respectable as anyone else in here,' Nell answered tightly. 'It wouldn't do you any harm to show her a little compassion.'

She got no reply and, biting back what she really wanted to say, walked back to where Kate, her face white, was resting her head against the cold steel bars of the bedrest. 'Nell, the bed is flooded,' she whispered anxiously. 'They're going to kill me.'

'No, they won't. Leave everything to me. I'll change your linen and make you comfortable. But then, you must stay another day. I'll come back for you, I promise.'

* * *

When Nell got back to the Connors' house, Róisín was skipping in the yard. She reassured the child that Kate was fine and would be home tomorrow. There was no need for Róisín to know more than that.

'Oh, goody! Will Kate be coming with us to England?'

'I hope so, pet. Now, I need to have a word with Mary and John.'

Nell's heart was heavy as she went inside. How would they take the news that Kate had been pregnant and lost her baby? She couldn't lie, as these things had a way of coming out when you least expected them to, so she told them.

John got up and put the kettle on and his wife placed her arm around Nell's shoulders.

'The poor child. But she's going to be all right, that's the main thing.'

'I hope so, Mary. I'm sorry to burden you with my worries. I'll ring Liam tonight and let him know what's happened.'

'Well, of course.' Liam's mother sat down, and her husband brought steaming mugs of tea to the table. 'You can bring Kate here, if you like.'

'Thanks, Mary, but Kate has a bedsit. I've not seen it, but I'll take her there and look after her.'

'You might be able to get a refund on the tickets, love,' Mr Connor said.

'Do you think so? I'll see what Liam says when I phone him later.' A sob caught at the back of Nell's throat. 'I never expected to see her again — at least, not this broken.'

Liam's mother patted her hand. 'Of course, the poor girl. You reckon some scoundrel took her down?'

She nodded. 'She hasn't told me anything yet.'

When Nell spoke to Liam, he said that another couple of days should make no difference to their wedding plans. He also said that it would give her peace of mind to have Kate with her. Liam's words had eased Nell's mind and she couldn't wait to see him.

When she took Kate back to the room, she was pleasantly surprised. It was tidy but the place was freezing, even though the sun was shining outside. There was no sign that a meal had been cooked recently.

'I'll settle you into bed with a hot-water bottle, and nip out to the shop,' she told Kate.

The walk from the hospital to the bus appeared to have tired Kate, and she didn't complain when her sister tucked her in, placed money in the meter, and lit the gas fire.

When Nell got back, Kate was asleep, and Nell set about cooking rice pudding made with milk on the hob. She made a pot of tea and sat down to consider the best way to help her sister come to terms with her loss. She hoped Kate would talk to her when she was ready, but for now she was more than happy to have her sister back.

She hadn't seen her for more than twelve months, and the thought of leaving her behind tore at Nell's heartstrings. Kate needed her and she wouldn't let her down again.

Later, over a bowl of rice with a dollop of strawberry jam, of which Kate managed a few spoonfuls, Nell looked closely at her. The girl was pale, thinner, her eyes dull, so unlike the

440

wayward sister she had known. Realising what she must have gone through to hide her shame, Nell wanted to wrap her in cotton wool. Nell was furious with the brute who had done this to her sister, and desperately sad that she had given birth alone, notwithstanding a stillbirth. Reporting it would only embarrass Kate, as the woman always got the blame. Fuming inside that the man would get away with it, she forced a smile to her face. 'Leave that if you've had enough.'

Kate swirled the jam round in the remainder of her rice pudding, then glanced up at Nell. 'Thanks for everything you tried to do for me when I wouldn't listen. I know now that you were right, and I hope, in time, you'll forgive me.'

'Oh, Kate, I never blamed you for anything. We were both grieving. I love you, and I don't want to lose you again.'

Kate's eyes widened in surprise. 'You do? Even after what happened to me?'

'Yes, and I'm not the only one.' Nell smiled at her. 'William came to the hospital, and I'm sure he'll be back.'

'William! Oh no! He'll hate me once he knows the truth. He won't want to have anything more to do with me.' She began to cry.

'He knows, and he still feels the same about you.'

'Oh God, I can't bear to look him in the eye.'

Nell reached for her hand. 'You can put it all behind you now. Start afresh with your family. And whatever you tell me, I won't judge you.'

'Oh, Nell, I've been a fool. I kept quiet, afraid

441

of being sent to the Magdalen laundries. But Miss Montgomery, my floor supervisor at Clery's, found out and I had to leave.' She blew her nose. 'I'm so ashamed, Nell. I blamed myself, although I couldn't stop what happened. His name is Jerry O'Shea, and he forced himself on me.'

'Him! I'll flaming kill him.' Furious, Nell glanced around the room. 'Was it here?'

'No, his place.' Kate's voice was little more than a whisper. 'Afterwards, I had to get away and rented this room. What am I going to do?'

'Do you know where he is?'

'No, Nell. I've not seen him since. He's probably gone to England.'

'Do you want to talk about it?'

'No, please let's forget about him. I never want to set eyes on him again.'

Kate sobbed and Nell held her close.

'All right, Kate, if that's what you want.'

The room wasn't luxury by any stretch of the imagination.

'Can you afford to stay here, Kate?'

'Without a job, I don't think so.'

'Then come to England with me and Róisín. Liam has a house big enough for us all. We're getting married.'

Kate smiled tearfully. 'Oh, Nell, that's wonderful, but he won't want me there. Not after the trouble I've caused.'

'He does. I've already spoken to him. The past is behind you now. And when you're fit again, you'll find plenty of work in London. It will be a new start for us all. Please say yes?'

442

'Oh, Nell, I don't want to stay here on my own.' She threw her arms around her sister. 'But there's just one thing. I'm not sure I can leave William. He's been so good to me, and if he can forgive me, then I think I might admit that I have feelings for him.'

'We're not leaving until you're well enough, and William can come visit us in London any time he likes. In fact, why not invite him to the wedding.'

'Can I?'

'Of course.' Smiling, Nell hugged her. 'I'll come back tomorrow to look after you, and I'll bring Róisín with me. How about that?'

Kate sighed. 'I can't wait to see her and tell her how much I love her.' She lowered her head. 'You haven't told her about . . . the baby . . . '

Nell shook her head.

★   ★   ★

When Nell brought Róisín to see Kate, she found her washed, dressed and sitting by the fire.

'You look better,' Nell told her. 'How are you feeling?'

Before Kate could do more than nod, Róisín rushed into her open arms.

'Where have you been, Kate? I missed you. Are you better now?'

'Yes, and I've missed you, too, Róisín. I've been very foolish. I lost my way, but I'm home now.'

Nell made them all a meal of sausage and mash, while explaining their future plans to Kate.

Before they were ready to leave, Nell wrote a long letter to Amy, thanking her for being there for her when she needed a friend, and informing her of her planned wedding to Liam in London. She wrote of her excitement to have Kate return to the fold. She omitted the bit about the baby. It would only embarrass her sister, if she ever wanted to return to Ireland in the future.

Once Kate had recovered enough to travel, Mr Connor dropped them at the airport. Mary said her goodbyes at home. She promised to see them for the wedding and would bring William with her.

As Nell relaxed on the flight, she glanced across at her sisters, chatting and laughing together, and tears of happiness rolled down her face.

A short time later, she was in the arms of the man she loved as Liam swung her off her feet, then he kissed the top of Róisín's curly head.

Kate, her head bent, looked a little uneasy until Liam gave her a gentle hug. 'Welcome to London, Kate.'

With her family back together again, Nell linked arms with the people she loved most in the world as they left the airport, heading towards their new life.

Epilogue

Nell and Liam's wedding was a quiet affair with the immediate family at the Catholic church on Brixton Road. But the church wasn't empty. Once word got round that there was to be a wedding, many worshippers came to church, along with West Indian families from the neighbourhood who arrived to see the new bride and groom take their vows. Nell looked radiant in a white midi-length tulle dress with a high lacy collar and long sleeves. She carried a posy of red roses, tied with a white ribbon, and her short veil was held in place with a sparkling chignon comb.

Liam couldn't take his eyes off her as she walked towards him on his father's arm to the altar. Smiling, he reached for her hand.

Kate, her long hair coiled on top of her head and decorated with tiny white flowers, looked beautiful in a pale peach crushed taffeta dress with puff sleeves. She looked happy and composed as she followed the bride. Róisín wore the same colour dress as Kate, except for a large white bow on the back. She stood next to Kate, holding a pretty posy of peach and white carnations.

Afterwards, they dined at one of Brixton's trendy restaurants. The table had been reserved for them and was paid for by Liam's dad. The food comprised a roast dinner, green vegetables with Yorkshire puddings, and pineapple upside-down cake to follow.

After they had eaten, a violinist walked towards them, playing a waltz, and Nell and Liam danced on the small square floor.

★ ★ ★

With all eyes on the bride, Kate had never seen her sister look so happy. She thought back to the previous night when Liam, his parents, Róisín and William had stayed at a nearby bed and breakfast, leaving Nell and Kate alone at the house where Liam had taken them a week before.

Nell had been rubbing Pond's cold cream on her face when Kate asked, 'Are you nervous, Nell, about tomorrow?'

'Yes, I am a bit, but I know it'll be okay.' She smiled across at her sister, already in bed. 'You mustn't let what happened colour your view of men, Kate.'

'I won't, Nell. I just hope William won't change his mind when he knows the whole story.'

'He won't, Kate. I think he loves you.'

'How can you tell?'

'The way he looks at you.'

Kate moved over as Nell climbed in beside her. 'I'm sorry about how I was before.'

'Why did you resent me? What did I do wrong?'

Kate sat upright and placed a pillow behind her head. 'You were always the strong one, like

446

our dad, and you were always his favourite. You passed your exams and went into nursing. He was proud of you, and so was Mam. I was jealous and felt such a failure. Mam understood me, then when she died . . . ' A tear rolled down Kate's cheek. 'Oh, Nell, we quarrelled that morning. I can't even remember what about now.'

Nell squeezed her hand. 'Go on.'

'You took away my last chance to say goodbye and say sorry. I couldn't cope with her loss, and the feelings of rage I felt towards you.'

'Forgive me, Kate. I thought I was doing the right thing for both you and Róisín, and with hindsight I should have asked you first.'

Kate nodded.

'I worried myself sick when you went off like that. What stopped you coming home?'

'No matter how bad things got, my stupid pride wouldn't let me.'

'Can we put it behind us now and make a new life for ourselves here?'

'I hope so, I really do.' The sisters hugged and then chatted until their eyes drooped and they fell asleep.

Now, pulling her attention back to the present, Kate was aware of William watching her.

He interrupted her thoughts. 'A penny for them?'

She felt a flush to her face. 'They're worth more than that, William.' She smiled.

The dancing was in full flow, and Liam's dad was swinging Róisín round. The child's laughter was infectious.

William got to his feet and reached for Kate's hand. 'Shall we?'

Kate stood up and felt her body tremble. This was how she had felt when she first met Michael, and a happy feeling consumed her.

William held her at a safe distance, then a little closer, until he wrapped his arms around her.

It felt good to have him hold her.

Then he whispered, 'You know I've fallen in love with you, Kate.'

She felt strangely fragile as she looked up at him. 'You don't know everything about me.'

'But I do, and wild horses can't drag me away from what I know to be the truth. It's our future I'm interested in, Kate.' He guided her back to the table.

Everyone clapped as the music grew faster.

William moved his chair closer. 'I don't want to rush you, but is there a chance we can make this permanent?'

'I'd like to think so,' she said. 'But what about your parents and your studies?'

'What about them? I'll soon be qualified to teach anywhere in the world.' He put his arm around her shoulders. 'I love you, Kate Flynn. You only have to say the word and, in a few months from now, if you're still living in London, I'll come and join you.'

'Oh, William,' Kate said. 'I love you, too.'

His kiss was gentle on her lips before they drew apart, when Nell and Róisín came over to speak to them.

Now Kate knew what love was. Like Nell, she loved someone whose love was sincere, and it was enough for her to leave her past behind and begin her life anew.

Acknowledgements

Thanks to:

My wonderful family, for their support and encouragement.

My daughter, Sharon, for accompanying me on research trips.

Just Write Group, who listened and critiqued many chapters of *The Dublin Girls*.

Lutterworth Writers' Group, for their friendship and support.

Jean Chapman's Peatling class, always encouraging and supportive.

Agent Vanessa Holt, my grateful thanks.

Amazing editor, Kate Byrne, and the team at Headline.

Copy editor Shan Morley-Jones, for her editing skills and useful timeline for *The Dublin Girls*.

Publicist Emily Patience, for promotional material.

We do hope that you have enjoyed reading this large print book.

Did you know that all of our titles are available for purchase?

We publish a wide range of high quality large print books including:
Romances, Mysteries, Classics
General Fiction
Non Fiction and Westerns

Special interest titles available in large print are:
The Little Oxford Dictionary
Music Book
Song Book
Hymn Book
Service Book

Also available from us courtesy of Oxford University Press:
Young Readers' Dictionary
(large print edition)
Young Readers' Thesaurus
(large print edition)

For further information or a free brochure, please contact us at:
Ulverscroft Large Print Books Ltd.,
The Green, Bradgate Road, Anstey,
Leicester, LE7 7FU, England.
Tel: (00 44) 0116 236 4325
Fax: (00 44) 0116 234 0205

Other titles published by Ulverscroft:

A PLACE TO BELONG

Cathy Mansell

It's 1943 and Ireland has escaped the worst of the war raging in Europe, but life is still hard. When fire breaks out at the convent in Cavan, orphan Eva Fallon barely escapes with her life. She's offered a bed for the night by Ma Scully, whilst her nephew Cathal helps battle the blaze. Seventeen-year-old Eva finds a job at Blackstock's farm, setting in motion a chain of events that will change her life forever. Amidst tragedy and hardship, the only ray of light is her growing, secret love for Cathal. And she clings to the hope that one day she will find a place where she can truly belong.

DUBLIN'S FAIR CITY

Cathy Mansell

On her deathbed, Aileen's mother reveals a secret she has kept for eighteen years, and pleads with her daughter to fulfil a last wish. Torn by grief, Aileen leaves Dublin, the Fair City, and Dermot, the man she has grown to love. Lonely and vulnerable, she unwittingly befriends a salesman at the seed mill where she has found work. Suddenly, her life is in danger. On a visit back to Dublin, Aileen discovers a devastating truth. When she finally decides to return to Dermot, and the family she loves, will the secret she too is now hiding tear her and Dermot apart?

WHERE THE SHAMROCKS GROW

Cathy Mansell

Jo Kingsley is transported from her turbulent childhood of domestic servitude, to the sophisticated life of the upper classes at the beautiful Chateau Colbert. Here she meets Jean-Pierre, the grandson of her employer, Madame Colbert, and visits Paris. But Jo's destiny takes her to America where she experiences more than her dreams of becoming a music teacher. During prohibition, in the mysterious haunts of Greenwich Village, she falls in love with Mike Pasinski, a son of Polish emigrants. However, loneliness, loss and hardship follow the Wall Street crash. Will the beautiful Jo let go of her demons and learn to love again?